Legacy

of

Shadows

Bernard Spilsbury

First published 2013 by Authorhouse, Bloomington, USA
This edition published 2023 by Kindle Direct Publishing.

This novel is a work of fiction. Aside from historical figures and events, and personalities clearly in the public domain in the 1980s, the characters in the story are entirely the work of the author's imagination.

Also available as an Amazon e-book.

For Patricia

Acknowledgements

I would like to express my thanks to Pat Barrow, the late Andy Nott, and to Peter Harris for their help, encouragement and suggestions in the preparation of this novel.

Bernard Spilsbury

THE FAMILY LINE

GEOFFREY MAYER
Born: 12 Aug 1937, Manchester.
Married: 12 Sep 1962 to Hanna Welkin.
Occupation: airline captain.
Children: David.

JAMES MAYER:
Born: 15 Sep 1903, Knutsford, Cheshire.
Married: 11 Dec 1934, to Ann Pendleton.
Occupation: Property-owner, grocer.
Died: 1954.
Children: Geoffrey.

WILLIAM ARTHUR MAYER
Born: 13 May 1871, Knutsford, Cheshire.
Married: Sep 1902, to Alice Drinkwater.
Occupation: General Practitioner.
Died: 5 Nov 1933.
Children: James, Margaret, Ellen, Jane, Mary.

WILLIAM MAYER
Baptised: 25 Feb 1851, Knutsford, Cheshire.
Married: 19 Jan 1871, to Ellen Carter.
Occupation: gardener.
Died: 1904.
Children: William Arthur.

THOMAS MAYER

Baptised: 29 Jul 1821, Styal, Cheshire.

Married: 3 Mar 1849, to Jane Wildgoose.

Occupation: tenant farmer.

Burial: 15 Dec 1868.

Children: William, Montague, Lavinia, Horatio.

JOSEPH MAYER

Baptised: 1 Dec 1796, Newcastle-under-Lyme.

Married: 18 Feb 1821, to Nell Platt.

Occupation: cotton mill apprentice, then spinner.

Died: 28 Nov 1826.

Children: Thomas, Ellen.

ISABELLA MAYER

Born: 3 Sep 1764, Newgate, London.

Married: 22 Nov 1796, to Ernest Betton.

Occupation: prostitute.

Died: 1809.

Children: Joseph (Mayer), Martha, Ann (Betton).

ELIZA MAIR

Baptised: 19 May 1735, Newgate, London.

Unmarried

Occupation: servant; prostitute.

Died: 1777.

Children: Isabella.

MIRIAM AYRE
Baptised: 21 Sep 1714, Newgate, London.
Unmarried
Occupation: prostitute
Died: 1764
Children: Eliza:

LUCY AYRE
Born: 1695, Kent.
Unmarried
Occupation: servant.
Died: 19 Jun 1719.
Children: Miriam.

If you can look into the seeds of time
And say which grain will grow and which will not,
Speak then to me, who neither beg nor fear
Your favours nor your hate.

Banquo to the witches, "Macbeth."
William Shakespeare.

CHAPTER 1

1983

The Boeing 737 was at 31,000 feet over the Mediterranean when it ran into the cat.

But this was no purring feline. Cat is pilot-speak for clear air turbulence. It has claws and a serious bite. Sensible flyers are wary; they treat it with respect.

So just two minutes earlier, when the captain of the Sunjet flight taking 130 sun seekers on a package holiday from Manchester to Malta told all passengers to return to their seats and fasten their seat-belts, because of possible turbulence, there was something about the tone of his calm but clipped announcement - not so much a suggestion as a polite but definite command - that hinted at urgency. It made everyone obey him. That was fortunate.

Only one stewardess, making a late dash towards her seat at the rear of the cabin after cleaning up a drink spilled by one of the dozen children on board, was not strapped in when the jet, in the blackness of the night sky, bounced twice, sharply, like a speed-boat crossing the bow-wave of a much larger vessel.

It brought several cries - half alarm and half a sort of worried humour - as stomachs floated in the motion; and it made the stewardess stagger, and fall to her knees in the aisle.

Two men, one either side, gallantly took a hand each to help her up. Then came the real cat-treatment...a plunge, not of some gentle fall, but one of being thrown downwards violently.

Everything that was not fastened down leapt upwards in response, in a melee of flying debris...including the stewardess, her feet up against the cabin ceiling, her head lower as she still held - desperately now - the two hands that had been helping her from the floor.

Her scream mingled in a shrill, discordant crescendo with those of terrified passengers as handbags, cups, books, magazines, girls' dolls, a teddy bear, a toy car, loose cash, all crashed into the cabin ceiling, thrown upwards by the horrifying downward force of the aircraft's fall.

The people would have gone up to the ceiling too, if it had not been for their seat belts. Their bodies felt themselves fighting to fly upwards, and their arms did. It was as if time went into slow motion. The stewardess, anchored by the arms, floated legs up. The two men, staunchly holding on to her, failed to notice their own fear.

And in the trance-like slow feeling of unreality, children screeched, high-pitched, terror adding an unbelieving urgency to their tones. Women screamed. A hoarse male voice shouted: "God...oh God." Hand clasped hand in the pandemonium which crescendoed briefly and died abruptly. Terror is the one tangible feeling now as the black falling, falling goes on and on...how long?

There was nothing to tell them how long they fell, or how far. But when they hit the bottom of the air pocket there was no feeling of landing on a cushion of air...nothing gentle about the shuddering crash which shook the aircraft to the core. It was as if they had hit the ground...many thought they had. The cabin lights flicked off, then on.

At the same moment the flying debris which had been stuck by the downward force on to the ceiling now crashed down...the stewardess too.

She was lucky. The hands of the two men had anchored her above the aisle. That was where she was flung down, in a bone-jarring, bruising heap, sobbing with pain. But from her training she knew, even then, that she was lucky, because she might have crashed down across the seat backs in a way that can break your back. So there was relief as well as pain in her cries.

About twenty of the summer-clad sun seekers were also hurt as falling objects hit them. Cut heads, mostly. No more falling now. But the cabin looked like a battlefield...and sounded like one too. For fear and panic took over. Children shrieked. Somebody was being sick. One man shouted: "For God's sake what's happening?"

2

It was the start of more pandemonium. Then, like a voice from the gods, a calm, professional, reassuring voice cut like a knife through the panic. "This is Captain Mayer. Ladies and gentlemen I'm sorry about that severe turbulence. We should be clear of it now. But please remain with your seat belts fastened. There is nothing to worry about. We will keep you informed. The cabin crew will be with you instantly."

The dazed and frightened passengers were silent. Then a child's voice piped up: "Are we crashing, mummy?"

It brought a nervous titter or two...then silence again, broken only by smothered sobs. Then the uniformed stewardesses unstrapped themselves and dashed into the aisle with first-aid kits...attending to a number of weeping and injured passengers and to their colleague now sitting in the passageway between the seats.

Gradually order began to be restored, and nervous, excited talking grew in volume. The stewardesses were bandaging, soothing, examining. The youngest of them, Sharon, had only been doing the job for a month, and she felt as if it was all some bad dream. It all had an air of unreality. She'd trained for this kind of emergency, but somehow felt that it didn't really happen. She looked into a gaping head wound, gently moved the woman's hair out of the cut and squeezed the edges together as her colleague Jean used scissors to clear an area of blood-soaked scalp, dry it with cotton wool, and use sticking plaster to keep the cut closed. Handing the shocked and sobbing passenger a wad of dry dressing with the instruction: "Keep the pad there for a while. I'll be back in a few minutes."

Then they moved on to another woman: elderly, this time. Her nose was bleeding copiously. Across the aisle Sharon could see two more stewardesses bandaging a woman's arm. The woman was crying with pain.

Then the pilot's voice again: "Ladies and gentlemen. I'm sorry about the rough ride. I understand that there have been some injuries, but I believe that nobody is seriously hurt in that clear air turbulence. It is, thankfully, a very rare event.

3

"For your information we actually descended 7,000 feet in a few seconds. But all is well now. We'll be starting our descent for Malta in a few minutes. We'll be landing at 2255 hours local time, thirty minutes later than scheduled, due to our late departure from Manchester.

"Please report any injuries, no matter how slight, to the cabin staff. And if there is any damage to your belongings please report that too.

"We don't expect any further problems. But please remain seated, with your seat belts fastened. Thank you."

*

The announcement, managed to combine the matter-of-fact with the efficient, the "we're all in this together" feeling with an air that said plainly, unquestionably: "I'm in charge here. I have everything under control and I know exactly what I'm doing."

The silence that followed it was broken by a small boy's voice, piped in a broad Yorkshire accent: "Are we all reet now, dad?"

Somebody shouted: "Three cheers for the pilot."

The first cheer was a bit ragged and uncertain. But the second was backed by nearly every passenger. And the third was a thanksgiving release of pent-up fears and panic...with nervous laughter and the sudden slackening of tension as the stewardesses began clearing up the mess, serving drinks, and helping life on board the sunshine jet to return to something like normal.

But it was more than normal. Everyone was smiling now. Knuckles that had been white with clutching the arm-rests and seat-backs were limply passing over perspiring foreheads. Drinks were taken eagerly. A group of half a dozen lads in their late teens and early twenties, seated in two lots of three, one behind the other, clinked cans of beer and yelped at each other. Shouted one, in the everybody-listen-to-me manner of lads in groups: "Bloody 'ell, I thought that were it, for a minute!"

"I'll admit, I were shittin' meself," bellowed another. "'Ow about you Dennis?"

4

"I wasn't worried about crashing," yelled Dennis. "I were thinking bugger this, I've paid three 'undred quid for this lot!"

The rising hubbub of chatter and laughter was suddenly stilled again as another lurch downward was felt in stomachs out to prove that they were a lot more wary than their owners.

Then again, that professional voice: "Captain Mayer, ladies and gentlemen. We're starting our descent. We expect to land in Malta in about 20 minutes."

Up front, Captain Geoff Mayer and his first officer, Ron Davidson, were busy. They had already informed Luqa air traffic control of the 7,000 foot drop in C.A.T., that they knew of no damage to the aircraft, but that passengers and crew had minor injuries. They were told in return that full emergency procedure and medical aid were being laid on, and that they had priority clearance to land.

Mayer radioed their home base at Gatwick to inform operations about the incident. A full structural check of the aircraft would be needed, delaying the return flight and running into problems with crew duty hours. That meant an overnight delay.

They also had to alert their ground handling agency at Luqa, preparing them for the inevitable delay to the planned return flight: its passengers, who would have already checked in, would have to go to an hotel for the night instead of flying home at the end of their holiday. Captain Mayer and his crew would need hotel accommodation. And they'd need engineers on the spot to assess if any damage had been done to the airframe of the Boeing 737.

And meanwhile, the descent continued down the night sky, positioning the aircraft as directed by air traffic control, using the navigational beacons, going through the check routines, lowering the flaps by degrees, undercarriage down, seat-belt signs and no smoking signs on, being updated on the situation in the cabin by senior stewardess Mary Beech, and all the time descending, slowing, turning.

Captain Mayer was handling the landing, leaving Ron Davidson to do most of the radio work and attend to the flaps, undercarriage and engine power. No problems. Lined up now on the instrument landing system's radio beam, the airport lights coming into view, two lines of brightness among a lot of other lights, some of them flashing blue, visible now as the runway came up to meet them, of the fire engines and ambulances standing by close to the landing strip.

Everything checked correct? Speed right? No tones on the instrument panel. Lined up OK...touch right, pull gently back as the runway comes up fast now, the aircraft flaring nose slightly up, its underside acting as a brake on the air...and one short "yelp!" from the tyres as rubber thumped tarmac before the 737 was speeding, easing, slowing smoothly along the runway. No problem.

"No problem!" shouted Dennis, who seemed to have taken on the role of informing his fellow-travellers of all major developments. But anything else he might have intended announcing was drowned by a wave of enthusiastic cheering and clapping.

"So much for the reserved English," said Mary Beech, the senior stewardess, grinning at the girl sitting next to her, strapped in for the landing in the backward-facing seats nearest to the cockpit.

That was Sharon Daniels, fresh out of cabin crew training school a month ago.

She smiled back. "It's given them something to put on their postcards," she said.

CHAPTER 2

1983

It was on the minibus taking them to their hotel in Valetta, after confirmation that there would be a long hold-up to the flight back to Manchester, as the other stewardesses talked endlessly about the fearsome fall, that Sharon was able to take her first real look at Geoff Mayer.

She had seen him, of course, several times before. She had been aware that he was the sort of man she had imagined meeting when she had decided to apply to join the airline. He was a lot older than she was, of course - at least 40, she guessed. He was not all that good-looking. He did have a kind of debonair style. That was something to do with his dark, slightly receding hair, swept back at the sides and with a hint of grey. And blue eyes. And it had a lot more to do with his uniform. Navy blue, with four gold rings on his sleeves, and the pilots' gold wings on his chest.

But that mid-air trouble tonight, which had terrified her as much as it had most of the passengers, had given Sharon her first glimpse of a totally new kind of attractiveness, one that she had never thought of before: whatever the outside of the man looked like, it was an inner strength - an ability to face the worst problems and remain calmly in control - that he'd shown.

It was a little strange to her. So was the idea of ending up in an hotel in a place like Malta without being on holiday...and she found the circumstances more than a little heady.

Even now, sitting there and being driven along at the front of the minibus, he was undoubtedly the Leader with a capital L, she mused. And it was not just the scrambled egg decoration on his uniform cap peak, and the gold rings on the sleeves of his dark jacket.

7

Up there tonight when there had been real fear in the air, there had been something about his voice that had lent an extra dimension that she couldn't quite define. To be honest, sitting there in the little bus, it looked more like arrogance.

Whatever it was, she felt it was somehow exciting. And it was definitely sexy. He was sitting almost sideways in his seat as he chatted to Ron Davidson, who was sitting just behind him. Mary Beech was with the injured stewardess, Lynn Welsh, across the aisle of the vehicle as it made its way through the warm night towards the hotel. Lynn had had a medical check-up and had passed as bruised, but not really in need of hospital treatment. She had insisted on staying with the rest of the crew.

Geoff Mayer looked relaxed, but not tired. Yet he had every excuse to be. Apart from all that had happened in the air, he'd had to give full reports to Gatwick Ops for the operations director and engineers; and he knew that the public relations people would be informed so they'd be able to field the inevitable press questions.

He had personally supervised that medical checks were being given to all the people who had been hurt, insisting on their going to hospital in most cases. He had done a good job, Sharon knew that. They all had. But he had led the team from the moment the doors of the aircraft had been opened, personally helping injured passengers, patched, bruised and limping, down the steps to the apron where other hands were waiting to conduct them to a fleet of ambulances.

They'd all helped...Sharon and the other stewardesses and Ron Davidson. Sharon had been inside the cabin. But she was aware of the flash of cameras outside as the stream of injured passengers disembarked. Some who had been quite calm up till now burst into tears with relief. It felt, and it was, dramatic.

Seventeen people were taken to hospital in Valetta. Captain Mayer saw them off with a word of assurance. Then he led the way, not as usual to the crew room, but through the passenger channel, carrying hand baggage, lending a hand here and chatting, with a few smiling words, there. He had led the way in helping his passengers to find their baggage and then to get on to the right hotel buses. His energy seemed boundless. And all the time there were those pressmen's cameras flashing away. He promised to talk to them when the passengers were all looked after. And he did, but only briefly, playing down the danger and the drama, very calm, very professional, Sharon thought.

As he talked, passengers kept arriving and shaking his hand. The flashes flashed again. He'd done a superb job, they told the newsmen. They seemed almost carried away with it, somehow, as if it reflected how very brave they themselves had been too.

Either way, the passengers had made it clear to the Malta-based reporters that Captain Mayer was a hero...he had saved them from certain destruction. And the stories they wrote were soon on their way to London and Manchester.

Captain Mayer had a slightly hooked nose, even if it was small, Sharon noticed. And nice smile lines from the corners of his eyes. But when he smiled he kept his mouth closed, and the corners of his lips turned slightly down. It gave him a slightly distant air. And he smiled a lot, particularly at Mary, thought Sharon with a stab of what she instantly recognised as jealousy.

Mary Beech had been a stewardess for years. She was Sharon's immediate boss on this flight. She had very dark hair and, although they were not visible to Sharon now, eyes to match. She had a nice figure too. But she was old, at least 30, Sharon thought, with a sort of satisfaction.

Sharon was sitting by herself. None of her particular friends were on this trip. She was definitely the junior. The other four girls were sitting in the row of seats behind her. One said: "It's nearly two o'clock now...what time do we have to get up in the morning?"

It was Mary who replied: "There's no chance of the aircraft being ready to go before mid-afternoon. It looks as if we'll get the morning off in town. But before anybody leaves the hotel I want you to talk to me. I'll give you my room number once we're checked in. Captain Mayer is going to get an update at about O-eight-hundred, and he'll

9

pass the information to me. So just in case there's a change, ring me unless I've already spoken to you.

"I suggest you have breakfast between eight and nine. Either way, we'll probably be wanted back at the airport around mid-day."

*

The luxury hotel was just the kind Sharon had dreamed about when she made up her mind to become an air hostess. The trouble was, she had found, that with Sunjet there were hardly any overnight stays in faraway places...not on these short Mediterranean flights. The planes went straight out and back - one duty trip for the crews. Unless something happened like this delay.

She looked admiringly around the big room. Then she got into bed. The crews all carried an overnight bag for such emergencies. She snuggled down, enjoying the privacy and the luxury of the surroundings. This is what I joined an airline for, she thought as sleep closed round her. She smiled to herself: and masterful pilots...

She woke to find the sun lighting up the ancient city of Valetta. Even in her air-conditioned room she could sense the heat beating on to the pavements outside, as she peeped round the window drapes.

Her bedside phone rang. "Sharon. Good morning. It's Mary. We'll be leaving the hotel for the airport at sixteen hundred hours. You've got the morning free. We're booked for lunch at mid-day sharp in the restaurant. See you then."

Sharon put the phone down, and, with a feeling of freedom she rarely got at home where she lived with her mum and younger sister Carol, slipped off her nightie and strolled into the bathroom.

As she stepped into the shower she stopped to admire herself in the mirror. She smiled at herself. A pretty, 19 year-old blonde smiled back, blue-eyed, not needing much make-up. She pulled her shoulders back and tightened her stomach muscles as she looked approvingly at her figure: slim, fair-skinned; and her boobs were not only bigger than

10

average, but, she assessed, pretty well-shaped too. Legs: could be better, perhaps, but she'd seen worse.

She ran her hands lightly up from her hips, over her slim waist, and up over her rib-cage, to rest gently lifting her breasts. Her thoughts switched to Geoff Mayer. And aloud she said: "Why not?"

There was no sign of the rest of the crew as she had breakfast. They were all friends, and fairly old hands at the airline game, so they were probably out already, looking at the town, she guessed.

Outside the hotel, as she set out to explore, an oven-heat enveloped her. Her eyes grimaced at the glare. Everything, as she stepped into the city street, seemed ancient. It was a feeling of being part of something enduring...not the sort of feeling you got in Benidorm, the only other place she had been to outside Britain. She had been there twice for holidays in the past, with her parents before dad left, and once with her friend Di, who had joined the airline with Sharon.

The street was crowded with swarthy-skinned, dark haired local people who mingled cheerfully with the obvious holiday lot. Holiday lot...I mustn't think like that, Sharon thought. Without them I wouldn't have a job...I wouldn't be here.

She wandered on, down the crowded street, looking in the shop windows, glancing up and down the side streets, and up at two large churches situated in squares just off the street she was on.

But it was aimless, she knew. She needed a guide book. She felt that she was wasting her chance to see this strange old place, so foreign yet with its English language everywhere.

It was so hot, too. She could do with a long drink of something cool...yet just sitting around would be wasting precious time, she thought as she glanced into a pavement cafe.

Then her eyes met Geoff Mayer's.

After her thoughts of an hour earlier she felt herself blush. It was as his eyes casually slid from her face to her blouse that Sharon knew that he had not recognised her. She was wearing just a blouse and skirt...she had left her uniform jacket at the hotel.

11

"Hello Captain Mayer," she heard herself say, determinedly. "Not your usual way of getting into the air!"

He started visibly as his eyes came back to her face. He knew he'd been caught eyeing up her figure...and damn it by what he now saw was that new stewardess.

She knew that he knew, too. But his smile - that closed-mouth, vaguely distant smile - was suddenly welcoming her: "Hello! Come and have a drink."

He stood up and got a chair for her. "I'm sorry...I was miles away for a moment...I didn't recognise you without your uniform. What'll you have? Sorry it'll have to be something non-alcoholic. Will you have a fruit juice?"

She went along with the idea and he hailed a passing waiter to order one. Then he said: "Is this your first trip here? What have you managed to see?"

"Nothing much yet. I was just thinking that I must buy a guide book...we've only got an hour or two."

"Yes, it's not long enough. There's a lot to see in Valetta if you like historic places. Tell you what, why don't I show you one place just round the corner from here...it's a quite amazing church."

The waiter brought the drink and Sharon took a long, cool sip. Churches were not really her scene. "I'd like that," she said.

Ten minutes later the baroque splendour inside the Co-cathedral of St John made her see that there are churches...and churches.

Its arched roof was richly painted, as were its walls, with their side chapels behind a row of arches pointing the way to the altar guarded by tall candles. But it was the floor of the building that made her accept Geoff Mayer's adjective "amazing" as the only fitting word.

It consisted, from wall to wall, of flat, decorated marble tombstones...richly decorated marquetry pictures in sombre-colours, skeletons, knights, swords and shields, scenes, with Latin inscriptions and names and places...Sharon could see that they were from many places in Europe.

"I've never seen anything like this floor. It's unbelievable," she whispered...the atmosphere made you want to whisper. "Who are all these people buried here? There must be hundreds."

"They were knights of old," Mayer told her. "This was the church of the Knights of St John...you know they were left over from the crusades and ended up in Malta.

"They came from all over Europe to defend Christianity. It's quite stunning, isn't it.

"What I find fascinating is the thought that perhaps one of my forebears might be buried here...you never know. Look at this..."

He led her across the floor to one of the dozens of tombstones. "Get the name," he said, pointing. Stooping Sharon read, among the Latin text, the name "Mayerei" under the inlaid picture of a knight in armour holding a sword vertically.

She looked round questioningly. Geoff Mayer told her: "I've always intended to trace my family's history. This has made me determined. We don't really know where we came from until we do, do we?"

They moved on slowly. He seemed to know so much about the place, and his enthusiasm was infectious. In the oratory he looked in silence for a long time at a massive painting. "It's the Beheading of St John, by Caravaggio," he said, almost reverently.

"I thought it was Salome wot done it," said Sharon quietly, but with a twinkle in her eyes. His eyes met hers. "I'll get you for that!" he said. As he said it he couldn't stop the half-formed thought crossing his mind that he was talking as if he'd known this girl for years...yet he didn't really know her at all.

He warmed towards her. New girl, young and obviously pretty unsophisticated. Not his type at all, he'd have thought. But with a little surprise he found that he liked her style.

They spent half an hour in the church before it was time to head back to the hotel. In the crowded street outside, at one point, she found herself jostled up close against him. She felt his hand firmly on her waist as he guided her through the crush.

13

It was then that they both saw the newsagent's poster: "HERO PILOT IN JET TERROR."

Mayer grimaced. "My God, trust the Press. They blow everything out of proportion."

But there was just a hint of satisfaction in his look, Sharon thought...and why not. They walked past the shop. They didn't buy a paper.

Back in the cool of the hotel he smiled as she thanked him for showing her the church. "Maybe we'll get more time to really show you the place one day," he said.

It was only after they had parted to go to their rooms that she realised that he had never once used her name. He probably doesn't even know it, she thought.

CHAPTER 3

1983

Back at Luqa airport the handling agency which looked after Sunjet flights was abuzz after reading the Maltese newspapers' dramatic accounts of the "cat" fall, which, in print, had assumed near-disaster proportions.

And there was a company message informing Captain Mayer that there was intense media interest in the incident, which had made the late editions of the daily newspapers, radio, and TV in Britain. It added that the company had received "much positive publicity" from the accounts so far, which had been full of passengers' praise for the crew. So a press conference and photocall had been arranged at Manchester Airport upon their arrival.

The crew should be prepared for this "photo-opportunity" and Captain Mayer, First Officer Davidson, senior stewardess Beech, and stewardess Welsh would attend the press conference for interviews immediately afterwards.

"Congratulations on a splendid job," added the message, which was from the company's operations director David Sanderson.

The English language newspaper was ablaze with it - and it was passed around with a mixture of giggling and cynical remarks by the stewardesses. But the pictures of dazed and bandaged passengers being led from the aircraft were dramatic enough. And the quotes from the uninjured passengers certainly backed up the "pilot hero" headlines.

The cabin crew also came in for glowing praise from the passengers. And there were pictures of Lynn Welsh, smiling bravely after her ordeal, and descriptions of her voyage to the ceiling as the aircraft had plummeted.

Geoff Mayer was scathing about it all. "Over-dramatizing everything - just like the bloody newspapers," he said shortly.

The flight back was uneventful. Ron Davidson was a touch nervous about the press conference. Mayer laughed it off. "I've never been to one, either," he said. "Just tell them what happened, play down the drama, and keep it short and sweet."

At Manchester Airport there were a dozen or more photographers waiting to meet them. The operations officer came on board to tell the crew to wait until the passengers were well clear, then to get on to the apron to be photographed.

Facing them was easy at first - a bit like a school mixed hockey team, Sharon thought. Then they wanted a picture of Captain Mayer and Lynn at the front. Then - Sharon could hardly believe it - one photographer wanted Lynn to stand on her hands with Captain Mayer holding her feet in the air..."just to show what it was like in the plane," he said. Geoff Mayer refused that, but smilingly. Then more line-ups. It went on and on.

But eventually the rest of the girls were free to go, and while the two pilots and Mary and Lynn went off to face the press conference, Sharon and the others were whisked away by crew-bus to the crew room, before making their separate ways home.

*

That evening it was all on the regional TV news. And the same Captain Mayer who had said in Malta how over-dramatized the newspapers made it, was now over-dramatizing the part the stewardesses had played, Sharon noticed. His own part had been nothing at all, but the cabin crew had been magnificent. Very professional. Exactly as he would have expected Sunjet stewardesses to be...they were trained to the highest standards to deal with emergencies even though such things were rare, he told the interviewer.

It was all very well done, Sharon saw, and Mayer looked good. Her mother and sister were full of it...and very proud of her. "I'm proud of them all," Mayer said, to conclude the interview. "Everyone was very professional as well as caring. It says much for the high standards of training that our cabin crews receive."

Later Mayer himself watched the TV news at his detached house in Prestbury - far enough from the airport to be unbothered by noise, but within 30 minutes' drive. He'd phoned his wife, Hanna, from Malta, and he'd spoken to her from the airport after the press conference, so she knew what had gone on.

She was slightly mocking about the TV interview. "Quite the little hero, darling," she said. "Sounds like a lot of bullshit to me. Perhaps it'll get you on the management ladder at last...you seem to have done all the right things for a change."

Mayer found himself irritated by the disparaging suggestion that he normally did the wrong things. But that is how Hanna is, he thought.

They had first met when Geoff was one year into his pilot training in the RAF. She was a natural blonde, with the easy ability to dress, to laugh and to enjoy life that made it very easy for the young officer to fall in love with her. Hanna came from the same sort of middle-class background as Geoff's, and he knew straight away that they were made for each other. They had married five years later, when Geoff had become a flight lieutenant. They'd had an idyllic love life before and after the nuptials. Slowed down now, of course. Only natural, I suppose.

And somehow, over the years, she had developed a critical edge which showed through from time to time...like now. Just hints; hard to define: it was as if she could not refrain from getting the digs in. Just nagging, thought Mayer. He'd accused her of it before now. She had an answer...somehow she always had an answer.

"Doctor Edith Summerskill always said there is no such thing as nagging: just the repetition of unpalatable truths," she had told him, several times.

"The repetition of unpalatable truths is better than nagging, is it?" he'd asked.

17

"If you'd shape up and get into management there wouldn't be the need to mention the unpalatable truths," she had said with that little air of final dismissal that was...yes...irritating.

Now, despite the irritation, he let it pass. He knew he had done a fair PR job for the company. And, to be honest, it had crossed his mind that this sort of thing did you no harm career-wise.

"Have you heard from David?" he asked.

"Yes, your son and heir rang to say his pals at university were asking him if his dad had passed his test to drive bloody aeroplanes."

*

The next day, looking at a video recording of the TV interview in the company's wood-panelled boardroom at Horley, Surrey, not far from the airline's main base at Gatwick, its chairman, Raymond Howell, chief executive Don Smithson, and operations director David Sanderson were certainly impressed.

"That was a hell of good job. We just couldn't buy that kind of publicity," said Howell.

"Write and congratulate him on behalf of the company, Don, and let's have him down here for lunch during the next couple of weeks. I'd like to meet him. He looks like management material unless he turns out to be one of those pinko union pilots. What do you know about him, David?"

"His record as a pilot is very good - came to us from British Airways five years back," said Sanderson. "I suppose he's in Balpa, but that doesn't mean he's a union type. I'll ask a few discreet questions if you like."

*

The following Friday, Mayer decided to look in at the party they'd been invited to at Ron Davidson's place, despite Hanna's refusal to go.

18

"I think the boss is going to be there. And there'll be cabin crew – it'll look odd if I don't turn up after that Malta flight," he told Hanna. "I'd better look in at it at least, but I shan't stay long."

Ron was a bachelor and had quite a reputation for his parties. It was one of those rambling, three-storey Victorian semi-detached houses in Bowdon, built of a mellow fawn-coloured brick...a great house for parties, Ron always said.

One of the first people Geoff saw, as he made his way to the kitchen to get a beer, was Sharon. Not that he remembered her name. But she was the cheeky little lass he'd shown around the cathedral in Malta...except that dressed for the party she looked quite a doll, he thought.

She was wearing skin-tight black velvet-looking pants and a short fawn linen jacket which was unfastened and revealed a very well-filled white polo-necked sweater. In fact, he found himself thinking, she looked very sexy - she was obviously young and had a beautiful figure.

Then he realised that she was smiling at him with exactly that look she'd had when she had caught him eyeing her blouse in Valetta...and damn it, the look said once more that she knew full well that he was enjoying the view again.

"Hello Captain Mayer," she said. "I have to tell you – you're my mum's hero. You were great on the TV."

"Not that hero stuff, please," he said, wincing slightly, but managing to smile too.

"Well mum's convinced you saved my life. She says you're very modest, but she knows the truth."

She had noticed that his wife was not with him. She had made enquiries and had found that he was married and lived in Prestbury. And the newspaper stories had revealed that he was aged 46: God knows why they always put people's ages in, she thought, but it was interesting to know.

She said: "Are you going to dance with me later, if I promise not to mention it again, or call you my hero?"

"It's a deal," he said. "But if you'll excuse me right now I'll go and get a drink."

And he went. It was later, as he talked to Ron Davidson and a couple he'd just been introduced to, that the subject of industrial action cropped up. "It looks as if it'll go ahead, according to several people I've talked to tonight," said Ron.

"The ground staff and cabin crews are getting very bolshie about the staff cuts the company wants, and they're going to ask for backing from the pilots."

"Well I for one will tell them to sod off," said Mayer. "Christ, haven't they learned anything from the 1970s? All the airlines are suffering from the recession and we've got to make a profit to stay in business...enough holiday carriers have gone under in the last few years to know it's not a con."

"Well here's the very man to tell to sod off," said the female half of the couple he'd just been introduced to, obviously relishing the moment. She worked for one of the freight agencies on the airport. She raised her voice. "John was telling me earlier that he's going to ask you pilots to back the strike."

Mayer looked round. It was John Cooper, one of the airline's operations rank and file. He knew him from the routine pre-flight briefing and paperwork, but he'd hardly exchanged more than the briefest "good morning" when they'd bumped into each other outside "ops."

Cooper was at his right elbow. He'd obviously heard Mayer's "sod off" remark - and the helpful woman's repetition of it - effectively flinging down a challenge between the two men.

"I didn't know you were a union type John," said Mayer immediately.

"What's a union type, Geoff?" countered Cooper, a hard edge to his question.

Mayer picked up the metaphorical gauntlet. "I mean the types who don't mind if they wreck the airline they work for if they think they can get a few more quid in their pockets...sheer greed most of the time."

There was a moment's total silence. "Asking for a big pay increase would be greedy if we were on the sort of salary that you are on," said Cooper quietly.

"After all, with the higher rates of tax removed for the well-off now, you must be a fair bit better-off without any increase in pay. For the rest of us, Mrs. Thatcher's sky-high interest rates of over ten per cent makes it damn difficult to pay our mortgages - and for some people it must be well nigh impossible."

Mayer was about to speak but Cooper cut him off. Raising his voice slightly, for the sake of the rest of the people who were in the room, and were all now listening, he added: "But this problem isn't about pay is it – it's about jobs."

The awareness that Mayer was umpteen rungs above him, in company hierarchy status, in the amount they were paid, in a sort of tacit assumption of social standing, hung unspoken in the air.

"Well it doesn't matter what it's about. I don't believe you or anybody else has the right to disrupt our flights for it...dammit man it's the passengers who pay our salaries and they are the only ones who suffer."

"Nobody's talking about disrupting flights. The idea is to persuade the management to think again about cutting staff...we're down to the bone already. Keep cutting back and back to save a few quid and in the end it's the service we give to the customers that will suffer."

"Bollocks! The only part of the service that we give that really matters is the cabin-service on board. On the ground we have handling agents."

"Well if you're saying we are overstaffed, all the company has to do is to show us why, and in which department, and really prove their point. Nobody is suggesting that we should employ people to do half a job. But everybody knows we've already cut back to the bone.

"All we're doing as a company is following the current vogue: if the profit isn't as good as we'd like it to be, just cut the staff by another ten percent...then pay the directors a bloody great bonus for increasing productivity per employee.

"You see all sort of firms doing the same thing, ever since Thatcher convinced the captains of industry that cutting back is the only way to make Britain great.

"There may have been some slack to take in over this last four years or so - but not any more...now everybody is getting rid of good, experienced people. You see them walking about, spending their redundancy money. When is it all going to end?"

Cooper's voice had been slowly rising, in vehemence and in volume, as he made his point. People who worked for the airline - more than half those present - began to take notice. Sunjet was a friendly company, a first-name company outside the public earshot. But Cooper was just an ops clerk, and ops clerks don't shout at captains.

Mayer picked up the spectators' interest. Some regarded him as being more than a touch self-opinionated, a mite too high and mighty for some people's tastes. He knew they wanted to see how he'd cope with this one. He spoke medium loud. "We have management people to decide how to run the company. They are paid to do it. And so far they haven't done it badly – we're profitable. If they say that's how to stay that way, it's good enough for me. What gives you the right to argue?

"Or are you saying that all the people who run companies are wrong to be cutting back in order to stay in business? With respect, perhaps that is why you are an ops clerk and not running Sunjet."

Cooper was getting angry now. Perhaps the drink helped. "So making a bit of extra profit matters more than people to you. Not just making a profit – making a *bigger* profit, which will probably go to giving the directors of the company an even fatter bonus.

"We've all seen our own publicity blurb time and time again saying it's the quality of Sunjet's people that matters – now they're saying hang the customers, and hang what it does to people who may have worked for the company for God knows how long...just sack a few more for the profit.

"And all we're left with in company after company right across the land is yes-men saying it must be good for us because the bosses say so."

In his anger he began stabbing the air with his forefinger in Mayer's direction. "Unfortunately since Thatcher conned everybody into believing that she was some sort of economic Messiah, all British companies can think of is sacking people.

"And this at a time when we've suddenly got North Sea oil pumping into the economy!

"It's bloody pathetic and so are the types of people who just accept it all and say yes sir, no sir...especially the ones who have the rank to influence the bosses."

And giving no chance of a reply, Cooper muttered a pointed "excuse me," and walked away.

Mayer looked after him and said loudly: "And that is the sort of left-wing crap that made Britain need Thatcher and all she's doing for us...my God where would we be now without her? The bloody unions would have taken over and bankrupted the nation by now."

It was Sharon who stepped in to end the awkward silence that followed. "What about my dance, Captain Mayer?" she said, actually taking his hand and leading him, almost child-like, to the room at the front of the house where the music was belting out.

Mayer was conscious of the strange role reversal: she was being mature and sensitive, ending the public squabble - about politics, of all things - which he shouldn't have allowed himself to be drawn into. Silly. Damn it. He had the feeling that he hadn't won the argument. But he was damned if he'd let that final insult rest there. Bugger Cooper! Who the hell did the jumped up little sod think he was?

But now they were among the dancers. And Sharon was already moving her nineteen year-old body in a way that took Mayer's mind off everything else for the time being.

CHAPTER 4

1983

His anger returned as he drove home and began thinking over the dressing-down Cooper had given him.

Two thoughts surfaced time and time again: one was that he was damned if he was going to be spoken to like that by a ruddy ops clerk; and the second was that Cooper was wrong.

Unions still hadn't learned the lesson: it is outrageous to take industrial action that hurts both customers and employer.

And, in any case, if companies didn't cut staff to keep costs down the means of employment for a lot more people would disappear.

So he'd make a stand.

He was off duty the next day. So he phoned the operations manager from home.

"Hello Ray, it's Geoff Mayer. Look, I'm sorry to do this, but I'm furious about a spot of bother I had last night at Ron Davidson's party of all places. Ended up having words with John Cooper about this industrial action they're planning.

"Thing is, I don't like being bollocked by a junior member of your staff, with other members of staff looking on, even if it is off duty...and that's exactly what happened.

"Can you have a quiet word in his ear? Don't tell him I complained - just say you heard about it from other people."

"I did hear about it, as a matter of fact."

Mayer gave Ray Ward, John Cooper's immediate boss, a brief run-down of what had happened, substituting only that he'd felt embarrassment (rather than anger) at being bawled out. He otherwise played the incident down...coming over as a very reasonable man, he felt.

Hanna, who had been asleep when he'd arrived home from the party, and knew nothing of the event, came into the room and caught the tail end of the conversation. He told her about the contretemps, and what he'd done to put it right.

"You should have squashed the little creep on the spot," she said, her eyes flashing. "You let people walk right over you. God, he'll be laughing behind your back, the way you've dealt with it...dammit you're a four-ring captain and he's nothing but a bloody clerk."

"He won't be laughing for long, will he though?" said Mayer. "Not when they come to decide who is going to get the boot in these latest redundancies."

"What do you mean?"

"Well, when you think about it, all the departmental heads are going to have to start drawing up lists of the people they might be able to do without. I don't think it's going to be easy unless there are definite black marks against certain people.

"If I were Ray Ward, that conversation I've just had would make me think of Cooper as a name for the list...although, of course, I certainly didn't suggest that."

"You crafty so-and-so! That's diabolical. I'm glad you're starting to think like that...that's the way to get to the top of the tree these days."

"Yes, well just leave these things for me to decide. I think I'm big enough to manage my own little fights now. Don't you bother your pretty little head about it!"

"God, you are a chauvinist pig!"

*

When Mayer arrived back at Manchester Airport, stepping lightly off the British Airways Shuttle from Heathrow, he felt pretty good. The lunch with the chairman and the chief executive had gone so well that it had left him feeling slightly heady...and it wasn't all due to the gin and tonics, the wines with the meal, or the XO cognac that had followed it.

25

The note he'd received inviting him to meet the chairman had just said: "The chairman would like you to join him for lunch next Monday in the boardroom. Confirm with my secretary that you can make it. David Sanderson."

He showed it to Ron Davidson, who was flying with him again that day. "I wonder what the hell this means?" he said to Ron. "It's not so much an invitation...more a command to attend."

"Perhaps they're going to give you the VC or something."

"They might be going to kick my backside."

"Come on! They're not going to invite you to lunch in the boardroom to give you a ticking off."

Of course Mayer knew that, from the moment he had read the note, which had been pinned to the flight documents he'd picked up in ops. When he told Hanna that evening she'd been ecstatic. "Fantastic! Who else will be there?"

"Haven't the foggiest. I'll ask David Sanderson's secretary when I ring in the morning to confirm I'll be there."

In fact half a dozen of the directors and departmental heads were at the lunch. They had drinks before the meal, and they talked about the CAT fall, the follow-up on the injured passengers, and the happy PR that had resulted from it, with all that praise from the customers and all that coverage in the media.

Someone said they'd all been lucky. Mayer spoke up: "It wasn't luck. We followed the procedures. The crew made sure the passengers were all strapped in, then they strapped themselves in. That's what the book says, and it came out right because we did what the book said. That and the fact that the aircraft could take all the stress."

"All except the stewardess who was hurt...nothing much though, fortunately."

Again Mayer spoke up. "Now she *was* lucky. If it hadn't been for those passengers on either side of the aisle holding on to her, she could have been very badly injured."

A sudden thought occurred to him. He said: "Chairman, I'd like to make a suggestion about that. We know who the men are - if we made

26

an official award of some kind to them, we'd get some good follow-up publicity."

"What sort of award?" The chairman was interested.

"Well we could certainly give them a free holiday...and there'd be more good publicity at the airport when they set off."

The marketing director, who had PR matters under his control, said they should be careful about reminding the public that everything on Sunjet's flights did not always go as smoothly as they might.

But the chairman, after a moment's consideration, said he didn't agree with that. It was another chance to stress that it was a one-in-a-million incident. It would do a lot more good than harm. And it could be done at very little cost.

"It's better to be looked over than to be overlooked...let's do it Gerald. Get the PR people on to it.

"It's a damn good idea Geoffrey."

All the other directors, seeing which way the wind was blowing, nodded eagerly. Gerald Smithies, the marketing director, nodded too: "OK, we'll get our heads together."

The lunch was pleasant. They talked airlines, trends, aircraft. And the threatened industrial action was raised. "What's your view, Geoffrey," asked the chairman in an apparent matter-of-fact manner.

Mayer sensed that this was no off-hand question. "I've already made it clear to one of the union people that I'm against any such action," he said. "Of course it's sad that people have to lose their jobs. But if they're any good they'll be employed again as soon as the economy looks up. There's nothing as important as keeping the company healthy. I told Cooper that in no uncertain terms."

"Cooper?" queried the chairman.

"Yes, he's a jumped-up ops clerk at Manchester who runs the clerical union set-up. Troublemaker like all union people."

"How come you were talking to him about it, Geoffrey?" asked the chairman. Again, Mayer had that feeling that behind the apparently guileless question was a purpose.

27

"Oh it was just a few words we had at a party the other night," said Geoff, seizing the opportunity to make a point. "He was shooting his mouth off. I had to put him straight. He wants the cockpit crews to join in."

"So how did you leave it?"

"I told him in no uncertain terms that he could count me out for starters. Anybody with any sense knows that any redundancies that have to be made will only be for the good of the company as a whole. I told him I was sure that they'd only be what's absolutely necessary."

The lunch had been pleasant, all round. As they lit cigars and had coffee the chairman said that the operations director had recommended Captain Mayer for promotion to deputy flight manager at Manchester when Raymond Hodges retires in a couple of months. There had been several "hear-hears" and applause round the table, and a lot of handshaking afterwar.

As he left, Mayer was drawn aside by the chairman.

"Congratulations again Geoffrey. And thanks for the very good idea of honouring those passengers who held on to the stewardess. I'm sure we'll be seeing a lot of each other. Good luck."

So Mayer was a very happy man arriving at Ringway. He had purposely not phoned Hanna. He wanted to see her face when he told her about the promotion.

CHAPTER 5

1983

A week later Hanna was away on a two-day girls-only shopping jaunt to London with her friend Mary when the official company notice was posted appointing him as the next deputy flight manager in Manchester. Mayer was leaving on a there-and-back Tenerife flight.

It was evening by the time they arrived back in Manchester. The congratulations from the rest of the crew had all been said by the time they got back to their home base.

Geoff wanted to celebrate, but most of the crew had to get home...wives and boyfriends waiting...duty next day...that sort of problem.

Only two of the stewardesses took pity on him and said they'd have a drink with him. One was Lynn Welsh, who'd just been told about the plan to stage another photo-opportunity, with the two men who had saved her on the Malta flight, when they would be presented with a scroll commemorating the incident, and a free holiday with their wives. The other girl was that Sharon lass he'd found himself fancying a couple of times.

She was very young...far too young and unsophisticated for the new deputy flight manager to associate with on anything but professional lines. But she certainly did have a great figure, and she smiled a lot...what the hell!

Both girls made a phone call, then they piled into his car, and he was glad of their company as he arrived at his big, empty detached house in Prestbury.

They had a scotch each. And then Lynn's boyfriend arrived to take her home, just as Sharon said yes, OK, she'd have just one more whisky. By the time Mayer returned from seeing Lynn and her feller off the premises Sharon had found and set playing a soft and smoochy tape. She turned from the stereo player as he walked in, and stepped up to him. "Let's dance," she said. It was a commanding sort of suggestion. So they danced. Close. Very close.

She felt different from Hanna against him. Softer. It wasn't just that she had bigger boobs, although that was certainly true. It was that she was...more flexible, pliant; and much more arousingly sexy...as simple and direct as that.

They were dancing like a prelude to making love, touching, pressing, from thigh to cheek. Then the impossibility of it...the sheer outrageousness of such an act of betrayal...made Geoff stop suddenly.

"Hey...this'll never do...you promised your mother you wouldn't be too late. I'm calling a taxi right now," he told her, feeling suddenly old beyond his years.

"I was just getting in the mood," she said, a little uncertainly now.

"Thanks for helping me to celebrate," he said quietly, looking her in the eye, then brushing his lips against her forehead. He stepped away to the phone. She sat down as he rang for a cab. There was an awkward silence. She went to the bathroom.

In the mirror she looked at the face of a woman with a sparkle in her eye. She felt a sense of victory. She knew that she had not imagined the feeling that he had wanted her...dancing as close as they had been had left no doubt.

She wasn't a virgin. Losing that had been easy enough, but the three lads she'd had sex with were never her type...it was just something you did. This would be different.

"So." She said it softly to the girl in the mirror. That single short word begged a question: where do we go from here? "I can wait," said the girl in the mirror, before she went downstairs.

They chatted easily as they sipped at another scotch and waited for the taxi. He told her about the house, and how long they'd lived there, he and Hanna. He spoke the name as if he was determined to show that he had nothing to be ashamed of, Sharon thought.

The room they were sitting in was big – a lot bigger than the three-bedroom semi that she shared with her mum. It was beautifully furnished, too. A monument to good taste really. No real bookshelves. No mess in corners. Very tidy. A bitch might think it was a tiny bit lacking in character, she thought, wryly. But it was all very expensive. I could live here. I could put up with it.

But I think I'd like some books around. As Sharon thought these things in between listening to what was fairly humdrum conversation from Captain Mayer now, the taxi arrived.

As she left he didn't kiss her. And he didn't say: "You must come again when my wife is here...she'd love to meet you," she thought wryly. Well he wouldn't, would he? But sure as hell she'd turned him on. And vice versa, she thought as the cab sped through the dark Cheshire country road, lined with trees, surprisingly high up above the yellow lights of the level land where she knew the airport, and her home in Chorlton in the southern suburbs of Manchester, lay.

*

After the taxi crunched off down the drive, and he prepared to go to bed, Mayer felt a pang of guilt. It was the first time he had even found himself thinking of being unfaithful to Hanna in twenty-one years of marriage. But he felt...good. As he turned off his bedside lamp he couldn't help thinking that almost everybody seemed to have had something on the side at some time during their marriage.

That is a bloody awful reason, he thought. Also, that very phrase: something on the side. I hate that. If I wanted to be unfaithful, it would have to be something more than that. Christ! I am only human. That girl is very attractive. And, dammit, she is making it feel as if she's available.

But she is very young. God! Another bad reason, he thought. Just think of the nods and winks if he had an affair with Sharon. It may be yet another bad reason, but I couldn't stand all the knowing looks, from cabin staff and even ground staff at the airport as well as the pilots.

31

Maybe they wouldn't know. Come on, they'd know. And he'd have to lie and cheat to keep such a thing from Hanna. Bloody hell! I'm just not into betrayal, was his final thought before he slept.

*

It was the sick feeling at the pit of the stomach that impinged on John Cooper first. Then anger. Then panic. "I regret to inform you that your post with the company is surplus to its requirements and we are therefore offering you the company's redundancy terms."

The letter said more. All bullshit of the worst kind...the hypocritical kind. In the next few hours he discovered that exactly the same wording was on the letters sent to each of the people being made redundant.

We thank you for the excellent work you have done for the company in the seven years you have been with us. You carry our best wishes for your future. Yes. Thank you and now bugger off.

Then the question: Why? Why me? I'm not the last in. I'm not the highest paid...they won't even save the most money out of me. I'm middle of the range in length of service. But of course I'm the union rep. Yes. The union. He picked up the phone.

At the Manchester branch office of the clerical union they'd received a list this morning of the ten people who had been offered redundancy in the company's "downsizing" arrangements. Yes, it's bloody outrageous.

Funny how the union rep was somehow always included in these redundancy lists - you can never prove that's why they're on the list of course. Rob Wills, the regional organiser, is talking to the management even as we speak.

I'll get him to ring you as soon as the meeting's over. He'll want a chat with you. He'll want to hear your ideas.

They called a meeting. It was well attended. But nobody was interested in fighting the management's redundancy plan. Let's face it, we've got our families and mortgages to think of. Great. What about mine?

*

"Anybody who is worth his salt will get another job sooner or later," said Geoff Mayer. "In Cooper's case he probably isn't worth his salt. Most union types aren't. All they seem to want is more. More for themselves without a thought about the consequences.

"Anyway it's a case of survival of the fittest. This country has been carrying far too many people who are too lazy or maybe not good enough to actually earn their keep.

"And you have to consider the long term good of the company in a world that is getting more and more competitive. Thatcher's right: we can't keep lame ducks.

"We'll come out of this slimmer and fitter. That's the way we have to think of it."

"We'll be rid of some of the bloody reds and union types who are a drag on everybody – that's the point if you ask me," said Hanna. "So that Cooper creep is for the chop?"

"Yes, as a matter of fact, he is. Serves him bloody well right, I agree. Bloody union Trots. But I'm not sure about everybody else. God knows what some of them will do - there aren't that many jobs about.

"I expect they'll get fixed up though.

"But the only thing that worries me is that there are so few jobs these days. I know Maggie is right about killing off lame ducks – you can't keep loss-making industries alive for ever. But the problem is: how is Britain going to pay its way in the world if most of our big industries have gone down the pan? Lame ducks, yes...I just hope we're not killing off the golden goose."

Hanna knew the answer: "We'll be a service economy. Never forget we've got the enormously successful financial sector. The City is big business – we're still a world power there. "The big banks are the mainstay of our economy now. We can always rely on them. And I'd rather rely on bankers than on coal miners. You'll see!"

33

"Yes, you're probably right. Now, how'd you like to go to the Northern College of Music tomorrow? There's a really good baroque concert and there are a couple of tickets going spare...somebody who can't make it at the last minute is offering them round."

"Sorry. I can't. I'm out at Donna's tomorrow...I did tell you weeks ago. It's one of those boring clothing parties, but I said I'd go."

"Don't worry...it was just an idea," said Mayer.

*

Jenny Cooper did not take it well. What hurt her husband most was that far from being supportive and sympathetic, her anger at first was aimed at him.

"How many times did I say that union job would do you no good. You didn't get paid for doing it, and now look where it's landed you – and us.

"I've told you and told you. You're a damn fool! Now you've really landed us in a mess! Well you'd better find another job PDQ. Because if you think I'm going to work my butt off supporting you, you've got another think coming."

"Hang on! It's not my fault...I didn't ask to be made redundant. I didn't have any choice! I..."

He could not halt the torrent of verbal vitriol from his wife, reacting to news that left her full of fear. It was a woman's instant perception of what it could mean...perhaps the loss of their home and certainly the way of life that they enjoyed. She saw the worst case scenario long before her husband.

She was having no truck with his excuses. If it wasn't his fault, whose fault was it? He should have kept out of all that union business. What about the children? What about the holiday they'd booked? What about the car: they still had half the HP to pay off. It certainly wasn't *her* fault.

She'd have to give up her holiday. And you've been promising the kids for months that you'd take them to the Caribbean. Without the airline concession we can't afford it now. We can't afford anything...and on, and on.

He knew better than to argue. She wasn't usually bitchy. But this was a bad shock for her. He'd told her about the company's plan to cut back on jobs, but he'd also told her that it wouldn't affect him...they'd go for the last-in-first-out routine, he'd said.

She'd said she hoped he was right, because the pay she got as an admin assistant at the high school wouldn't go very far if he lost his job. But she accepted his assurances that he wasn't under threat. He'd believed it too. That night, in bed, they made it up. They were friends again. But as she clung to him afterwards her fears came rushing back: "Do you think you'll be able to get another job...things are so bad these days?"

He told her he would get something, even if it meant leaving the airline business. "You can't do that - you love that job and you know it," she said. "I don't want you to end up being a filling station attendant or something...it's just not fair."

"It'll work out all right for us...just you see if it doesn't," he said, sounding a lot more confident than he felt.

CHAPTER 6

1983

Hanna had gone out to her clothes party. There was damn-all on the TV. Then Geoff remembered the book he'd picked up when he'd been spending a few minutes browsing in the airport bookshop. He'd chanced on the title, "Tracing Your Ancestors," and the passing thought he'd voiced in Valetta made him decide to buy it.

Straight away there was a snag. The book advised starting out by chatting to older members of your family to pick up as many details as possible about names of grandparents, where they came from, and what lines of work they were involved in. Geoff's parents were both dead. He had been their only child - his mother had died giving birth to him, he'd been told. His father, James Mayer, had been a prosperous grocer – with six shops, all in Manchester. He had paid somebody else to run them until he had died after a stroke when Geoff was seventeen.

He had a definite curiosity about his mother. He'd always wondered about her, for as long as he could remember: what would home have been like with her in it? What was she like, as a person? He'd asked his father, but had never got any clear vision of her from his answers. It was a void in his life. But somehow she was so remote from him that it was the Mayer family history which really interested him - after all that was his family name. But there was nobody close to him who would be able to tell him anything.

In fact it only left his father's younger sister, Aunt Margaret, who was now a widow well turned seventy, and living in Bournemouth. They always sent each other Christmas cards but they had never been very close, and he hadn't seen her since his father's funeral. With a twinge of guilt, he realised that was nearly thirty years ago.

He picked up the phone and rang her. She was surprised to hear from him, but she seemed quite pleased. And she was very helpful. She knew his father's date of birth – September 15th 1903. His grandfather had died before Geoff was born, and he knew nothing about him, except that he had been a doctor. But Aunt Margaret not only told him his grandfather's name, William Arthur, but also that his grandmother had been called Alice, and Drinkwater had been her maiden name.

Everybody knew William Arthur as Wam because of his initials. He had been a G.P. in Knutsford. But Wam's father had been a gardener. He'd lived in Knutsford too, she'd always been told.

Wam was 62 when he died, and Aunt Margaret was pretty sure that was in 1933...she remembered going to his funeral. His wife had died quite a few years earlier.

Geoff was grateful for the information. He asked if his great grandfather had owned a market garden, but she said no, she understood that he had just worked as a gardener, presumably at a large house. He rang off, dismayed by the lowly position in life of his forebear, and puzzled, too.

He had always assumed that he sprang from at least middle-class stock. After all, his grandfather had been a doctor in the days when that meant wealth and status, and his father had been pretty well off too – he had owned half a dozen shops in Manchester's better-off southern suburbs.

And as a true blue Tory city councillor he had been a pillar of the local establishment, in the days when the Conservatives had been a force to be reckoned with in Manchester.

Yet two generations back, if Aunt Margaret was right, the head of the family had been a nothing more than a gardener. "So how the hell did he have the money to pay for his son to get the education to be a doctor?" he said aloud to himself. Geoff's curiosity - and appetite to solve the riddle - was whetted.

In his book he read about the ways to get further back into his family tree: checking birth, marriage and death certificates, each giving a little more information about the previous generation. Once you got

100 years back, you could use census returns, which had been made every ten years since 1841, giving details of family names, children, ages, jobs, and places of birth.

And before that, the use of parish records on baptisms, marriages and burials to get more names and dates: playing detective to fill in the void of information generation by generation. With a lot of luck you could go back as far as 1538 when it had been decreed that all parishes had to keep records of christenings, marriages and burials.

Geoff knew immediately that he was hooked on the idea. It would be fascinating to know more about his roots. And he'd always had an unconsummated interest in history which, he knew at once, could tie in nicely with finding out about his ancestors: who they were, where they lived, and what they did for a living.

It might mean doing a fair bit of bookwork to catch up with the historical background as he worked his way backwards in time tracing his forebears; but somehow he hadn't done a lot of reading in recent years, and this would provide a reason for getting back into the habit.

He had an early start the next morning, so he went to bed at ten. He was not awake when Hanna got home. He was dimly conscious that her breath smelled of drink. But she hardly disturbed him as she slipped quietly in under the covers, assuming him to be sleeping. She's very thoughtful...that was the last thing he found himself thinking as he slipped again into a comfortable sleep.

*

The very fact that Geoff hadn't the vaguest notion that the man he thought was his best friend was screwing her was the one thing that above all made Hanna despise her husband.

It had started as a secret, disturbingly exciting, thing. God! How worried she'd been that Geoff would somehow find out. She had this terrible anxiety, after the sex – the wonderful sex! – with Adam that he might sense that she had shared her body with someone else. But not

Geoff. He was too bloody boring for such thoughts to have entered his head.

Now it was so easy that it was almost routine. He always brought home a full copy of his duty roster so that she would know exactly where he was, and when. My God, it was almost like taking candy off a child, she thought.

And Geoff was childish! He was so damn stupid that he never once suspected what had been going on for months now. And what had been a daring experiment for her had turned into much more than that. Adam Davies certainly was in love with her. She knew that. He couldn't get enough of her.

And perhaps that was why he had proved to be so good at hiding it from Geoff. The two men saw a fair bit of each other ever since Hanna's best move. Even now she felt like hugging herself when she thought how simple it had been, that ploy. She had persuaded Geoff that with his job taking him away so often, he lacked friends in Prestbury. "Why don't you go out for a drink occasionally with the boys?" she had suggested.

It was true that he had not got any special pals. "You should have, you know," Hanna had said. "A man needs male company. Why don't you team up with one of the chaps we see at church. There's Adam Davies, for instance. He seems a pleasant guy."

And he'd fallen for it. He rang Adam a couple of days later and asked him if he fancied popping out to the Admiral Rodney for a pint. After that it was not uncommon for Adam to ring the Mayer household...and if Geoff was in, he was just calling for a chat or to suggest going out for a drink.

It had been at St. Peter's, the ancient parish church in the centre of the village, that Adam and his wife Jill had first met Geoff and Hanna, a couple of years back.

Later they bumped into Hanna and Geoff at a fund-raising event at the golf club. After that they had met a number of times socially. And the first thing that attracted Hanna to him was that he chatted to her as if they had been friends for years – they got on so easily. They were

39

interested in the same things – antiques, as well as pop music of the 1960s and jazz, which bored Geoff.

Geoff always left them to it and went off to talk golf to the guys at the bar. It was at one such event at the golf club that Adam had confided in Hanna about the time a couple of years back when Jill had told him she had had an affair with some young chap in the office where she worked.

He had been so devastated that even as he told her about it Hanna had sympathetically reached out and put her hand on his. But only for a moment. She felt an almost electric shock as his eyes – those lovely brown eyes – had looked up into hers, and she had pulled her hand away, knowing that she was suddenly, ridiculously, blushing, of all things!

But he wasn't looking at her face, so perhaps he hadn't noticed. He was looking at her sweater. And then she had first known that she wanted him to look.

Now, lying in bed alongside her sleeping husband, Adam was all she wanted.

Geoff stirred in his sleep and his arm moved on to her hip. Hanna moved away, irritated by the revulsion she felt. She may be married to him, but she did not want him to touch her, asleep or awake. Having sex with him was nasty. "Creep," she said to herself, with an amazing self-righteousness. "I can't stand creeps."

To avoid his getting suspicious she had vowed to carry on having sex with Geoff. But she avoided it as much as possible. She decided that she would treat it as a duty, to be gone through solely to keep him happy enough to suspect nothing – that way she would be able to continue to love Adam as often as they could manage in the discreet but urgent way they had now come to think of as their right.

She had found it easy to pretend to Geoff that she had orgasms with him. In fact the whole thing made her shudder, and he was so damned stupid that he thought it was passion!

*

Geoff bought a card-index and a loose-leafed A4 notebook to record his family history research. He wrote a card for himself containing all the information that his book advised him he would need each time he identified an ancestor. His birth certificate, which he had not so much as glanced at for years, was easy to find, because he always kept such documents in a large envelope in a drawer.

Sure enough, as his book told him it would, it gave not only his date and place of birth, but also his mother's maiden name – Pendleton - and his father's profession. And there was his first surprise. For it didn't say, as he expected, "grocer." It said "property owner."

Geoff's memories of his father were distant - his dad had died when he was only seventeen. I never really knew him, Geoff thought. For his grocery shops and his duties as a city councillor in Manchester had kept him out so much of the time - daytime and evenings.

They had had a live-in housekeeper, Mrs. Mullery, who had looked after him. She was Irish, a widow of a motherly sort of age, loving and caring, and she had looked after Geoff until he had been sent away to boarding school. Come to think of it, Mrs. Mullery was probably no more than forty at the time, he thought - certainly not as old as I am now.

In his younger days at school it was to her that he turned for advice and help with his reading and homework because he never knew what time his father would be arriving home in those days. And he would usually be too tired to want to bother.

Yet he had been a kind and generous father. On Saturdays after the war he used to take him to Maine Road to watch Manchester United, under the captaincy of Johnny Carey, weave their Matt Busby brand of attacking magic on that very green turf. Maine Road was Manchester City's ground, but United played there after the war because their own stadium at Old Trafford had been damaged by bombing.

And he had always provided Geoff with pocket money in amounts that had made him the envy of some of his pals, for it was obvious that his dad was pretty well-heeled. "I always thought that was the result of his shops doing so well," said Geoff aloud. "But I never knew about him owning property for a living."

It made him keen to find out about his forebears. William Arthur, the doctor, must have provided the money to set Geoff's father up in business. But how could his grandfather have been able to afford to become a doctor if his own father had been a gardener? Despite what Aunt Margaret had told him, he must have been more than that. More likely the owner of a market garden, decided Geoff. Anyway, he'd find out.

CHAPTER 7

1936

Ann Mayer frowned as she read the letter. It had been hand-delivered long after the morning postman had called. It was addressed to her, yet she did not know the handwriting.

Intrigued, she opened the envelope to read this appeal...this pleading for help that she immediately knew was genuine, yet, unbelievably, cast her husband - the only man she had ever loved or wanted - as a creature she could not recognise.

The writing was not that of someone who was educated or mature. It was from a woman who signed herself Jane Dawson. Ann felt anger against this woman. Then she read the letter again. It must be a mistake. She knew exactly what to do. She would ask James. He would explain everything - how this Jane Dawson could be so mistaken.

Her husband's arrival home from business was timed almost to the minute: 6.35pm. Always. James Mayer did not believe in being late for his glass of whisky and his perusal of the *Manchester Guardian* before dinner at 7.15 sharp.

His kiss was perfunctory, as ever, a moment's pause as he headed for the decanter on the sideboard. He had had a trying day and he needed it.

"Darling, I have had a most peculiar letter from a woman who says she is one of your tenants," she began. "What?" His voice was strangely abrupt, almost menacing, she thought. He had stopped short, the cut-glass decanter in one hand, the matching whisky glass in the other. His tone was one of shock. And anger. "Why should one of my tenants write to you?"

"This Mrs. Dawson says you have given her notice to get out of her home because she is behind with her rent - but she has a new baby and she is short of money because she has been too ill to work."

The decanter and glass thumped down on to the sideboard and James was striding across the drawing room. Ann could see that he was in an instant towering rage. He snatched the letter from his wife's hand, scanned it briefly before crumpling it and throwing it with some force into the fire.

"How dare she write to you," he raged. "How does she know you?"

"Darling, she doesn't know me. I don't know why she has written to me - I have never heard of her."

"Liar! Why should she write to you otherwise?"

The word "liar" struck Ann like a blow. Her husband had never spoken to her like this before. As the import of the word sank in she felt anger rise to her face. She felt herself redden as she heard herself snap back: "How dare you call me a liar."

The impact of the back of her husband's hand smashing into her face was something she knew had happened, but there was at first no physical pain - just a sense of unreality. Her hurt was this sudden realisation that this man was a complete stranger: a violent, unpredictable savage in his expensive businessman's suit. Then she felt and saw the pouring of blood from her nose and mouth and the first sharp stab of agony surged through her.

Dimly she heard her husband's harsh, unrepentant tones: "I dare because you are my wife and I say you are a liar. So never talk to me again as if I am one of the servants!"

And he strode from the room, slamming the door behind him.

For Ann, the cosy middle-class world she inhabited had collapsed for ever. She knew that she would never trust her husband again. And what she felt towards him was an intense hatred.

And she knew, too, as her bruises healed over the days that followed his attack, that nothing would stop her visiting Jane Dawson and finding out what sort of man was James Mayer, to whom she had been married for three years, and who, she now saw clearly, she did not know at all.

She remembered the name of the street in Gorton, from the letter. The next day a taxi took her there. And it took only one question to a pinafore-aproned woman at a doorway to locate the mid-terrace house where Jane Dawson lived. Ann had never been in a neighbourhood like this. She was nervous, but determined to go through with it.

She introduced herself and said she had come in response to her letter. As she eyed Jane Dawson, the dingy, dark room, with the milky baby aroma was mixed with what she recognised from some distant childhood memory, as the cloying, pervasive smell of rot.

Jane Dawson was, she guessed, in her mid-twenties - about her own age - but thin and ill-looking. Her brown wool dress was patched and threadbare, what could be seen of it outside her apron. But her hair was combed and pulled back, albeit not too tidily, and below that her blue eyes were alert. As they started, haltingly, to converse, she seemed bright enough despite her pallid face, Ann thought.

Jane saw the bruises on her visitor's face and drew her own conclusions, but she made an instant decision to say nothing about them.

She told Ann that she hoped she had not minded her writing to her, but she was desperate...she had written to Mr. Mayer explaining her illness and promising that she would catch up with the rent payments as soon as she could get back to work, but the only reply had been the notice to quit. "He didn't seem to understand – that's why I wrote to you," she said.

"I've nowhere to go. My parents turned me out when they found I was expecting, and me not wed. They are big churchgoers. They won't have me back – they've made that plain. And I've no one else to turn to," she pleaded.

Tears brimmed in her eyes as her own words reminded her again of the awfulness of her predicament.

"How much do you owe?" asked Ann.

45

"Three pounds rent - and I owe the grocer nearly twenty shillings too," sobbed Jane.

Ann opened her handbag and took a five pound note from her purse. Jane's eyes opened wide as she saw the big white banknote being held towards her. "Take this. You don't have to give it back," said Ann. "But never tell anybody where you got it."

She paused. "Especially...anybody in Mr. Mayer's office."

Their eyes met. Ann knew that Jane knew exactly which "anybody" she meant. She stood up and walked towards the door, then stopped and turned. "Did they give any reason why they were giving you notice to leave your home?"

"No. But it didn't really surprise me. Mr. Mayer doesn't stand for people being behind with their rent - or asking for repairs to be done. They always get thrown out..."

Jane stopped, suddenly becoming aware of what she was saying. She added quickly: "I'm sorry, but it is the truth. He is a very hard landlord. Some say he's the worst in Manchester. But he's got a wife with a heart of gold - I can't thank you enough, Mrs. Mayer. I'll pay you back one day. I promise."

Back home, Ann suddenly found herself feeling terribly guilty. She fought it off, determinedly. But the feeling that she had betrayed her husband persisted in her mind, despite her mental arguments to the contrary; despite telling herself that her secret intervention had been for the good.

It was not helped, of course, by the growing perception that she had begun to loathe her husband. What had happened on the day of the letter had come as a massive shock. She had never imagined that her husband could be violent. She had decided then, as she struggled alone with the mental and physical pain, to be strictly dutiful as a wife, but nothing more. Ever.

He didn't seem to notice that whatever else happened, her mind was hating him...as they ate their meals, sorted out the household bills, had sex. She found that she could avoid antagonising him - for loathing was

46

mixed with fear - and yet refrain from offering him anything except that which was required strictly as the duties of a wife.

Her visit to Jane Dawson, her confirmation that James Mayer was viewed by his tenants as a terrible landlord with little humanity, had hardened her feelings of dislike for this man she had thought she loved. But there was this terrible foreboding – a kind of foreknowledge that she could not win.

*

The bailiffs were brutally efficient. It wasn't their concern: they were just doing their job. They went about their business with the swagger of bullies who know that the might of England's incomparably even-handed legal system was all on their side.

*

The Law in England had always, in its amazingly learned way, taken the obvious view that the wealthy - by virtue of their money and the influence they were thus able to wield – were superior to the poor, and therefore so much more needful of, and, indeed, entitled to the support of the courts' judgements.

Not only that: the poor, by virtue of their not having any money or influence, were plainly inferior, and needed all the chastisement and punishment that the law could find an excuse to mete out.

For judges themselves had always been among the moneyed elite; and below them in the legal chain of command, the magistrates and the lawyers were all in that class which was comfortably off. They knew where their interests lay.

The bailiffs refused to have anything to do with the five pound note that she offered them, telling them that she was intending the next day to take it to Mr. Mayer's office.

"You should have thought of that before now," said the man who was obviously in charge. "Our orders are to put you out."

They took away everything saleable, ignoring Jane's pleas and appeals for mercy for her baby. "It's your problem missus, not ours," was the extent of their response.

They physically pushed her and her baby out on to the cobbled street, along with a few pathetic possessions – an old pram, a blanket, a worn rug, and a pair of old shoes.

The rest of the contents of her home they put into their lorry. They locked the door with the keys they had taken from her. Then they drove away. Job done. Very satisfactory.

*

It was a week later when the envelope arrived in the post. Fortunately Ann recognised the handwriting and hid it before James arrived to look at his post.

When James had left for his office she opened it, to find just three one-pound notes inside, and a scrap of torn paper with the words "Thank You" written on it.

Ann's initial pleasure that Jane had been able to pay back some of the money so quickly was followed moments later by a growing puzzlement. It kept nagging away at her every time she thought about it. But it was another week before she took a taxi again to the terraced street where Jane lived.

Had lived. There were already new people in the little terraced house that Jane had called home. Neighbours had no idea where Jane had gone.

"And her with that sickly little baby, too," said one. Ann found genuine concern, but nothing more. She regretted not asking Jane where her exceedingly Christian parents lived. She went home full of doubt and more than a little worry. In the few minutes she had had with the young mother she had developed her first real feelings of concern for somebody who lived in the slums of Manchester.

But there was nothing she could do for the moment. She didn't even see the single paragraph story in that night's *Manchester Evening News* headed: "Drowning tragedy."

It wasn't until the report of the inquest two months later when she read of the finding of Jane Dawson's body in the Rochdale Canal, still clutching her dead baby, that she knew.

It was all the worse because Ann was now expecting her first baby. But she knew that her pregnancy had to take precedence over any feelings of remorse and anger over Jane Dawson. When her little boy was born on August 12th 1937 they called him Geoffrey. He was a handsome little thing - everybody said so. And so like his father. It was that that started her depression.

They said that she would soon get over it. You always do, they said, once you get to know your baby and how to cope with his cries for food. Once your milk comes easily. Once he grows and starts to smile at you.

But it didn't. Geoffrey cried more and more. Her depression grew worse. She could not stand the baby to be near her. Her mother came and tried to help. But Ann found no comfort at all. They tried to reason with her. The doctor tried being firm. The district nurse tried being stern and blustering. She wept most of the time. She refused to eat. There was no controlling her.

Milk fever, they called it. So they put her in the asylum.

*

Ann got worse. She could not face her husband's visits. Her tears, her refusals to speak, her occasional ranting, were embarrassing. So he stopped going. Her parents, who lived several miles away in north Manchester, called once a month for the first year, despite the length of the journey by two changes of bus.

After that, their visits were much less frequent. That their only daughter was a hopeless mental case was destroying them. Ten years later, after the war, her father, who was ten years older than Ann's mother, retired and went to live in Colwyn Bay. After that an annual visit was all they managed. And that stopped after her father's death.

When her mother followed him to the grave in 1972, nobody came to visit. And so she came to be a non-person, for James Mayer had told everybody who asked that she had died in hospital. And he told his son that she had died in giving birth to him.

And in the asylum in 1977 she did die, forgotten, twenty-three years after her husband, whose life had ended after a stroke, aged just 51. The cause of her death was pneumonia, following influenza.

Her records didn't mention postnatal depression.

CHAPTER 8

1983

Another phone call to Aunt Margaret provided the answers. Geoff's father had invested his share of their GP father's will in buying up swathes of cheap terraced houses in the worst-off areas of Manchester - Gorton, and Openshaw.

"Everybody tried to talk him out of it at the time. I told him it was old, broken-down property, and to even think of investing in it was ridiculous," she said when Geoff phoned. "But James was always headstrong. When I spoke to him about it he told me to mind my own business. It was his money and he'd do whatever he wanted with it.

"The thing is, he was right. While I was taking good advice and putting my legacy into safe investments, he was already getting a decent income from so many rents, even if they were peanuts individually. I don't think he ever spent much on his houses, mind.

"He didn't do much repair work or modernisation, even though he was told they were needed.

"He said it kept rents low, and there were lots of folk who wanted cheap housing, and he was carrying out a social service.

"He was certainly right. He had a very good head for business. Within a few years he'd been able to buy his first grocer's shop on the proceeds. And by the time he'd got six shops he was coining it - enough to sell some of his property at a price well above what he'd paid for it.

"And getting on the city council didn't do him any harm, either. Being a Conservative he mixed with all the right people, of course. Yes, he did very well, did James. Our father would have been proud of him."

"I never knew all this," said Geoff.

"Well, when your father died you were away at school. What were you...seventeen or so? And as soon as you'd done your A-levels you went into the RAF, and I don't suppose you ever really thought about such things. Before that you were too young to want to know about his business affairs - not that anybody knew that much," said his aunt. "And honestly, since then I've seen very little of you. And you've never asked before."

Fair point, thought Geoff. "The thing that I'm really puzzled about, though, is if my great-grandfather was a gardener, how on earth was he able to afford to educate his son to be a doctor?"

"Well, that's been a little secret in our family for years, but I suppose there's no harm in telling you now," said his aunt. "The fact is, your great-grandfather, who I think was also called William, was a very good sprinter.

"Apparently he could always run faster than anyone else, and when he was a young man somebody from the local rugby club saw him running in some May Day races on the heath, and he was asked to play for Knutsford, even though he was only a working-class lad, and all the other members were gentlemen – in the old sense of the word. I seem to remember that the team was called the Dirty Dozen. I suppose they had to teach him how to play first.

"I was told this by my mother when she was ill, just before she died. She said that William Arthur's father played regularly for the team for some years.

"The players were all well-off sort of men, except for him. And, between you and me, after each game, when he got changed, he used to find a golden guinea in his shoe. He used to pocket it quietly, and he never asked where it came from. But they all added up, those guineas, and he was able to send your grandfather to a grammar school and then medical school on the proceeds."

"My God, now I've heard it all! You're telling me that he was secretly paid for playing rugby union. It has always been a prime rule that you didn't play for money. Everybody has to be amateur!" said Geoff.

"You're really saying that the family's wealth all sprang from my great-grandfather being an underhand professional rugger player!"

"Yes, I suppose you could say that. Of course it had to be kept very quiet," said Aunt Margaret. "Even when I was told, which was years later, I was sworn to secrecy. I was told in the strictest confidence."

"Oh! I'll keep mum about it! Frankly I wouldn't want my friends or anybody at the airline for that matter to know that my great-grandfather was a ruddy gardener. And as to being paid to play rugger, if they'd known about it in my RAF days I'd probably have been drummed out of the officers' mess!" laughed Geoff.

"Nonsense! It's different these days! They'd have admired you for having such a talented great-grandfather. Remember, Geoffrey, it's not how you made your money...the only thing that matters is that you made it!"

*

Geoffrey Mayer was deeply disappointed. He had been nurturing a belief that his father's wealth had somehow filtered down from aristocratic roots, way back.

Ever since his RAF days, when he had first seen that name on the tombstone in St John's co-cathedral in Valetta, he had been holding on to the vague idea that his family must have had a noble history going back - perhaps, who knows? - as far as William the Conqueror.

Thoughts of knights of old had been beckoning him to find where his family history would lead him. It wasn't the idea of wealth that intrigued him. It was the simple fact that he had always felt a bit above the common herd.

Going to boarding school, then taking a commission as a pilot in the RAF, had lifted him into the rarefied atmosphere of those who frankly never felt themselves to be one of the ordinary, common sort of people.

Since his father had died, as a youth he had never had a home or family to go to. But he had been very well looked after. His education had been taken care of. Then the RAF had become his family. By the time he decided to leave for civilian life he was flying Hercules transports.

Curiously enough his becoming an airline pilot had, to some extent, brought his feet nearer to the ground. It was one of those uppish businessmen passengers, who had certainly been drinking, who fired the first shot, taking him to task over the braid on his British Airways uniform in the days before he joined Sunjet.

It had all been over a delayed flight, grounded for hours because of a major engine snag. Geoff, feeling that his seniority called on him to help out when he saw a group of passengers besieging one of the check-in desks, spoke up and tried to put this troublesome, rather loud, if expensively dressed, man in his place.

"Christ! It's the bloody admiral!" the man had derisively greeted Geoff's opening, placatory, remarks. "It's a wonder the compass doesn't swing round ninety degrees when you get on board with all that brass on you," he had added, encouraged by the sniggers that had greeted his first riposte. "Who are you? The cabin boy?"

"I am in fact the First Officer of the aircraft that is due to take you all to Dusseldorf," Geoff had stated, feeling that this would silence this twit at a stroke.

"Are you?" said the businessman, now in full cry. "Well as far as I'm concerned you're just an airborne bus driver. Sorry! Assistant bus driver!

"And if you had any authority you'd be fixing us up with a replacement plane or telling the ground staff to transfer us to another airline," he added belligerently.

"I've paid to get to Dusseldorf in time for a very important meeting, and I don't expect to be given a load of rubbish from the likes of you, scrambled egg on your hat or not!"

In the face of applause - actual clapping, would you believe! - from some of the other passengers, Geoff had been forced to retreat after muttering lamely: "I was simply trying to help!"

That was the first time that it had crossed his mind that ground staff were not necessarily inferior to cockpit crew - for it was quite obvious that the girl behind the desk had been handling the situation better than he had managed to do.

But it had not materially changed Geoff's general feeling that he was somehow a bit above the masses - and not only after take-off!

So he had, without thinking about it, been clinging to the idea that he was...well...high-born.

He sent away to the local register office for the birth, marriage and death certificates of his grandfather. Geoff discovered that William Arthur had died on November 5th 1933. He had been born, in Brook Street, Knutsford, on May 13, 1871. His father, sure enough, was William Mayer, a gardener, and his mother was Ellen Mayer, formerly Carter.

In the following weeks he found that Dr William Arthur Mayer had married in September, 1902 in Knutsford. His wife, Geoff's grandmother, had been Alice Drinkwater. In the marriage certificate she was described as "Spinster." She would have been proud to marry a doctor, Geoff surmised.

One thing occurred to him: if his forebears hadn't been rich or aristocratic, obviously they had intellect - it took a good brain to qualify as a doctor.

And he had obviously been a very good doctor. For when Geoff sent away for a copy of his will, it showed that he had left more than £35,000 to his children.

"That must have been a tidy fortune in the 1930s!" he said to himself.

*

Geoff discovered that he didn't have to travel 30 miles or so to Chester to study the microfilms of births, marriages and deaths at the Cheshire County Records Office - the Central Library in Manchester held copies of the micro-films of BMDs and the ten-yearly census returns not only for the city and for Lancashire, but for Cheshire too. The only census returns available to check through were from 1841 to 1881...they weren't released to the public until they were 100 years old.

He found that going through the parish records for Knutsford was a painfully slow process. Sometimes the film was not easy to read.

After one particularly hard session of poring over the faint, ill-focused screen at the Central Library, Geoff arrived home to find that Hanna was out, again. There was a brief note: "Get your own supper, I'll be late."

After his meal - a frozen curry concoction in a packet, which turned out to be not at all bad - Geoff poured himself a beer and began looking over the notes he had made at the Central Library.

He entered his findings into a loose-leaf A4 notebook and his card index where he was slowly assembling more and more information on his forebears. He now knew that his family had lived in Knutsford for well over a hundred years.

A new thought struck him. I wonder if my grandfather got his brains from William the gardener - or from his mother? We'll never know. There's a lot we'll never know, despite all the records. I mean, how the hell did my grandfather become so well-off? All right, he was a doctor. But he was in a small country town. There must have been limits, even though Knutsford had some well-heeled citizens who no doubt would pay well for a good doctor's services.

"Or was he some kind of specialist...or a miracle healer?

CHAPTER 9

1894

Of course the gentry knew he was the son of a mere gardener – everybody in Knutsford knew it. But whereas the people of his father's class didn't really know how to place him in the hierarchy of the town, the men of the moneyed sort seemed to have made an instant, collective decision: give him the cold shoulder.

So there he was, newly qualified as a doctor - proud of his achievement in getting his degree in medicine – setting up to practise in the very place where his father lived his lowly life and worked his lowly work. But where on earth were his patients going to come from?

At first, as he had approached the end of his six years at the Manchester University Medical School, William Arthur Mayer had considered joining an existing practice far from where his background was known.

No questions asked: he'd be a general practitioner, respected for his knowledge as a doctor. Life would be sweet.

But as he'd pondered where to go and practise, the thought of Knutsford and its rigid attitudes towards serving and servitude, to being of "good family" or not, of being "the right sort of people," kept intruding into his vision of how he wanted his life to go, and where he fitted in.

In effect, he knew, the one place he seemed to face exclusion from polite society was Knutsford, because he was pretty sure that the gentry there - the only people capable of paying a doctor's bills - would not want to be treated by the son of a local gardener, a man of the lower classes.

He may have been educated; but how had that come about, they'd ask. His father must have obtained money somehow. It was inexplicable, except, perhaps, from crime. It could surely not have been by fair means. That's how the higher echelons would view it, William Arthur knew.

He smiled as he thought about his dear old father, honest as the day he was born, and the suspicion and puzzlement that existed about how on earth he had managed to get enough money to educate his son to be a doctor.

Well let them puzzle. Damn them! William Arthur Mayer - Wam to his friends at the medical school, a name he liked and had become accustomed to - had decided that he was hanged if the prejudiced snobbery of the "better" people of his home town would prevent his practising there.

But how could he? If the people who could pay his fees wouldn't use his services, and the people who might want to attend his surgery couldn't afford it, how was he to live?

Anyway, why give himself the problem?

It was something, he knew, about honouring his father. But not all. There had been a moment, when he was in his final year at medical school, when he was in Knutsford for the Christmas holiday...

Close to the railway station, he had come face to face with Sir Galahad Whiteside, one of the town's wealthy cotton grandees, and Lady Whiteside.

He had raised his hat and said brightly: "Good morning Sir Galahad...Ma'am."

The noble gent had looked at him, pulled down the corners of his mouth into the sort of expression that would be worn by one seeing something truly revolting, and uttered a sound that to Wam's ears sounded like "Huh!"

Then Sir Galahad had walked past, saying loudly to his lady wife: "The lower classes don't know their place any more. Dress 'em up as you might – they're still the lower classes."

And Lady Whiteside muttered, as they stepped away: "Disgusting! Absolutely!"

At the Manchester Medical School William Arthur's intellect and ability had made him accepted as the equal of his considerably wealthier fellow-students, who respected and liked him. It had established a degree of self-confidence in him.

So, confronted by Sir Galahad's attempt at rebuff, he had been unable to resist saying, with an equal volume, to an imaginary companion: "Such a perfect gentleman! And what a lady! Absolutely!"

And, unspoken, it had planted a seed of determination to stand his ground, and to fight the stupid prejudices of so-called class...which really meant the possession or otherwise of money.

*

In the end it had been a lot easier than he had expected. He had made it clear that he would treat people who couldn't pay his fees straight off. They could pay by instalments, when they had the money to do so. His father had spread the word about that.

Like most doctors, of course, he would treat the victims of accidents or other emergency cases without expecting payment if they were too poor to be able to afford it.

And within days of setting up in his newly-rented surgery in the town centre a farmer brought in one of his young labourers who had caught his fingers in a mowing machine. Wam happened to be the nearest doctor.

Even in the blood and mess he could see that the youth's hand would have to come off. Wam's surgical skill had earned him high marks at the medical school, and he put it to good use now.

The lad, aged just fourteen, recovered well, and the care he received kept it infection free until the stump of his arm healed.

His parents were always grateful to Dr Mayer. The word began to spread that he was an exceptionally good doctor. It brought in patients, mostly poor people.

Those who couldn't pay immediately were allowed to contribute a shilling each week, entered into a book by the doctor's father, who discreetly called at their homes in the evening, until they'd paid for their treatment.

He got a lot of patients that way, and that brought in quite a few shillings each week, even at the start.

In those days the labouring classes were not expected to use the services of a doctor unless they were at death's door.

And they did worry about death's door. It opened all too easily.

The biggest health dread of most people was consumption. That was because there was no cure, and it was a not uncommon ailment because much of the milk that people drank was infected with tuberculosis.

And there were constant reminders of other dread diseases that could bring you down – pneumonia, bronchitis and influenza among the lesser ones, epidemics of smallpox, typhoid and diphtheria even more likely to prove fatal.

It was hardly surprising that, like many country people, the less educated in Knutsford held on to beliefs in the old ways of warding off the dangers.

For a medical man they could be exasperating...or amusing. They appealed, in the main, to Wam's sense of humour.

Sometimes it was difficult to avoid smiling when, confronted with the deep-rooted beliefs in the life-saving methods taught by old people's parents and grand-parents, he tried to suggest more up-to-date cures.

William Arthur saw a lot of the poor people because he volunteered for the unpopular and not well-paid task of administering medical care under the Poor Law Union rules.

These patients were, some of the gentry observed disparagingly, his kind of people. But he'll never make much of a living out of them, they bumbled.

Wam might have agreed, if they had asked him. But it gave him a start, and he approached his early work with good will and a cheerful approach to his patients.

Looking at the records of Poor Law treatment given in the past, he was interested to see that mostly it consisted of recommending the provision of mutton, oatmeal, broth, or milk to help people's recovery.

Men, women and children, even small babies, had also been given brandy and gin to make them better, for the more expensive medicines – such as quinine, cod-liver oil and sarsaparilla – cost too much for the tight-fisted Poor Law guardians to accept.

Anyway Wam knew that when they became poorly many people preferred the old traditional medicines, which were mostly, but not all, herb-based.

One or two could even quote John Wesley, who had stated that a celandine kept under the foot was a sure cure for jaundice. No less an authority than their Methodist preacher – a man whom Wam knew to be a kind, yet austere fanatic – had told them so. So no good arguing with that!

However some old cures he definitely discouraged: "Look, Obadiah, it may be true that your wife's cousin in Norfolk swears by it, but in my opinion your grand-children's whooping cough definitely will not be cured by eating fried mice."

Opium was about the only analgesic that eased the pain of rheumatism. It eased many pains and troubles. In a mixture with treacle and sassafras it was found to have a quieting affect on babies when their mothers were away from them, working in the fields.

Wam thought it was a wonder it didn't quieten them for good.

Slowly the shillings rolled in as the months rolled by. It paid the rent.

He was freshly taught in the latest medical techniques, so his cures tended to work. Over time that made him popular, and it gave William Arthur a very great sense of satisfaction.

It wasn't going to make him a wealthy man, he knew.

But gradually there was one thing that really did bring in patients: Wam was a very good-looking young man.

61

He was always well-groomed. He looked his best when he smiled. And when attending to his patients he smiled a lot. He was that sort of chap.

The better-off sort of males may be giving him the cold shoulder. But it was the apparently well-heeled ladies of the town who didn't seem to be too worried about his father's lowly position in life.

Because a handsome young doctor, who knew how to treat a lady – something he had learned during his six years in Manchester among well-brought-up medical students – as well as having a lot of up-to-date knowledge at his delicate fingertips...well, that was something the ladies found hard to resist.

He had, they said, such a wonderful bedside manner. He was so...understanding.

Somehow they needed to see the doctor quite often. A woman needs help in so many areas of life. And being healthy was so important, wasn't it?

He amused the ladies too: "A cold, if not treated, will last for seven days," he would say with no hint of a smile. "Properly treated it will last only a week."

He gradually became quite a popular doctor.

Some of his lone women patients, he quickly realised, were not as well-off as they appeared. Well brought-up, yes; well-dressed and housed; and determined to keep up appearances as gentlefolk. But short of money.

Such people, especially the widows and the elderly unmarried women, lived very carefully, spending little because they had little, often slowly starving themselves in an effort to husband their meagre resources whilst retaining their status in the town's rigidly stratified society.

If they fell ill, sometimes it was their friends, or even their servants, who called him in. In their position it was not easy to refuse to see the G.P. But they could not really afford doctors' fees.

Wam felt a great sympathy for such women. They were intelligent, educated, decent people who did not deserve to descend into an entirely unaccustomed penury.

He genuinely liked many such women, and when he was sure that their inability to pay was a real, distressing shortage of funds, he did not press for payment, but gently suggested the same solution that had helped the labouring classes...pay a shilling or two each week, and don't worry about it, he would tell them. Nobody would know.

Wryly, Wam thought of his offer of "treat now – pay later" as his own form of medical advances.

So his practice slowly grew. Women told their friends: "I go to Doctor Mayer now – he is such a nice young man. And he knows all the latest treatments."

And whilst some of his elderly lady patients were genuinely poor, others were very well-off indeed, and well able to pay his bills.

When they were ill – and even when they were not, sometimes – they asked him to visit them. He lavished care on them, and often became their confidant, adviser and friend.

They seemed to need to tell him their innermost thoughts and hopes and fears, as well as the town tittle-tattle that brightened their days, and his.

Because he was a sensible man, with rather more learning than most of the people they tended to meet, the advice he gave them was found to be well worth listening to. In any case, it always sounded wise.

It surprised him how many elderly widows had no family other than relatives almost as old as themselves. And, being just as wealthy, they didn't need more money. What would they do with it when they were eventually called to meet their maker?

He suggested that they seek out long-missing nephews and nieces, or cousins far removed. Some did.

But one or two told him that they had decided to leave in their wills a small token of their gratitude for his care and friendship over the years. They hoped he didn't mind.

Well of course not. It would have been rude to have refused.

63

But please don't make your family, your relatives, feel deprived on my account. You must look after them first. Of course you must!

The first time one such old lady – who knew of no relatives – left him £200 in her will, he was surprised but of course not displeased. He felt honoured, if slightly uneasy about it. But nobody else knew, except her solicitor, who was bound to professional silence.

After two more women – both spinsters, lost to any but far distant family, and without any relatives who might have wanted to care for them – had left him bequests, he began to surmise that this was where the real money lay. For although he was by now beginning to find himself comfortably off, these sudden, unearned additions to his bank balance began to make him a wealthy man.

Wam never actually suggested that anyone should write him into their will. But he did, when asked for advice, help his elderly patients to crystallize their thoughts on disposing some of their wealth to their "most trusted friends and advisers" when they eventually went to a better place.

Especially those, he suggested, who could do most good for the community.

And a number of them took the hint.

*

1933

He had married, in September 1902. His bride, Alice Drinkwater, was ten years younger than Wam, and the daughter of a fellow doctor in Knutsford. She brought a fresh sparkle into his life, for she found pleasure in everything, it seemed. She was a joy to be with, both inside and outside their home.

It brought him a wider circle of friends, and the Mayers often entertained them.

64

Like all doctors, he made up his own medicines from the array of glass-stoppered and labelled bottles that he kept on the shelves in his surgery.

It amused visiting friends to his home that when he poured a gin and tonic, or a whiskey and water, he always held the glass up to his eye level, and poured in the liquids from a bottle at the same height...just the same way that he poured in the ingredients of his medicines.

It was a habit he kept all his life.

In 1903, a year after their marriage, they had their first child, a boy they called James, a fine healthy lad who was, people said, the image of his father. Wam's father lived long enough to cuddle the baby whenever he could, and to see his first birthday. He died in 1904, aware that Alice was pregnant again; it filled his mind with thoughts of his long lost wife Ellen.

In 1905 Alice gave birth to a stillborn child. Three years later, in 1908, they had a daughter, Margaret, a sturdy girl. But although Alice bore him three more girls, Ellen, Jane and Mary, none of them survived.

One terrible summer, despite all his medical skill, the three little girls died of scarlet fever, one after the other, aged two, four, and five.

James and Margaret were both away, staying at the home of school friends in Northwich and Sale during part of the holidays, and William Arthur sent telegrams asking their friends' parents to keep them away from Knutsford until the epidemic had died down.

So James and Margaret were saved. But the grief of losing her three little girls left Alice a sad shadow of the fun-loving beauty William Arthur had married.

She became listless. She lost weight. She seemed to lose interest in living. And in 1918 she died. Her death certificate gave the cause of death as influenza. But her friends were sure that she died of a broken heart.

*

Over time the legacies left to him by his patients became not uncommon. The Great War, which left so many families bereaved, their menfolk killed and often lost without trace in the mud of northern France and Belgium, meant there were more widows with no son to whom they could leave their wealth.

William Arthur Mayer discreetly benefited from that. His wealth grew. His patients kept quiet about leaving him cash bequests, and so did he.

Some left him small amounts, others willed him substantial sums. He was not short of money to live on, so these gifts were put into the bank, and slowly grew, until he had amassed a considerable fortune by the time he died suddenly in 1933, aged 62, of a heart attack.

To his son James, then aged 30, the news that his father had left in excess of £30,000 went a very considerable way towards assuaging his grief.

*

1983

Geoff was puzzled about his grandfather's wealth. Somehow it didn't seem to add up.

The train of thought made Geoff return to the boxes that his father had left in the attic. He had never really examined everything in them. He knew there was a lot of old paperwork. Probably boring old bills, he'd concluded at the time. But they might show just how old grandfather Mayer had made his pile. If not, he could throw them out.

It was in the third box of half-a-dozen that he found a smaller box containing copies of a lot of old wills. There was one, obviously drawn up by Alice's parents, leaving her a legacy of £3,000. But the rest were wills of women - mostly - whose names meant nothing to Geoff, but who had left Dr Mayer various sums of money.

The amounts ranged from £100 to one lady who had bequeathed £2,000 to her "trusted friend and doctor of many years".

Working his way through the pile of wills, Geoff found that the total amounted to nearly £20,000 over a period of years from 1903 to 1933.

"He must have been a hell of a good doctor," said Geoff, speaking to the empty room. He paused, and heard himself say: "Or a hell of a good con-man. I mean, the odd legacy might be OK, but this is something else."

He lapsed into silent musing. Isn't there some kind of rule against this sort of thing? I mean, a doctor's in a special position of trust. A GP was probably invited into his patients' homes quite often. He might be in a good position to influence some of his rich old patients, especially widowed old ladies.

They'd probably be very grateful for the medical help they received from him. I suppose they could please themselves who they left their money to. No, it's fair and above board. It was their money. They could do what they wanted with it.

He paused again. "It's a hell of a lot of money though. Assuming they were all his patients, how come so many of them put him in their will?"

Looking around him at his large and pleasant house, he added: "Thank goodness they did though. It made his fortune, and Dad's, and mine to some extent. It certainly gave me a flying start."

He stopped, suddenly aware that he was talking aloud to himself again. Still, Hanna can't hear me. She'd give me hell if she came in without my knowing and heard me talking to myself.

Mind you, she's not in all that often these days. Where is she today? She probably told me but I can't recall it. She's got a very good circle of friends – she's that kind of girl.

He felt a warm and comfortable glow as he thought of her, having a nice time with her friends.

CHAPTER 10

1983

"Got to go. My boring sod of a husband will be wondering where I am."

Hanna pulled herself from Adam's grasp, and got out of bed. She walked into the bathroom and stepped into the shower. As she soaped herself down she thanked her lucky stars that had provided the flat for her use, pretty well any time she wanted it.

It belonged to Robin, an old boyfriend of Julie, one of Hanna's friends. The man was married, and he had finally taken his wife off to live in Spain. He'd kept the upstairs flat, furnished, in a nice part of Hale, on the outskirts of Altrincham, because he wanted a pied-a-terre for visiting. And he felt he had to have a place in England if he ever wanted to leave Spain. The beauty of it was that it was gaining in value all the time, even with nobody living in it, he had told Julie.

"And if you're ever available when I'm over and we're both feeling lonely, well, it's available for us," he had said.

Julie had promised to pop in from time to time to keep an eye on it. And she was quite happy to delegate the duty to Hanna, whenever Hanna wanted it...which was quite often these days.

It was perfect. Well, almost. There was just one thing that stood in the way of the flat's being an absolute bliss. And that was the owner's Aunty Maud. She was always there. Never moving. Never speaking. And Hanna had never actually seen her. But she was there. She was, in fact, in the urn standing on the mantelpiece in the lounge: Aunty Maud's ashes.

Julie told Hanna that Robin had ended up with them because he was her next of kin. He'd always intended to scatter them in some appropriate place.

Aunty Maud had never been married, and she had never said where she wanted her ashes to be scattered. The only place he could think of where she had been happy and would want to end up was her old garden in the house in Altrincham where she had lived alone with her cats for forty years.

Problem was, of course, that somebody else lived there now, and Robin just could not bring himself to go and ask these complete strangers if they'd mind.

So in all the ten years since his aunt had died, he'd never done anything about it.

"I think if it's left to him you'll be here for good," Hanna had told the ashes. It didn't exactly worry her, of course. Why should it? Not at first, anyway. Then it began to irritate her. Just a little. Then more than that. And when she focused on the source of her irritation, it increasingly annoyed her.

One afternoon, after another stolen hour with Adam, and after he had left - they always left separately - she hit on the solution.

No sooner a word than a blow. She went to her car, which was parked on the roadside a few hundred yards from the flat, and emptied her shopping into the boot. Then she took the plastic bag back to the flat, and emptied about a quarter of Aunt Maud into it.

Next she took the bag back to her car and drove off to Dunham Park, the National Trust grounds surrounding a stately home a few miles south of Altrincham.

She carried the bag into the garden behind the house, and, after glancing round to make sure nobody was within sight, emptied the first instalment of Aunt Maud over an area of soil under a bush.

I'll be back with more some other time, she thought. I seem to remember that ashes are good for plants. The dear lady would be pleased to think she's doing some good.

She smiled as a new thought struck her: she'd be very pleased to find that she's ended up with aristocratic roots!

*

1983

When you have no job you think yourself towards despair. For John Cooper the optimism he had voiced to his wife about getting employment had turned out to be unjustified. The name of the game in Britain in the early 1980s was, as he had told Mayer, "cut back."

Because of those cut-backs there are three million people unemployed – it hasn't been this bad since the 1930s, he thought bitterly.

Even now the bank rate is only a shade under ten per cent. Admittedly that's better than the 17 per cent this damn government raised it to back in 1979. Of course, they could blame it all on Labour then.

Now unemployment is sky-high. A lot of businessmen think that dumping staff keeps costs down by getting more out of the ones who are left to cover the same work.

In the so-called "golden triangle" of North Cheshire - an area that included Prestbury, Alderley Edge, Wilmslow and Hale Barns, all situated in an arc of well-being around the southern and western fringes of Manchester Airport - you could hear in any wine bar snatches of conversation as the better-off-than-ever businessmen and their wives aired their view that Maggie was the woman to sort out the unions once and for all, and how a good dose of unemployment was what this country needed.

There was much guffawing at the beating unions were taking. But what it meant in practical terms for John Cooper was that Sunjet, the airline he had loved working for, could and did put the boot in every time he applied for a new job and they were asked to supply a character reference.

"Union activist," they wrote, killing off any chance of new employment.

He suspected that that kind of thing was happening, and that was why he never got an interview. But a frustrated job-applicant had no right to know what a former employer was saying about him or her.

It's an absolute calumny if that is so, he thought. Yes, he had become chairman of the Sunjet branch of the union. Basically because nobody else would do it, and he believed it was important.

Led by our beloved Prime Minister and supported by Britain's wildly triumphant right-wing newspapers, there's now a great anti-union feeling among people who don't seem to know that a big proportion of the population are members of one union or another. Apparently their interests don't matter a jot.

"I'm sorry I voted Conservative, now," he couldn't help muttering.

But I always have...I always thought of the Tories as reasoning people. Until now. They say unions are militant. But Margaret Thatcher is a lot more militant than they are. Of course there has been trouble from some unions. But certainly not all.

And there's no way anyone can accuse me of being the sort of union man who, according to the Press, was trying to wreck British industry.

This government has decided that all the nation's ills have been caused by the unions. By people like me.

And it is a lie. It's the highest-ever bank rates that are killing off businesses. No wonder there are so few jobs to be had.

If you're made redundant you're trapped. Yet there's a sneering, belittling attitude about...and more than a suggestion that the unemployed are simply work-shy. The truth is that thousands of honest, hard-working people, who have never been out of work in their lives, are being thrown unceremoniously out of their jobs, only to find themselves condemned as lazy skivers.

It was typified by Norman Tebbitt, one of Thatcher's guru supporters in the government's openly anti-union drive, who had calmly suggested that all you had to do was to get on your bike and ride down the road to find work, like his father had done when he had lost his job in the 1930s.

"Oh yeah, it's that easy, isn't it...thanks so much for the helpful information, he found himself saying aloud as he walked down Grove Street, the main shopping area of Wilmslow.

Half a dozen of the shops were empty, their business ruined by the fall in people's buying-power: it added to his feeling of utter despair. God! At a time when we've become an oil-producing country! All the oil income is doing is paying for millions of people to be unemployed, if you ask me.

"It's all about killing off lame ducks – that's Thatcher's big thing. Survival of the fittest.

"Where on earth is all this leading us?"

Thatcher reckons she's all for the free market. But there's no free market when it comes to wage bargaining now.

As for the people like me, you can now be thrown out of your job with no reason given and no redress.

If directors lose *their* jobs, through redundancy, takeovers, or even incompetence, they're given huge golden handshakes.

He passed a young man sitting on the pavement outside a shop begging. You never saw that in Britain, not during my lifetime, until now, he reflected bitterly. "I'm damned if I'll beg," he said out loud to himself. "I'll bloody well die first."

In the end, the constant failure to get a job meant humiliation...and for what? It wasn't as if there was any prospect of things changing in the near future. Now John Cooper's marriage had been wrecked by the strain of it. In a fit of anger Jenny had told him that she and children would be better off without him. She knew people who had been able to get new jobs. Why couldn't he?

He had walked out, telling her that she needn't expect to see him again. Pride, of course. But he had quickly found that if you didn't have an abode, you couldn't get what they used to call "dole money."

And without an address, how could you even apply for a job?

What the hell can I do? Whatever it is, it isn't enough, he silently told himself. You are surplus to requirements...an unwanted spare part. You're dead, Cooper. By starvation if nothing else.

He shouldn't have walked out. But what else could he do? He had spent the last few nights in the recessed doorway of a shop. But last night the police had moved him on. He had walked around nearly all night, finally settling down on a bench in The Carrs, the leafy country park where he now found himself again.

He climbed up into the wood. The first few slugs from his bottle of whisky numbed the pain. He took another three or four swigs of the warming liquid. Then he began taking the tablets. Three. Seven. Twenty. More whisky. Hazy now. Tablets. Unreality. Whisky. A strange feeling of floating away, away from all the pain.

But he did not die peacefully. During the night when he was lying on his back unconscious, his vomit choked him to death.

CHAPTER 11

1983

Geoff was now spending much of his spare time working on his family history. He found it irritating that Hanna kept asking him if he had found himself to be connected to the aristocracy yet.

Far from finding anybody rich or famous, he'd found that it was going the other way. Perhaps it was a good thing that she was out of the house so much these days.

Working back in time from the birth of William Arthur in 1871, he quickly found the marriage of his rugby-cheat great-grandfather William, for it was in the Knutsford parish records on microfilm at the Manchester Central Library: January 19th, 1871, to Ellen Carter, spinster of this parish. Wait a minute! When exactly was William Arthur born? He checked his grandfather's birth certificate: 13th May 1871. So! Naughty, naughty! Gardener Willy had got Ellen Carter into trouble, and had to marry her! No doubt her father had turned up with his shotgun!

Well his running speed didn't help him there, did it! Anyway, it was before the age of cinemas...there was probably nothing else to do in those days.

The problem now was to find William's birth or baptism. Assuming that 17 would probably have been the youngest that he might have had to get married, Geoff turned back the Knutsford parish baptism records to 1854. Then working back in time, it didn't take too long to find what he was looking for: February 25th, 1851, William, son of Thomas Mayer, and Jane his wife.

So he now knew not only when his great grandfather was born – or, at least, christened; he also knew for the first time the names of his great-great grandparents.

"My God! What a bore! A gardener! Born in Knutsford, married in Knutsford when he wasn't 21. Probably to the girl next door. The poor sod probably never went out of Knutsford in his life! I suppose that's where he died too.

"Still, he did get enough money to give his son an education and become a doctor. And thinking about it, I suppose there was something to be said for life in the 1870s. They wouldn't have the same sort of stress and complications of life in the 1980s. It must have been very pleasant to take a straightforward job like gardening, marry your first sweetheart, and just let life take its course.

"You'd know your place then. No rat race. Just take life as it came. No worries. No pressure. I'd say they were bloody lucky."

*

1871

William Mayer remembered that his mother was always telling him that one day he would be a rich farmer, with a farm much bigger and grander than his father's, so he'd be able to live in comfort, and care for her in her old age.

Wrong. Wrong. Wrong. After his father's experience of farming, he'd decided to be a gardener, even though it would never make him rich. And since his father's death two years ago now, he was alone in the world.

The thought brought back his feelings of guilt. I should have done more to help him. He didn't have to die. I just didn't realise. If I had helped him more, he might be alive today.

William didn't like to think about it, yet he found it impossible not to.

But he definitely could not think about what had happened to his mother and his two brothers and his sister. He had closed off the memory.

Yes. I'm alone. Well, I was. Until now.

Today I am getting married.

75

Not because I want to. Because I've got to. I've got to marry Ellen Carter. Because the parish overseers say so. Even though she's nearly twice my age.

They say so because she went and told them that she is with child, and that I am the father. How does she know? She is the sort of woman who does it with lots of men. Everybody knows she has had three babies already, although she's never been married.

She had to take them to church to be christened. But each one died. Not one of them reached a year old. Whether she didn't know how to care for babies, or whether she neglected them on purpose, I don't know. Maybe she killed them. But anyway they died, each of them.

And now I've got to marry her.

It's true that I lay with her. I admitted that to the overseers. But she'll go with anybody. Everybody knows that.

There was a knock on his bedroom door. It opened enough to let Mary Sutton push her head in and say cheerfully: "Come on. Time to get up. It's your wedding day, God help us. You'll want to look your best, even if your poor father will be turning in his grave at who you're amarryin'."

Mary used to be his father's dairy-maid. Now William lodged with her and her husband, John.

Ellen Carter! It was the first time, and so far the only time, that he had had what the overseers called "knowledge" of a woman. But then, he was not yet twenty.

How come she didn't have to marry the men who fathered her other babies? Perhaps she didn't know who to blame. Or maybe they just denied it.

I should never have admitted it. "You're too honest for your own good," he told the mirror as he shaved.

It had happened back in August, the Saturday he had joined the harvesting to earn some extra money after his morning's work at Caldwell's nurseries, where he was employed full time.

Everybody who wanted the work went and helped with the harvest while the weather held. It was hot, sweaty work. But he was with a lot of friends, lads and girls, and there was always plenty of laughing and larking about.

Ellen Carter was there too. She was older than most. She was a servant at a big house, but, like many of the others, she had been allowed the day off specially. It was hard going, but the farmers paid well for casual labour.

When they finished for the day they all went to the nearest pub, the Snig and Skewer.

That wasn't its real name, of course, but it was what everybody called it. Officially it was the fine-sounding Sword and Serpent, but the regulars, with the Englishman's cheerful refusal to put up with the grandiose, saw the signboard as depicting a snig – which is what the locals called an eel - and skewer: it satisfied their sense of the ridiculous and even protected the alliteration.

With money in their pockets, it was good fun, that summer evening. Everybody was having a good time, joking and singing. It just happened that Ellen Carter sat next to him. And after a couple of drinks they put their arms round each other, just like other lads and girls were doing while they were singing.

The thing was, Ellen was not only much older; William didn't think she was exactly pretty. Yet when she laughed her face changed – sort of lit up, he noticed.

And one way or the other he felt his old urges. For a long time now the sight of a pretty girl, or a buxom figure, or even, sometimes, a certain way women walked, did something to him that he couldn't control – or want to.

When the party broke up, he and Ellen left the Snig together, lurching a little as they stepped into the night. He couldn't help feeling the way he did. And, emboldened by the drink that he'd consumed so merrily, he tried his hand at fondling her as they walked. And instead of telling him to get his hands off, like several girls had done in his limited experience, she told him how much she liked it, and she wanted him so much to carry on.

77

So there was more feeling and fondling, and things became heated and breathless.

And near the house where she worked and lived, she'd led him to a haystack, and on the loose hay lying on the ground alongside it they had made love.

It was dark. There was a tumult of breathless fumbling, which Ellen calmly slowed down while gently encouraging and guiding and helping and responding...then the delicious moments of plunging relief...and Ellen's little groans of pleasure...all in the darkness.

And for a few moments of ecstasy he now had to marry this woman. And it wasn't just for today. He had to vow to live with her for life.

"It doesn't make sense. Why should that mean this? I mean, it was something it's true I've wanted for a long time, but it didn't seem to have anything to do with her having a baby.

"Well, I know that's how they get made, but one thing doesn't seem to add up to the other. Somehow there doesn't seem to be a connection."

Despite everything, William half smiled. No, there was a connection all right, that night!

But that was that. Now I'm marrying her. I hardly know her to talk to!

"It can't be. I don't deserve it," he said to his bedroom at large. "What am I going to do?"

He had an idea. "Perhaps the baby will die, like the others she's had. That will help.

"But even then, I'll still be married to her. I know! I'll have nothing to do with her in bed – I'll sleep on the floor, that's what I'll do. Downstairs.

"You can take a horse to water, 'tis said, but you can't make it drink.

"Can a marriage be unconsummated if the bride is already pregnant?"

He didn't know.

78

But at the moment it seemed his only way of escape.

*

He walked to the church with John and Mary Sutton. John was going to be a witness to the marriage. They didn't talk much. Mary several times pointed out what a nice day it was, for January.

Ellen was already there when they arrived. She was with a friend called Ann Lobb. Funny name. Well it's the only one she's got! She's from Cornwall.

Ellen was wearing the dress she normally wore on Sundays. She had a kind of lacy thing on her head and over her shoulders. She smiled at him. She had dimples and she looked nice with her face framed by the lace. He couldn't help smiling a thin smile back.

The vicar spoke his words. The verger gave Ellen to be married to this man. William gave her a gold ring that Mary had given him as a wedding present. She'd told him it had been her grandmother's. Ellen looked surprised.

Then off they went to the small cottage he had rented to be their home, the two of them. Oh God!

What was he to say to her? What could they say to each other? She took off the lace head-dress. She normally wore her hair in plaits, held together by ribbon. Today her hair fell free like a golden cascade over her shoulders.

He stared at her, transfixed.

She said: "Come here husband," and she smiled her dimpled smile that lit her face. She held out her arms to him, and he couldn't help stepping into her embrace, and putting his arms round her as she kissed him a long and passionate kiss that pressed her body against him and turned something over inside him – his heart, his stomach, his loins: he didn't know which; maybe all.

She whispered: "Take me to bed. You can't make me pregnant anew. I've wanted you so much. There's nothing to stop us now we are married. We've got to get to know each other really well. I'll show you how well we can know each other..."

If William's senses were simmering before, now they danced. Ellen was not inexperienced. She knew a few things about what men liked. She did them. William, who had until now never seen a grown woman unclothed, gave his all.

But he learned some things. One was that whereas he had always thought that having his way with a woman meant a male sort of aggression to which a female might submit, with Ellen he found that he went where she led him.

She talked in a way that he had not expected. He'd kind of expected that women being naturally modest would be silent, pretending that it was not really happening.

That first married time Ellen showed him what she wanted him to do. She told him how much she liked it. She said: "You're so big and strong. I want you to love me until I sing all over."

William was overwhelmed by her. She could not get enough of him. And during that first day and night of their marriage he learned to love it. And so he learned to love her.

All right, maybe it's lust. Well it's what I need and I don't care what anybody else says. I had no choice but to marry her, so I might as well enjoy it. I've never felt like this before.

Ellen had been allowed to keep her job in the laundry at the big house, despite moving out to live in the cottage. For the moment their earnings combined to keep them fed if not well-clothed. And they were happy together.

She told him it was not just by chance that she had ended up with him that night after the pub sing-song. "I'd seen you and I'd watched you. I made sure we'd walk home together. I wanted you to make me pregnant so you'd have to marry me because I knew you'd make me the husband I've always wanted.

"Don't speak. Just listen. I wanted you and I've got you. I want you to love me. Because I love you, William Mayer."

Ellen didn't mind talking about her past. "You tell me about your urges that you can't control – well I'm the same ...I've always been the same, for as long as I can remember.

"I've seen the way men looked at me ever since I was thirteen or fourteen. I grew a nice figure early on. I told my mum about how men looked at me, and she said I must be very careful and not allow them to take any liberties.

"But the thing was – I wanted them to take liberties when I saw them looking at me and I could see what they were thinking.

"I was fifteen, though, before I let anybody touch me. I'm not saying names, but he was a married man, and after he'd touched me here and there I'd have let him do anything he wanted – and he did, in the wet grass in the field alongside the road.

"Of course I got pregnant. It was terrible because everybody told me how wicked I was. But I wouldn't tell them who the man was. Anyway he moved away with his wife and family before the baby was born."

"Why did it die?"

"I left her with my mother so I could go back to work. But ever since my dad died she had been drinking. She left the baby alone in her house while she went to the pub for a jug of beer, and when she came back hours later she was dead – I don't know why. But I couldn't tell anybody that it was my mother's fault, could I?"

"But you've had two others that died too."

"They were both boys, and they were both sickly little things from the start. One cried all the time and wouldn't feed properly – he seemed to be in pain.

"The other had a hare lip. He was the wrong way round when he was born and he only lived a week and a half."

"Didn't you get a doctor?"

"I didn't have the money. But I would have gone and got someone to help except that I was slow getting over the birth and I couldn't get out at first. My mother was so drunk I had a job keeping her away from the little mite. But he was never going to live, I could see that.

81

"Believe me, I would have loved to have kept those little things. That is why I can't wait to have your baby – I want it so much."

"Well you'd better make sure that nothing goes wrong, wife, or you'll have me to answer to.

"Nothing will go wrong. I'm sure of it. And you'll be here to help me. We'll be the best mum and dad in all Knutsford!"

CHAPTER 12

1871

Just before the baby was due William took Ellen to see the recently established May Day parade. The streets were sanded into patterns and pictures in the way that Knutsford's specialist artists had made their own, the May Queen looked pretty as a princess, and on the heath the big May Fair was throbbing and ready to go.

Ellen was big indeed with child, so William insisted that she took it gently. They walked slowly, with stops to sit down whenever the chance arose. Amid the bustle their pace was careful. They felt that they were not quite taking part – just watching from the outside.

But when the racing began, William decided that Ellen might be sitting it out, but he was damned if he wasn't going to enter for the 100 yards dash.

He had always been able to outrun his friends at school. He didn't know why. His father used to say he could run like the wind. Funny thing to say really. Sometimes the wind was slow, and ever changing direction.

Anyway what the young William could do, and enjoyed doing, was breaking into a high-speed dash. And here was his chance to see how he compared with others now that he had reached the ripe old age of 20. But above all, there was a prize of half a guinea.

All who wanted to compete had their names written down, and it was then explained that as there were twenty-four entrants, there would be four preliminary races, each with six men competing. The first two in each would then be in a final race for the half-guinea prize.

It was a lot of money for a labourer – more than half a week's wages even for a top farm hand - and the 100 yard track across the grass was lined with dozens of people keen to see the event.

William was in the second preliminary dash, and he easily outpaced the other five competitors. He watched the other three races, and he could see that there were one or two very quick runners.

So he was in determined mood as he lined up with the other seven finalists in the prize race. He knew Ellen was watching and he wanted to impress her with his speed. He also wanted the half guinea.

They lined up at the start-line. The starter held aloft a white handkerchief. Ready. Steady. William tensed every muscle and concentrated his mind on the one thing that mattered – the finishing line 100 long yards away. Go!

He was alarmed to see from the corner of his eye that three of his competitors were already inching ahead of him with only ten yards gone. That was good. Because it brought even more resolve to William.

Drawing on every ounce of energy, he felt himself draw level, then leave behind the others. He didn't slacken his pace. Eyes on the white tape held across the finishing line, he reached it a good yard ahead of his nearest rival.

He had been oblivious to the cheering of the spectators all along the track. But now he became aware, as officials and his defeated rivals shook him by the hand, patting him on the back, and congratulated him on his speed.

There were more cheers and handshakes as he was presented with the small gold coin.

Then through the crowd came Ellen. She flung her arms round him and kissed him, in front of everybody! He was overjoyed to see her joy. And he gave her the half guinea there and then, and told her: "Let that be put towards the well-being of our baby.

"Perhaps it is a sign."

*

"Have you ever heard of rugby?"

The man who asked the question was of the gentleman class. That was obvious to William. The man's tweed suit, his upper-class accent and the large, sweet-smelling cigar that he was smoking, all made it clear.

"No sir," answered William. "What is it?"

"It's a game, a bit like football. But a lot more fun."

"Why do you ask, sir?"

"Because we have a rugby team here in Knutsford. We call ourselves the Dirty Dozen. It's a real rough and tumble in the mud, and we're getting more spectators to watch us play. That's why I thought you might have heard of it.

"Thing is: with your speed I think you'd be an asset to the team. In rugby you need a real speed man, and I've not seen anybody faster. Do you think you'd like to have a trial at it?"

In the euphoria of winning the race William was prepared to say yes to almost anything.

"But I'm a working man. I don't have time for games. I have to work on Saturdays. Mr. Caldwell might let me off for the afternoon, but he'd dock my wages for it, and with our first baby due, I couldn't afford that."

"Look, I know Caldwell. I'll have a word with him. I don't think you'd lose by it if you can catch a ball as well as you can run!"

"Well, if it's all right by Mr. Caldwell, and if I'm not to lose by it, I'll have a try."

"Have a try! Yes, that you will, I'm sure! That's what we call it when we get a try at kicking a goal!

"Tell me your name and where you live, then I can get in touch with you to let you know when and where to turn up."

After he had written down William's name and address, he said: "Let me shake you by the hand. I think we'll be meeting again, soon."

He raised his brown bowler hat in polite farewell to Ellen as he left.

*

A few days later Mr. Caldwell came over to talk to William as he was busy in the big market garden. He said he had been asked by some of

85

his important clients to let William off work on Saturday afternoons, and he had agreed to do so.

Although in normal circumstances this would reduce his wages, he had decided that as he was now a married man, his baby was due any day, and he was a good worker, he would increase his wages by exactly the same amount that he would lose by not working Saturday afternoons.

"So the effect is that your wages will stay the same, William. You've made a good move, getting to know these gentlemen."

He paused, and smiled. "You're moving in exalted circles, you know. I've heard it said that football is a game for gentlemen that's played by hooligans, and rugby is a game for hooligans that's played by gentlemen!

"The players are all of that class, and they want you to join them. You're a lucky man. It could be the making of you."

William couldn't for the life of him understand that. But it all seemed a happy thing, to be let off work to play a game instead of working, and without losing any money.

So the following Saturday he did turn up early to be instructed about how to play his first game of rugby. A number of weekly practice sessions followed.

He learned that although you could kick the ball, the main thing was to throw it from player to player as you tried to run it over the opponents' goal-line and put it down on the ground – this gave the man who got the ball over the line a try at kicking a goal.

But unlike football, you had to kick the ball *over* the cross-bar instead of under it. That wasn't as easy as it looked. But William was told that there was talk of making the ball oval instead of round, and if that happened, it should make goal-kicking a bit easier, as well as making the ball easier to throw and catch and run with.

There were even some, he was told, who quite liked the element of chance that an oval ball's unpredictable bounce might bring to the game.

And he quickly learned that although punching and tripping had recently been banned under new rules for the game, it was quite all right for your opponents to bring you crashing down by diving at you and grappling your legs, or your body, if you were carrying the ball.

On the other hand, he didn't like the idea of attempting to do the same to the other side's players, because they were not only big and tough, but they were all of the gentleman class and all his life he had known that the one thing you don't do is to show violence to this sort of person.

But what he could do, and did do – even in his heavy working boots - was to get the ball, tuck it under his arm, and run as fast as he could while avoiding their tackles if he possibly could,

Only three times in his first match did it come off. But as a result he got three tries at kicking to score, and succeeded on one of them. So he contributed to a narrow win for his team.

The other players in the Knutsford team congratulated him during the game, and afterwards every player came to him, patted him on the back, and said: "Well played William. Well played."

He was proud of their gentlemanly accolades, and felt that he had done quite well. But the once-white shirt, the short trousers and his boots were all very dirty. He was told not to worry about them. The shirts and trousers all went to the laundry, and the boots he could clean at his leisure. He was asked what size boots he took so a new pair which would be better for running could be provided.

He dressed. Then, as he put on his working boots, he felt something inside one of them. He took it off and put his hand in to check what the obstruction was – to find himself holding a golden guinea! His face showed a mixture of puzzlement and shock.

Then his eyes met those of the man who had spoken to him after the races. The man winked and with his forefinger gently patted the side of his nose twice, before turning away to talk to one of the other players.

So William earned his first money from rugby. Over the next few months he found that it was strictly against the rules to be paid for playing the game...but after each match there was a guinea in his boot.

He didn't have to be told that this was all right as long as he didn't ever mention it to anyone.

He did tell Ellen, though. "Put it with the half guinea I got for winning the races at the May Fair," he said, after his first game. "We'll call it our baby fund."

Then a few days later the baby was born, and they named him William Arthur. The Arthur was after Ellen's father, who had died when she was young.

William Arthur was a fine, healthy baby. But Ellen, after the birth, suffered pain and bleeding. William cared for her with tenderness and broth. Ellen's concerns were all for her baby.

She neglected her own health. She recovered only slowly. William Arthur thrived. And, as Ellen had promised, there were no better parents in Knutsford...nor happier.

Fourteen months later their second child was due. But as her time approached Ellen knew that something was wrong. "It isn't moving," she told William, a look of fear on her face.

The baby, a girl – was born dead. Getting her into the world was a long, bloody business.

Ellen grew weaker as she lost more blood. It went on for a week. William, desperate for help, called in a doctor, and spent the precious few guineas he had saved for their son's future.

But Ellen, now in a fever, had lost too much blood to be saved.

At first William felt numbly that it was the end of his world. His new-found joy and love had been snuffed out.

He tried to be brave when friends talked to him. But alone, in his cottage with little William Arthur he wept bitter, angry, hopeless tears.

Mary Sutton took over the care of the little boy during the hours when his father was at work. She was happy to do so because she and her husband had never had any children of her own, despite many years of wanting and hoping.

She cared for William Arthur as if he had been her own, and built up a wonderful bond with the child.

But William made it clear that he would have his son back at home when the working day was finished. "I am very thankful to you for looking after him while he is so little, but I can not let you have him, Mary. Ellen said she would care for him and now she is gone I will do it in her stead, the best I can."

William changed his job, to work at a big house in the wealthy Chelford Road, newly built and needing a good, hard-working gardener to put its acre of surroundings in order.

It gave him all Saturday as well as Sunday off, and he was well-paid.

Meanwhile as William Arthur grew, each week when his father played rugby, his fund of gold grew too. The money was put into a local savings bank. William wouldn't spend any more of it after paying for Ellen's treatment. It kept on growing, and earned interest too.

The little boy was quick to start walking, and quick to start talking, probably because Mary used to sit him on her knees, and chat to him in a fully-grown-up way.

She knew he wouldn't understand it at first. But she liked doing it, and William Arthur plainly liked it too, because he used to smile at her and gurgle away happily in response to her words.

*

When William Arthur was old enough to go to the local school, they found that he was quick at learning everything they taught him.

At ten William had enough guineas to send him to a school set up in a converted barn at his vicarage by the Reverend Lawrence Riley, the first vicar of St. Cross Church, a red-brick place of worship built on the unfashionable Mobberley road in Nether Knutsford.

Mr. Riley was the former headmaster of the Knutsford Grammar School, and was known to be an excellent teacher. Under his tuition William Arthur was found to have an exceptional memory for everything he was taught, and shone at everything...except running, strangely enough.

89

By the time he was ready to leave, his teachers had identified him as an outstanding scholar. Plainly, they saw, he could go far in a profession.

Seeking to help him in his choice of future direction, they discovered that William Arthur Mayer had impossible ambitions to be a doctor.

His headmaster often moved in Manchester's exhilarating academic circles, and now he made a special trip to the city. He was determined to do his best for the complete education of his star pupil.

William Arthur's father had amazed Mr. Riley by being able to pay to put his son through his fee-paying school. But he was sure he would not have the money to send him to the medical school.

He came back with good news; but he kept it to himself until it was confirmed a month later: William Arthur had been awarded one of two entrance scholarships worth 160 guineas to pay the fees for him to study at the Manchester University Medical School.

His father could hardly believe it. William had long since given up rugby, but the money they had saved had provided all that their son needed so far. Now, as a result of William Arthur's own efforts, aided by his teacher, came benefits that William had never dreamt of. His gratitude, and his pride in his son were inexpressible. And he knew that he would succeed.

For six years William Arthur attended the lectures at the university.

For the first year he studied chemistry, botany, medicine, elementary dissection and physics.

In the second year zoology, anatomy, histology, and physiology.

By the third year he was attending lectures on pharmacology, and he had his first taste of hospital work.

Next there was pathology and systematic surgery as well as bacteriology, obstetrics, and gynaecology.

Systematic medicine, forensic medicine and psychology, ophthalmology, diseases of the ear, nose and throat, orthopaedic surgery, and anaesthetics were on his timetable in the fifth year.

And in the approach to his final exams he studied tuberculosis, vaccination, infectious diseases, dermatology therapeutics, children's diseases, and mental diseases.

"Who'd have thought there are so many ologies," said William, wonderingly.

At the end of each academic year there was a tough examination which had to be passed, for the Manchester Medical School had a high reputation that it was determined to keep.

And at the end came his final examination, which, with the help of his determination and his prodigious memory, he passed.

And so he became a doctor. A doctor and a real gentleman, his patients said.

CHAPTER 13

1983

Back at the Central Library in Manchester, Geoff was on the hunt for the birth of his great-great grandfather, Thomas Mayer.

That record, of course, would give the names of Thomas's parents...and so take Geoff another generation back.

But first it would be a good idea to find his marriage to somebody called Jane. Assuming that it wouldn't have been too long before the birth of their son William - which he had already found in February 1851 - Geoff worked backwards through the microfilmed records. And if William had not been their first child, he'd presumably find the baptisms of earlier children of Thomas and Jane Mayer. Eventually he'd find their marriage.

There was no sign of earlier Mayer children being christened at Knutsford, it turned out. Nor, despite a long search back, could Geoff find any marriage of Thomas and Jane.

So if they didn't marry in Knutsford, where? Perhaps the ceremony would have been in Jane's home town – where perhaps her parents still lived. But where would that be – it could be anywhere. And where on earth had Thomas come from?

Geoff pondered. Ah, yes. Now he remembered that in his family history book it had said that the censuses gave birth-places. So far Geoff hadn't looked at census records.

He checked it out in his book. It told him that the censuses had been held every ten years in England since 1801, except for 1941 when the Second World War had got in the way. But it was only from 1841 that names had been put into the census records; and in 1841 it didn't give the place of birth - only whether each person had been born in the county where they were living.

After that, from 1851 onwards, they recorded the actual place where everyone in the census had been born.

The censuses were not made public for 100 years. That should mean that if he could find Thomas Mayer in any of the 1851, 1861, 1871 or 1881 censuses, he'd be able to find where Thomas was born.

Back at the Central Library again, it worked like a dream. He knew that William had been born in Knutsford, so it was the town's census records that he had to check.

And there was the family, in the 1851 census - which had been held on March 30th, Geoff noted - living at Shaw Mill Farm in Knutsford: Thomas Mayer, age 29, married, farmer of 50 acres, born in Styal, Cheshire; his wife Jane, age 27, born in Middlewich, Cheshire; and their son William, aged one month, and born in Knutsford.

Now he got out the Middlewich parish records microfilm, because probably that was where Jane's home was. Starting from February 1851, when William was born, counting back nine months to May 1849, and checking back in time from there, it did not take long to find the marriage of Thomas Mayer, farmer, of Knutsford, and Jane Wildgoose, of this parish, on 3rd March 1849.

"So her maiden name was Wildgoose. Interesting name. Unusual, too. At least it should make it easy to find if I ever decide to trace the female lines of my family some time."

Back to the census. This time the microfilm of the 1861 census for Knutsford. Thomas, Jane and William were still at Shaw Mill Farm, but their family had grown. As well as William, now aged 10, there were Montague, age 8, Lavinia, age 5, and Horatio, 2, all born in Knutsford.

What was important was that it was another step forward. But later, reflecting on what he'd achieved, exciting it was not.

"But to be quite honest it is pretty boring," he told his car as he drove home from Manchester. "Far from finding nobility in my family, I'm not even finding gentry. Farmer of 50 acres! Wife and four kids. Big deal!

"In fact all my ancestors seem to be totally uninteresting. But Thomas seems to be the most boring of all so far. Apart from fathering four children, his life seems to have been without anything notable happening."

However Geoff was on the trail of his ancestors now. He carefully wrote it all down. And a few days later he returned to the Central Library.

The 1861 census had given Thomas's age as 39, so he must have been born around 1820 or 1821 in Styal, which was part of Wilmslow. Geoff couldn't resist trying to find when his great-great grandfather Thomas was born, looking in the Wilmslow baptism records, working back in time from 1822.

Hooray! There was the christening of Thomas Mayer on July 20th 1821, son of Joseph Mayer, cotton spinner, of Styal, and Nell, his wife.

Geoff went back to the census – this time for 1841. But the family was not there.

He searched through the whole of Styal. No sign. His neck and shoulders were aching. He leaned back in his seat.

He suddenly noticed that he had been in peering at the viewing screen for nearly four hours, and it was late afternoon.

Feeling his eyes straining from viewing the often unclear images, and weary in the neck and shoulders from sitting still for so long staring at the viewer, he decided to call it a day.

It was at that moment that he became aware of a woman standing close to him, and, of all the cheek, looking at his screen. He looked over his shoulder at her...a plump, unattractive woman, not young, he noticed as he felt irritation at the interruption.

His distaste failed to get through to the woman. She spoke kindly to him: "Are you stuck? Can I help in any way?"

"No thank you: I'm fine," he said coldly.
"It happens to us all, sooner or later," she said. "We just can't find someone that we know ought to be there. It happens."

She wasn't going to go away. He half turned in his chair, intending to be rude if necessary to get rid of her unwanted presence.

His irritation started with the implied suggestion from a total stranger that he needed help. Dammit he knew exactly what he was doing.

And, as he looked at her again, it was clear that she was not the type that Geoff admired: she was...well...untidy.

She seemed to have no sense of style in her dress. She was, frankly, overweight, if not exactly fat.

She certainly had the beginnings of a double chin. And her hair, once black but now streaked with grey, seemed to have been put in place by nothing more than fingers combing it back from her forehead.

It wasn't unattractive, but it wasn't perfectly groomed, the way Hanna's hair always looked.

Yet he couldn't stop himself, in his frustration at suddenly finding himself getting nowhere, from saying: "Do you ever feeling there's a brick wall that's sealing off the past?"

"Yes, I've felt like that plenty of times. And some of my brick walls are still there.

"But I just try another branch of my family tree until I find I can make progress. I come back to the first problem later...there's no point in banging your head against a brick wall, if you'll pardon the expression."

"That's true," said Geoff.

"So do you fancy a cup of tea in the café downstairs? That sometimes helps."

"Why not. I've had enough of this for one day, to be honest."

Over the cup of tea Geoff found his initial distaste melting away. Her name was Rose. She talked sense. She made a couple of good suggestions that he might look into – one was a possible change of spelling of the Mayer surname. It might be Mair. Or Mayor. Or even changed to Major...sometimes the hand-writing in parish records wasn't too brilliant.

"It sometimes happened in the old days, when the parish clerk filled in the registers. He would certainly be able to read and write, but his spelling and his memory might be very dodgy," she pointed out.

Rose had been widowed for ten years or more. Her husband had died in a car crash while on business, she told him. Somehow chatting with her was very easy. She was happy to talk. She had been a secretary employed by a big chemical firm. She had volunteered for redundancy a year earlier. What with the pension she got from her husband's company, and her redundancy money, it gave enough to live on, she said. And that way she could pursue some of the things she was interested in – like family history.

Later, back home in Prestbury - where there was a note from Hanna telling him to get his own supper because she'd be out until late with "the girls" - Geoff found himself thinking about his chat with Rose.

She was one of those people he couldn't categorize. His first impression had been a definite dislike of her appearance. She was almost frumpish – not smart like Hanna.

Hanna looked good. She kept weight down, she dressed well...she almost looked better now than she had when she was much younger, when he'd first courted her.

She's aged well. Obviously Rose hasn't. I wonder how old she is. At least mid-forties, I'd say. She's nothing like as pretty as Hanna, and she simply doesn't seem to care very much about her appearance.

Still, she's been doing family history for a lot longer than I have, and she knows a lot more than I do.

She knows what she's talking about. And, somehow, she's easy to talk to. I must admit, it's nice to have been able to talk to someone – makes a change from all my sessions at the Central Library until now.

And the thought occurred: Rose had told him she was often at the library: in the future she'd be there to chat to, or to ask a bit of advice if he needed a bit of help. That was quite a good thought.

*

Still intrigued to know what manner of people he originated from, Geoff went back to the library at the next opportunity, a week later.

Rose gave him a wave as he walked into the room where the microfilm viewers were. Pleasant to see someone he knew.

He switched on a vacant machine, loaded the film he'd selected, and got down to work. He was being methodical, reasoning that this was the best way of keeping everything in good order so that he could draw a family tree as he worked his way backwards in time, step by step.

What he had to find now was the marriage of Joseph Mayer and Nell. Using the same method that had paid off for finding the marriage of Thomas and Jane Wildgoose, he started his backwards search in November 1820...nine months before Thomas's baptism.

No sign of a marriage in the Wilmslow parish records, though. Where could they have been married? Suddenly a thought occurred to Geoff. He now worked his way *forwards* in time from November 1820. And there it was! On 18th February 1821: just five months before their son Thomas was christened. Joseph Mayer and Nell Platt, both of Styal.

Another case of a shotgun marriage! "Unless, of course, my forebears had found a way of doing pregnancies quicker!" he told Rose, straight-faced.

She smiled. "In the old days you'll find that a lot of marriages were well within nine months of the first baby arriving," she said. "No cinemas, no TV, what else was there to do?" he responded.

All right. So now we know. But it didn't help in going even further back in his family history. For there the trail ended: no earlier records of the Mayers in Wilmslow, despite long hours of searching. So where had Joseph come from?

Could be anywhere, and there were no census records in 1821 to give a clue. Ah, yes! Check the 1851 census to find his birth place.

But despite an extensive check, they were not there in the Styal census records, nor in the Wilmslow census. When did they leave? I know: check the 1841 census. But again, no sign of Joseph and Nell and young Thomas.

Where the hell were they? Geoff went back to the Wilmslow parish records of baptisms. There was one mention: Joseph and Nell had one more child, a daughter they called Ellen, baptised on 23rd August 1823. Then nothing. Where could they have gone?

Rose had a suggestion: it might be worthwhile to check the records of adjacent parishes – Alderley to the south, Bowden to the north.

"But Bowden is a good way from Styal...four miles at least. I wouldn't have thought that was worth checking," objected Geoff

"Ringway, where the airport is now, was a farming area then, in the Hale chapelry of Bowden parish," she told him. "So the Bowden parish boundary divided Styal from Ringway. I reckon you could live in the southern part of Ringway and work in Styal, very easily.

"When was your Thomas born...1821, did you say? Why not check the 1841 census for Bowden, in case the family had moved just across the parish boundary? Thomas might have been still living with his parents then."

So Geoff checked the 1841 census for the Ringway area. He made an intriguing discovery: living in Ringway, at Oakwood Farm, were Jack Harper, farmer, whose age was given as 55, Nell Harper, aged 47, farmer's wife, and what were obviously their children, Harry, who was 28, and Jack, aged 26. And there were three younger girls, aged 12, 10 and 8, all with the surname Harper. The youngest girl was described as "scholar." Alongside the others it said "ag lab" – which Geoff knew meant farm labourer.

But the important thing was: there were two other people listed with the Harpers. The first was Thomas Mayer, aged 19, "Ag Lab" by way of occupation; and there was Ellen Mayer, who was 17 and described as "servant."

Was farmer Harper's wife Nell the same one who had been married to Joseph Mayer, then widowed? If not, why would she have Thomas and Ellen Mayer living with her, as well as her Harper family?

The 1841 census, unlike the later census records, didn't give the family relationships to the head of the household, but Geoff felt certain that they were Nell's children from her earlier marriage to Joseph

Mayer. Thomas and Ellen were the same names that he had seen in the Wilmslow parish records of baptisms.

This was being a bit like being a detective. How could he prove it?

Thomas, son of Joseph and Nell Mayer, was baptised – and probably born - in July 1821. He'd have been a month short of twenty by the time of the 1841 census. And his younger sister Ellen had been christened in August 1823. She was two years younger than Thomas – just like the Ellen in the Harper household in the 1841 census. There was a fair chance that they were the children of Joseph Mayer, Geoff reasoned.

It looked as if Joseph had died, leaving Nell a widow with a son Thomas, and a younger daughter Ellen; and she had remarried, to a man who had been widowed.

To make sure, he got the Wilmslow Burials microfilm, and worked back from the end of 1826. He didn't have to go very far back to find it: the burial of Joseph Mayer of Styal on 3rd December 1826. It even had the date of his death – five days before the burial – and his age: 30.

"God, he must have been born in 1796...I'm back to the eighteenth century!" was the thought that came to Geoff as he drove home from Manchester. He had died young, but that seemed to have been not uncommon in the early 1800s, Geoff had noticed. The parish burial records didn't say why people had died.

The next week Geoff checked the Bowden parish records, and found the marriage of Nell Mayer, widow, to Jack Harper, farmer, at Ringway on 10th July 1827. It all fitted! Geoff was satisfied that Nell was the widow of Joseph, and that the Thomas Mayer living at Ringway was his great-great grandfather.

"Eureka!" he exclaimed. Rose came over to the screen where he was working. "You've found him?"

"Yes, thanks to your suggestion. I've found a Thomas Mayer living at a farm at Ringway. My Thomas's father had died, and I'm sure his mother remarried, because in the following year I've found the marriage of Nell Mayer, a widow, to a farmer in Ringway. Living with her and her new husband and his own children were Thomas Mayer and Ellen Mayer...and their ages fit exactly the Thomas and Ellen who were the children of Joseph and Nell."

"But do you think that's proof enough that it's the right Thomas Mayer?"

"Well, you could check the 1851 census for the Harper family...that gave the relationship to the head of the household of every person in the household."

"And it would be very time-consuming, but you could make sure there wasn't another Thomas Mayer by checking the whole of the area to see if there are any other Mayer families that he might have come from. If Thomas and Ellen Mayer are step-children of Jack Harper, that would certainly be proof enough for me," she assured him.

"Let's celebrate. Cup of tea?"

CHAPTER 14

1983

His check of the 1851 census was a great disappointment. There was most of the Harper family at Oakwood farm, Ringway, but no Jack Harper. Nell Harper was head of the household, and she was described as a widow. But Geoff's concern was that Thomas Mayer and Ellen Mayer were not there. Of course! Thomas would be aged 29, and Ellen 27. They'd have flown the nest...probably married with homes of their own. But where?

It would have been nice if he could have proved absolutely that the Thomas Mayer, living at Oakwood Farm, Ringway, was his great-great grandfather. On the other hand it didn't affect his ancestor search. He already knew that Thomas was the son of Joseph and Nell Mayer of Styal, and that Thomas's son William was his great grandfather.

He'd been quite excited to find a Thomas and Ellen Mayer living in Ringway – which after all was next to Styal. It had all added up so neatly, and it was probably the right Thomas Mayer.

What was satisfying to Geoff was that now he was moving into unknown territory as far as his family history was concerned. Here were two new generations that not even Aunt Margaret had heard of: Thomas and Jane, and Joseph and Nell, taking him back to his great-great-great grandparents.

Geoff felt a strange elation. He knew that he now had to move on further into the past in order to find Joseph's parents. More searching in the parish records...but where? Obvious place to start was Wilmslow. But Joseph's parents might have come from anywhere: he had died in 1825, long before there was any census record that might have shown his birthplace.

"This is becoming a little like hard work," he said to himself. Then Geoff felt a sense of ennui coming over him.

And what am I getting excited about? A gardener! A farm labourer! A cotton spinner! How boring can my ancestors get? he found himself thinking.

*

1826

The empty shock, from the first eternal moment when his mother told him: "Your daddy has gone to heaven" stayed with Thomas Mayer for a long time.

The aching emptiness in their cottage, dominated by the big wooden box in the parlour was one thing. Seeing his father in his coffin, the face that he loved for its smiling eyes and ever-present cheerfulness and joy, now frozen, pallid, unmoving in a terrible, cold stoniness, was a horror that he could not forget.

It brought the first anger into his life. Why? Why don't I have him any more? Why can't he just wake up? He cried. Through his sobs he told his mother: "I want my daddy."

But even as he said it he knew that it was hopeless. And although he did not see his mother cry he could see from the strange, numb expression on her face that she was just as hurt and empty as he was.

At the big church there was weeping from women. And then the awful moment when he saw the box lowered into a big hole in the ground, and his mother's strained, sad face as she grasped his hand and tried to smile as she said: "It will be all right, Thomas, never fear."

But he did fear. He was five years old and he feared that she would die too. And he feared that *he* would die, especially after the well-meaning neighbour had assured him that everyone had to die sooner or later. They said never mind, his father had gone to heaven. But he did mind. And he most definitely did not want to die: he'd seen what happened to his daddy.

People kept saying that he'd gone to heaven, and Thomas wanted to believe it. But he couldn't. So he pretended to the grown-up people that it must be a good thing, just to make them feel less sad.

But he saw a shaking of heads, and he heard that people talked to his mother in low voices. They were not happy.

So it came as a nice surprise one day when his mother took him and his sister Ellen on a long walk to a farm at a place that she told him was called Ringway. There were cows and pigs and horses and hens and ducks. Two big boys called Harry and Jack showed him and Ellen all the exciting things on the farm.

There was a big black and white dog called Jess, and she licked your face and got excited and barked, and if you threw a stick she would run after it and bring it back, no matter how many times the big boys threw it.

Thomas loved it all. They kept going back to the farm, and mother made the big house clean and tidy while he and Ellen played outside.

Then his mother told him they were going to live there. Not long after that she told him that he was going to have a new daddy, and she got married to Mr. Harper, the farmer.

Thomas liked him. But he knew he would never be like his real father. And the two boys told him that he'd better remember that Mr. Harper was *their* real father, not his. And he always did remember it.

Yet they became like big brothers – bossy and sometimes mean to him. But they taught him to look for eggs laid by the hens and ducks. They showed him that you didn't have to be scared of the cows, but you did have to be scared of the pigs. And he watched them milking the cows. They taught his mother to do it. They all laughed when she couldn't get the milk out of the teats at first, and when finally she did, it didn't squirt into the big shiny bucket that she held between her knees.

Then one day, when he was six, they taught him too. And he became a proper farm boy.

But his mother made sure that he learned to read, and to write and do sums. She had been taught these things at the apprentice house at

103

Quarry Bank mill, where she and Joseph had worked when they were young. She was determined that her children were going to learn too.

She talked to him about the things that he saw around him – the trees and the birds, the clouds and the rain. And she explained how the earth went round the sun, and the moon went round the earth, and how it all changed the seasons. And how God had made these things, their sights, their sounds, their colours and changing moods.

He was growing up. One day she gave him something new to read – the old copies of Cobbett's "*Political Register*" that had belonged to Thomas's father, Joe. At first he found some of the words difficult. But his mother helped him.

And when he asked questions about what it all meant, she did her best to explain. He began to understand about rich and poor people, and how they all had to work in their different ways to get money for food and clothes.

He read all the old Cobbett "*Registers*" and he talked to his mother about the unfairness of the government that they told him about. But Nell warned him never to get involved in fighting the way things were done, because the government had the law on its side and would always win.

What he had to do, she told him, was to learn all he could, and work hard, so he could have a happy life and a good wife and family when he grew up.

As he became bigger he did more of the work on the farm, helping his step-brothers. He got used to the smells of the farm – he had to because the boys made him clean the cowshed with a shovel and a big, stiff brush. But until he became nearly as big as Harry and Jack they pushed the wheelbarrow to take it all to the muck-heap.

He learned about ploughing, watching his step-father keep the two big horses in straight lines as the grass turned into earth. He told Thomas that the ground at Ringway was the best farming land in Cheshire.

*

1839

When he was eighteen, one Saturday afternoon, Harry and Jack took him to the pub for the first time. It was near the church, and not far from the farm. Everyone called the pub the Romper, though its real name was the Red Lion.

They said that a few years back a painter had made a new sign for the pub, but the regular drinkers laughed at his efforts. One wag declared that what was on the pub sign-board didn't look like a lion rampant – it looked more like a kitten romping. In the general laughter another wit declared that the pub ought to be renamed "The Romper." Somehow the name stuck.

They bought Thomas a drink of beer, brought up in a big jug by the landlord from a cellar, then poured carefully into the half-pint glasses.

Harry and Jack laughed uproariously – and so did the other half-dozen men who were in the pub – when Thomas pulled a face at the bitter taste as he took his first sip. They told him he'd get used to it and he'd like it; and they were right.

After they had downed their ale they said that he must buy the second one. It was one penny for half a pint. They were pulling his leg, because they knew that he didn't have any money. They laughed again when he took it seriously and told them with a shamed face that he had none.

Harry and Jack knew it perfectly well because Thomas had never had any money. He had never been given any pay for working on the farm – it was just expected of him and he had never thought of being paid for it. After all, he did get his clothes and he was given good food. What more could he have wanted?

But the experience set him thinking.

Harry and Jack were evidently given money by their father, so why shouldn't he? He was now doing a lot of the work on the farm. He spoke to his mother about it, and she said she'd talk to his step-father.

One Friday soon afterwards he mentioned it to his step-brothers too. They made it quite clear that they did not like the idea. All three of them were milking at the time. When they asked him what he'd want money for Thomas said: "If I'm not paid money for my work, how can I buy you a beer at the Romper?"

Another thought struck him, for he had been taking an interest in the farm finances, under the guidance of his step-father. So he smiled as he said: "Think of it as extra pay for yourselves, given in the form of ale, with the money just passing through my hands."

Thomas was pleased with his own wit. He thought he'd been quite humorous. And he grinned into the warm flank of the cow as he added: "I believe father would call it liquid assets."

But Harry and Jack didn't see anything funny at all. The fact was, Tom thought, they just haven't got much of a sense of humour.

Harry said: "You might live here, but you're a farm labourer and nothing more. So don't try being clever with us."

The conversation ended there, because the two of them were off to Wilmslow again, a habit they had got into recently. When Thomas asked them why they were going there, they told him they were going for a drink.

"Why go to Wilmslow – what's wrong with the Romper," he asked innocently.

"Well there's more pubs and more lasses in Wilmslow," Jack told him. "Pity you can't come, but somebody's got to be on the farm to help dad with the work – and anyway you've no money."

So when he'd finished his work Thomas walked alone to the Romper. He wasn't telling the lads, but his mother had given him some coins so he could buy a beer or two. It was while he was sipping his ale that he got into conversation with old Bill Perkins, who he'd seen sitting there and smoking his pipe every time he'd been to the pub.

"You got some money then?" Bill asked him through a cloud of smoke as he relit his pipe.

"I couldn't help hearing what you said about having no money the first time you come here with the Harper lads."

"Yes, my mother gave me some," said Thomas.

"So you're still not getting a proper wage for working on the farm, then?" said Bill.

"No. Not yet. But I'm going to ask my step-father about it one of these days."

"See you do, lad," said Bill firmly. "It's not just for your own good. Word gets round, and if farmers can get away without proper pay for them as does the work they'll try it on with others

"They want as much work as they can get out of you but pay as little as they can get away with.

"There's fellers round here with wives and a dozen or so children to support. They need more money, not less. Times are hard enough as they are."

"The truth is, I don't know how much I should be paid," said Thomas. "That's why I haven't asked about it yet."

"Don't tell Mr. Harper that I told you, but the rate for the job round here is twelve shillings and two pence a week for a married man. At your age, if I were you, I'd be asking for six shillings and one penny a week, bearing in mind that you're fed and clothed as well," said Bill.

"That seems a lot to me," said Thomas. "I could buy a hell of a lot of beer for six shillings a week."

"Listen lad, it's not just beer we're talking about. It'll not be long before you're like the Harper lads are now – looking for girls to spend your time with. And that leads to courting, and courting leads to marriage, and children.

"No, don't think it won't happen to you," he added as he saw Thomas start to laugh at the idea. "Mark my words: in a year or two after you turn twenty-one you'll be wanting to have your way with the lasses, and you'll end up married sure as eggs is eggs. Then you'll want enough pay to live on for yourself and your family. So you ask for six and a penny a week from Mr. Harper and don't take no for an answer.

"Them lads of his won't like it, I can tell that. But never mind them. One day you'll thank me for what I've just told you."

*

It was a week before Thomas raised the matter, at the dinner table one warm summer evening, when all the family were busy eating. "Father, you know I'm the farm labourer round here, he began, addressing Mr. Harper. "At least that's what Harry and Jack keep telling me that's all I am."

His step-father nodded without speaking at first. He cast a sideways glance at Nell. When she didn't say anything, he said: "Yes. That's right. We all have to earn our keep."

"I pull my weight, don't I?" said Thomas.

He was a big lad, strong and healthy. . .the hard work and fresh air during the long hours in the fields and about the farm, with the good food it provided, had seen to that. His stepfather knew that without his work on the farm he'd have to pay to employ at least one labourer – maybe two.

Mr. Harper readily agreed that Thomas was a good worker. He knew it was true – more so than could be honestly said for his two older sons, who had begun to absent themselves from the farm, far too often for his liking.

Sometimes they were off the farm when they were needed. Thomas and his step-father had to get through more work because of it – and it had caused several rows. But it hadn't stopped them. Harry said there were more girls in Wilmslow, and that had become important to them, so they weren't exactly apologetic.

Their father had angrily pointed out that he had to make enough profits to pay the rent for the farm, and their going out wenching wasn't helping.

At the dinner table Thomas pressed on: "So I should be paid as a farm labourer, shouldn't I? You can take the cost of my food off. But I should have the proper rate for the job if I'm nothing but a farm labourer round here. I've been asking around and it's twelve shillings and tuppence a week for a married man.

"I think I should get half that, to take account of my food."

108

"You live here and you don't pay no rent, remember," chimed in Jack. "And you're definitely not married either."

"Yes, that's true," said Harry. "And it's not as if you're our real brother, so don't think you should get everything that we get."

Thomas felt a new determination rising within him. "No, I don't think that. I don't think I should go off to Wilmslow for hours at a stretch when there's work to be done. I wouldn't want that kind of privilege."

He'd hit a sore spot. "It's bugger all to do with you what we do," retorted Jack, his temper visibly rising.

"Who the hell do you think you are?"

"We'll have less of that kind of language at my dinner table, young man," cut in Nell. "Remember where you are. This is not the public house. And we are a family."

An uneasy silence followed.

Then Thomas, his voice calm and even, said: "It is something to do with me because father and I are the ones who have to do your work as well as our own when you're not here.

"Am I right?" he added, looking at the older man.

Mr. Harper knew he had to make a judgement there and then. He'd already told Nell that he would consider paying Thomas a proper wage. "He's right about the work," he said, slowly but decisively.

"It's only fair he should get regular wages now he's eighteen and doing a man's work. Rent doesn't come into it. But his food has to be taken into consideration. He'll be paid five shillings a week. That's my decision."

And as both his sons began to speak he cut them short. "And I don't want no arguing about it. That's it.

"You two get more than your fair share and it's only right that Thomas should get paid now he's a man."

"Seems to me you take his part rather than your own sons'," was Jack's surly response.

"Look. This is the final word. I've said it once. What I've decided is right, and it's fair, so I want no more arguing. And that's final," he ended with an emphasis that left it impossible for anyone to say another word.

CHAPTER 15

1841

"Yes. It's grim down south."

Hal Brown lived next door to the brother of one of the long-distance stagecoach drivers who regularly visited the south of England. He was a fount of wisdom. He brought a lot of information into the pub.

He refilled his pipe and took a long pull at his pint of ale. The half-dozen regulars in The Romper, including Thomas, were all ears.

"We all know about the Captain Swing trouble going back a few years," continued Hal. "Rick-burning and machine breaking all over the south of England because farm workers are being thrown out of work. And them that are working can't earn enough to live on.

"Captain Swing! Fat lot of good it did them. Some people were hanged for it, and a lot more sent to prison or transported. Worst of all, it didn't do any good at all for raising wages.

"They still get paid a lot less than we do in the north, and that's certain."

"Who's Captain Swing?" asked Thomas, feeling a bit foolish because everybody else seemed to know.

"Nobody knows," said Hal. "Fact is, between you and me, I don't think he exists. But whenever there was a riot or some machine breaking or rick-burning they'd find a letter signed with the name Captain Swing, saying he'd organized it.

"But whether he was a real person or not, it stirred things up right enough. And with wages as low as they are in the south the farm workers are desperate.

"These new machines can do the work of ten men. And something's got to be done. Otherwise there'll be thousands starving to death – men and the women and children who depend on men's wages."

"How much does a farm labourer get down south then?" someone asked.

"Well it might vary quite a bit, but from what I hear they're lucky to get seven shillings and sixpence a week," said Hal.

"And it's been like that for years – ever since the end of the French war. I believe that ten years back whole villages in the south were in the hands of the overseers because nobody could live on the wages they were getting. Whole villages!" said Hal.

"I reckon we're damn lucky to be in Cheshire. Even in Lancashire and other places up here in the north of England farm workers don't get wages as high as ours – very few get twelve shillings a week, that's what I hear."

One of the old codgers in the chimney corner broke in through the fug of smoke from his newly-relighted pipe: "You make it sound as if we're all well-off, but that's not the way it feels to me!"

"Well if you feel hard done by, just think how lucky you are that you don't live in the south," that's all I can say," said another regular Saturday afternoon imbiber of The Romper's ale.

"That's true," said Hal. "Look at all the riots and trouble down there. For nigh on twenty-five years now they've had regular bouts of haystack firing and smashing the threshing machines. Stands to reason they've not been doing that because they're happy.

"Truth is, there's lots of people starving down in those southern counties.

"The trouble is there's damn-all you can do about improving wages...whatever anyone does to try to raise pay is illegal, and that's a fact."

Thomas chipped in. "William Cobbett said in one of his newspapers that many of the labouring people in the north of England used to eat pig-swill for sustenance – but that was better than they got in the south."

"We all heard about that couple in Stockport, not five miles from here, only a few weeks back - found guilty by the Assizes of poisoning three of their children to defraud a burial society," said Bill Perkins.

112

"I don't understand," said Thomas. "How would it help them to murder their children?"

"It's like this, lad. The burial society paid them three pounds eight shillings on the death of each child to cover the burial costs.

"People that could afford it had joined these societies after the terrible cholera epidemics years ago that killed thousands, so they say.

"Of course I don't imagine these parents spent the money on funerals...you can bet they buried their children in their back garden, or on waste land, so it would have cost nothing.

"The money would have been their due if the children had died naturally. But you can't go poisoning children to get the money. That's not only murder...it's fraud.

"The law takes a dim view of fraud.

"No. The money they got was used to feed themselves and the children they'd got left, I shouldn't wonder."

"But that's the most terrible thing I've ever heard," said Thomas. "To kill their own children!"

"Ay, we don't know the half of it, living out here in the country," said Hal. "In the towns, like Manchester and Stockport, the living conditions are terrible, I've heard tell.

"There's dozens of folks crowded together in cellars because there's nowhere else to live that they can afford.

"We don't know how lucky we are living this far north but in the countryside."

"But how come we're so much better off in Cheshire?" asked Thomas. "Don't they work as hard down south, or is the land not as good for farming?"

As usual Hal had the answers: "It's like this, lad: up here we're mainly a dairy county. We get plenty of rain, and that means good grass. Cheshire's famous for its rain and its pastures...and that means good cheese, you must know that. These days we send big quantities of milk and cheese to Manchester and it pays well. The main thing here is pasture and cows. Arable farming comes a poor second, although this particular area is good for vegetables too.

113

"The thing is, you need men to do the work on our farms.

"Down south where it is mostly corn growing, these new machines that they've been bringing in can do most of the work, and they can do without most of their farm labourers.

"And where you've got more men than jobs the farmers can cut wages to the bone because they know there'll always be men clamouring for what jobs they do have.

"That's why they've been smashing machines on farms in the hope of keeping more labouring jobs. But farmers aren't fools – they know it's cheaper to buy a new machine than to pay more men to do the work. Once they've bought it a machine will last for years, doing the work of ten men.

"We haven't been affected by it because dairy farming doesn't use much machinery."

He took a sip of ale. Then he said: "There's another thing. There's a shortage of farm hands in the north because so many people have been drawn off the land to work in the mills.

"I wouldn't work in one...I've heard tell as it's like hell on earth in some of 'em. But they do provide work. They do put a crust on the table."

He changed tack: "And I'll tell you something else – why it's grim down south: ever since they brought in that new poor law you can't get parish relief if you're able-bodied but out of work.

"They said the old Poor Law was against the natural working of market forces...I suppose that meant it saved people from dying for want of food.

"But now, if you get thrown out of work, you can expect slow starvation – that's the way the new law works. It's done on purpose because they say some people preferred to be on the old parish relief instead of working.

"They say it's necessary to encourage people to work. So if you're unemployed they have to make sure you're a lot worse off than the lowest-paid labourer.

"The result is there are lots of families down there living on nothing but potatoes and bread and cheese."

"I heard say they believe that bringing people to the brink of starvation will increase their spirit of self-reliance," said someone.

"Ay, I suppose they'll be really full of self-reliance by the time they drop dead!" said one of the gnarled old farm workers present.

"But if there's no work to be had because the machines are doing the work of ten men, what on earth can they do about it?" asked Thomas.

"I suppose they could move somewhere else, where there is work," put in someone.

"Ah, but it seems to be the same, all across the south of England," said Hal, "That's the problem: there's nowhere to go."

He drank down the last of his beer before adding: "But I have to go, so I'm off."

And he went. Through the window they saw him step away from the pub. "He knows a lot, that Hal Brown," said Shadrach Short, a Styal man. "But he doesn't know everything.

"I've heard that the parishes in the south have been paying to send hundreds of families over the sea to Canada to save paying relief to men without work.

"And Mr. Greg has brought thirty families to Styal from a southern place called Great Bedlow for employment in his mill.

"But Hal's right about one thing. One of them, a chap called John Howlett, has been working at Beech Farm, and he's been telling people that with all his family who can work at the mill they've been earning one pound four shillings a week altogether, and that's twice as much as they could earn where they come from."

"Now they've done away with the combination laws you'd think these unions they're forming would be able to do something about wages in the south, that's what they're supposed to be for" said Tom Younghusband, a labourer, not much older than Thomas, and recently become a young husband, as the regulars at The Romper found delight in repeating every time he came in to the pub.

115

"They might have done away with the combination laws, and they might be forming trade unions as a result, but it doesn't mean they can actually do anything about improving wages," said one of the older contingent. "Only a couple of years back there were five union men charged with conspiracy, in Essex if I remember right. And they were damn lucky to get off."

"What were they supposed to be conspiring to do?" asked Thomas.

"They were charged with conspiring to raise wages!" said the older man.

"But they were found not guilty?"

"Yes. Even though the clergy were preaching against them, and saying that what they were trying to do was unchristian."

"No bloody wonder the churches aren't as full as they used to be," said Tom. "You always know whose side the vicar will be on. That's why so many of them are magistrates – they can always be counted on to do what the local gentry tell them. They know where *their* bread's buttered."

"Increase the labourers' spirit of self reliance! Like hell it would! All it does is to give them a choice: steal their food or starve...them and their wives and children.

"Well I know what I'd do. And it wouldn't be starve to death!"

"But if you were caught you might hang," said Shadrach. "Or they might transport you for life. Then your wife and children would starve anyway, like as not.

"They talk about self-reliance! The working man always used to be self-reliant – he had to be.

"Now they talk about self-reliance and at the same time cut wages and bring in machines that take men's work, so there are fewer jobs.

"All you can do is to hope you keep your job, work at it, and hope you can pay your way. But if you've no job you're buggered. So it's well nigh impossible for a lot of people to be self-reliant.

"Self reliance my arse!"

*

1983

We must aim to increase the spirit of self reliance, Prime Minister
Margaret Thatcher told her eager cabinet of ministers.

"The trouble is that there is far too little differential between the
lowest-paid jobs and the income you can get in benefits...it is a
disincentive to work."

So short-term social benefits – for unemployment, sickness, injury,
maternity and invalidity – were reduced by five percent, and taxed.
Mrs. Thatcher had become Britain's first woman Prime Minister in
1979. She was fiercely against the kind of compromises she felt Tory
prime ministers had made since the war, adulterating their Conservative
beliefs with consensus politics.

One of her government's first actions was to cut the standard rate of
income tax from 33 per cent to 30 percent. The highest rate was
reduced from 83 per cent to 60 per cent.

At the same time it increased Value Added Tax from the two-tier
eight and 12.5 per cent to fifteen per cent, so increasing the price of
most things except food. Inflation, around ten per cent when she took
office, doubled.

Mrs. Thatcher and some of her most trusted colleagues had
developed a belief in keeping down inflation by restricting the money
supply. This was monetarism, but it came to be known as Thatcherism.
It was by no means a proven theory in practical terms.

In the event, record high bank interest rates, brought in to combat
inflation, killed off much of Britain's manufacturing. Unemployment
soared. But she refused to change course.

The people she really wanted to target were the workshy – the people who sponged off the state and had no intention of ever doing a day's work if they could avoid it.

"We have got to tackle this problem of people being better-off out of work," she said.

She believed that freely-distributed welfare benefits encouraged illegitimacy and the breakdown of families, replacing encouragement to work with incentives for idleness.

*

"About time these lazy so-and-sos found their game is up – at last we've got a leader who will tell them their free ride on state benefits is over," said Hanna.

"There are far too many so-called workers doing as little work as they can. Some haven't done a day's work in their lives, if you ask me!"

"She's absolutely right to cut benefits unless people are too disabled to work. Once they find they're out of house and home because there's nobody to bail them out and pay their rent they'll soon learn self-reliance."

"Trouble is, half of them will turn to crime rather than find work," said Adam. "Work is the last things these lazy sods want."

They were lying in bed at the flat in Altrincham, relaxing after their weekly romp. He could always get an afternoon off without anyone checking where he was. He told them he was on the road, visiting various of his firm's offices.

"Speaking of which – finding work, I mean – I've been offered a job in Australia."

For once Hanna was shocked. "What are you going to do?"

"Well I think I'll apply if nothing else. It's always a good thing to show that you're interested in promotion. And the job would be a big step-up for me if I got it. I don't think I'd be able to turn it down."

"But what about us?" said Hanna.

118

"This is why I mentioned it. If I'm offered the job, I'd want you to come with me."

"Bloody hell, Adam!

A long silence followed.

"What about Jill?"

Adam turned and stroked Hanna's arm. "I think it's time we stopped pretending about our home lives. Don't you want to be with me instead of Geoff? Because I want to be with you instead of Jill.

"It might be bloody awkward here, but if we went to Australia it would be the ideal moment to make the break. Whatever people might say, we'd be twelve thousand miles away. Sod them."

"What about the children – yours as well as David."

Adam thought about his twin sons, aged 11. "They'd soon get over it. And your David is at university – he'll be off making his own life anyway before long.

"We can't let concerns about other people affect what we want. It's our happiness that counts. They all have their own lives to live – and so do we."

Hanna was shaken by the proposition. "Leaving Geoff wouldn't bother me at all. But I'm not sure I can just walk out on David."

She got out of bed.

"Of course it may never happen. You haven't actually got the job yet. But it's a hell of a thing you're suggesting. Oh God! I need time to think about it."

CHAPTER 16

1846

The walk from Ringway to Knutsford took Thomas less than two hours. It was only half the distance he walked in a day's ploughing. And far from the heavy work of guiding the plough straight behind the two sturdy horses on the farm, he was travelling light, carrying nothing with him except the two shillings and sixpence that he had saved up from his wages, and was determined to enjoy.

For he had been told by the experienced hands at The Romper that the fine old town was a sight to see when a fair visited – as it always did for May Day.

There was, he had been told, dancing round the May Pole, roundabouts and swings, and the streets were decorated with sand-pictures for which the Knutsford townspeople were acknowledged experts.

And in any case, the travelling fair, he had been told, was one of the wonders of the age, with jugglers, magicians who could produce an egg from your ear, a boxing champion taking on all challengers, and swings and roundabouts that whirled you until you were dizzy. There was a fortune-teller too, and Thomas was keen to know what was going to happen to him in the future.

It had been a sunny Saturday so far. He had asked for a rare day off just so that he could go and see the things he had heard about. He walked through the country lanes and footpaths that took him across the fields to Mobberley, then on to Knutsford. Walking down Hollow Lane hill he began to sense the excitement special to the day. He became part of a drift of people heading towards Canute Square in the town centre.

And sure enough, there were the sand-patterns, in colours and shades wonderful to behold. Thomas had never seen anything like it. He knew the seven-mile walk was going to be worth it.

*

The colours of the fair were vivid. There was excitement in the air. There was movement everywhere, and music from a brass band. There was a noisy crowd round a Punch and Judy show...a hubbub and a jostle of more people than Thomas had ever seen before.

There was a tall red and yellow structure with a slide circling down round its outside – young women, their skirts billowing, screamed in mock terror as they sped downward, round and round. And a chorus of regular screams came from some things called swing boats. There was a notice saying there'd be prize fighters; there were rope dancers, and vaulting and tumbling displays. There were coconut shies, with prizes...and hoop-la and skittles too. Cheers as someone won, and groans when people failed, filled the air with cheerful excitement.

Thomas had never seen anything like it. He felt himself responding to the atmosphere of fun and crowded festivity. There was a big roundabout, and he decided to try that first – it looked quite gentle, and it cost only a farthing to ride.

Young lads ran and pushed until they were red in the face to keep it turning. Giggling with delight as they tried to hold on to the whirling wheel, girls shrieked to each other and held on to their bonnets; young men were shouting raucous comments as they saw the girls' skirts swirling. You could see their ankles.

When it stopped Thomas paid his farthing and stepped aboard. Once in motion, the unaccustomed movement made the whole thing seem faster than it had looked from standing on the ground. Faces and trees and reds and yellows and greens whirled past. He planted his feet firmly, determined to show that *he* didn't have to cling on.

But when it stopped and he stepped back on to the ground he found himself lurching half sideways, like being drunk.

121

Then he banged into a little group of four lasses who were excitedly talking. He quickly grabbed the nearest girl's arm and tried save her from falling. But she and the others all fell to the ground in a welter of arms, skirts, and indignant squeals. And Thomas fell on top of them.

He heard an older woman standing nearby mutter: "Drunken lout!"

He felt himself going red with embarrassment. But he quickly picked himself up and helped the girls to their feet, apologizing as he did so, and asking anxiously if they were hurt. "I'm not drunk. I was dizzy from the machine," he heard himself saying. "I just lost my balance. I hope I haven't done you any harm."

They seemed remarkably affable, all considered. In fact they seemed more inclined to giggle than to complain, and to assure him that they were quite all right.

But for Thomas his dizzy spell seemed to come back. He felt a lurch in his stomach or his chest or somewhere, as his eyes met those of one of the girls. She was the prettiest lass he had ever seen. She had yellow hair and big blue eyes that seemed to look into his soul. He was in love.

But he had not entirely lost his senses. He knew that somehow he had to stay with this girl; he could not just let her walk away.

"There's a lemonade stall. Let me get you all a drink to help you get over the shock," he said, adding: "It's the least I can do after knocking you all down like that."

And when one of the girls said coolly that no thanks, they were quite all right, he looked deeply into those blue eyes that held him captive and said: "Look. I feel so bad about it. Please don't send me away without a chance to make up for it in some small way."

She was called Jane. Jane Wildgoose. It was like poetry. She seemed to understand how he felt. She almost seemed to know what he was going to say before he said it. She had a gentle smile that made him feel happy. She was a servant in a big house in the town.

But she came from Middlewich, a place he'd never heard of. She told him it was in Cheshire about ten miles away. To Thomas the very name of this unknown town seemed imbued with magic.

"Are there many witches?" he asked. When they saw that it was a serious question Jane smiled, and her three friends giggled. No, it wasn't that kind of witch at all, she assured him. And there were other places with witch in their name – Northwich and Leftwich and Nantwich were ones that she had heard of.

Her friends sensed that they should leave Jane and Thomas alone. They said they were off to try the fortune teller.

Thomas felt suddenly older and wiser than he had been up to now. He looked at Jane and said seriously: "I think *you* may be a witch."

She looked startled. He felt his heart pounding as he heard himself saying: "I think you have bewitched me. For a start, I feel as if I've always known you – yet I'm sure I've never seen you before. And..."

He felt his face burning again. But he went on, determinedly: "And I can't stop looking at you. I don't want to look at anything else. I want to stay here for ever, just looking at you. You've done something strange to me!"

There was only a hint of a smile as she said: "I don't think you really *can* stay here for ever looking at me. First of all I won't be here. I'm going to catch up with my friends and have my fortune read. You should come and see what the gypsy lady says about *your* future. They say she never gets it wrong.

"Perhaps she'll tell you what kind of girl you'll marry."

"I'm coming. I've got more reason than ever for wanting to know."

They caught up with two of Jane's friends by the fortune teller's booth, waiting for the third to emerge. All were in service at large houses in Knutsford. Their working lives as servants were strict. The day of the fair was their freedom to be young women having fun.

The third girl stepped out, of the fortune-teller's tent: "I'm going to have many children," she shrieked, dissolving into laughter.

"So are we," chorused the other two. "I'm going to marry a very tall dark man," said one of the girls.

"She told me I'll live to see many grandchildren," giggled the other. "Come on. Your turn now Jane."

123

Jane went inside the coloured tent. Thomas stood awkwardly, wondering what to say to the other girls. He couldn't think of anything.

When Jane came out, she had a quizzical look on her face. "I don't want to say what she told me," she told her friends and Thomas, who couldn't help hearing it. Then Jane turned to him: "Go on, you're next."

Inside the light was dim. There was an old woman with a scarf round her head, and big earrings dangling by the side of her swarthy face. She sat behind a table which was covered with a cloth, on which stood a round, glass ball.

She took Thomas's silver threepenny-piece, her dark eyes fixed on his. She paused. She took his hand. She peered at it by the light of a candle, running her fingers along the lines in his palm. She seemed to pause again, as if uncertain. Then she looked straight into Thomas's eyes.

"You will marry a girl you already know. You will have a good life. You should go and marry your love and be happy."

She stopped.

"Is that all I get for three pence?" said Thomas, indignantly.

"I could tell you more, but some things must remain hidden...it is the lore of the all-seeing. I can tell you are a good man."

She peered again at his hand. "Your children will be few."

Again she paused. She looked hard at Thomas. What should she tell him? "I see success. You will be loved. I see much good in your life."

She stopped again. She seemed to be struggling. She looked at his hand again. "But I see...betrayal...someone close to you...you must try to rise above it by the goodness that is within your heart.

"Go now."

That was a command. Thomas felt more than a little nervous in front of this sage. So he went out, still feeling it wasn't much for three pence.

The old woman watched him go. She sighed. She had powers...feelings...that even she did not understand. She had seen many young people anxious to know what the future held for them. She liked

124

them to go out from her tent feeling happy. But she would not lie. Instead she tried to choose her words carefully.

She knew that most of what she did was a bit of nonsense to make her look mysterious and darkly wise: crossing her hand with silver; peering into a glass ball; staring at their open palms. But the real thing was the feeling that she sometimes had the moment a person stepped into her tent.

A sense of foreboding came to her at these times. She felt it quite clearly. She felt it now.

Outside, in the sunshine, Thomas was aware only that he wanted to know about Jane, who was waiting with her friends. "Jane, can I talk to you by yourself?"

"We know when we're not wanted," said one of the others. "We'll be at the juggler's tent."

"Jane, I need to know what she told you about your future."

"Well now, that would be telling," she responded in a teasing tone.

"Jane, can I visit you when you have your day off from work? I couldn't bear to think that I might not see you again. I don't know if I'm being daft, but I feel that I want to talk to you, and to listen to you. Well...what I feel is that I want to be with you. I've never felt like this before. Maybe I never will again.

"Will you let me walk out with you?"

There. He'd said it.

"Well, I don't know that I should. I don't really know you."

"Well I feel as if I've known you all my life, even though it is for such a short time," he said earnestly. "Perhaps I could write to you. Can you read and write?"

She smiled. "Yes. Yes I can and yes you can."

She told him the address of the house where she worked.

He knew she would be off now to join her friends. "Bless you Jane. Today has been my lucky day. I'll write to you and the next time I can get off from the farm I'm going to come and see you."

*

125

The sense of loss as she disappeared was something he had not expected. He wandered aimlessly through the happy crowds for a while, then decided that he would go home. Something had happened to him. The day could not offer anything better.

Once on his way back to Ringway he felt as if the very air was different: new, exciting. He felt elation. He felt astonishment. And he knew that he had to spend the rest of his life with her.

CHAPTER 17

1846

Thomas was used to writing. He did much of the accounts for the farm, and he wrote business letters for his step-father. Because of his mastery of words, allied to his ability to tot up figures fast and accurately, Thomas had become a great help to Mr. Harper, quite aside from the labouring work on the farm.

But now he turned his quill to writing in a way he was not used to. He gave it a lot of thought.

Oakwood Farm,

Ringway.

Dear Miss Wildgoose,

We had a short time together when we met in Knutsford yesterday. I would like to see you again when you are free from working, for I can but feel sad that we parted so soon.

If youd like me to come please write me a note to tell when you are going to be free, so as I can arrange with my step-father to be away from the farm.

Thomas Mayer.

When he had written business letters for his step-father he had always finished them "Your Humble Servant," before "Jack Harper."

But he found himself mentally rejecting the term as being seemingly servile on the one hand, yet too "routine" on the other. He couldn't think of an alternative that seemed right. So he settled for his name only.

It was three weeks – three anxious, despairing weeks – for Thomas before the reply came. In roundish characters Jane told him that she would be free the following Sunday and would be in Knutsford for two hours in the afternoon.

It was short, and not particularly sweet; but it was a willingness to see him – that was all that mattered!

He had four days to make his arrangements, for, as Mr. Harper put it, the cows couldn't milk themselves.

His mother had been aware from the start that Thomas was in love, even if he hadn't told her that he had met a very pretty lass called Jane when he went to Knutsford.

Nell knew that he had written to the girl, and everyone in the family was aware when the reply letter arrived addressed to Thomas.

When the day came Nell insisted that he wore his best clothes, and she had carefully washed and pressed one of her husband's best shirts, using the heavy irons that had to be heated on the black kitchen range. She polished his boots too. So he looked pretty smart as he set out to walk to Knutsford.

*

He found Jane easily enough in Canute Square, where all the principal roads met in the centre of the town.

His heart seemed to stop for a moment when he saw her. It seemed to him that she was lovelier than ever, although she was wearing the same dress that she had worn at their first meeting.

He took her to a café for a glass of lemonade. The sun was shining and there seemed to be a special, strange new feeling in the air. They took a walk on the heath, just across the road from the White Bear inn. Thomas found that talking to her, and listening to her, was so easy. Words flowed between them. It was as if they had known each other for years. And it was not the problem that he had feared to tell her that he loved her and hoped that one day she would be his.

She didn't say yes. She expressed surprise. She pointed out gently that they hardly knew each other. She wouldn't want people to think that she was the kind of girl who rushed into such things so quickly.

128

"But Thomas, I feel that we have already become friends. We have had such a lovely afternoon together, and I should like it very much if you can come again the next time I am released from my work."

It fascinated Thomas that she spoke very much like a lady. The girls that he'd talked to in Ringway and Wilmslow had a broad Cheshire way of talking. On his walk home he reasoned that she had become used to speaking that way when addressing her master or mistress in the big house that he had seen from a distance when he escorted her homewards.

It was called Shaw Hall, and was a mile or so from the centre of Knutsford. It was the seat of the Hardman family who were enormously wealthy and one of the biggest land-owners in the area, Jane had told him.

Strangely enough, Jane was also taken with Thomas's accent, which was not the local Cheshire way of sounding. He had never thought about it himself, but he had partly absorbed the way his mother spoke. Nell had been brought from a workhouse in London to be an apprentice at Styal, and she still retained to a small degree her southern accent, with the more drawn-out "aa" when she said words like "path."

Jane was attuned to the upper-class world in which the Hardman family lived. She knew, of course, that as a farm labourer Thomas was certainly not among the moneyed classes. But his step-father was a farmer, a husbandman – and a definite step up the social scale.

There had been talk recently among the gentlemen who called at her employer's house, which she had overheard when serving refreshment to them after the ladies had withdrawn – talk of rising prospects for farmers now that the French wars and their aftermath had stabilized. New machines were being brought in to cut farmers' costs, even in some parts of Cheshire. It seemed that a new era of prosperity faced farmers in the next few years.

She had also heard mention within the family of one of the estate farms becoming vacant in the not-too-distant future, for its aged tenant could no longer cope with the work of running it.

Jane Wildgoose was not a young woman who would fail to make a connection – tenuous and by no means fully formed as yet, but still a connection – between these interesting facts and the attentions being paid to her by a good-looking stepson of a farmer.

For she had ambitions. She did not intend to remain a maid at the big house, comfortable though the position was in some respects. To be the wife of a farmer in prosperous times appealed to her sense of her place in the world. Thomas, she could see, could be the important keystone in the bridge that she was building, in the privacy of her thoughts, between what she was today, and what she could become in the future.

The more she thought about it, the more she liked the idea. And over the next few months she actively encouraged Thomas to court her. He would always remember the day he found himself and Jane briefly hidden from public view behind a hedge so that kissing her for the first time was accomplished in a trembling moment of ecstasy.

She smelt clean – she tasted of soap, he thought. And she felt soft and fragile. Her waist was so small, and it swelled into hips that sent his senses spinning. It was the moment when love became something more determined.

*

When Thomas told her that he would like to take her to meet his mother and step-father, she readily agreed. Thanks to Nell's and Thomas's care with the farm accounts, and on several occasions Mr. Harper's adoption of new methods for fertilizing the ground and for selling produce at the best price, he had been able to buy a pony and trap which had opened up new horizons for Nell. She could now get much more quickly to Wilmslow and Altrincham.

Now the trap, she insisted when Thomas told her he was bringing his young lady to visit, was to be used to bring her from Knutsford.

For Jane it was a heady new experience to be riding like a lady through the countryside, with smartly-dressed Thomas driving. She loved the idea. She loved the envious looks of people they passed by.

But she was still able to observe carefully when she arrived at the Harper farm, seeing that it looked well-kept outside.

She looked Nell over as she came out to greet them, followed by Mr. Harper. She met Nell's eyes as Thomas introduced them.

And once inside the farmhouse, she cast a critical eye over the furnishings and the sparse décor, the way the kitchen was equipped, the attempts at comfort in the sitting room. But most of all she was assessing Nell.

And Nell was assessing her right back. She had been deeply curious to meet Jane from the moment that Thomas had told her that he had met a young woman in Knutsford over a year ago now. She was five years younger than Thomas. Nell knew that this was the girl he was going to marry.

What she saw was a very pretty young woman, fair-hair neatly pulled back and pinned, looking well in the best dress she was wearing. But as they chatted she heard, too, a woman who was as neat as her dress, a woman who knew what she wanted, and was not afraid to voice her likes and dislikes.

And, Nell instinctively knew, a woman would have things done her way, a woman who would win, a woman who would rule.

Nell could not like her.

And somehow that feeling, secret and unexpressed, was known to Jane. The knowledge that she was to take something precious – her son – away from this older, wiser, and obviously able woman, gave Jane a feeling of power. So she did not care what Nell thought

But politeness was the order of the day. Mr. Harper was enchanted by Jane. Thomas was ecstatically happy to have the two women in his life meeting for the first time. He was unaware of any undercurrents. All he saw was his mother, learning to love the woman he loved. It was all as it should be.

CHAPTER 18

1847

Old Mrs. Hardman was a widow who never had to question her position in society. But she was a gentlewoman with a keen sense of parenthood – not only towards her own children, but also to the band of young women servants at Shaw Hall. She had a proper sense of responsibility for them

Some, like Jane Wildgoose, did not see their own parents more than once or twice a year. Despite the great social gulf between herself and them, Mrs. Hardman enjoyed a chat, at carefully selected moments, with the young women whose work brought them close to her.

She enjoyed her private feeling that, whilst these chats were, of course, never to be thought of as between equals, they were "woman to woman," and that there was a way that females could sympathise in a cosy, private kind of atmosphere.

She took a genuine interest in the lives of her servants. She knew what their parents did, where they lived, how many other children they had had, how old they were, what their state of health.

She had almost a parental fondness for the young servants, and was constantly aware that young men of the household, and of the town, all too often attracted their attention.

That they would one day want to marry was something that she knew quite well. But she felt a responsibility to do all in her power to ensure that they did not get themselves involved with young men she felt to be "unsuitable."

Mrs. Hardman was therefore immediately alert and interested when Jane, deputising for her regular maid – who had been allowed off to attend her father's funeral – informed her that she had a follower.

Mrs. Hardman had asked Jane if she had a special interest in any young man. Now she wanted to know all...these things were interesting. And she did feel that she had a responsibility to enquire into them.

She was a little surprised when Jane told her that matters had progressed to the point where she and Thomas, her young man, had an understanding, and intended one day to marry. She was more surprised to learn that Thomas lived not in Knutsford, but some miles away in Ringway.

"What is his station?" she asked.

Jane told her that Thomas lived with his mother and step-father, who was a husbandman farmer. She also described how Thomas's step-brothers often conspired to leave the bulk of the farm work to Thomas and their father.

And Jane told her how Thomas had been taught by his mother to read and write, and how he had taken on the farm accounts.

From finding them hardly making sense he had sorted them out. And he had personally gone all the way into Manchester and met some market men and had arranged to sell much of the farm's produce to the traders who paid the best prices for a steady supply of good quality vegetables, butter and cheese.

And, she finished triumphantly, Thomas had taken to reading the new information about the latest farming methods, and had persuaded Mr. Harper into adopting better fertilizers that he had read about...and they had improved things greatly.

"And is he a handsome young man, as well as being clever?" asked Mrs. Hardman with a smile.

"Oh yes, ma'am, or I shouldn't have talked to him in the first place when I let him bump into me."

They laughed again, almost conspiratorially, and their little chat ended.

*

Jack Harper's death was sudden, unexpected, and a shattering blow to everybody at Oakwood Farm. He had always been a man of oak, with a strength and durability that made him master in more ways than one. He had never been ill. Not until the fateful day when, after haymaking, he had had a furious argument with his oldest son.

Suddenly he complained of a splitting headache. His speech became slurred. He wasn't making sense, and he seemed to lose his co-ordination. Then he fell to the ground, with his face strangely contorted. They tried to get him to his feet, but his right arm and leg were paralysed. He kept trying to talk, but his words were a meaningless jumble.

Nell sent Thomas in the pony and trap to bring a physician from Altrincham, but before he arrived her husband died. He was sixty-one. And at fifty-three herself, Nell knew that her days as matriarch of the farm were numbered.

Harry's argument with her husband had been over a pregnant local girl who had made a complaint that Harry was the father of the child she was expecting. He denied all responsibility.

She had come to the farm and had tearfully told Nell that she had never been with a man until Harry had had his way. He had persuaded her after making her tipsy on gin, and she had not been with any man since. Her baby's father could be no other than Harry. She had believed him when he had told her that he was doing it only because he loved her.

Now she knew that it was a lie. That was the worst thing – worse even than having her life ruined by giving birth to a bastard, she had sobbed.

Confronted, Harry had accepted that he had had his way with the girl, but claimed that she was well-known to be the village whore who had been with many men. So Nell said: "Name one."

And when met by silence she said: "Take me to three or four of the many who know that she has been a whore. Only do that and I shall believe you."

But he couldn't. Nell told his father so. And honest Jack Harper vowed that his son would not bring dishonour on his name, and would marry the lass.

The blank refusal was the cause of the last, bitter argument that finished the life of farmer Harper, and the well-earned comfort of Nell as a farmer's wife.

For in his will Mr. Harper had left the farm to his two older sons – the sons of his first marriage.

The will decreed that Nell should be suffered to live at the farm as long as she desired, as should their younger children. To Thomas, his step-son only, and no blood relation, but whose diligent work had brought the prosperity that Mr. Harper recognised, he left the sum of one hundred pounds – equal to four years' wages.

*

It was a large enough sum to marry and set up home with Jane. Thomas had already been building up a fund from his wages, which had been increased to ten shillings a week in view of his plans to marry. Now it was only a matter of finding employment at a farm paying him the going rate, and finding a cottage.

But Jane had other, better, ideas. The farm on the Hardman estate, she knew, was about to become vacant at last. And Mrs. Hardman had asked after Thomas several times since their little chat. Jane boldly asked for an audience with her mistress, told her of Thomas's financial ability to take the tenancy, and asked if she thought the master might consider offering it to Thomas and herself as his wife.

Thomas could hardly believe it when he was invited to be interviewed by Mr. Trevithick, the estate's agent, and, in view of his status as son of a husbandman farmer, his knowledge of the latest agricultural practices, and his means of bringing in profits from the market trade contacts that he had established, he was offered the tenancy.

*

The elation, the successful application, the setting up home in his own farm ready for his marriage to Jane, took Thomas clear of the new enmity from his half-brothers, and the break-up of the family life he had grown to love since he had gone to live in the Ringway farmhouse at the age of five.

He invited his mother to leave Oakwood Farm and come to join him and Jane at Shaw Mill Farm in Knutsford.

But to his surprise Nell refused. Oakwood needed a woman to run the house and the dairy, and to keep the accounts since her step-sons wouldn't know how, she told him.

Also, she said to herself, Shaw Mill Farm will already have a woman, and that was enough. She knew that she and Jane would never be able to live together in harmony.

But she set to work to sew and stitch and knit to make cushions and curtains and table cloths to adorn Thomas and Jane's home – and baby clothes to adorn their firstborn, whenever it came.

For Thomas the wedding, meeting Jane's parents and brothers and sisters, the ecstasy of loving his new wife, were but a prelude to the challenge of making his farm what he was determined it would be: productive and profitable.

It was fifty acres only, average for the area, though smaller than Oakwood Farm at Ringway. He had bought the existing herd of cows after finding them in fair condition, and checking their milk yields. He had also bought up the former tenant's two heavy horses and his machinery too, out-dated though much of it was. But it was cheap, and a start.

And a start was what he needed. His predecessor had been an old man without children, and at the end there had been too much neglect. Now Thomas threw himself into repairing and hedging and ditching,

136

ploughing and fertilizing and sowing by day, planning and book-keeping by evening candlelight. The routine of early to bed and early to rise came naturally to him.

To Jane, released from service for the first time since she was twelve, the housework was something she was used to. But milking and dairy work were new, and had to be learned. Thomas kept on the former tenant's dairy-maid, a woman very experienced at her work. And Jane was a quick learner.

The work was hard, but the weather smiled on their efforts, and the first three years were productive in the fields and, towards the end of 1850, in Jane's swelling figure.

*

Back at Ringway all harmony had disappeared from Oakwood Farm. Jack had now made a girl pregnant too. They resented Nell's despairing attempts to get them to see their responsibilities.

But now two things caught up with the brothers. The first was in the shape of four very large men who were friends of the two girls' brothers.

Their brief and blunt explanation of what would happen to Harry and Jack if they did not marry the girls, struck fear into the two farmers...until the big men left. Then the pair struck a pose of not being worried by that lot.

Then the vestry overseers and the constables caught up with Harry and Jack, and they found themselves faced with having to pay to bring up the children on pain of imprisonment...or marriage. So each brought home a young wife who soon produced a baby apiece.

Nell's help and advice were welcomed at first. But the girls' mothers – both younger than Nell – saw it as an interference with their rights as grandparents. They quickly saw that Nell might have a right to be there as Jack Harper's widow. But she had no bloodline to her step-sons, much less to their children.

The grandmothers didn't like the thought that Nell, with children of her own, and a son who was also a farmer, might somehow come to muscle in on the Ringway farm that had now become their daughters' home-ground and their grandchildren's birthright.

*

Nell had no money of her own. She had to move out. She was adamant that she would not go to live with Thomas and Jane – she knew in her heart that it would be disastrous, for she simply could find no liking for her son's wife.

Anyway, she had always had strong feelings against men's mothers living with their sons when they married. "Too many women," was the way she viewed it.

So she went to live in the Altrincham Union workhouse in Wilmslow. She had started her life in a workhouse in London, in the times when they were seen as a haven for paupers who could no longer support themselves, and conditions were strict, but often not unkind.

Unfortunately for Nell she hadn't believed the stories about the grim turn they had taken after the new Poor Law was enacted in 1834...the punitive philosophy in workhouses stemming from the conviction that people were poor because they were too lazy to work. The Royal commission on the Poor Laws, upon whose findings their 1834 Amendments were based, had stated boldly that paupers had reached that condition as a result of nothing less than fraud, indolence or improvidence.

Nell's thinking was that the workhouse solution meant that she would not be too far away from Thomas and his wife and family. She might be of help to them from time to time. But much more likely, she might need Thomas fairly nearby as old age took her in its grasp.

Now she was 53 she knew she would not live much longer. She had lived to see two husbands dead, but Thomas was set up as a farmer, and she knew in her bones that he would be a success.

More than that, though, he's the sort of man that I wanted my son to be. He's intelligent, and he's also so nice and pleasant. Everybody says so, except those Harper brothers.

I'm just glad that Thomas didn't turn out like them. I just hope he'll be happy in his marriage. But I could not go and live with him. He's going to marry a wife that is one that won't put up with another woman being around. There's something about that Jane that I can't take to. But he loves her and that's that.

Two of my girls are married. Eliza and Joanna are happily placed too, working for farmers who were good friends of Jack's. Pity I don't see them any more. But they've their own lives to lead, and I say bless them and keep them well and happy – as I have been with both my husbands.

I've been lucky. Like a lot of people I've ended up a pauper, but I've nothing to be ashamed of. I've passed on everything I could give to the next generation...we all have to give way in the end.

That's what life is. You bring up your children and watch them grow and blossom and marry and have their own children. And then you know you've played your part and the wheel has turned full circle. It's as it should be and I'm content with that.

There was no stone on her grave in the churchyard to record her death three years later.

But Thomas knew the spot, and made sure that in each season there were flowers there, in memory of his beloved mother.

CHAPTER 19

1851

The birth of their son, assisted by a local woman much experienced in such matters, was uncomplicated. Jane emerged exhausted but triumphant, and the baby was called William, after her father.

For Thomas it was a big relief from the anxieties that had built up in him over the last stages of Jane's pregnancy. He was very happy to pay the woman three shillings for her attendance – sixpence more than she had asked.

He was used to seeing the birth of farm animals, normally a simple and natural event. But he knew that occasionally there were problems, and his love for Jane was such that he could not help worrying, especially when he could not persuade her to stop working so hard about the farm.

If he had loved her before, now the sight of her with the tiny mite in her arms, or suckling at her breast, filled him with an intensity of emotion and joy that he had never experienced before.

Among the first to congratulate them on the safe delivery of their firstborn was Crispin Trevithick, Mr. Hardman's land agent, who made a special call the day after the birth with a bottle of wine to toast with Thomas the "health and happiness of the mother and baby."

He gave Jane a bunch of roses picked from his own garden.

For Thomas and Jane it was a matter of great pride to be accorded such attention from Mr. Trevithick, a gentleman of impeccable manners, and who, it was commonly known, was greatly respected and relied upon by Mr. Hardman himself.

He had been appointed agent nearly eight years earlier, and had proved to be an able man of affairs, softly-spoken yet well-versed in the latest farming techniques, who ran Mr. Hardman's estate more efficiently than it had ever been in the past.

He had increased Mr. Hardman's profits from the five tenanted farms that he owned, yet had pleased the farmers too, by keeping their buildings in good repair, whilst making his insistence on good farm practice sound more like friendly advice.

On the other hand, he was always ready to listen to the farmers' problems, and to pass on such information to his employer. When it meant that Mr. Hardman had to spend money to improve the farm buildings or fencing, or any other matter for which he was responsible, Mr. Trevithick was not afraid to say so.

These days Mr. Hardman left the running of his Knutsford estate in his hands entirely, for he and Mrs. Hardman were frequently away, in London, or taking the waters in Bath or Cheltenham, or residing at their much larger estate in Norfolk.

For the agent, it wasn't just the concerns of the tenant farmers and their ability to pay their rents that occupied his time. He handled the estate's flow of money, making sure that there was cash to pay the bills, and the wages of the estate's outdoor staff, as well as the wages of the home farm workers and the hall's domestic servants.

His responsibilities were great. Yet Mr. Trevithick never seemed to be weighed down by his cares.

At the time when William Mayer was born, he was a man in his thirties, suave to a degree, always impeccably turned-out, well-spoken and plainly well rewarded.

He was equally at ease talking to farmers or mixing with the upper echelons of society in Knutsford, a handsome man much talked about by the ladies, yet so far unattached.

He was the youngest son of a big landowner in his native Cornwall, and his Cambridge education had not entirely removed a hint of his West Country way of speaking.

Despite all his responsibilities he always seemed to have time to stop and talk to the estate workers. He made it his business to know something about everyone living or working on the estate, and little escaped his attention.

For a bachelor he seemed much taken by little William, and often called at the farm. He delighted Thomas and Jane by attending the baby's christening. He even presented William with a little silver cup to mark the occasion.

"He is so kind, Thomas," said Jane when the ceremony was over, and they were home at the farm. "I don't know what we have done to deserve it."

"He's just that kind of man – a gentleman with a heart of gold, if you ask me," replied Thomas.

And turning to the now-sleeping William, he lowered his voice and said gently: "You may not have been born with a silver spoon in your mouth, but Mr. Trevithick has made sure that you'll always have a silver cup to drink from.

*

In fact Mr. Trevithick had long had an unexpressed admiration for Jane. He had noticed her soon after he had become Mr. Hardman's agent, when he was twenty-four.

He had seen the 17 year-old servant Jane in the hall, in her neat dress and white apron and cap. Her pretty face, and her full-breasted figure, accentuated by her small waist, and which the apron couldn't entirely hide, had taken his eye immediately.

He had, over the next few years, secretly admired her, although, of course, the gulf between their relative stations in life had forbidden anything but routine pleasantries to be made on the few occasions when they had come face to face in the course of Jane's duties.

Then, suddenly, he had the opportunity to do her a tremendous favour: for it was he who had to interview Thomas for the farm tenancy.

He knew that he was Jane's intended, because old Mrs. Hardman, who always stayed in the Knutsford hall, had told him so.

There were a number of applicants for the farm, and not a lot to choose between them as to their suitability. He awarded the tenancy to Thomas, of course, and was delighted by his secret pleasure in so doing.

Now it was his duty to visit the farm to ensure, in Mr. Hardman's interests, that the tenancy was going well, for a profitable farm generated the rental to the estate, and that was Mr. Trevithick's business.

Often when he called unexpectedly, Thomas was out in the fields. He would leave a note, asking some question, or raising some issue, and have a few words with Jane. Now that she had her baby, he always wanted to have a look at the little boy, for he was fond of children.

He was always complimentary to child and mother, often bringing small gifts and tokens of his esteem. But the suspicion slowly grew in Jane that she was the object of his visits, not Thomas, or even the baby.

The idea – admittedly nothing more than just a vague feeling that she had formed, and certainly had not mentioned to anybody – that perhaps she was being courted by Mr. Trevithick brought a secret pleasure in the space of an instant's thought.

She had a sharp eye and ear for the nuances, and she felt instinctively that there was more than business on his mind during these often apparently pointless visits.

Once alerted to the possibility, she became more and more sure that Mr. Trevithick wanted her. She saw his eyes wander from her face to her figure. In handing her a sweet-smelling rose his hand would accidently touch hers, and linger for a second, no more.

He was a gentleman, a man of high reputation in the town . . . and she was sure that he harboured a secret love for her. Naturally she was flattered by the idea.

It was common gossip among the ladies of all ranks in Knutsford that he would make an excellent husband for the right woman. Ladies of his class could be seen posturing and simpering to him in the hope of capturing his regard.

But if she was right, Jane knew that she had a head-start on the society ladies, for all their fine dresses and polished manners.

There was a competitive urge in Jane. There was also a desire to raise herself above her working-class background: she wanted to be a lady.

She had never told a soul that that gypsy woman at the fair the day she met Thomas had told her that one day her lover would be high-born. But Jane had never forgotten it, even though she had not believed it at the time.

Mr. Trevithick was not only a gentleman born and bred, but he was smooth-mannered, worldly-wise – and handsome.

There was even the thought that encouraging Mr. Trevithick to admire her would help Thomas. After all, he was, as a tenant farmer, an independent businessman. To better relations with the man who represented his landlord could surely be no bad thing.

It was not difficult. One day, as they stood in the farmhouse kitchen, looking through the window to see if there was any sign of Thomas, she made sure that her ample breast pressed against his arm. He moved ever so slightly towards her. She stayed there. He didn't want to move. She had him in thrall. A power was in her. And she very much liked the feeling.

No. No sign of Thomas. What a shame. She drew away. Mr. Trevithick was flustered. He had lost his poise. She could see that. He said: "I must go. I'll call again tomorrow."

And he took her hand and kissed it in farewell. He had never done that before.

*

The next day Jane made sure she could hear what important matter Mr. Trevithick had to discuss with Thomas, who had busied himself within the farmyard until the agent rode up.

It was some trivial enquiry about the state of the crops, followed by news that wheat prices had fallen again since the Corn Laws had been repealed by Peel more than four years ago now.

Neither was a matter of immediate urgency. Thomas told Mr. Trevithick that what was more important than anything for Knutsford was to get a railway to Chester and Manchester so that farm produce could be got to market so much more quickly and easily.

He told Jane after Mr. Trevithick had left: "Hardly worth his coming specially. I think he only wants to see our little William, I really do.

"Anyway I can't afford to waste half a morning hanging around in the yard just to hear him talk about nothing that matters much. He'll have to come and find me in the fields in future."

It just added to Jane's growing conviction that Mr. Trevithick's visits were, more often than not, to see her.

The next time he came, a week later, sure enough Thomas was out in the fields. But Mr. Trevithick said he would not go and find him – what he had to talk about could wait.

He accepted Jane's invitation to step inside for a small beer, and to take a peep at the sleeping William. Several times he went to the window to see if Thomas was come back.

Jane deliberately didn't go and stand by him, although he twice asked her if she could see Thomas.

"I know he won't be back yet. He said he was hedging down in the long meadow," she said.

A week later the agent was back at the farm. This time Jane did join him as he looked out of the window. It was a hot day, and she was wearing a loose smock. When she saw Mr. Trevithick some distance away she had quickly tied a cord round her waist. It outlined her figure nicely under the thin material, and, gentleman or not, it had taken his attention instantly, she could see that.

Alongside him, at the kitchen window, she had stood close to him, pressing her breast against his arm. They had stayed there for some minutes, pretending to be looking for Thomas, enjoying the unacknowledged intimacy, until Mary, the dairy-maid, came into view, walking towards the house.

Before he left, Jane gave him a dozen eggs. He made a pretence of his not being able to accept – then accepted. The next time she saw him, Mr. Trevithick told her he had never tasted such excellent eggs.

Jane said he should have some more.

CHAPTER 20

1984

It was with a feeling that she was taking a crucial step in her life that Sharon read the letter from Sunjet accepting her application to transfer to Gatwick.

But it was mixed with regret too. Her mother was getting older and would miss her being around. Although Sharon had moved out of the family home into her own flat, she was only a couple of miles away in the Withington area of Manchester.

But there were more destinations on the airline's route-map out of Gatwick, and it had recently added flights to the Caribbean. Snatching a few hours on palm-fringed beaches fronted by the warm blue waters appealed strongly to her: it was what she had always wanted, and it was one of the main reasons she had joined an airline.

The regret at leaving Manchester had another element. There was a feeling of defeat over her ambitions concerning Captain Geoffrey Mayer.

She had tried everything to interest him, and all he was, was . . . friendly.

She had tried wearing very short miniskirts at parties when she knew he'd be there. She had tried wearing tops that showed off her cleavage. It only attracted men she didn't want.

And although Geoff expressed admiration, it was clear that he didn't intend to do anything about it.

They had developed a special relationship of sorts. They were friends, kind of...within the context of their relative positions in the airline. But Sharon knew he was never going to be her lover.

And what was really irritating was that Geoff's attitude towards her had become avuncular – almost paternal.

She'd tried going out with young men in flashy sports cars in the hope that it might make Geoff jealous, but he'd just been concerned about drunken driving and her safety.

Damn! She knew what she wanted. But he didn't.

Short of carrying a placard round her neck saying "come to my flat and ravish me" she'd tried everything, yet she knew that nothing was going to seduce him.

Part of her felt angry...she did not like being rejected: who would? She knew that she ought to say "Oh to hell with him then," and forget him, but she couldn't actually feel like that.

Yet she knew she had to move on, and Gatwick was the move.

*

Two months after Sharon moved south, the airline laid on a dinner for its senior staff to celebrate its tenth anniversary.

It was the first time for ages that they had been out together as a taxi took Geoff and Hanna from their hotel to Gatwick airport, where the celebration dinner was being held.

After being greeted by the chairman, champagne was offered on silver trays carried by a number of Sunjet stewardesses who had been more or less dragooned into the evening job as drinks waitresses. One of them was Sharon.

Having seen Geoff arrive with a blonde woman who was obviously his wife, she was in position to offer the couple their first glass of bubbly.

First, Sharon was curious to know how Geoff would greet her. Their strange friendship had only ever been in informal, off-duty events. But this was formal, and Geoff was in a sense as much on duty as she was – and anyway directly under the eyes of both his wife and other senior managers and *their* wives.

Sharon also was curious to get a close-up look at this wife of his to whom he was obviously so devoted.

148

He was quietly enthusiastic in his greeting. "Sharon," he exclaimed. "What a nice surprise!"

And as he took a champagne for himself and Hanna he said to his wife: "Darling, this is Sharon – one of the veterans of that Malta flight. She's recently moved to Gatwick."

OK. There couldn't have been anything more effusive – even a handshake from Mrs. Mayer – because Sharon was holding a tray full of drinks.

But this thin, angular lady's response of a cold smile, distant and somehow conveying boredom, might have been followed by, say, the word "hello," or any small verbal offering, considering Geoff's greeting.

But Hanna just moved on into the room with hardly a glance, with her husband dutifully following.

Then there were more guests to greet with the champagne, so Sharon had to concentrate on that. But she did find moments to take a look at Mrs. Mayer: cold, playing the sophisticated wife, too soignée for words, as Geoff introduced her to the gathered executives.

During the meal that followed, when Sharon and her colleagues had to continue to serve wine, refill water glasses, and generally act like airline stewardesses – God knows whose damn silly idea that was! – she couldn't help observing how little contact there was between Hanna and her husband.

It was puzzling: Geoff plainly thought the world of Hanna, and here were two people obviously happily married, yet it didn't actually look like it now she was seeing them together for the first time.

Sharon kept a discreet watch, but there was never a moment of silent sharing between them; from Hanna, no air of pleasure to be with him; no small smiles; no incidental touching; no sense of happiness at all.

And later, as she drove to her new apartment in East Grinstead, Sharon said to herself: "Yes, she is a cold fish. OK, they've been married for a long time, and it was a formal gathering, but all evening she didn't have anything to say to Geoff that made him smile or even look generally happy.

"Maybe they'd had a row or something."

And as she drove she found herself saying: "Surface glitter but cold and rigid . . . like an iceberg."

After a pause she added: "And she's got no tits to speak of, either!"

*

Three weeks later Sharon was in Manchester for her mother's birthday. She'd got three days off after a long series of days on duty, and was staying with her mum in Chorlton.

They had gone to their favourite restaurant in Didsbury, which, like Chorlton, was a village that had been overtaken and absorbed by the growing city in the 19th century.

They always enjoyed it – the atmosphere friendly, the menu not too extensive, and the food good. They had gone early – Sharon's mother didn't like eating late – and had got their favourite table in a corner, tucked away.

They were into their main course when Hanna walked in. Not with Geoff. With a slightly older man. Expensive suit. Overweight, bearded, and inclined to a beer-belly. Sharon read him as a businessman at play.

Hanna sat at a table at right angles to Sharon. She didn't see the younger woman, the air stewardess she had met so briefly and for the first time three weeks earlier at Gatwick; she was too tied up with the man she was with to glance around at other diners.

Their evident intimacy was almost embarrassing. It would have been even if Sharon had not known who it was. Hanna could not keep her hands off her companion. She stroked his wrist. She wasn't playing footsie under the table – the game was leggie. Their eyes were locked on each other's eyes. There was nothing furtive about it...Sharon formed the impression that at any minute they might start tearing their clothes off and have sex on the restaurant table. That was what their body language looked like.

150

It was most definitely Hanna. Sharon kept thinking that she must be mistaken. But no: it was her alright. Yet the contrast between the cold, hard lady she had seen with Geoff was very marked.

This was a woman relaxed...almost abandoned...and wildly in love. The man had taken off his jacket, and hung it on the back of his chair, and several times Hanna ran her hand down his arm as they waited for their chosen dishes to arrive. She put her hand on his, under the table.

What might have been a charming, mature couple obviously in love, or on passion bent, was, to Sharon, an outrageous, vulgar display; plainly Hanna was betraying her husband, thinking she was safely out of the way of anyone who would know her. Or maybe she didn't care.

Sharon found it difficult to take her eyes off her. But she was there for her mother's birthday, and she couldn't spoil that. With difficulty she tried to concentrate on her mother.

Afterwards, lying awake in bed at her mother's house, Sharon tried to reason it out. Look girl, if you'd had your way you'd have been doing something similar with her husband, so get off your high horse.

But that's the point! I have made advances, but Geoff has always made it clear that he was happily married and faithful to his wife.

The fact that I'd have made him unfaithful might not make me as good as Snow White. But I am a free agent, unattached in wedlock. Hanna is most definitely not.

So what's the difference? Most men seem keen to have a bit on the side – so why not a wife?

These days a woman didn't have the fear of getting pregnant just because she had sex. So it wasn't a question of cuckoos in the nest.

So what am I saying? Sauce for the goose is sauce for the gander? Yes that's pretty apt.

And yet. Sharon was sure about Geoff. She was quite certain that he was faithful to his wife – she should know! Yet here was that wife, plainly enjoying herself with another man.

Did Geoff know? Of course not. So what was Sharon going to do about it?

Well nothing, of course. How could she? And anyway, it was really no business of hers. OK. But it didn't stop her being concerned.

And maybe it was double standards, but she felt hatred for Hanna, a hatred for her betraying a man who wouldn't betray her.

But hadn't this kind of thing always gone on – wasn't it par for the course? Yes, of course it was. It's all part of life's rich pattern, Sharon thought, as sleep began to make its demands on her musings.

"You absolute unspeakable bitch!"

*

1851

The eggs for Mr. Trevithick became a weekly routine at the farm. They were always ready for him when he left. He always thanked Jane profusely.

At first she used to reply simply that it was a pleasure. As their acquaintanceship ripened, she would add with a smile the occasional cheeky compliment: "We must keep your strength up, Mr. Trevithick;" and "They do say they're good for the virility!"

Actually Jane had wondered about Mr. Trevithick's virility. Of course he was the perfect gentleman, and would never do anything improper. Yet their secret little intimacy did not develop beyond standing at the window together, touching yet not acknowledging.

Didn't he want to put his arm round her waist . . . press her to him, kiss her?

She felt sure that he did want these things, but somehow could not make the next step.

And the suspicion that man-of-the-world though he was, sophisticated and educated as he plainly was, at ease talking to the well-bred ladies of the town, yet, thought Jane, he has no experience of women. To talk to, yes: to make love to, no.

Her suspicion was heightened when, one day as she stood in the grocer's store in Knutsford, she overheard two well-dressed ladies, standing just ahead of her, talking together.

Mr. Trevithick walked past in the street, and they saw him though the shop window.

"Such a pity he is not married," one lady said.

"Such a handsome man," said the other.

"He does not seem to have any female attachments."

"So strange."

"I wonder."

"You wonder what?"

"Just wonder."

"What, exactly?"

"Perhaps he's one of those men who, you know . . . don't like women."

"Oh, no! He is always most polite and complimentary – I've heard him."

"I didn't mean he's impolite. I have been wondering whether he's...not attracted by women. I mean in the way of ever getting married."

"What! You mean he's..."

At that point the women put their heads close together and their voices dropped to an inaudible whisper

Jane knew exactly what they meant. The same thought had crossed her mind. Homosexuality had been talked about by her fellow-servants at the hall. There had been lively if discreet discussions below stairs, centred on one or two of Mr. Hardman's occasional guests.

However, Jane knew something that others did not know concerning Mr. Trevithick, and it made her pretty certain that the two ladies' speculation must be wrong. She knew he enjoyed her closeness.

On the other hand, whatever it did for him, it led to nothing else.

Why doesn't he turn and kiss me, she thought. Could it be that he is one of those men who can't make love to women?

Or maybe he just never has, and doesn't know how to begin, for all his gentlemanly knowledge.

It was a dilemma. There didn't seem any way of finding out. But Jane was aching to know. She decided to take matters into her own hands and find out.

So one summer morning, when Thomas had gone with the carter on one of his periodic trips to Manchester to discuss prices with the market men, Jane left William in the care of Mary the dairymaid, and took a basket of eggs to Mr. Trevithick's house.

She found him at home, and went inside at his invitation.

When she left, almost an hour later, Jane had the answer. Mr. Trevithick was no longer a virgin. And, although she didn't know it yet, Jane's second child had just been conceived.

CHAPTER 21

1853

As soon as she became aware that she was again with child, Jane knew with certainty that it was Mr. Trevithick's.

She had been keeping Thomas away from her, pointing out that feeding and looking after William, as well as doing her farmyard and housekeeping duties were as much as she could manage.

She was tired at the end of the day, and had taken to sleeping in a separate room from Thomas, who rose at 5 a.m. in the summer and needed his sleep.

Initially it had been to let Thomas be undisturbed by the baby's crying for his feed in the night. It was, thought Thomas, very thoughtful of Jane, and typical of her devotion both to him and William.

He loved her all the more for it.

But as soon as she suspected she was pregnant Jane slipped into bed with Thomas for the first time for two months. For Thomas it was the return of bliss.

For Jane it was to ensure that Thomas would not think that he had not fathered her second child.

In fact it never crossed his mind, even when the baby seemed to have been born prematurely, yet perfect, and almost as big as William had been at birth.

It was just a joy that all had gone well with both Jane and the baby boy, and he had a second son.

For some reason that was beyond him, but with which he was not prepared to argue, Jane insisted that they name the baby Montague. It sounded noble, and it went well with Mayer.

What she didn't say was that it was Crispin Trevithick's choice, being the name of his father. Nobody in Knutsford would know that.

*

It was agreed between Jane and Crispin that they were in love, that they would always be so, and that they could not envisage a future in which they did not make love.

But that there had to be absolute discretion and secrecy was apparent to both. Neither wanted scandal. Crispin knew it would cost him his position as well as his reputation. Jane's reputation was just as important to her.

They discussed these things. The found it easy to talk to each other about anything. They felt that spiritually they were man and wife, with their own child – but it was, of course, essential that nobody else knew about it.

Thomas knew that there was something different. Jane, since the birth of William, had not been the same with him. And the change in her was even more marked with the birth of Montague.

Something had gone. It was probably due to her new status as a mother. Or tiredness. Or worry about ending up with a dozen children or more, and, like most women, worn out and old by the time they were forty.

But he never questioned her love.

Three years later Jane gave birth to a daughter. She called her Lavinia. "God know why," Thomas confided to a friend.

He didn't know it was the name of Mr. Trevithick's mother...but then he didn't know that Mr. Hardman's gentleman-agent was the child's father.

And it never entered his head that he was a cuckold.

"Funny word that – cuckold," he said one day.

He was having one of his occasional visits to a local beer-house, the Half Way House, on Town Lane, the road that led to Mobberley and Wilmslow.

He had just been told, over a glass of ale, about a labourer at a neighbouring farm, whose wife was known to be consorting with another man – they'd been seen on more than one occasion slipping out of some local woodland, and now everybody seemed to know about it except the woman's husband.

Poor "bugger doesn't know he's a cuckold," Thomas's drinking companion had told him. "Still, 'tis his own fault. He should look after his wife better. If a woman's not getting enough from her husband she'll start to look elsewhere."

"I suppose it's something to do with being a cuckoo – rearing somebody else's young in your own nest," Thomas ruminated.

"Reckon that's about it," confirmed his informant. "It's one thing I'd never stand for myself. I'd kill my missus if I ever found she's been with another man. That's what I'd do.

"I'd kill her. And then I'd kill the man in question. That's what anybody would do. It wouldn't be murder – it'd be standing up for your rights.

"But poor old Ben Williams doesn't even know about his missus. And nobody's going to tell him, you can bet your life on that.

"Perhaps it's as well. They say ignorance is bliss. But he'll always be a bloody cuckold to everyone round here. Likely he'll never know everyone is laughing at him behind his back!"

"I wonder why everybody despises cuckolds, though," said Thomas. "I mean, a man in that position is the one person who is not at fault.

"It's his wife, and the other feller who are doing wrong. He's innocent.

"But every time I've ever heard it discussed, it seems to be the cuckold that comes in for all the scorn and ridicule."

"Well, stands to reason, doesn't it. If you're a married man it's up to you to make damn sure your wife keeps herself to herself when you're not there.

"Any man as doesn't, deserves to be despised, I'd say."

"Yes, but how does a man make sure his wife stays faithful?" insisted Thomas. "When you're not around how do you really know what your wife might be up to?"

"Well, that's just it – any man with any sense would know if his missus was up to no good with someone else. It'd be obvious enough to any married man. I know I'd know. Wouldn't you?"

"Yes, I suppose you're right. I'm sure I would," agreed Thomas. "But you wouldn't really kill her, would you."

"Well, I'll tell you what I really would do: I'd half kill her, then I'd throw her out. Out of the house."

"Then you'd be left to look after yourself and the children."

"No! The children would go too. They'd go with her. Because I wouldn't know which ones I'd actually fathered, would I? So she'd go, and they'd go with her. And good riddance."

"Come on!" said Thomas. "I don't believe you'd do anything of the sort. I mean, she'd been your wife for how long?"

"We've been married thirteen years. And that's *why* I'd throw her out – her and the children. Because all those years I'd have worked hard to keep them fed and clothed as best I could, and I'd have cared for the children that I thought were my own flesh and blood.

"But if I found out that my missus had been enjoyed by another man, it'd mean that she'd not only been a whore, but she'd been a liar too – she'd have had to tell a lot of lies."

Thomas thought for a moment. "I'd say a wife who cheats on her husband is worse than a whore. At least a whore is probably a poor woman who needs the money.

"And a man who makes her so is as bad. Any man who takes another man's wife can have no decency – he is the worst kind of thief. Even if it is with the woman's agreement, he is still taking something he has no right to.

"It is that man and the woman who should be despised and regarded as lepers among decent people.

"But I still think it would be a terrible thing to turn out not only the guilty wife but the innocent children too. I don't think you could do that - not to a woman you'd cared for and loved for years, never mind the little ones."

"Don't you see that it's *because* you care for someone over years and years that makes it worse, not better. And not more forgivable, but less."

"But what about married men going to other women – isn't that just as bad?" said Thomas. "Shouldn't a wife be able to turn him out of the house in that case?"

"Well, it's different for men," the beerhouse landlord chipped in. He only had the two customers. "At least men can't get pregnant as a result!"

"No. But they can make the other woman pregnant," said Thomas. "If she's a married woman she's going to put someone else's child into her husband's family, and it's him that has to work to raise the child.

"And if she's not married, who's going to look after her and the child? The workhouse?

"You call that fair treatment? I can't think of anything worse."

"Maybe there's something in that," responded mine host. "But you know men are naturally ever in search of a mate. It's the way we are made. And God made us, they say, so it can't be wrong!"

"Well to me it is wrong. It's the betrayal of your wife that would be wrong – breaking your vows of faithfulness, made when you get married in church and before God. I couldn't do that," said Thomas emphatically.

"And now I'm off home before my Jane begins worrying where I am – I wouldn't want her thinking I'm dallying with some other woman!"

And off he went. Off towards home, thinking how important was faithfulness in marriage, and how lucky he was.

CHAPTER 22

1866

Thomas's decision, 16 years ago now, to concentrate entirely on dairy and root crop farming, had gone well.

Cheshire had once been famous for its wheat. But Thomas had reasoned that wheat prices were subject to too much fluctuation. If the weather was favourable and the crop good, then prices fell, under the law of supply and demand.

That gave poor returns for the hard labour involved in ploughing, fertilizing, and harvesting and carting.

Yet Thomas could not force himself to pray for terrible weather so that the wheat crop would be poor, and prices high.

But there was one other thing – and an important one, Thomas thought. The Corn Laws had been repealed in 1846 amid much fear from the farming communities across Britain that wheat prices would drop as cheap grain came flooding into the country from abroad.

In fact everyone had been surprised at how little it had affected prices.

There just wasn't a mountain of unwanted wheat in other European countries waiting to be shipped to England. So prices had held up well.

But Thomas reasoned that it was from American grain that the problems would come for British farmers. So far the Americans did not seem capable of organizing the movement of vast amounts of wheat to Britain.

Also, the cost of transporting wheat across the Atlantic had delayed any great imports.

But Thomas was convinced that it could not be long before American wheat *would* start to arrive in large quantities. When it did –

as it was bound to sooner or later – it would hit British wheat farmers hard.

People kept telling him he was wrong...wheat prices were bound to stay at decent levels for as long as anyone could possibly foresee.

Thomas wasn't prepared to wait and see. And anyway he didn't have the big acreages necessary to make wheat-growing his main source of income.

Dairy farming needed much less space. And the returns were quick, especially for milk. He was convinced that he was right to look to the fast-growing city of Manchester and its need for milk, butter, potatoes, carrots and other vegetables to provide the market for everything he could produce.

He had agreed steady market prices with wholesalers in Manchester, and it had served him well.

The city's population had grown massively during the first half of the century, and its food traders were greedy for Cheshire's dairy products. And what Thomas really wanted was a means to get milk quickly from his farm to Manchester.

He had said from the start that a railway was the key to making bigger profits, giving the ability to get fresh milk and vegetables into Manchester's markets.

"I can't understand it...villages like Wilmslow and even Chorley have had a railway for nigh on twenty years. Some people in Knutsford have been fighting against it...they reckoned it would spoil the town," Thomas had complained. "Well, for farmers it would have been the best thing they could have wished for."

It had certainly been long talked about. But now they had the first part of their railway, with trains to Manchester, opening the line in 1863.

Heading west, the line only went as far as Northwich. But soon it would be extended to Chester.

Already it was reaping rewards for Thomas as he sent milk to Manchester on a daily basis, as well as sending fresh vegetables to the city.

His farm was profitable, his rent always paid on time, his income was steady. Things looked good.

Until the cattle plague ruined him.

His herd, cows that were a cross between the Holderness and Welsh breeds, had been his pride and joy. He had taken great care of his cows. They were regularly inspected by the veterinary surgeon, and any sign of sickness had been dealt with speedily. He was meticulous in keeping his shippens clean. No farmer's cows were in better condition than Thomas's.

Now they were all dead.

And the farm was dead. The silent, deserted cowsheds, he knew, meant the end of him as a tenant farmer.

But he had a wife and growing family to support. It was no use crying over spilt milk – he couldn't help a grim smile at the epithet – and so he became a labourer again, earning fifteen shillings a week, and feeling thankful for that despite the bitter taste of failure.

It would have been easier to accept but for something that took him by surprise: Jane's disparagement and rejection. That was what he felt was most hurtful of all.

They had, he reflected, been so happy...he and Jane and William, Montague, Lavinia and little Horatio – a happy family, respected and paying their way, due to his astute farming and marketing.

The terrible irony was that all along he knew it would only be a matter of time before Knutsford had a train station. A railway to speed his products to market, he was convinced, would be the making of him.

Now it had come – but it couldn't save him.

He had tried hard to escape the worst effects of the plague. As soon as he heard about it's being in the London area in 1865 he had acted decisively. He had sold some of his cows, and had turned some of his land over to wheat, and even more to potatoes, carrots, beans – anything to offset possible problems if the cattle plague reached Cheshire.

He remembered his step-father's dire warnings about such a killer disease, based on *his* father's stories, passed on from the previous generations, about the terrible devastation of farming caused by the cattle plague in the 1740s.

Thomas had stopped buying cows. He had tried to isolate his herd. But the news was not good as 1865 saw the foot and mouth disease spread northwards and westwards.

In 1866 it arrived in South Cheshire...then mid-Cheshire...then Knutsford. Some farms stayed miraculously free of the disease.

But one by one Thomas saw his cows become sick. Parliament had brought in a law earlier in the year, requiring all the infected cattle to be immediately killed and buried.

Seeing his beloved cows being strangled and thrown into a pit was the worst thing that had ever happened to Thomas.

His awful feelings of doom were not made better by the soothsayers – those who saw the plague as a punishment from God for the supposed sins of the time.

One, Thomas Rigby, actually had some good practical advice to give – keeping cattle in the open air as much as possible, keeping their shippens well-ventilated, cool and clean, and placing a three-month ban on the entry of all cows from abroad.

But he made it clear that he believed the cattle plague was the design of divine providence. He urged a reading of the Book of Amos, chapter 4, in farmers' bibles.

Thomas turned to it. "Hear this word, ye kine of Bashan, that are in the mountain of Samaria, which oppress the poor, which crush the needy, which say to their masters, Bring, and let us drink," it began.

"The Lord God hath sworn by his holiness that, lo, the days shall come upon you, that he will take you away with hooks, and your posterity with fishhooks.

"And ye shall go out at the breaches, every cow at that which is before her; and ye shall cast them into the palace, saith the Lord."

"I'm hanged if I know what it means," said Thomas, scratching his head after reading it three times.

"But I can't see that it helps anyway. What I need the Lord to do is to provide a miracle."

But most of his income dried up, almost overnight.

A compensation scheme was drawn up. But in a dairy county like Cheshire the majority of the people who had to pay to finance the scheme were the farmers – the very people who needed the help.

Thomas's annual rent became due. He had the money saved, and he paid up in full. But now there was little money left.

He struggled on, but his new crops couldn't grow and produced earnings instantly, like his milk would have done.

Under Mr. Trevithick's pleas, Mr. Hardman had reduced the rent, and had promised more time for its payment.

But as time passed, it was obvious that Thomas would not be able to pay his next year's rental.

So he gave up the tenancy. There was no choice.

*

1866

Losing his proud status of husbandman, and becoming a labourer again, was a bitter blow to his pride.

But his wife and children needed food. He had to have an income.

He walked three miles to the relatively isolated village of Peover, to a farm which had miraculously escaped the plague.

Thomas had heard that one of the farmer's older labourers had taken poorly, and was not likely to live long, his doctor had confided to Mr. Trevithick, who was as ever most sympathetic to their plight, and had told Thomas.

The afternoon that Thomas arrived at the Peover farm, the labourer died of the consumption. So Thomas got the job as his replacement.

"I'm a hard worker – always have been – so I'm sure you'll not regret taking me on," he told his new employer.

There was even a cottage included with the job. The farmer took him to see it.

It was, in truth, a tumbledown, verminous place that had been home to his widowed predecessor.

But it could be cleaned and put right, with a lot of hard work, he thought. He was willing to do anything to keep his family together, under one roof.

Except for William, of course. That was another piece of fortune: there was one less mouth to feed, because their oldest son had, months back, taken a job as a gardener, with Caldwell's nurseries in Knutsford when he saw the approach of the cattle plague.

Now he was earning his own keep, and was lodged with Mary Sutton, the former dairymaid at Shaw Mill Farm, who lived with her husband John in a cottage at the bottom of Hollow Lane, on the outskirts of the town.

"I can repair the things that need looking to," Thomas told Jane, when she arrived with the children at their new home.

But what he couldn't repair was Jane's rejection.

She was humiliated by their change of fortune. And she had Crispin Trevithick to turn to. But his fortunes, too, were finely balanced as Mr. Hardman saw his own income threatened by the farmers' difficulties.

Every farmer affected by the cattle plague had problems paying his rent. But none had specialised to the extent that Thomas had, so most others were not as devastated.

CHAPTER 23

1867

Thomas was, as he had told his new employer, a man accustomed to hard work in the fields and on the farm, early rising and long hours at haymaking and harvesting.

Although their income was cut, it was, as he pointed out to Jane, regular.

And they didn't have the worry of balancing the books, like they'd had when they had their own farm.

He worked at the cottage, too, first cleaning it from top to bottom. Then repairing the windows, the doors, the roof. He did it after his daily labours and on his one day off each week.

It took six months. It was hard and tiring work after his outdoor labouring on the farm. But at last he began to feel that the cottage was a fit place for Jane and the children.

Then, one day, when he returned to the cottage at the end of his working day in the fields, expecting a welcome from his family and a meal awaiting his arrival, he found the house empty.

It was mighty odd. It was six o'clock. The old timepiece he had brought with him from Shaw Mill Farm told him that. Where on earth could they be?

There was no sign of his family in the immediate neighbourhood of the cottage, he soon established that.

Jane must have taken the children into Knutsford, to see William or to buy something that she needed, he decided. He took a piece of bread to assuage his hunger, and set out along the Knutsford road to meet them.

He reached the town, without any sign of them. Alarm was rising in him now. Had something happened to William?

He went to the Suttons' cottage. William, Mary and John were there – but they hadn't seen Jane or the children.

Something must have happened – but what could it be? William and John set out with him to scour the town in search of them. But there was no sign. Thomas went to Shaw Mill Farm, in case Jane had gone back to their old home. But she was not there.

He decided to return to Peover. Surely she will be home by now, he told William, never fear.

But Thomas himself was full of a strange fear – a fear of the unknown. As he walked back along the road from Knutsford, he looked about him.

But there was no sign of his wife and family.

And when he arrived back at the cottage his heart sank when he saw that it was in darkness, and was obviously as deserted as when he had last seen it.

He could not rest. He set out again for Knutsford, calling into the gathering darkness. But there was no reply.

He returned to the cottage. Still dark. Still empty. He walked the country lanes in an agony of fear, calling into the blackness of the night.

He kept at his search until dawn crept into the fields. Nothing.

Where can they be? They cannot have vanished into the air. Jane's parents were dead so she would not have gone to Middlewich. He could think of nowhere she might have gone.

He knocked at the farmhouse door of his employer. He had seen no sign of them. Thomas went again to Knutsford. Work will have to wait.

He found William again. "I have a fear that I will never see them again," he told his son.

He added: "No. That cannot be. There must be an explanation."

There was an explanation. But Thomas never did see his Jane or Montague, or Lavinia, or Horatio again.

For they were in Liverpool, on their way to Australia. On the ship's passenger manifest Jane had given their surname as Trevithick. And nobody questioned that. For Mr. Trevithick was with them. The whole family had a cabin for their comfort.

*

1868

For Thomas life became a torment. His loved ones were gone. Where? How? Why? Not knowing was the thing that turned his mind.

He took to wandering round Knutsford, asking everybody who would stop, if they had seen his wife and three children.

No, they always said. No. No? No. You are sure? Yes. Yes you've seen them? No. I have not seen them. I mean yes, I am sure that I have not. Good day to you.

How many times he asked the question, how many times he heard the word no, he could not count.

His eyes grew wild. He was dismissed from his labouring job. With all the sympathy in the world the farmer could not continue to employ him.

He ceased to eat, other than scraps that he found, and more solid fare that William took to him, if he could find him.

William begged him to come and live at Mary and John's cottage. But he would not.

Nor did he live at the cottage in Peover, even before he lost his work: he could not go back, and see the things they had left behind.

It was noticed, by others at first, that Mr. Trevithick had disappeared too, and at the same time.

Ann Lobb, a young Cornish woman who worked as a servant in a house just outside the centre of Knutsford, mentioned to her friends that it was strange – how Thomas's youngest three children had the same Christian names as Mr. Trevithick's parents and brother.

She came from the same part of the Tamar valley as the Trevithicks, and although she had never met them, being from a much lowlier station in life, she knew the names.

So people began to put two and two together, although nobody had any idea where they might have gone.

But it seemed a clear case of a married woman running away with another man, and taking her children with her – all but her oldest, who was now eighteen.

William knew that he had to try to look after his father. But he also knew that he had to keep on working at Caldwell's, earning his keep, hoping for something to happen, hoping for his mother's return.

He too heard the rumours, the suggestions rather, that perhaps his mother's disappearance on the very day that Mr. Trevithick disappeared from Knutsford, may not have been coincidence.

But such was his father's distress, that he did not mention such an idea to him.

It was more than a year before a letter arrived for William from his mother. She enclosed a sealed note for Thomas.

William read his mother's words of assurance that she was safe and well, and so were the children, and that they were living in Australia. What! Why? He went out and found his father.

He was in Brook Street, where the shops were, among the passers-by.

He handed over the envelope with the one word "Thomas" on the outside.

His father instantly recognized the handwriting, and uttered a cry of joy.

He tore open the envelope, and read the short note. Then he sank to his knees on the ground, and wept inconsolably.

William took the note from his hand and read it.

"I hope you will not take it too badly. I am with the children in South Australia, living with Mr. Trevithick. We have taken his name. We are very happy. We feel like we are married.

"We have loved each other for a long time, and Montague, Lavinia and Horatio are Crispin's children, not yours. But not William.

"Do not try to find us. It would be no good. I do not want to see you. Jane Trevithick."

169

He took his father home to Mary and John's house. But his mind, it seemed, had gone.

Nothing could be done to console him. Nothing could calm him.

They could not keep him from going out, eventually.

They found his body drowned in the Shaw Mill pond, not far from the farm that had been his joy, his hope, his home, his love.

They brought William to see him. The contorted features of his face were those of a man who thought he was in heaven, and found he was in hell.

CHAPTER 24

1984

Geoff found the burial of his great-great grandfather in the parish records. 1868. December 15. Thomas Mayer. That was all.

"I said he was boring. Born 1821 in Styal. Married 1849 in Middlewich. Died 1868 in Knutsford. Travelling between those three places was probably the most exciting thing he ever did. As far as I can see, absolutely nothing else happened in the whole of his life."

He was talking to himself again. It had become a habit. There wasn't anybody else to talk to about his family history. Hanna wasn't interested. And David isn't interested either, he reflected.

Sad really – it's his family history as well as mine.

But you can't blame them. I'm fast losing interest myself. As far as I can see all my ancestors except my doctor grand-father seem to have been country yokels.

To be honest it's hardly worth the trouble finding out about them.

No. Surely it's not too much to ask that further back just one of my forebears made his mark in the world and did something worthwhile. Or just something interesting. On the other hand, I can't just give up now.

Thomas was born in 1821, and I already know that his father died in December 1826, aged 30. So he must have been born around 1796. I know his name was Joseph. But finding his birth won't be so easy. Where did he come from? There weren't any censuses that far back to help.

But I'd like to get back another couple of generations. That would be quite an achievement, to get back as far as the eighteenth century.

171

Mrs. Thatcher's reign has been nothing short of a revolution for Britain. She called for a return to Victorian virtues, and her government has led the way.

"We now have beggars on the streets. And people sleeping rough in shop doorways and under railway arches...just like it was in the nineteenth century. We're right back in Charles Dickens's time - just what she wants, apparently.

"The big difference is that in Charles Dickens's novels you never seem to get rows of shops standing empty and forlorn, covered in fly advertising, in what were once busy and prosperous towns and villages across the land," said the man who was being interviewed on Radio 4.

"Switch the bloody thing off," ordered Hanna. "I don't know who the hell he is, but he should never be allowed to talk like that on the radio. It's nothing short of anarchy.

"We pay for the BBC and it is our government. They should not be allowed to criticise the best prime minister this country has ever had."

"It's the sort of subversive rubbish you hear all the time on the BBC," said Geoff. "Discussion programmes they call them - what a laugh! The Lefties have taken over at the Beeb...I'd sack the lot of them. Give them a taste of being out of work. It'd serve them right."

"They are trying to bring down the government. It's treason and they should be given more than the sack. They want a public flogging!" said Hanna. "Who the hell do they think they are, these faceless Trots and communists.

"Britain voted for her to run the country, not them."

*

Arthur Scargill, general secretary of the National Union of Miners, had led the pitmen's opposition to the coal board's plans to shut down uneconomic pits. But he had not held a ballot before calling for an all-out strike. Now he led their striking pickets towards the solid lines of policemen barring their way.

The National Coal Board had stated its intention earlier in March of closing down twenty-one pits and making twenty thousand men redundant.

Make the mining industry profitable...easy: shut it down, or, at least, a large part of it. Oh yes, just incidentally, add twenty thousand to the jobless total...you know, the list of people who are too lazy to work.

Mr. Scargill and his national executive committee decided that mass picketing of mines and storage depots where work was still going on would soon bring supplies of coal to a halt, and force the government to change its mind.

Some miners did not want to go on strike. Mrs. Thatcher was absolutely determined that coal workers who wanted to continue working should not be prevented from doing so. The message went out loud and clear from the government that the right to work would be upheld.

She didn't seem to notice the irony.

The miners' strike was the result. It was nothing short of insurrection by Mr. Scargill, she fervently believed. But there was no way that the coal miners could fail to fight the closure of dozens of pits with the loss of thousands of jobs. They were incredibly hard-working men employed at jobs that most people would not be capable of doing...hard men doing hard labour in communities mainly in the midlands, Wales, northern England and Scotland - a world away from the affluent Home Counties that were the territory of the powers that ran the United Kingdom.

Coal mining had always been the toughest of jobs. It was more than a job: it was a way of life. Of course miners got dirty...it wasn't like Westminster at all. Sure it brought in good money in return for the hard graft in terrible conditions. Down a pit, miners had always worked in terrible heat, danger and dust.

Mechanisation had speeded up production, but it didn't make life much easier for the men, often working a thousand feet or more

173

underground. The black dust still got everywhere. Including your lungs. When miners became too unfit for work because of the coal dust they had breathed for years, there was no compensation.

They were expected to go quietly away and cough until they died. But their homes, their families, their neighbourhoods were all around the coal areas, and the shared difficulties of life had made the people into communities – it was their traditional way of life and they did not want it to end.

Although miners in Kent were on strike too, it was the Yorkshire miners who filled the news on TV.

In the northern coalfields, towns that for generations had grown from villages to supply the needs of men working in the pits, faced devastation as thousands of miners who wanted nothing more than to carry on working faced enforced idleness.

Their prospects looked utterly bleak. No wages. Nothing to keep up the payments for cars, freezers and televisions. No treats for the kids. No holidays. No future.

A plague sent to wreck their lives as well as their livelihoods: that was how it looked to the miners.

They marched forward. Police in massive force and the latest riot gear, brought in from all over the country, blocked the miners' way like an army. The police lines stood. They met. And violence from both sides broke out big time as they clashed. Then policemen on horseback charged into the protesting miners, breaking their ranks.

The police won. They had riot shields and truncheons, they had had training, and, of course, they had the law behind them: mass picketing had recently been banned by Parliament. Of course the policemen lost their tempers. And if they got a man down they weren't going to pussy-foot around.

The miners had gone to the Orgreave coking plant in large numbers. That evening television audiences were able to enjoy the spectacle of police batons smashing into the unprotected heads of the men who wanted to keep their jobs.

The defeat of the miners went on for weeks on end. The Sun newspaper, which saw Mrs. Thatcher as the saviour of the nation, called the pitmen the scum of the earth. Strange that it had been their favourite newspaper.

Mrs. Thatcher's government described the unions as the enemy within. She believed that the coal mining industry had come to symbolise everything that was wrong with Britain.

Her determination was to snuff out the threat of Marxism which she devoutly believed was being imposed on Britain by the evil that she saw threatening the country's democratic rule...the hard left revolutionaries whose three bases were, she said, the Labour Party, local government, and the trade unions. Scargill's refusal to ballot his members on whether to strike was sure evidence of this evil.

The prime minister spoke about it all on the television: the coal board and the government wanted only a prosperous industry, she said. Yet the miners were blatantly attempting to substitute the rule of the mob for the rule of law.

"It must not succeed!" she declared.

On the television the miners, armed with stones and bricks, marched towards lines of police. As the two sides clashed you could see that only the police could win. They took the first wave of miners, then, thrashing at them with truncheons, they charged at the pickets.

When a man fell he was set upon by three or four coppers who laid in with their heavy sticks, blow after blow until the bloody recipient of Mrs. Thatcher's special brand of law and order was dragged away, a shattered relic of the cocky, determined Yorkshireman who had marched forward to try to save his job and his family from ruin.

"It was dreadful what the police did with riot shields and batons against people wearing trainers," said one miner, still unable to believe what had happened when he was interviewed by his local newspaper.

"Men were put in cells in shackles. The police kept asking you if you knew any trade union leaders or communists. This is Britain! Not South Africa or somewhere."

"Thank God they're getting what they deserve at last," said Hanna, watching the battles on her TV screen in Prestbury. "They want to give the police sabres, not sticks. Finish the ignorant bastards off."

"They ought to give the police guns. That way there wouldn't be any rioting. It'd stop the buggers in their tracks if they had to face the barrels of police rifles," said Geoff.

"Well at the very least when they've finished giving them the beating of their lives the police should take them away and sentence them to a public flogging. They need to bring back the birch. They might understand that!" Hanna contributed.

"Who the hell do they think they are? They think they can defy the government. Well they are finding out what they'll get if they try it. And that Scargill needs stringing up. I'd do it myself if I had the chance.

"They are just like all the working class bastards - vicious and nasty and out to bleed the nation for doing as little work as possible. OK, if they don't want to work, sack the lot of them. Then they'll expect the rest of us to support them with dole money of course. I'd starve them until they begged for mercy."

That what the miners wanted *was* to work seemed to escape her.

CHAPTER 25

1819

It was the obscene crimson surge from the livid, gaping wound in the woman's head and the shocked look still on her dead face that kept coming back to crowd Joe Mayer's mind.

All the way home to Styal his hands were shaking, and several times he found himself crying like a child. He tried to explain it to himself and to John Booth. But he could not get the haunting, sickening image from behind his eyes.

They had gone to the great rally for Reform at St Peter's Field in Manchester to hear the famed orator Henry Hunt. They knew he was going to tell of the progress towards reform - change in the way that Parliament was chosen.

It might even lead towards votes for ordinary working men like them. And change to get some justice at last for the working men and women who knew only oppressive poverty despite their labours.

The Manchester magistrates had considered whether Hunt's meeting was illegal. They had decided it was not.

Joe and John had walked the twelve miles to Manchester that bright August morning in 1819 with a dozen other men and women from Wilmslow and Styal. Many thousands of people from towns and villages round Manchester were converging on St. Peter's Field. It was a daring day out, with a promise of good things and a carnival joy in it. There was a feeling of hope in the air...a feeling that change was going to come soon.

They all wore their best jackets - the ones they kept special for church. Their talk was full of cheerful hope. The women wore their gayest Sunday bonnets, for they knew that it was a very special event - a really grand day out.

177

Of course the feelings were strongest for the people of Manchester itself, which had grown into Britain's second biggest city, but did not even have a single member of Parliament - there was nobody to tell the Government about the hardships and the terrible deprivation among working people labouring to make a few men very wealthy. But Reform of Parliament was a matter of much wider concern than for any one town, no matter how big.

The writings of Cobbett and Hunt and others had impressed millions of workers to become politically aware of what could be achieved if only every man had a vote.

They fervently believed that it would relieve the dreadful poverty of the labouring classes who only knew that no matter how hard or how long they worked, they and their families were suffering a deprivation that brought them very close to starvation. Yet they were working in the huge money-making enterprises that were the new mills and factories.

That great belief developed as the crowd grew in St. Peters Field. Many marched as if they going to a fair.

In the field there were babies as well as older children. There was cheering intermittently as some new contingent arrived, banners flying. Optimism was in the air. The workers and their families had to stand up for their rights...if they didn't make a stand somewhere they knew that they would never get out of the dire and unceasing circle of work, near-starvation and poverty that was their lot in the early 1800s.

Meanwhile the magistrates, seeing the huge numbers attending the open-air meeting, suddenly changed their minds about its legality. "Arrest Hunt," was their order sent out to the troops who had been placed on standby to deal with any trouble. The people heading for the rally didn't know. Hunt didn't know.

Nobody seems to have noticed the 1,500 mounted part-time soldiers of the Cheshire Yeomanry from Knutsford and the Manchester and Salford Yeomanry Cavalry – all men intensely proud to represent the interests of the major landowners who commanded them - gathered in nearby streets.

The crowd, already big, grew bigger. Then the speakers stepped on to the raised platform to massive cheers. The air of expectancy and hope grew in the certainty that change was bound to happen - history was being made...it was almost tangible.

It was then that the cavalry men rode up, men in red and blue coats, their sabres glinting in the sunshine. There were some fearful cries of "The soldiers are coming."

Hunt saw them and told the crowd to give a cheer for the brave guardians of Britain's safety - the very symbol of the military might which had defeated Napoleon at Waterloo after more than 20 years of war with France.

The crowd cheered and made way for the horsemen as they rode towards the platform. They stopped cheering as they realised that they were there to arrest Hunt, who had no means of knowing that the magistrates had made a last-minute decision to disperse the crowd, now estimated to be at least 60,000 strong.

Hunt did not resist. But suddenly the officer in charge of the Yeomanry shouted "Have at their flags!"

Now the cries from the crowd on the far side from where Joe and John stood turned from happy cheering to screams of horror.

The clatter of hooves, and the strange flashing of sunlight on the blades of the soldiers' sabres rising and falling as the yeomanry hacked their way into the crowded people, spread fear and panic like wildfire in the street. And still the sabres, red with blood, flashed as the soldiers and the horses pressed on.

Now they were joined by the 15th Hussars, professional soldiers who had been told by the watching magistrates that the crowd was attacking the Yeomanry. Like good cavalrymen with a long history of riding headlong into the enemy no matter how strong, the Hussars fearlessly charged into the defenceless crowd of ordinary men, women and children, their swords hacking and stabbing.

Joe felt the fear surge through his veins. *This could not be happening!* Everything was unreal...it was before his eyes and yet he felt that it could not be.

179

Then, shouting and cursing, the mounted soldiers, in their splendid cavalry uniforms, their swords finding no opposition, were near him. He forgot all else as he struggled to get away.

But he was surrounded by more people, shouting in terror and fear. For the mounted soldiers were not on the defensive. They were shopkeepers and businessmen whose interests were on the side of the gentry. They *wanted* to kill and maim these vile beings who were lower than the beasts of the field...these splendidly-uniformed representatives of law and order and might and right and government in 1819 Britain wanted to murder labouring-class men and women, and children too.

Years of education and talk about the awful scum, dirty and ignorant, nasty unspeakable creatures too low to be called properly human...all their superb English upbringing had come to a culmination in this, their supreme moment that properly asserted their superiority at last...*at last.*

At last they are getting what they deserve, by God!

The Yeomanry soldiers – the manufacturers and traders' classes on horseback, led by the landed gentry – were imbued with political hatreds, and their moment had come!

"Run them through! Kill the rabble and teach them a lesson they'll never forget!"

A woman with a baby in her arms was ten feet from Joe when the sabre sliced into her shoulder. Her scream was stifled as another cut from the sword hacked into her head and she fell to the ground, still holding the baby, blood and brains spreading like an evil cape over both of them.

Joe saw no more of her. Everyone was struggling to get away. His legs took his panic beyond his shame. He dashed through the crescendo of screams as he pushed weaker people aside and found a gap in the struggling panic of flying feet and stumbling, falling men, women and children, and headed into an alleyway between adjacent buildings.

In the relative shadow his hands found a recessed doorway with a sort of alcove. Joe was in the corner in an instant, jammed against the wall, and out of the melee of fleeing terror. But he found himself shaking uncontrollably and crying like a child.

In the alley he could hear the screams, the stampede of feet, the clashing of horses' hooves, and the cursing of soldiers, so full of hatred, dying away, leaving behind the horrific screams and pitiful cries of injured men and women, and terrified children.

He looked out fearfully, saw no one in the alley, and ran in the direction that the fleeing, pursued crowd had taken, reasoning in an instant that that way he was less likely to be overtaken by more soldiers.

He turned left down a narrow street where there were only a few shocked and bewildered people, and crossed the wide Deansgate, finding another narrow road taking him further away from the carnage. Then, lower down, another left turn took him across Peter Street and away, running parallel to Deansgate, then re-crossing the main road near Knott Mill and headed towards Ardwick and home.

Home. That was where he had to go. Away from something so terrible, so unreal that he could hardly believe that it had happened.

But the image of the dead, bleeding woman and her screaming baby kept filling his mind. He turned back. He must help. But how could he? His footsteps faltered as he faced the stream of shocked and limping people getting out of Manchester. But he saw the woman again in his mind, and carried on, back towards Knott Mill. Then he saw John Booth, his best clothes stained everywhere with blood, limping towards him.

"For Christ's sake, Joe, where are you going? Get away, man! Don't go back there! The constables are beating up the ones that aren't dead! Let's get away!"

"Where are you hurt, John?"

"I'm not badly hurt - just got my foot trodden on by a horse...lucky for me the soldier's sword was on the other side."

"But you're bleeding!" said Joe.

"No...it's off an old chap that I tried to help. I thought I could get him away. But it was too late...he died in my arms.

181

"Joe, it was murder! Plain bloody murder! And people were saying the magistrates will be hunting us all down, and them they find will be transported or hanged.

"That's why we must get away quick. I'll find something to cover the blood on my clothes...but don't let's stand here. Come on!"

They headed southwards for Styal, going with the flow of dazed and shattered men, women and children who, an hour earlier, had been full of fun and hope.

"It's back to the mill tomorrow, and tell nobody where you've been today. We'll have to find the others and tell them to keep quiet about it too."

"Well, that is the end of reform," said John. "Votes for all men...fat chance! I knew in my heart they'd never let it happen. Why should they? In England they've got too many slaves to want to give it up.

"And that's what we are - slaves. That's what we all are, us that aren't rich. The high-ups have got the means to make sure it stays so.

"The rest of us haven't got a say in it...and we never will have. We have to work for starvation wages because it delays dying. And it will never change. Not in our lifetime, anyway. Slaves our class has always been and slaves we'll stay."

*

1984

"Britons never never never shall be slaves! Rule Britannia..."

The feeling of pride at being British was overwhelming as Geoff and Hanna stood, like the rest of the flag-waving audience in the last night of the proms.

He had been offered the tickets through the airline, which had paid for a box for senior staff at the night of unalloyed nationalism-with-nostalgia.

They sang it again, smiling at the sheer euphoria, the splendid chance to be proud to be British: "...Never shall be slaves!"

182

"We don't wave the union jack often enough," said Geoff as they made their way back to their hotel afterwards.

"It's nice to be demonstrative for a change.

"It's quite true that we English have still got stiff upper-lips. It doesn't apply to the Scots or the Northern Irish or Welsh. They are always waving their flags and shouting about their country.

"I wonder when we English became so damn lacking in pride about our homeland."

"I should think it was about the time that Labour got in in 1945 and introduced the welfare state and all that bloody socialism," said Hanna.

"There's nothing like socialism for reducing everything to mediocrity."

Geoff decided not to point out that it ought in that case to apply to Scotland, Wales and Northern Ireland too. He didn't want an argument.

Hanna had become much more militantly Conservative since Mrs. Thatcher became Prime Minister, he thought.

"Well we damn well should be proud," he said. "We've been a civilizing influence all over the world, pretty well, for centuries.

"In two bloody world wars we've stood our ground and fought for freedom and democracy – and in both cases long before the Americans came in."

"What does that book you're reading say about it – the Harold Nicholson diaries?" asked Hanna. "He was right at the centre of it all when the second war started, wasn't he?"

"He certainly was. He seems to have known everybody who was anybody at the time. He was amazingly well-connected."

"Of course he was married to that novelist...Vita Sackville-West, which couldn't have done him any harm. She was frightfully well-connected too, I seem to remember. Didn't they live in a castle or something down in Kent?"

"Yes, but what I think you don't seem to realise is, that he was a National Labour MP."

"You're joking! How could he have been? He was very upper-class, wasn't he?"

"It was the way his beliefs were at the time. But he doesn't seem to have been a committed socialist, to be honest. In fact he was in the *National* Labour party, and that was not the same thing as the Labour Party – I seem to remember from my school days that it was a right-wing breakaway group that had some big names but never really caught on.

"Anyway some of the things he has to say in his diaries shook me, I can tell you," said Geoff.

"Like what?"

"Well one bit I remember was just before the war, in 1938 I suppose, some peers told him they'd prefer Hitler in England rather than a socialist government.

"I mean...bloody hell! How close to fascism did we get?"

"Well a lot of British people did flirt with fascism in the 1930s you know – it wasn't just Mosley."

"Yes, I think it was a question of being anti-communist more than anything else. The thing was, they equated Labour and its supporters with communism – they were all 'reds' to the upper classes in the 1930s."

"Still are! But about socialism wrecking the country: is there anything of that in his diaries?" asked Hanna.

"There was no question that even during the war the upper classes feared a lower-class take-over which would take away their privileges and influence and their comfortable life-styles.

"In fact, come to think of it, that was just what the Whig and Tory politicians of the early 19th century feared above everything...they were afraid they would lose their land and their money and their influence because they were sure there was going to be a revolution from the masses just like had happened in France.

"Anyway during the second world war there was a strong belief among the upper and middle classes that if Labour got into power it would turn Britain into a third-class state."

"They damn well did too – till Maggie came along and put them out of business for good...Labour and the unions. Thank God she's turning it round now."

"Yes, but it worries me that we seemed to have had such fascist leanings in the 1930s," said Geoff, determined to get Hanna off her high Tory horse for a moment.

"I read somewhere that even before that – as long ago as 1910 or 1911 I think it was – in Parliament Churchill advocated sterilization of the feeble-minded.

"And the same kind of thing was proposed in some of the furore about Darwin's Origin of Species in the mid-19th century."

"What on earth has Darwin got to do with it?"

"Well evolution is all about the survival of the fittest.

"When Darwin explained how natural selection worked, everybody screamed blue murder at first – the idiots complaining that he was trying to make us all out to be monkeys at heart.

"Then the religious zealots came out of the woodwork. If human beings weren't created by God, with a divine purpose to fulfil – if we are just a chance mutation, an accidental event in the survival of the fittest – then what is the purpose of life...that's what they were asking.

"To be honest, I think a lot of people ask it secretly even today."

Hanna looked at him quizzically. He added quickly: "The thing is, in the 1930s Darwin's theory of natural selection was taken by some people to justify the sort of race-violence that the Nazis embraced...creating a master race...the kind of thinking that was behind the holocaust.

"In fact, when you really think about it, it's more like the very opposite – it shows the human race is essentially one...we've all sprung from the same source and we're all part of the same family."

They reached the hotel as he spoke. "Quite the little philosopher you've became, haven't you," said Hanna tartly as they stepped towards the reception desk.

"You know, I hate you when you became all pompous like this.

"And frankly you're starting to sound like a bloody socialist!

185

"OK, so you've been reading a few books. For Christ's sake loosen up. We're here to enjoy ourselves, not discover the meaning of life!"

CHAPTER 26

1805

Joe Mayer would never forget the day when he first saw Greg's mill at Styal, the day he stopped being a little boy and became an apprentice. It was the day his life changed.

Joe couldn't read. Like his ma. His pa was dead. Joe was nine years old, so it was not a surprise when the Overseers came to the workhouse one day and told his ma that he was going to be taken to a cotton spinning mill up in Cheshire to be an apprentice.

He'd seen other boys and girls taken off over the years. They never came back. Joe and his pals supposed that they made their fortune as workers and became rich enough to get married and have their own children.

Then once grown up a lot of people seemed to become poor again. Like his mother. His friend Bill told him they were something called "paupers," although they never really knew what that meant.

Except that you didn't ever have any money. And you ended up in the workhouse, like the one he called home, at Newcastle-under-Lyme in Staffordshire..

Once you had been thumped a few times by the men and women in charge, you got used to watching what you did and what you said in case you annoyed anyone and made them angry.

Like saying you were hungry. Ma said the food was terrible. He knew it didn't taste very good, but he couldn't remember eating things that did. Except apples. You could steal them from people's gardens if you were quick. But you had to wait until the weather turned colder and the apples turned red. Everyone knew that.

Now he was going to be an apprentice. At first he had been brave. His mother had told him that now his dad was dead he was the man of the family. The older of his two sisters was only six, and she looked up to him as a very big brother. It made him feel important, from the moment that ma had told him that he was being sent to work in a cotton mill far away in Cheshire.

Joe had no means of knowing that parish apprentices were much sought after because, as the cheapest form of labour in the textile mills, they were making their owners very rich indeed.

He did not know that children like him often worked longer hours than slaves in the sugar plantations of the West Indies. Nor did he know that the arrangement admirably suited parishes round the land whose overseers were extremely keen to rid themselves of the burden of feeding pauper children.

He was just glad that he did not have to live in the workhouse any more, because sometimes he could hear his ma crying when she thought they were all asleep. And in the street other children shouted names at him.

So he put on his bravest smile when he kissed them goodbye and got on to the cart with his butty in a cloth and his spare shirt rolled up and tied with string.

He didn't know why, but the parish officers had given him almost new trousers and a jacket that was only a bit too big. In them he felt special. But in his stomach he had an uneasy feeling: a secret despair at leaving his ma and his sisters; and a very great worry about what lay ahead in a place he had never even heard of, miles and miles away, in the next county.

He was deeply scared and worried. But being nine he absolutely could not show it.

Ma had told him he would have to work, and he would get food and a place to live...but he had to behave himself too. And maybe he'd come back to see her when he was grown up.

He did not know much. But he knew somehow that that meant he would never see her again. She gave him a big hug and told him not to cry...everything would be all right. But she was crying, so he knew then that it wouldn't be all right.

He turned and waved to Ma and Martha and little Ann as the horse drew him further and further away. But when he couldn't see them he didn't feel brave any more. He couldn't cry, though, because there were two girls on the cart and they kept looking at him. They were bigger than him, and they were holding hands and snuggling together, so they were making themselves brave together.

Soon Newcastle-under-Lyme was left behind, and towards the end of that day the man driving the horse said they were in Cheshire. It looked just like Staffordshire, Joe thought, and that cheered him up again.

They stopped at a farm when it was nearly dark, and Joe and the two girls who were also going to Greg's mill were told to sleep on the hay in a barn. He was glad they were there because it was very dark, and he had never been alone at night.

On the cart they had asked him his name and they told him they were called Annie and Mary. They were sisters, and their father had died a few weeks earlier. Their mother was going to live in the workhouse too, with their six younger brothers and sisters.

When they reached Styal next day a dim sense of foreboding that had been growing inside Joe reached a new level: a fear of the unknown; a fear that his mother wouldn't be there to comfort and guide and hug him. Not now. Not ever. He knew that all that was left behind. He was cut off from her and his sisters...from his childhood.

He didn't put it into tangible thoughts or words, but they were there, just the same. A door, invisible, strange and impenetrable, had closed behind him.

They went first to the Apprentice House. Inside, its walls were whitewashed. It was November and there was a fire in the first room they went into, but it still felt cold to Joseph...well, at least, he shivered.

Up in the attic, under the roof, it *was* cold. He rubbed the top of his arms. The iron-stern lady who had met them at the cart gave him a look that stopped his rubbing. She told them she was called Mrs. Sims, and from now on they would do exactly as she, or her husband, told them. Or else, she said. Joseph was just about to say "Or else what?" but something made him bite back the words and keep them inside his mouth.

All three were given a fixed wooden bed to sleep in, but Joe was in a different room from the girls. They were to share a bed, but Joe was told he would be sharing with another lad called Sam.

All the other apprentices were at work in the mill, they were told, but, being new, they didn't have to start until the next day.

"This is where you live now," Mrs. Sims told them. "Do as you are told and speak civil and you won't get into no trouble."

That last word hung in the air. Joe didn't like to ask what trouble. But somehow he knew, there and then, that trouble could come easily at Mr. Greg's Quarry Bank mill, and a fearsome foreboding overcame him. Girls or not, he could not stop the tears from coming out of his eyes, and, even worse, a sob escaped.

"And we don't want no snivelling," said the woman. "Any more and you'll get no supper."

*

When the other boys and girls came back after their work, well after dark, they cheered him up quite a lot. They told him that in the Apprentice House they had food that was much nicer than they'd ever had before.

"It's mainly porridge, bread, milk and potatoes," said one lad.

"But we get meat, sometimes, and vegetables too," said a tall girl who looked much older than the others. Joseph instantly liked her.

And at weekends they had lessons. Mrs. Greg and two of her daughters, who all wore lovely clothes and smelt nice, came from the family's big house next to the mill to teach the apprentices, he was told.

That was how Joe learned to read and write, over the months. Like the other children, he also learned about Jesus and other people in the Bible. And they had lessons in music and gardening...which was where the vegetables came from. So he learned quite a lot.

190

Even so, he never knew that learned and earnest men, concerned about the treatment of apprentices in textile mills, were comforting the middle classes with the information, in pamphlets and booklets, that they had themselves inspected the mills, and that those who laboured therein were among the most favoured in the land. With the mechanisation of steam and water power their work was light and easy, with only occasional calls on their attention and dexterity to engage their working hours.

Working hours, Joe learned, meant thirteen hours daily, although not, of course, on Sunday. They woke you up in time to eat a piece of bread and then stumble the few hundred yards to the mill for six o'clock.

They brought porridge for breakfast at half-past eight, and you were allowed ten minutes to eat it. You got an hour off for dinner in the middle of the day, although you had to finish cleaning up the workrooms, and that was counted as part of your break.

There was another break for tea at half-past five.

And at the end of the day in the mill, at eight o'clock, you walked back to the Apprentice House for supper...which was quite often a piece of bread, and broth.

You got a clean shirt once a week. And when your clothes wore out you got new ones.

The other children told him that he would be an apprentice at Greg's Mill for a long time, almost for ever, until he was eighteen or even twenty-one.

What *is* an apprentice?

There was laughter from the three or four boys who heard Joe's question. It means you work all day in the mill. You don't get holidays, or pay, except for overtime, which is written down in a big book. And if you do anything wrong or break anything they take something off whatever's in the book. You don't get any money of course.

"Except if Mr. Greg sees that you're working extra hard, or you've done something really well – sometimes he gives you a penny to keep for yourself.

191

It's not bad unless you get into trouble with the overlookers. And don't think of running away. They always catch you and bring you back. Then you are really for it.

"They take off money from the overtime book, to pay back what it costs to bring you back. And they lock you up on your own for a week.

"And all you get to eat is bread and gruel twice a day. And they cut off girls' hair too, sometimes, to teach them a lesson," one lad told him.

Nobody mentioned slaves. They didn't know that that was what they were, albeit with a benevolent master.

Mr. and Mrs. Sims, the superintendents in the Apprentice House, were strict and definitely not to be argued with. They got the fifty children out of bed in plenty of time to eat a piece of bread and get to the mill for 6 a.m.

After supper it was off to bed. There was a bit of larking about, some laughing, an adult shout from below, snuggling into the little bed with Sam, who, being ten, took up most of the space. And, at last, silence.

At the end of that first day it had not been so bad, Joe thought. It was a bit like the workhouse, but not so strict. It was all a bit strange, but he was not downcast. Until he wondered what his ma and his sisters were doing. An empty longing, such as he had never known before, overtook him, and a strange fear.

He felt a tear run down his face. And – he could not stop it – a sob shook him. And another.

A voice in the darkness growled: "Shut up!"

Joe sniffed. Then another sob. He stopped. He thought again. He could not stop a sniffling sort of sob.

Suddenly his head was ringing and a pain stopped his breath with surprise and a violent aching. The punch had hit him on his left ear.

"The next time I'll really thump you!" said the voice of a big boy. "So shut up now if you know what's good for you."

The fear of that was worse than thinking about his ma and his sisters. The pain from the blow began to spread, and his ears throbbed. He lay still. And in the tumult of feelings, he slept.

It was still dark when Joe was woken up by a shaking and shouting. At first he did not know where he was. Then he remembered: he was not with his ma and his sisters – they had been left far behind. He was in this prentice house with all these other boys. He cuddled himself up in his blanket against the memory, trying to shut it out.

"Get up now. Quick! Here's Mr. Sims! Quick!"

Fear soaked up the words. He leapt out and began putting his boots on. He was ready to start work.

*

Even in winter it was hot in the big work place with its clattering, incessant machines. But Joe's first impression, the day he hesitantly stepped inside to do his first day's work, just over twelve hours after he had arrived at Quarry Bank, was the noise.

It hammered at your ears...it filled your senses...it battered at your mind, until he got a cuff on the ear for not paying attention to the big man in overalls who, he came to understand, was telling him, Annie, Mary and another new boy, what to do.

Joe saw that he was speaking in a funny way, widening his mouth as he spoke each unheard word.

He still didn't understand. But another boy pulled at his arm and showed him.

Some boys had brooms. Joe did what others did and picked up bits of cotton fluff, from around the whirring machines. It wasn't too hard. But after a while when he needed a rest he found that there was no stopping...not unless the machines stopped.

Breakfast was brought in. There was milk to drink, very thick porridge that you could eat straight out of your hand, and an oatcake. Ten minutes. Then back to work.

Hour after hour it went on. By dinner time Joe was so weary that the only thing that stopped him going to sleep was his hunger. For thirty minutes the children had to clean the floors and oil the machinery. Then they could eat their potato pie. Food had never tasted better. Thirty minutes. Then back to work.

The day seemed endless. The work went on relentlessly. The only time the machines stopped was when the cotton threads broke and the apprentices who were piecers quickly tied the ends together.

The machines - the most modern you could get, he was told - never tired. But Joe did.

By seven o'clock at night he kept falling asleep. So did other apprentice boys and girls. The overlookers kept poking them with sticks and hitting them with the back of a rough hand to remind them to stay awake. And the work went on and on.

The apprentices were so young and ignorant that they did not know how easy their jobs were. One of the government's Factory Commissioners made a careful calculation to prove it.

Three quarters of the children in cotton mills were piecers, their job being to dash forward and tie together any loose ends of broken threads in the spinning mules, which rolled backwards and forwards on the mill floor during their operation.

But because the piecers could only work when the machines were *not* moving, it meant that they stood idle for about three quarters of a minute in each sequence of the machines. Obviously, therefore, the Factory Commissioner said, the young apprentices only worked for a quarter of the time.

So in a 13-hour working day in the mill they spent nine hours doing absolutely nothing at all. Nine hours at leisure, as he put it.

So they only actually worked for three hours a day. Unless, of course, the piecers worked on two mules at the same time, which was, in fact, usual. Even then, the children only worked for six hours a day, the commissioner pointed out triumphantly.

It was a little surprising that he didn't expect the apprentices to pay the mill owners for the sheer pleasure of it all, some people thought wryly.

The end of each working day brought relief, a quick stumble back to the apprentice house, and food – such good food! Then bed. Now Joe was too tired to think much after getting under his blanket - the sleep of exhaustion took him too fast.

*

All the apprentices had coughs, Joe noticed, and some had sore eyes. As the weary weeks and months went by, so did he. His job had been changed to cleaning the spinning machines.

It was while he was coughing and using a cloth to clean cotton fluff from among the whirring spindles, which were spinning so fast that they appeared to be still, that something grabbed the cloth, and his hand jerked and jammed into the machinery. The searing agony made him scream.

Within seconds the machine had been stopped. Hands pulled his arm free, and a terrible pain filled his senses. He fell backwards. The crimson hurt filled his brain. He screamed again before fainting.

Everyone came running when they saw blood pouring from his hand. At first Joe couldn't apprehend that he had lost the forefinger of his right hand. When he saw the shattered bone, blood and strange trailing bits he fainted again.

When he came to life again found himself in the Apprentice House with a man putting a bandage on his hand, which throbbed with a terrible agony. He cried out again as tears flowed.

But Mrs. Sims told Joe that the man was Doctor Holland, and he was very lucky that he chanced to be at the mill that day. So he must stop all this crying and wailing and he must do exactly as the doctor told him.

As the doctor began attending to the injury Mrs. Sims stroked Joe's head, murmuring: "There, there."

It reminded him of his mother, so gentle. Later Joe realised that Mrs. Sims was always kinder when the doctor was around.

But for now it was fear of Mrs. Sims that made him obey, subsiding into muffled, painful sobs. And it was only when the other apprentices came back from the mill that evening that he was told that he was

195

lucky...he would not have to work for days and days, maybe a week or more.

Much later he realised that he *was* fortunate. Mr. Greg, the mill owner, made sure that Doctor Holland always attended if there was an accident, or if any of his apprentices became sick.

They suffered all the diseases of childhood. And they coughed. Some children coughed so much that they died. Nobody knew why. Nobody knew that the millions of cotton fibres that filled the air, and were daily breathed in by the workers, was the cause. Nobody cared. The word byssinosis had not been invented. But it still made the children cough, despite the doctor's best endeavours.

The other children were quite cheerful about Joe's injury. They told him terrible stories about an apprentice who had been killed by a machine. All *he'd* done was to lose one of his fingers!

Over the next few weeks the doctor came back several times and took off the bandage. The congealed blood made it difficult to get it off. The last part, where the material was stuck to the bloody bit at the end, was the worst for Joe. The doctor soaked it in hot water till it came loose. He tried not to cry. But somehow it made him want his ma. He didn't know why. But he couldn't stop the tears.

At first he could hardly look at where his finger had been...it made him feel sick to see it. Then he had a fresh bandage. Each time Joe could see that it was getting better.

Joe had to go back to work in the mill, but he was given jobs that kept him out of harm's way. One day the doctor took off the bandage for the last time. Over months the skin healed fully over the joint. Eventually he hardly noticed it.

And he no longer noticed the things that had terrified him at first in the mill...the smell, the heat, the dust, the bashes from the grown-ups, the occasional bullying from other children.

Joe often thought about his mother and his sisters. He had an empty feeling and it made him cry at first. But he got used to not seeing them. The other children at the mill became his family. Except that you couldn't trust some of them...the bullies thumped you and stole your food.

There were others who'd go and tell the overlooker if you'd done anything that you shouldn't...they thought it got them the odd favour. But some were friendly. He especially liked a lad called Harry who also came from Newcastle. And there was a big girl called Lizzie who looked after him when his damaged hand was throbbing and hurting enough to make him cry. She even threatened to bash up a couple of boys who started to tease him and call him "Fourfingers."

They didn't do it again. But he noticed that one of them had a black eye, and the pair of them kept well away from Liz.

CHAPTER 27

1816

Joe's apprenticeship had been extended until he was twenty-one. It was an act of kindness, for he now had no family and no home to go to. And Joseph Mayer had been noticed as a sensible lad, and a hard worker.

The daily grind of hard labour and long hours in the deafening noise and heat of the spinning rooms had become his normal way of life, along with all the other apprentices.

Most lived through it to the end of their apprenticeship. And some were offered adult workers' jobs in the mill.

Samuel Greg, forced by the Factory Acts to cut children's working hours, yet reluctant to give up his apprentices – the cheapest form of labour to be found – could foresee the end of the lucrative child labour system upon which he had based his highly successful cotton spinning mill at Styal.

He was a hard-headed businessman, but he had a kindly streak. The children he took as apprentices were almost all paupers from poorhouses and workhouses, as far away as London.

He was giving those children a chance to break away from the often terrible conditions in which they were being brought up in penury...albeit to spend their youth working for next to nothing in his mill.

Some of the apprentices could not wait to get away from Styal and Mr. Greg and his Quarry Bank Mill. But he could see that some had become useful workers, trained from the age of nine, and willing to stay and earn pay as adults at the end of their indentures.

And he had begun to form the idea that if he had to employ adults, it would be in his best interests if they were already bent to his will. They would live on his land and pay rent to him in houses that he would build for them; they would buy their food in his shop, and they could even worship in a church that he would build – all close to his mill. Time-served apprentices would be ideal.

Mr. Greg, a strict Unitarian, was a highly sensible man with Christian principles. And he knew that healthy workers were cheaper to employ than those who were sickly.

So he drew up plans for houses that would be well-built, terraced, but with plenty of space between the rows, each with a cellar, and each with a garden so their occupants could grow their own vegetables...just as the apprentices were taught to do in the prentice house garden.

They were then only plans. Years later they were built, just as Mr. Greg had planned, but by his son.

For in 1834 the founder of Quarry Bank Mill died of pneumonia in the aftermath of breaking his hip when he was butted by the pet stag that he kept in his garden, adjacent to the mill.

*

Even in the early days, once he had become used to the long hours, the heat and the noise and the dust, Joe found that some things interested him. Styal was not at all like Newcastle-under-Lyme.

For a start there were the woodlands and the steep valley-sides enfolding the mill, alongside the River Bollin which powered the machinery through a great water-wheel.

In the winter the trees were bare and forbidding. But he delighted in seeing the beech trees' buds unfolding in the Spring, bringing leaves of the freshest green that seemed to alter the sun's light, softening it, in a way that he couldn't explain, but which seemed to spread a calmness through him.

He knew that it was a sign that the harsh, cold days were numbered, and it heralded the warmer, happier days of summer, when the early-morning stumble from the Prentice House to the mill didn't make you cough so painfully.

And in the autumn, when the green leaves turned to yellow and orange flame, its beauty overrode the knowledge that winter could not be far behind.

*

1817

As he approached the end of his apprenticeship, Joe liked to think about how the mill's machinery worked. He knew of course that the mill was powered by water from the River Bollin. The mill's water-wheel drove big metal cogs and shafts that had to be greased and carefully looked after by the mechanics.

They knew the mysteries of it all, and whenever he got the chance to see the millwheel he was always asking them what was this for...how did that work...where do these go...what happens if there isn't much water in the river?

In fact the mill itself, which was entirely devoted to cotton spinning, was getting busier. Despite the general contraction in trade after the end of the wars with France, more and more spindles kept being brought in by Mr. Greg...more than 4,500 by 1817.

A big extension was being planned – meaning even more capacity for spinning. And it needed more power.

There were rumours of a massive new water wheel being needed to make all the new machinery work. It was to be sited inside the building, in the basement.

Sure enough, work began on a tunnel, three-quarters of a mile long, to take the tail-waters from the new wheel back to the river much lower downstream than the existing water outlet.

Soon, engineers began planning the huge iron wheel, the like of which nobody at Styal had ever dreamed of.

It was going to be 21 feet *wide*. Enormous!

It would be 32 feet in diameter.

And when finished it would weigh 44 tons.

Tom, a mechanic Joseph got to know, told him that it was so big that it would be rated at 100 horse-power...it was one of the biggest water-wheels in the whole of England.

It was a good few years now since Joe had first sneaked out to watch the old, much smaller, mill wheel at work, and Tom had explained how, through a series of iron cog-wheels, metal shafts and huge leather belts its power was taken up into the spinning floors of the mill, to make the spinning machines work.

It fascinated Joe. "It's like magic in a way," he said wonderingly to Tom. "Yet in a way it is so simple. It's a thing of beauty and purpose at the same time.

"The wheel only borrows the water from the river for a short time, yet it turns the gentle current into strength and power to make the machines work at its bidding.

"It's like God's almighty hand, moving though all things – it makes one of gentle nature and brute machinery."

"Aye, and those are wise words, young man. But the only thing is...all you apprentices are just people, youngsters at that, and far from fully grown, most of you," said Tom

"We don't have the strength of the machines – they outpace and outlast us...and they will outlive us too.

"Whereas the water and the wheel and the shafts and the belts and machines can keep going on, almost for ever, with any worn-out parts replaced, you can't. We human beings can't go on without sufficient rest and food and sleep.

"Somebody has to understand that.

"Here I think Mr. Greg is aware of what work children can do, and what they can't. But there's plenty of cotton mills up in Manchester not ten miles from here where the mill bosses don't know or don't care, and children are worked near to death tending their machines.

"So you hang on to all the magic you can find, me lad, because there's not too much of it about these days."

"What do you mean?"

"I mean that a few years back a man and his wife or his mother would work at making cloth in their own cottage – the women at a spinning wheel making the thread and the men at their hand-looms weaving it into cloth.

"Then they'd sell it to an agent, and so make their living. It was hard work to make much money, but they had the freedom to work at their own pace, in their own homes, and the more skilful they were the better the cloth

"You worked hard to get a good reputation for it.

"Yes it was hard work, but families could work together and they felt happy in their labours even though it was in a small way.

"They felt that the cloth they produced was the work of their own hands...they were proud of it.

"Poor they might have been, but there was a feeling of family labours well done. Their work and the spinning wheel and the loom put together fed themselves and their children.

It worked like magic for them...their own private magic.

"Now them that keep on at the home working have been driven to ruin by these mills that we work at. They can't sell their cloth against the output of the mills, with their power-machines, and these days if you can't compete you are lost."

Joe thought about it. "So we're lucky to be working at Mr. Greg's mill? It doesn't seem like it. Some apprentices hate it and want nothing more than to escape from it.

"The days are so long that they say all they want is peace and the open air."

"Maybe," said Tom. "Well they might find a job on a farm. They'd get plenty of fresh air there.

"But they won't get much pay. And if they can't get a job because there are more people than jobs these days, well that's all they'll get to eat...fresh air!"

*

It was Tom who first made Joe aware of the desperate struggle for survival that was going on beyond the boundaries of rural Styal, across Britain, from the farmlands to the industrialised towns.

For it was a time when the more thoughtful of the moneyed classes who ran the nation – almost always for their own benefit and profit – felt sincerely and carefully that what politician Edmund Burke had called "the swinish multitude" should not be paid more than would enable them to barely survive.

Indeed, for well over a century the great and the good of the land – used as they were to a life of plentiful luxury and untroubled ease – had been expounding the view that grinding poverty among the less great and less good was not only an excellent thing in itself, but an absolute necessity for the proper functioning of the British economy.

These philosophers saw quite clearly that if you had, for the sake of argument, a nice round pie, and you had to share it with a lot of other people, you would get less of it.

Great numbers of people should be not just poor, but wretched, it was said. Good for the economy. Good for society. Good for civilization. Essential, actually.

Such revelations come quite clearly when one is in that blessed mood of contemplation that follows the consumption of a large dinner washed down with a bottle or two of goodly French wine.

And one had to voice such profound thinking when, every so often, a bishop or some such foolish cleric would blatantly preach that it might be unchristian to keep in abject poverty the mass of the people who laboured to bring home the bacon for their masters. The sin of avarice, they kept calling it. Well, bishops should keep to their proper business. One cannot stand interfering prelates.

Yet the Anglican Church was a body not to be swept aside: it was the biggest and richest organization in the kingdom; and the two dozen or so bishops were the leaders of around ten thousand parishes throughout the land. All this added up to power that even parliament had to heed, or at least to respect.

203

Now, in the early part of the nineteenth century, the reasoning of the parliamentarians had crystallized in a way that could not upset the church. And it was even easier to understand. It was this: if the labouring classes had more money than starvation wages they would obviously use the money to get drunk. And the equally obvious by-product would be that they would breed even more starving children who would be a further burden on the public purse. It was the parishes that had to raise the money to alleviate the distress of the poor. So lower pay, less drinking, and fewer children would ease the burden on the parishes.

Worst of all, if the labouring classes *were* to be better-paid, they would not work so hard, or so long. They would feel that with money in their pockets, they could afford to do less work...and that wouldn't put money into the coffers of the mill-owners and land-owners who were the parishes' more influential people. Well one couldn't stand for that.

Whatever their conflicts on many things, this was an issue on which Whigs, Tories and the Church could all agree.

It was Tom who pointed out to Joe the simple truth that if you were a rich man of business, a wealthy farmer, or a man of property, who spent your time squeezing every last drop of profit from your workers by paying them as little as possible, the last thing you would then want to do would be to pay rising parish rates to support these very workers just because they and their many children were dying for want of food.

Tom lived in Wilmslow, on Church Street, in a cottage about half way between two public houses – the Ring o'Bells, near the top of the hill and just across from the old market ground, and the George and Dragon, which was near the bottom of the hill, next to the parish church, St. Bartholomew's.

Being sensible, he was not a big drinker, but he did like to spend much of his spare time in one pub or the other, for what he liked above all was the conversation, the exchange of views that could be voiced with little fear of reprisal, on life, work, and the need for more money.

He read things, too. William Cobbett's news-sheets were passed eagerly but surreptitiously from hand to hand. They were read aloud in little groups, for the benefit of those who could not read. They opened up a new world of knowledge, chiming with what people could see happening around them.

"Somebody said an attempt had been made to shoot the Prince Regent," said Joe one day in 1817. "Have you heard about it? It's terrible if it is true."

"I did hear it. But they say the shot missed," Tom replied. "I suppose they'll blame Thomas Paine. But they can't hang him for it, for he died...oh, eight or nine years ago now."

"What do you mean? Who was Thomas Paine?"

"He wrote two books called The Rights of Man, back in the 1790s. He was against having kings and queens. He preferred the idea of having a republic, like America and France have, rather than a monarchy like ours.

"More important, he contended that all men are born and always continue free and equal in respect of their rights to liberty, their property, safety, and freedom from oppression.

"The land-owning class took that to mean that he wanted all their property to be taken off them, and distributed to the poor. So they wanted him imprisoned or even put to death for sedition."

"What does that mean?"

"They were accusing him of trying to bring down the state. He had to live the rest of his life in France and America. If they had caught him in this country he would have hanged, for sure...for the law's interests here are the same as the interests of the landed gentry. If you're not of that class you've very little chance being treated fairly by the law.

"That was another thing that he said...in France, since the revolution there, the law is the same for everyone – all are equal in its sight."

"It is not so in England?"

"It is not, and that's for certain. The law is the instrument by which the workers like us are kept in our place...which means perpetual hunger for many, many people. Yet we do not rise up against it, like they did in France. Perhaps it is because no matter what state of penury the working man or woman is left in, we love our king and we are loyal to him. It's the way we are.

"So most ordinary people live in wretchedness – that's how it is in England."

"But the king will always protect the working people, won't he? That's what all the apprentices say."

Tom took a long, silent look at Joe. He looked around before speaking. "I don't think I'd count on that. The days of Robin Hood are long gone, I'm afraid. The poor will always stay poor."

"But how can parliament suffer it to be so?"

"It suffers it because the members of parliament are all of the class and wealth that benefit from keeping the working people at the point of starvation. Why should they change what is good for them?"

"But if they don't like it, the people who elect them can decide against them when they vote, can't they?"

"Well, first, the only people who can vote are of that same moneyed class – the men of property and wealth who also benefit from having a starving population eager to work for a pittance in order to get food for themselves and their families.

"And second, the membership of the House of Commons is a very odd matter. Money and family interests play a big part.

"They say there was one member of parliament in the 1700s who had fifty relatives who were also MPs. The more family and the more money you have, the better your chances of getting into parliament and making money from positions of power in the government. In some places there are only a few voters, so they can vote for the candidate who pays best. It's called democracy but it's really bribery.

"Manchester, which has a population of sixty thousand people, has no member of parliament at all. But Thomas Paine's book says there's a place called Old Sarum, which has less than three houses in it, and it has two members of parliament.

"They pay money to win their places and go and vote for things that will bring them more money – that's how it is. The truth is that it is rotten to the core.

"If a*ll* men could vote, things might change. But I fear it will never be any different."

*

Joseph's mother had died only four years after he had left for his new life at Mr. Greg's Quarry Bank Mill. He remembered the anguish and empty fear he felt when he was told that she had given up her struggle for life.

He did not know what had happened to his sisters. Newcastle youngsters arriving from the workhouse told Joe that they certainly were no longer at their former abode.

Probably they had been sent away to work as apprentices. For parish officers were always keen to get rid of pauper children who were a burden on the rates.

Now, as Joe approached twenty-one he was secretly dreading the day he finished his apprenticeship. Some were simply turned away and left to their own devices on the day the mill had finished with them. Some of them found work locally. Some were sent back to the place they'd come from. Where would he go? What would he do?

It was a time of major economic depression. Jobs were hard to come by. Many thousands of people were out of work. Hundreds of thousands of ex-soldiers and sailors, discharged from the army and navy since the end of the wars against France and America, were wanting work.

At the same time, mills and factories were forced to cut back from their peaks of wartime production, because war-torn European nations were in no position to import British goods. That meant reducing their work forces, and their wage rates.

Men vied to offer themselves for lower wages in order to get work, on the principal that anything was better than nothing. Death by starvation was by no means unknown.

The effect on the labouring population in the years after 1815 was devastating. Many families faced desperate privation. Privation bred hunger. Hunger bred anger. Anger bred violent protests.

The Government, which had long feared a French-style revolution from the low-bred rabble who toiled to produce the riches for the noble moneyed classes, acted with the ruthlessness of advantaged people determined at all costs to protect their advantages.

They sent in troops to quell the demonstrations and protest meetings, with orders to shoot at unruly agitators. And the troops did shoot into various crowds. "Serve 'em right, what!" you heard the better type of person declare.

Parliament, convinced that the threat of insurrection was very real, went into secret session to consider the Government's so-called proof that the protests were part of a revolutionary conspiracy to seize power. And so Britain was turned into a country ruled by State oppression.

And with the help of spies' reports they did find a number of men bent on trouble and even, in some cases, keen to bring down the government which in no way represented them. As a result habeas corpus was suspended.

Free speech was all but stifled. For criticism of the Government was now a criminal offence, punishable by imprisonment without trial.

The well-fed people who ran the county and its businesses could not comprehend that it wasn't revolution that the labouring classes were crying out for.

It was food.

CHAPTER 28

1984

Increasingly Mrs. Thatcher spoke on the television news as if she saw herself as Boadicea.

She knew that the two big threats to Britain's freedoms had to be stopped. Communism and the trade unions: the enemy at the gates and the enemy within, bent on opening the gates.

Since her accession to the premiership in 1979 her voice had been getting more strident. The pursuit of wealth, she believed, is one of mankind's most important driving forces...and it should be achieved by honest endeavour and hard work.

She spoke admiringly of Victorian virtues. And the kind of virtue that she wanted to restore was to distinguish between the deserving poor and those people who had lost the habit of working.

So her government began to work out a new welfare policy that discouraged dependency on the state, and encouraged self-reliance. She believed passionately that everyone had a moral responsibility for their own lives. The state had been doing far too much.

She wanted to improve people's lives by making them see that self-betterment was their best course. It was the way she had been taught. But for many caught in the poverty trap, it was a foreign language. More than three million people were unemployed. There were few job vacancies to be found. Self-improvement? How?

She faced much opposition, not only from the recipients of welfare, but also from within her own government...from the colleagues she disparagingly called "wets," the people who wanted to temper her crusading spirit on matters like major cuts in public spending. But the lady, she had already declared to much applause, was not for turning.

It was a time when politics became polarized. Every day, it seemed, the news was full of politics...with strong voices either totally for or totally against. Britain was a nation divided.

Gone were the soft tones of her 1979 entry into 10 Downing Street: "Where there is discord, may we bring harmony...where there is despair, may we bring hope."

Those honeyed words, her worshippers knew, hid a woman of steel. The Iron Lady. At last...the leader we have been waiting for! The leader who will put the spongers and the trade unions in their place.

Many people saw her as the long-awaited saviour that Britain needed. But those who did not love this increasingly strident woman found her new, hard-edged voice irritatingly arrogant.

Away from the public gaze, of course, she was different. "Oh Brian!" she said in smiling admonishment when the broadcast journalist Brian Redhead, sitting face-to-face with her in a taxi along with several other politicians one evening, remarked: "I never realised what lovely knees you've got, Prime Minister!"

It must have been the first time in Britain's history that those words had ever been spoken!

Mrs. Thatcher never used sex-appeal in her rise to the top in Britain's political life. But whether she knew it or not, and whether she liked it or not, men who liked an attractive face allied to intelligence and drive in a woman did find her sexy...and it may well have been one of the stepping stones that took her to 10 Downing Street.

They were going to the BBC for another chance to tell the country what was right and what was wrong.

Among the things that she knew were terribly wrong was the hidden agenda of certain powerful union chiefs in Britain who, she was convinced, were leading a communist conspiracy to hand over the nation to Stalin's successors.

*

"Thank God we've got Mrs. Thatcher. I really think she's the only thing between us and national ruin."

Hanna was speaking at the candle-lit dinner table as they entertained their friends Ron Davidson and Mary Beech.

Before dinner, over gin and tonics, most of the talk had been about the engagement ring that Mary was wearing with a gleam of gold and diamond.

But as the meal got going, the conversation moved on to other, weightier matters. Hanna brought up the subject of Mrs. Thatcher, hero of the hour, still basking in post-Falkland war glory.

Talking politics was OK when you knew there wasn't any chance of giving offence.

And obviously, if people were your friends, they would not be devoted to anything other than Thatcherism, she assumed.

"All these union Trots and leftie Labour people – they're nothing but Commies, the lot of them, if you ask me," she declared, looking for approval to their guests.

"That's a bit extreme, isn't it?"

Mary was not the kind of person to keep silent for the sake of her hosts' comfort when she disagreed with what they were saying.

"I mean, they're surely not *all* Communists. In fact some of our friends are Labour voters. We know that because they've told us so.

"They've also told us that they admire some of the things Maggie is doing, but simply don't agree with others.

"For instance they said her decisiveness made her an ideal leader at the time of the Falklands War. But they think her economic policies are rubbish."

"Well I hope you put them right on that," challenged Hanna.

"No, of course not," said Mary, who was not going to tell them that she normally voted Liberal. "Because that's just a normal political view.

"I'm certainly not going to tell them they must change their politics because I don't happen to agree with them!"

She'd said it! O.K., you don't usually argue politics with your hostess. But she was not going to be dictated to, even in Hanna's own home.

Geoff stepped in to ease the awkward moment. "But you must agree that something's got to be done about the trade unions. They're out of control.

"If they had their way they'd bring the country to a standstill, with their strikes and works-to-rule, and restrictive practices.

"Until Maggie took them on they were a huge drag on industry.

"And you've got to wonder who are their political masters. It's a known fact that a lot of the union leaders are communists."

Now Ron stepped in to rescue Mary. "Well maybe they need watching. But it isn't just union leaders, is it? I've heard they've got MI5 watching people making genuine ethical protests – like CND, Greenpeace, and the peace women camping out at Greenham Common to make their point about the evils of nuclear warfare.

"These are people making serious points, and as a nation we've always prided ourselves that protests like these are accepted as a part of free speech and the right to be heard.

"Mrs. Thatcher might not like activists who are opposed to her policies. They might be a danger to her party. But that doesn't make it subversion. Being opposed to the government doesn't make them a threat to the State."

"But there are all these loony left Labour people in town halls as well as parliament. They're not coming from the old Labour of Atlee and Gaitskell, bad as they were!" countered Geoff. "They're taking their orders direct from the Kremlin, or I'm a Dutchman."

"If that was proved it might be different," said Mary. "But until it is, we have to accept that it is legitimate political opposition."

"Well I for one am glad that we've at last got a prime minister who'll stand up for our country and our way of life," stated Hanna.

"And I'm glad she's a politician with the same kind of beliefs as people like us. I'm sure she's right when she says that the permissive society is undermining family life, for instance.

"This country needed a woman in charge. She speaks her mind. She knows what she wants. And she goes for it.

"And at least we've made sure that Labour never gets in power again. That's for certain!"

*

1817

In the midst of it all, Joe was lucky. Almost all the trouble - riots and protests against the harsh conditions and low pay - was in the towns and cities. Styal was a rural backwater.

Like a lot of the older, more experienced apprentices, he had been taught carding, then spinning. He was even paid a shilling a week.

He was known to be a sharp-minded and industrious lad. And at the end of his apprenticeship in August 1817, he was offered a fully paid job as a spinner.

Samuel Greg, with a shrewd eye for the future, foresaw the days not too far ahead when new laws to protect pauper children would cut off the supply of parish apprentices upon which his enterprise had depended for so long.

He wanted the good workers, still young enough not to expect high wages, to form the basis of a permanent work force in Styal.

Most of the spinners were girls, but Joseph took what he was offered. Work was work, and not everybody had it.

There was a terrible post-war slump, and he knew that when trade was bad, workers were laid off

Suddenly he was getting a proper wage – four shillings and six pence a week. He lodged in the village with John and Alice Booth. They were both former apprentices who had been sweethearts and had married. They rented one of the houses that Mr. Greg had bought in Styal.

The bad times when they were children at the mill were something that they could smile about now, when they talked over the old days.

213

There was plenty of laughter, especially when they had finished work...although laughing often made them cough.

They laughed and coughed as they remembered how they had played tricks on other apprentices. The bolder ones had been naughty, despite the threat of big fines if they were caught - five shillings for stealing apples.

They had always been hard up. But they had used their time off, especially in the warm, summer Sunday afternoons, to venture through the woods that ran alongside the River Bollin, even going as far as the big village of Wilmslow, a mile or so away.

They knew the way because each Sunday as apprentices they had been marched to St. Bartholomew's Church to attend morning service.

*

Joe's mechanic friend Tom seemed to like the way he talked and asked questions. Joe thought of Tom as a guide, full of wisdom and knowledge...like a father.

He told Tom about the workhouse in Newcastle, and about his mother's struggles to keep the family together. And Tom told Joe about why people were poor yet doing all the sweating whilst Mr. Greg and his family didn't seem to do much at all, but were very rich.

Tom knew everything there was to know about the mill at Quarry Bank, it seemed. He had served his apprenticeship there, starting shortly after the mill first opened in 1784.

It was a dirty, greasy job. But the mechanics were a set apart. Upon their skills depended the livelihood of everyone else. Half a day lost through the break-down of a machine could be very expensive for Mr. Greg.

That was the kind of problem that Mr. Greg had to worry about, and make decisions about. "He is the one who has to work out how to make this mill – and his other four mills – profitable," said Tom.

More than half of the workers were not paid wages because they were apprentices. But Tom also pointed out that if the children didn't

214

actually receive money, they did get free board and lodging and clothing which had to be paid for out of the mill profits.

*

It was Tom who told Joe about Reform, and especially about William Cobbett who was fighting for the right for all men to vote in elections for Parliament, which would give everyone a fairer deal, and enable workers to get a decent wage for their labours.

"It is a simple truth that there's a profit to be made from the economic hardship of others," said Tom. "As some people starve, others profit by it.

"Take these enclosures...it's a clear-cut case of robbery of the poor by the rich."

Cobbett had been a constant critic of the Government, Tom told Joe. The Government had been looking for an excuse to bring him down, and they got their chance when through his own newspaper, the *Political Register*, Cobbett poured contempt on the Government's German Legion which, in a dispute over pay, had flogged part-time British militiamen in Ely for refusing to obey orders.

For telling the truth about it, Cobbett was found guilty of seditious libel, and sent to Newgate prison. After two years he had come out of gaol determined to fight on for reform of Parliament.

The big-wigs in the Government hated Cobbett, but it didn't stop him. He'd kept writing his stinging articles for the *Register* even when he was a prisoner in Newgate.

But the war with Napoleon had gone on and the labouring people had got poorer. Some years before, people they called Luddites had begun rioting and breaking machinery in mills and manufactories because the new machines were taking work from men whose families were already close to starvation.

Now, as ex-soldiers and sailors looked for work after the end of the war, and many thousands of families began starving for want of work, the riots had started again.

Tom knew about it because he could read, and he had actually got copies of some of Cobbett's news-sheets, contemptuously labelled "twopenny trash" by parliamentarians who had been lashed by their criticisms...a label proudly and ironically taken up by their author.

"But don't let anyone else know what I've been reading – Mr. Greg can't abide trade unions or anybody that fights for higher pay," he said.

Joe soaked up the new knowledge from Cobbett's newspaper. It fascinated him more than anything he had ever heard before. It seemed to him to offer hope of a way out of the crippling poverty that had blighted his early life, and the lives of his parents, and many, many like them.

He knew he was lucky, working at Quarry Bank, because Mr. Greg was a kindly master, for all his stern ways, and although wages were lower than in many other mills, especially in Manchester, it was much healthier to live in the countryside where there was fresh air and cottages for the adults to live in.

Tom had been to Manchester where many people lived in terrible places, sometimes dozens to a room, sometimes in cellars where there was no light or fresh air.

"Not that there's too much fresh air outside, come to that! The air is full of smoke. You're better off here, lad," Tom had said.

He pointed out: "For all the hard times here, you've been fed and clothed since coming to Styal. You've been looked after and kept out of trouble. You've even had a doctor when you had your accident and when you've been poorly.

"And they taught you to read and write. That's something your mother and father never had in all their lives...nor their parents and grandparents before them. And if you've any sense you'll stick at it here.

"Now you must make use of all the good things you've been given. Use it to better yourself.

"I'll bring you one or two old copies of William Cobbett's newspapers and you can read them for yourself. But don't let anyone see you with them . . . it could land you in a deal of trouble."

It was the first time Joe had ever read anything other than the learning books, the Bible, and the hymns in church. He found that he could master most of the words easily.

The first pamphlet, entitled "An Address to the Journeymen and Labourers," said that Britain's wealth had been produced by people like them, and that in the recent wars with France and America the country had depended on the men in the ranks who had carried muskets, or who had manned the fighting ships.

So they were not to be ignored or despised. "With this correct idea of your own worth in your minds, with what indignation must you hear yourselves called the Populace, the Rabble, the Mob, the Swinish Multitude," it said.

Joe couldn't wait to talk to Tom about it. But Tom counselled him to caution.

"The Government can do what it wants with the likes of us," he said. "They've been hanging these Luddites and folk making violent protests, when they've caught them.

"Above all, don't forget you can be shot just for criticising the government now."

But from then on Joe missed no chance of listening when his fellow workers complained about their pay and conditions, and talked - usually despairingly - about how they should be improved.

Tom kept him supplied with pamphlets from Cobbett, who had now become the hero of many of the manual workers.

Joe felt a great urge to do something to better the lives of the disadvantaged that he now knew were the majority of the labouring classes.

It didn't affect him at Styal. He was young and single, and had enough money to live on. But there were many, many people with large families who were not getting enough to eat.

It was not reasonable or right that a man should work hard, long hours of labour six days a week, and still not get enough pay to support himself and his family.

Surely something would be done soon. Reform! That was the thing to hope for!

CHAPTER 29

1820

Joe tried to forget the horrors he had seen at St Peter's Field in Manchester. People were calling the terrible episode "Peterloo" in ironic reference to Britain's glorious victory over Napoleon at the Battle of Waterloo.

Eleven people had died, men women and children. And the newspapers said that hundreds were known to have been injured by the charge of the fearless mounted soldiers who had been brave enough to ride with sabres into an unarmed crowd.

It earned official thanks from a grateful government.

The injured hadn't dared to get medical help. They were too afraid that the magistrates would hear that they had been at Hunt's meeting in St. Peter's Field. They feared they could be hanged or transported just for being there.

So their wounds festered painfully. Some got better. Others didn't. Death came slowly and agonisingly.

It was more than a year ago...it's all over now. I must put it behind me. I must think of good things. I must think about happy times.

But the images kept coming back. They haunted him, especially at night in the darkness of his room. The pleasure he had first felt three years earlier when, on completing his apprenticeship aged 21, he had moved in to lodge with his old mill friends, the newly married John and Alice Booth, had been followed by the feeling of intense loneliness when he went off to bed, for he had never had a bed to himself before!

Now, alone at night, the terrible thoughts came back unbidden, night after night. And by day the sound of a baby screaming or a woman's high-pitched yelling sent a coldness down his back that made

219

him shiver, and - shame of all shames - an urge to cry. Tears in a grown man! And at nothing. Nothing that he could explain to anybody.

So he hid his terrors. When the feelings came on he found an excuse to blow his nose or look away, then find some seclusion until they subsided.

He had always been one for company - one of the jolly crowd. Now he took long walks alone on Sunday afternoons, avoiding the groups of young men and women he knew so well from the years of the deafening work in the mill.

One Sunday in October he was returning to Styal after a lone walk up to the top of the steep slopes called Alderley Edge, above the village of Chorley nearly four miles away. He had set out seeking a change of view, feeling a kind of black despair, although he did not really know why.

First he walked through the woods alongside the River Bollin to Wilmslow. It was only a mile or so.

But he could see Alderley Edge, a line of raised ground two miles further on, and decided to climb the hill. He reached the village of Chorley and climbed the slope from the Mottram Road to a sandstone buttress that everyone knew as Castle Rock.

The view from the rock, 300 feet above the verdant, sunlit Cheshire plain, green fields, and trees in their autumn gold spread before him, with the Derbyshire hills blue-misty in the distance, suddenly turned his grey mood to a quiet wonder at the beauty of it all.

He stayed, not too close to the edge of the giant rock, gazing at the splendour before him, until a family arrived with children shouting noisily. They were having a good time, but they had disturbed the magic.

He walked back down the sloping track and made his way by road and across the fields to Wilmslow, then into the woods towards Styal, aware that he had become happy again.

He met a mill girl, Nell Platt, who was also alone, and in his lightened mood, he greeted her cheerfully. He had known her since they were youngsters at the mill, although she was a year or so older than Joe.

She was pleasant enough, sort of top-heavy, but definitely not one of the prettier girls. He told her where he'd been. She seemed impressed when he told her how beautiful the views had been from the Edge.

She told him she had something beautiful to show him. She led him from the path into a secluded place among the trees. She took his hand for support. Suddenly she placed it on to her breasts. They were so soft and yielding under his hand that his initial shock disappeared in a moment. It was exciting and breath-taking...his heart was beating as if it wanted to get out.

Nell lay down on the soft woodland floor and pulled him down to her. She pulled up her skirt. Her nakedness was magnetic. He had never seen a girl like that. He had only one urge now. She made it easy for him. There was an ecstasy of feelings that overwhelmed him.

Then it was over, and he felt a mix of pride, shame and panic, but Nell seemed strangely in control. She told him to wash himself in the river. And then she walked away slowly, leaving him in a tumult of thought.

*

He had to marry her. The under-manager at the mill told him so.

It was nearly four months after their encounter in the woods. Nell Platt had informed her overlooker that she was expecting, and that Joe was the child's father. So that was that.

He had gone to the under-manager's office thinking that he had been summoned to be told something about his work. Joe's shock was that of a young man whose world has abruptly lurched into a new direction.

"But I don't love her," he heard himself saying weakly.

"You should have thought of that before now," he was told. "You'll marry her and be done. You're a good worker, and you're lucky - Mr.

Greg thinks well of you. There's a job coming up for you in this next six months as an overlooker, and a cottage coming vacant in a week or so. The rent'll be taken from your wages.

"It'll leave you enough to live on, and Nell will be able to work until she's due. Now back to your work. And work hard – you'll soon have a wife to support, and a baby too before long."

*

1984

Geoff's decision to walk along the Bollin Valley from Prestbury through Wilmslow to Styal had, he decided, been a good one. The sun was shining. The birds were singing. The countryside was green and beautiful. The scents of spring blossom were everywhere.

He couldn't remember ever walking out in the country alone, but he found it a good experience. Even the few people he met coming in the opposite direction, seemed to be nicer than if you met them in the village...almost all smiled and said good morning. It was almost like a brotherhood of pilgrims making their way to places unknown, he thought.

And, come to think of it, going back to his great-great grandparents, this was probably the only form of travel that they would know! It was a strange thought. He couldn't quite reconcile himself to the fact that his forebears were among the common herd, poor and probably uneducated working-class – probably not able to read or write.

He had decided to go and visit Styal to see the place for himself. He didn't know exactly where his ancestors had lived - the parish records didn't give people's address - but Geoff felt a great curiosity to see the locality where they had lived their lives.

He knew Styal as an interesting, if very small village. It was once peaceful, but standing as it did against the southern boundary of Manchester Airport, it was now a very noisy place. Strange: his ancestors once experienced nothing but peace and quiet, he thought; now he was among those shattering the silence with the enormous power of the aircraft he piloted.

Geoff had been to its one pub, the Ship, and he knew there was a cricket field, and not much else apart from an old water mill on the outskirts of the village, which he had heard about but never seen. Was that where Joseph had worked? He knew there were purpose-built houses that had been planned and constructed for the mill workers and their families.

For most of the four miles or so his walk took him alongside the River Bollin. It, too, had changed over the years. Back in the 1800s its water had probably been clear and unpolluted, but now, in the 1980s, it was tainted by a dark-coloured effluent from a dye-works or some such industrial concern.

"Bloody outrageous!" Geoff said aloud to the unpeopled verdure. There was nobody else within sight, so he could talk to himself if he felt like it. And he did.

"Just what right have people to pollute a river like this."

It wasn't a question...it was a statement.

He lost the irony; didn't see the connection with his own aircraft noise pollution's affecting the residents of modern-day Styal.

"It really is time that this country got back to the way it used to be. Back in Victorian times, I bet people used to walk along here and let their children paddle in the river, having a wonderful time on a Sunday afternoon, just enjoying the fresh air.

"Working people used to be happy with one day off a week, which they would spend with their families. No TV. No football hooligans. Simple needs. Simple pleasures. And if anyone did step out of line they'd very quickly find out that they were in trouble with a capital T.

"It must have made everybody's life so much easier and better. And because they didn't ask for too much, we were not only a rich country, we were the most powerful nation on earth.

"That's what Mrs. Thatcher wants to bring back - Victorian virtues and Victorian success as a nation. The only flies in the ointment are the bloody trade unions, with their constant demands for higher and higher wages, and their constant threat of strikes.

"They've got to be stopped, and I am one hundred percent with her. So is every right-thinking person!"

His walk took him out of the valley through Wilmslow, then into the Carrs parkland along the river again and into the woods leading to Styal.

It was mid-week, and although he kept passing a few people, for much of the time he was alone. It suited his mood.

On his way he didn't realise he was walking only a few hundred yards from the wooded slopes on which John Cooper had died his lonely death, defeated and thrown on the scrap-heap of life, just one of the many who lost their livelihoods in the 1980s.

Somehow the beauty of his surroundings made Geoff angry. It all got back to ignorant, money-grasping workers who were simply envious of those who had worked hard to make something of their ability and their education, so that they naturally got more responsible jobs, and the kind of salaries that reward responsibility.

Class hatred: that's what it's all about. And in the end you are talking about just one thing: envy. In fact, come to think about it, that is the one thing that drives the Labour Party and all the socialists and Trots and general bloody lefties: they have at least as much hatred for the people in charge as they have compassion for the underdogs.

And what is really sinister is that the lefties are trying to take power insidiously, taking over city councils, pushing their socialist ideas through the local people when they've been pushed out of government for ever.

At least I hope the British people are never stupid enough to vote them back in again. If they do, I for one will bloody well emigrate...I won't live under them.

Well thank God more companies are now managed by people who have got the guts to show the lazy sods the door! Half of the people working in this country do as little as possible for their pay and a lot of them are now finding that because of that they are expendable...that's why they are finding themselves unemployed - and unemployable.

But for the rest of us - our companies and the nation as a whole – we'll come out stronger. It's a shame we didn't have Margaret Thatcher in charge years ago, before the loony left took control and wrecked the economy.

He had a brief chat with an elderly couple walking their dog. They told him that the wide and well-trodden path he was now starting on was called the Apprentices' Walk. "Presumably the apprentices mostly lived in Wilmslow and came this way in big numbers in the old days," he said.

He walked on, alone again. "Apprentices. That's what we need nowadays. Make youngsters learn a trade the hard way. It would be good for them. Good for the firms employing them because they know they'll have a good supply of well-trained workers for the future. Gives the older workers a sense of responsibility to know that part of their job is to teach the younger people."

Now the outlying parts of the old mill came into view...a pond, an obviously man-made waterfall, a water-course with wooden gates and sluices. Then the mill itself.

He'd seen photographs of it and felt that he already knew it...standing amid the greenery of the valley, with its rows of Georgian windows and its one now-smokeless chimney, it was far from the "dark satanic mills" stereotype of the William Blake poem.

It looked businesslike, yes, yet a thing of beauty. "Well the people who worked here were lucky, I'd say," he said aloud. He stopped short as he realised that several people were looking at him as he spoke to himself. There were a surprising number of people about.

His immediate thought was: what a lovely place to work, surrounded by greenery, with a pleasant flat grassy area across the river where, he immediately envisaged, the mill workers would have been able to spread their picnic lunches and enjoy the fresh air during their meal-breaks.

The mill had been taken over by the National Trust as a museum, and Geoff had intended for a long time to visit it...somehow never getting to it until now. He paid his entrance fee and set off into the building.

*

Geoff Mayer's visit to the pleasant place to work was a jolt which opened his eyes to the wider history of the period in which his ancestor Joseph Mayer had lived.

Geoff discovered that the enterprise established by Samuel Greg in 1784, when he had his spinning mill built alongside the River Bollin at Styal, had grown into one of the biggest cotton companies in England in the mid-19th century.

It was therefore an important part of the huge surge in manufacturing that became known, later, as the industrial revolution.

Greg was a very wealthy man, his riches built on the profits from his five cotton mills. The other four had been built on the profits of Quarry Bank Mill. Those profits, certainly at Quarry Bank, depended on the grinding, sometimes-dangerous, 13 hours-a-day unpaid labour of pauper apprentices.

And one of them, it turned out, was Geoff Mayer's great-great-great grandfather, Joseph.

Geoff was surprised to realise that that impinged on his own feelings of right and wrong. It surprised him because he didn't think that he would really care. He certainly had no great-great-great grandson feelings towards Joseph Mayer, he thought.

Geoff phoned the mill museum's archive department the day after his visit, when he had first asked a member of the staff about his ancestor. They called Geoff back a few days later. The records had been well-kept, and they showed that Joseph had been taken on as a nine year-old pauper apprentice in 1805, and that he had come – as so many others had - from the Newcastle-under-Lyme workhouse in Staffordshire. He had lost a finger in an accident the same year.

That brought a mixture of feelings to Geoff. One feeling was embarrassment: his great-great-great grandfather was from the workhouse.

But he couldn't stop his mind dwelling on the thought of his own son, when he was nine.

Geoff had bought a book about the mill which told him that in the early nineteenth century the apprentices got no pay - they worked thirteen hours a day in return for just their board, lodgings, and clothing. They got up for work at 5.30 a.m. to be at the mill for six o'clock, they had ten minutes for breakfast and an hour for their midday meal, and they ate their tea while still working. They got back to their accommodation in the nearby Apprentice House at 8 p.m.

"How on earth could little children cope with that? How could anyone force children into it?" he asked himself indignantly.

It also told him that Samuel Greg was a benevolent employer, who cared for his apprentices rather better than most cotton mill owners of the time, making sure they were well-fed, clothed, and taught to read and write.

"Bloody hell!" he exclaimed aloud as he read it. "I should think that's the very least he could do...it was these poor children who were bringing him his wealth!"

"What on earth are you talking about?" asked Hanna, who had been busy reading the *Daily Mail*.

Geoff hadn't been keeping his wife up to date about his family history. She knew that he had walked to Styal to see the old mill, now a museum, but Geoff had found that she had been easily bored by his ancestors, and had told him that she didn't want to hear about them unless he came up with some that were members of the aristocracy.

But now he told her about Joseph.

"My God! Fancy having ancestors who were in the workhouse!" she reacted in the contemptuous tone that he had come to expect of late.

"What, honestly, is the point of working out your family history, if this is all you're finding?"

"Well first of all I find it interesting to know where I sprang from. And it will be of interest to David...maybe not now, but perhaps in the future, when he has his own family," said Geoff.

"If I were you I'd keep quiet about it, and give up the entire thing. Your family's history is only worthwhile back to your grandfather. At least he was a doctor. Before that they seem to have been the lowest of the low.

"Paupers in the workhouse! Just don't tell me any more. I'm beginning to wonder what sort of family I married into, all innocent, all those years ago.

"I'm just glad David doesn't take after you."

"OK, but you did ask. And in any case, high or low, they are the people I'm descended from...their genes are in me, I suppose."

"That's exactly why I'd keep quiet about it! If you know what's good for you, you'll let people think your family has always been on the upper side of middle class at least...that's the way to get on in life. Who's to know unless you tell them all this about paupers and peasants and bloody gardeners?"

"I'd say it shows staying-power and determination to get from the workhouse to the status we enjoy now," Geoff countered. "It's certainly better than the people who have been born with a silver spoon in their mouths and have managed to lose it all...many of the aristocratic families have had that happen to them."

"Well I'd say that it explains quite a lot about you," said Hanna tartly.

"What exactly do you mean by that?"

"Well, for instance, your failure to progress to senior management. You haven't exactly blazed your way forward in your airline career, have you?

"What I'm saying is that all this about your ancestors doesn't really surprise me – I've been convinced for a long time that you're simply not made of the right stuff to get to the top."

"And all this is from the fact that my ancestors were poor? I'd say it is more than a touch high-handed of you Hanna.

"What I find fascinating is the thought that I carry their genes...a mix from a great many different people way back in the past. We all do. You might just look exactly the same as one of your ancestors, just as some people closely resemble one of their parents or grandparents...you might *think* like one of your ancestors...who knows how far back it goes.

"You remember what I was saying about Darwin? He was the first person to realise that genes are passed from generation to generation. Now there's this amazing discovery of the way it works, in the shape of a double helix, with bonds linking the two spirals and infinite variations in the way they are linked...all carrying inherited characteristics from parent to child.

"Wouldn't it be wonderful if they could find, say, a happiness gene. Perhaps there's a kindness gene...or an anger gene. One day they might be able to find out why some people seem to be perpetually happy, and some are always angry.

"I'd like to understand it more. In a way it is a bit like discovering the innermost secrets of life."

Hanna was not impressed. "It doesn't alter the fact that most of your ancestors were low life...a gardener, a farm labourer and a cotton spinner were bad enough, but now it's workhouse paupers...and what I'm saying is that it shows sometimes.

"I accept that all families have a skeleton or two in the cupboard. But that's the best place to keep them...hidden in the cupboard.

"You keep on about how you're made from the genes of your ancestors...well, there you are: you're just not made of the right stuff, and that comes from not being from the right sort of family.

"Of course you can't help it. It's just the way it is. But you just don't have to tell anybody. Because quite frankly I find it embarrassing, and I wouldn't want any of our friends to know about it. Or anybody else who knows us, for that matter. God, we'd be laughing stocks! We do have a position to maintain, you know."

Geoff didn't know whether she was deliberately trying to irritate him or not. But he knew that she was certainly succeeding.

"Look, inherited characteristics can't be specific to actual behaviour. Our ancestors may have been criminals...so why aren't we?

"It might mean I'm tall or fat or have blue eyes or go bald. But it can't possibly mean that succeeding generations are carbon copies. That would mean that all brothers and sisters would be the same, and have the same way of thinking – and it's patently obvious that they are not.

"No. It can't be all that simple. Although I suppose the DNA principle must apply to the structure of the brain as much as any other part of the body.

"But I refuse to believe that every person doesn't have a choice as to how he or she behaves."

Hanna stuck by her guns: "All I'm saying is that you seem to have inherited your ancestors' inability to rise in the world, whether it's by genes or helixes. And bugger Darwin!"

Geoff knew he was getting nowhere with Hanna. But he knew for certain that whatever unwelcome facts he was finding about his ancestors, he was going to continue to pursue his search for them. He wanted to know what they did, and where they came from. And so would David, one day. Whatever Hanna said.

And he also knew, on the instant, that it was pointless to argue about it, because when Hanna made her mind up about something, it was useless to try to change it.

So he closed his book, walked over to the TV, and said: "Let's watch the news – it'll be on in a minute."

CHAPTER 30

1821

Marriage to Nell, Joe found, was the best thing that had ever happened to him. Making love to her was something he could not get enough of, almost up to when the baby was born. Nell had been taught to cook and sew when she had been in the apprentice house, and she made their little cottage in the village cosy and comfortable.

The baby was a boy. They called him Thomas – the name of Nell's father, as well as Joe's friend. It was a new world for both of them. But Nell had talked to other women. Two of them came to the cottage and helped with the birth. And Nell seemed to know how to look after the little thing. The baby's hands and feet fascinated Joe. "They're so small...yet perfect," he said with a quiet wonder when he first saw them.

His eyes met Nell's proud gaze. He smiled his impish smile: "How did you know how to make him?"

"Oh, we women know a thing or two that you men can't comprehend."

"I know that now," said Joe. "But do you know this: I love you lass - more than I can tell you."

"Yes. I know that too," she said. "But I also know that you'll have your work cut out in the next few weeks to help with things I can't manage in the house while I'm looking after our baby.

"And he'll cry to be fed in the night. So we'll both be tired all the time. Yet you'll have to work harder than ever to earn enough to keep us in food and fuel."

For Joe the very thought of his wife and baby was a spur to greater effort, tiredness or not.

At the end of his day's work at the mill he looked forward to the strange, milky smell inside their cottage. He didn't mind extra chores. At the end of the work he would sit by the fire, gazing as Nell suckled little Thomas. He'd tried calling him Tom, but Nell would have none of it. "His name is Thomas, and that's how he's going to be known," she said firmly. "Not Tom!"

Joe had taken to smoking a pipe. He'd seen other men with their pipes and looking contented with the world, and he liked the smell of the tobacco smoke. It seemed the right thing for when he and Nell sat by their fire at night. But it made him cough, even more than he normally did.

Nell was a good cook, and as she recovered from the baby's birth, she used her time at home to make sure Joe always had a tasty meal to greet him when he finished work.

The baby thrived too. They took him to be christened on the 29th of July 1821. "I'm a lucky chap," he told his friends at the mill. "I never knew what I was missing until I became a family man."

*

1826

Joe, now an overlooker at the mill, loved watching little Thomas as he began smiling, and gurgling with evident contentment, lying in his arms. He could see that Thomas was beginning to recognize things, handling and sucking at a little blanket that Nell had given him. He grew and began to crawl. Then he tried his first faltering steps just as he reached his first birthday.

It was a time of real joy to Joe, compounded six months later when Nell told him that she was going to have another baby. They looked forward to it with all the experience of the first baby behind them.

The new baby was a girl. They called her Ellen. She brought the same delight to Joe. Even when she was only a few weeks old he loved nothing more than to sit her on his knees, gently bouncing up a down, sometimes singing to her, and at other times talking to her, in proper

232

grow-up fashion, about matters, as he said, "of mutual interest to a man and his daughter."

For Nell life in their little cottage had become very busy, keeping an eye on Thomas as he dashed about, demanding constant attention, while she had to look to the needs of her new baby, at the same time preparing food, washing clothes and keeping the cottage clean. She had little time for rest.

When she did sit down she worried about how they could manage to care for their growing family on Joe's low mill wages. And she had one other big concern: Joe continued to cough. He gave up the pipe. But the cough got worse.

She had seen too many children in the apprentice house suffering from the coughing sickness. She knew that it could be a serious matter. The cough began to wrack Joe's frame. He grew pale and much thinner.

It was Thomas's fifth birthday when Joe began to cough blood.

His health declined rapidly, and he began gasping desperately for breath. His face ashen, he leaned back in his chair, and struggled to draw in the air. Nell kept a brave face. But secretly she cried the tears of a woman who fears the worst and knows that it is going to happen.

Work, of course, was out of the question. He grew worse. Nell insisted that he stay in bed. Every breath seemed a fight for survival.

Mr. Greg's Sick Club did bring in some money. Four agonised months later Joe breathed his last, a long, rasping, terrible breath, holding tightly to Nell's hand.

The Sick Club paid for his funeral. He was interred in the churchyard at St Bartholomew's, the parish church in Wilmslow. But his grave was not marked by any stone. So Joseph had no permanent memorial, no message of loving regret at his passing: there was no money for that nicety.

*

1827

Nell held Thomas's hand as she pushed the little home-made baby cart containing Ellen into the farm-yard. It had been a long walk from Styal to Ringway, and although it was only April, it was a warm day.

But Nell knew a thing or two about this farm. She knew the farmer's wife had died four months earlier. She talked to the Styal village women and as a source of information they had no equal - until you came to the next village!

Nell paused as she turned her back towards the house and opened the tie-ribbon at the neck of her shift.

She took off the little jacket, that matched her skirt, and put it in the baby carriage. She checked how far down the shift opened, where her ample bosoms could be glimpsed.

They walked up to the open farmhouse door and five year-old Thomas was allowed to knock on it. A dirty, untidy youth came to the door, and when Nell asked to see farmer Harper he pointed to some pigsties, where she could find him.

Half way across the yard Nell paused, and checked her shift again. She walked on then, and found the farmer, clad in a smock-frock, brushing one of the sties.

He seemed to be a man of about forty, solidly built, with the brown face of one who had spent his working life out of doors – nothing like the pale-faced mill people that she knew so well. But not as handsome as Joe, she thought.

His eyes swept down to the cleavage between her breasts as they stopped a couple of yards away from the sty wall. "I'm Nell Mayer," she said. "I'm recently widowed, and I need some vegetables, but I can't afford the village shop prices now. Can you let me have some potatoes and cabbage and carrots?

"I could pay for them by doing some housework for you. I know your wife died a little while back, and I know how you men are usually too busy to be able to keep the house proper.

"I'm a good cook. I could get your meals for you and your sons too, if you want. I'd have to have my children with me, but they wouldn't be any bother. It's so hot today, isn't it?"

She moved a few steps forward. Her shift moved in a way that transfixed farmer Harper. When he eventually raised his eyes to hers, he said: "Well, I don't know missus. P'raps we can discuss it over a cup of tea, and see what can be done."

They went into the farmhouse. Nell could see instantly that it needed cleaning. There were good brass pans and a brass kettle on a shelf in size order. She knew they must have been someone's pride and joy once, but their shine had gone. There were dirty pots piled up in the sink. And something didn't smell too good.

Farmer Harper put the kettle on to the kitchen fire and soon made a pot of tea. Then his sons were sent outside with Thomas and Ellen with instructions to show them the farm animals and keep them amused while the grow-ups talked.

After the children were outside he tried to put his hand on Nell's bottom, but she was having none of it. She gently moved away and sat down at the kitchen table.

An hour later she walked out, the newly employed live-in housekeeper to farmer Jack Harper and his two teenage sons.

*

1984

Geoff Mayer finished his paperwork, looked at his watch, and decided that as he was listed as standby crew, and there was no possibility of being called on to take a flight in the next couple of hours, he'd take a stroll in the passenger areas of the Manchester Airport terminal building.

235

When it had first been opened as an airport in 1938 it was called after its locality: Ringway. Now it had grown enormously, and had dropped its old name.

Geoff walked into the concourse, where he was always struck by the ludicrous giant chandeliers that hung from the ceiling. "Like rather tired udders," he recalled somebody remarking.

The idea seemed to have been to make an impression on everybody who saw them, and, at least, they did that. Whether it was the right impression was another matter, Geoff thought with a suppressed smile.

He wandered into the W.H.Smith shop and bought a Daily Telegraph, then went to the buffet, bought a coffee, and found a seat alongside the windows looking over the airfield.

Outside, the sun was glinting on half a dozen aircraft parked and in various stages of arrival, or of getting ready to load and go. Beyond the concrete apron, the taxiways and the grass of the airfield, with black hangars on the opposite side, were the hints of the greenery of the Cheshire countryside immediately to the south.

As he took in the pleasant prospect he was suddenly aware that somebody was sitting down on a seat on the other side of the small circular table on which he had placed his coffee.

Glancing up, he saw that it was a white-haired, very old man, who, having settled in to his seat, looked at Geoff and said: "It's a lovely view, isn't it – I never get tired of it."

The man didn't look like a passenger. There was no feeling of being ready to go aboard and take off about him.

"Do you come here often, then?" asked Geoff.

"Yes. I live fairly near, just down the road on Shadow Moss Road. I enjoy the walk to get here, and I enjoy watching the planes and people."

"Don't tell me you are an aircraft spotter," smiled Geoff.

The old man smiled back. "No. I wouldn't call myself that. But I've been involved in this place nearly all my life...and that's ninety years!"

Geoff was intrigued. "How have you been involved? It must have been just green fields ninety years ago. And incidentally, you don't look anything like that age."

"I was born in a cottage that stood on this land that is now the airfield, and it is where I grew up. It was all green fields when I was a boy. I worked on a farm on this very land from being about ten years old. My father was a farm labourer too.

"I worked on the farm until 1936 or 37 when the whole area was bought by Manchester Corporation to be made into the airport – over 600 acres of good farming land it was, too."

"So what did you do then? Was there work to be had elsewhere?"

"Well if you can't beat 'em, join 'em, I thought. So I came and got a job at the airport as a porter. And even during the war I stayed here through all the changes that have gone on, until I retired in 1959.

"Now I live with my daughter on the Wythenshawe council estate, and I can see the aircraft landing – in fact I can hardly miss them, they're so close to where we live.

"I suppose the aircraft must get into your blood. I must have seen thousands of them over the years, but I still can't help looking up whenever I see one, and watching them land or take off.

"There's something about them. They're so big and obviously heavy...yet off they bound into the sky and they're away to places all over the world...I still think it's something of a miracle."

"Yes, I suppose it is – although it's a long time since I thought of it that way," admitted Geoff.

"Who do you fly with?" asked the old man, looking at his uniform.

"I'm with Sunjet."

"That's one of the newer airlines. It didn't exist when I worked here."

"Well you said there had been some changes! But it must have been interesting to watch it all happen. Wasn't it a grass airfield at first?"

"Yes until during the war they realised that grass wouldn't take big aircraft in all conditions."

"You were living nearby during the war?"

237

"I was living in a cottage on the edge of the airfield. It was demolished years ago when the airport expanded."

"What flew from here during the war? There was no civil flying presumably."

"No. It was used by Avros at first – the Manchester bomber and then the Lancaster made their maiden flights from here. But the main thing was that it was Britain's first parachute training school.

"They brought thousands of very worried people here to learn how to jump out of aeroplanes. First they taught them in a hangar – how to land without damaging themselves. Then they took them up in a tethered balloon and that was their first parachute jump, here, on the airfield.

"Then they had a variety of aircraft that they flew from here over to Tatton Park just outside Knutsford where the troops made their first drops from planes...troops and spies, too. They brought them here, very hush-hush, and they had to learn how to parachute into German-occupied Europe, at night, I suppose. It must have been a terrifying experience for them, women as well as men."

"So a runway was built then?"

"Three runways were built, running in different directions, so the aircraft weren't grounded by cross-winds. Aircraft then all had tail-wheels. They were badly affected by cross-winds – even taxiing was a problem in strong winds. They sometimes had to have a couple of men sitting on the tail-plane to weigh it down until the aircraft was lined up for take-off."

"Then after the war it was just civil airline flying, I suppose."

"Not entirely. You should have been here in the 1950s and 60s! A company called Airwork had those hangars on the south side of the airfield, and they had a contract to service Sabre jets that were being moved from the American and Canadian air forces to the Greeks and the Turks, under a NATO contract I seem to remember. So Sabre jets were screaming around every day, taking off and landing in between the airliners.

"Then Airwork began servicing American B26 bombers, and they joined the mix. At the same time Fairey Aviation were building Gannets and Fireflies in their hangars on this side, and they were being test-flown. "Added to that, at weekends the Auxiliary RAF pilots based here were roaring around in Vampires and Meteors. They were very noisy jets, and they started early. Not many people round here slept late on Sundays.

"It was like Farnborough most days!"

"I had no idea...I'd have loved to have seen it then," said Geoff. "I was a lad then – and mad on aeroplanes. But I was away at school most of the time. When I came home for the holidays I spent most of the time with my father until he died in 1954. My mother had died when I was born."

"That is a terrible thing for you," said the old man. "I can't imagine how I'd have felt if I'd had to grow up without my mother – she was the centre of our family. She didn't have much, but she managed and fed us all – dad and me and my five brothers and sisters – and we never went hungry even though times were hard."

Geoff suddenly thought of his family history. "I've been working on my family tree. I had an ancestor who worked on a farm at Ringway," he said. "It was way back in the 1840s. His father had died and his mother remarried – to a man called Harper at Oakwood Farm. I don't suppose you knew that one, did you?"

"Oh yes, I remember Oakwood. It wasn't anybody called Harper lived there in my time, but I believe I've heard my father talk about them. It was his father who knew them when he was a lad.

"Ringway was all farms then. It was a country community, with its pub – the Romper – and St Mary's, the church - they're still there!

"But as for the rest, it's all history now...it's all gone. But I'm glad you're looking into your own family and who you came from. I think it is important that we all know something of those who were here before us. In my younger days it wasn't written down, but it was talked about.

"Nowadays I have the feeling that people move about so much from their origins that they just don't know or care. You keep up the good work!"

"Well you've told me a lot that I didn't know," said Geoff. "By the way, I'm Geoff Mayer. I'm the deputy flight manager for Sunjet. It's been really nice talking to you. But I must get back to my office."

He extended his hand, and shook that of the old man. "It's been nice meeting you," he told Geoff. "My name's Eric Perkins. All the porters and baggage loaders know me."

*

Later that day, back in his office overlooking the airfield, Geoff found himself musing on the chat with old Eric Perkins. Somehow it had seemed an almost tangible link with the times that his ancestors had known.

He had a tantalising feeling that his forbears were almost within touching distance.

For some reason I hadn't really connected this airport with the Ringway that Nell Harper and Thomas Mayer lived in. I know it was a long time ago. But I suppose it is quite likely that they walked on the very ground that I'm looking at now.

Strange that I earn my living, in a sense, from the same patch of earth where they earned theirs a hundred and fifty years ago.

It seemed to add a new dimension to both the airfield and the family history that Geoff had been slowly uncovering.

Of course all you can get is the names and the dates of when they were born, married and died – or at least christened, married and buried. That and their occupation if you're lucky. They are the bare facts on paper.

But they were real people, after all. I should always try to remember that. OK, so Thomas was only a farm labourer. But he lived out at least part of his life here.

The other thought that then came to Geoff hung on the unuttered thought: only a farm labourer.

Eric Perkins was only a farm labourer too, until the airport took all that away. But he was surprisingly articulate. He wasn't exactly the classic idea of the country yokel.

And Geoff had seemed able to talk so easily to this old man whom he didn't know. He had found himself warming towards Eric Perkins.

He had a good memory for the way things used to be, and yes...he had a sense of history, and how maybe we shouldn't forget the ways things were long before we were on the scene.

Maybe Thomas Mayer was a lot more than he seems. Looking at the records it seems as if nothing happened at all in his life.

What if he was alive to the world around him, like Eric Perkins obviously was? Maybe his life was full of excitement, even if he didn't travel the world as we do these days?

Excitement? Well, for a start, he'd have to meet a girl and court her and marry her. At that time, in anyone's life, it's an important time, and yes...exciting.

And he became a farmer in Knutsford. He was probably only a tenant, but where did he get the money to set up as a farmer? He couldn't have been paid a lot as a labourer in those days.

There's a heck of a lot that I don't know, and I suppose I never will.

The telephone rang. The present had caught up with Geoff. He found himself quite resenting it.

CHAPTER 31

1805

"Goodbye Joe. Goodbye. Wave to him, Martha. Let's wave 'til we can't see him no more. Look, he's waving back. Goodbye. Goodbye Joe."

"Why are you crying ma?"

Isabella Betton picked up her twenty-one month-old toddler and led the girls back inside the workhouse.

"I'm crying because I'm sad now your big brother's gone, and I know we'll all miss him, that's why."

"Where's he gone?"

"He's gone to be an apprentice in a place far away in Cheshire, so we won't see him for a very, very long time."

If ever, she thought.

"He'll be grown up when he comes back. He has to stay there 'til he's eighteen. Think of that...Joe a grown-up young man!"

"Will he be able to take us for walks to see the lambs and the flowers in the fields, like you said?"

"Well yes, but you'll be quite grown up too, you know, by then. You're six now. You'll be fifteen and even little Ann will be turned ten. Maybe you'll both be apprentices too by then."

"What's an apprentice?"

"It means you have to go away from here to learn a trade, so you'll be able to earn enough money to buy food and have your own house and your own children when you grow up."

"Where will we have to go?"

"Will you come too?

"I don't want to go by myself.

"I don't want to be sent away.

"Ma, don't let them send me to be a prentice.

"I want to stay here with you and Ann."

Martha's questions and pleadings seemed to be never-ending. Then there were tears. They continued as her mother took her two daughters into the workhouse, its door clanging shut against the outside world and its freedom.

For only a little time had been allowed for them to say goodbye to nine year-old Joe. Now Isabella was required to return to the laundry to get back to work, endlessly washing clothes and bed-linen.

Martha had to work too. She had already been shown how to spin wool. Now she joined all the other young children who lived in the workhouse – three-quarters of the total – in doing so, with varying degrees of success, under the stern discipline of Mrs. Hugget.

Mrs. Hugget was not unkind. But she knew that the latest thinking was that harsh conditions now might persuade these children, when they grew up, that hard work for little pay *outside* a workhouse was infinitely better than hard work for hard lodgings and meagre diet *inside* the walls.

It wasn't necessarily true, but for the parish rate-payers and the overseers who were answerable to them it was cheaper for the parish if families slowly starved in their own homes.

For the family, as for all the inmates, the work was how they paid for the accommodation and food provided by the Newcastle-under-Lyme Workhouse.

Working in the laundry was hard, and wearying, but the washing and putting up to dry and folding and ironing to the background chit-chat of the other women, and the laughter that kept breaking out despite the miserable conditions, kept Isabella's mind occupied until, by evening, supper finished and her little girls now asleep, she could lie on her bed and give way to her despair.

Yet, even as she silently wept at the knowledge that she was never likely to see her lovely son Joe again, and that her girls would all too soon be sent away too, there was a feeling that she had given them a chance in life – with luck they might have better than had been her lot.

243

Lying there, listening to the snores of other women, many of them much older than herself, Isabella couldn't help thinking about how her life had turned out.

Life in the workhouse might be hard and nasty, but at least she had escaped her past. Well...almost.

I never wanted to be a whore. It was a nasty way of life. Not just the men having their way. It was having to pick their pockets, nick their money. Because men could be dangerous once they found that you'd robbed them.

Mind you, I was never badly hurt...just punched and kicked a few times.

For two years I was never taken before the justices. I knew that would mean a death sentence. Or transportation to Carolina if you were lucky. Although from what I've heard there wasn't much to feel lucky about if you were sent there.

Then I *was* caught - red-handed - and I knew I'd hang for sure. So once I escaped from Newgate I couldn't stay in London.

I was only in that stinking, filthy dungeon for a few hours. I'd only been there a few minutes before a woman told me I was young and pretty and I'd have the men prisoners queuing up for me, and she'd look after me and the money I'd make.

I felt a despair so deep that I felt death would be better. But I was so scared of dying. My, was I scared! It made me think about things in a way I'd never done before.

That's what really made me decide if I could get away I would never go back. Because I could see clear as daylight that that way of life might have its excitements, but it never had made me any better off...and it never was going to.

Suddenly I was sick and tired of the dirt and the stink and the pick-pocketing and thieving.

It was no good being tired of being a street woman because that was not going to change – and, to be honest, it still hasn't, in a way. Back in London it was the only way I could live. And it still is, if I'm honest.

Dan gave me some of the money, true. But not much. It's obvious really. I can see that now. He wouldn't have wanted me to have become well-off so I wouldn't want to go to work every day. I was his means of eating and drinking and enjoying himself.

The thing was that I really saw him as a loving father...well, a step-father...at first. When he started to have me in his bed I was daft enough to think that he loved me. I've got to admit he taught me a lot.

It took being put in Newgate to see that all I was to him was a sort of work-slave, taking all the risks, running all the dangers of arrest and disease and pregnancy.

He did care for me. Like a farmer would care for his horses and his cows, only because he needs them to bring in his money.

But he was smart. Where did he learn all the tricks?

From somebody else, I suppose. Just like I learned the tricks of pick-pocketing. And whoring: he was a good teacher, considering he had never been one!

My mother would have been proud of me. She must have been a good whore. She was smart too. A real professional. Just like her mother before her, she told me.

I come from a family of whores.

The stealing was new. Now that was the hard thing to learn. Picking pockets ain't easy. And if you're caught, well you could end up dead. And I was caught all right.

Did I do right to run away from London? It's terrible here, but at least the law can't find me.

*

Isabella found it easier to think back over her life than to lie for hours, trying to make herself go to sleep. Sleep never came easily to her.

She felt safe when she took up with Ernie Betton. He really did care for her and he looked after her. All he wanted in return was her company, the chance to satisfy his needs, and something to eat.

It hadn't started out like that. He was just a customer who paid to have a few minutes of pleasure in a dark alleyway.

But afterwards, instead of making off without so much as a goodbye, he put his arm round her, and talked to her. He asked her where she lived, and could he see her again next week.

She told him she needed money to look after her baby, who she'd left alone in her lodgings. And he said, after only a moment's hesitation, that she could move in to live rent-free at his house. He told her his wife had died nearly two years before. He said he'd enjoy some company. Perhaps she could cook for him in return.

Above all he probably wanted the pleasure free, too!

She told him her small baby might keep him awake with his crying. But he said it was all the more important that she should have a decent place to stay, and a bed to sleep in.

She knew he'd want something more from her: they all did. But she went with him to his terraced house in Newcastle-under-Lyme after picking up her sleeping baby, wrapped up in his shawl. She had to find somewhere to live, for her baby's sake. I can always leave if things start happening that I don't like, she reasoned.

But nothing bad did happen. And she stayed with Ernie. She knew that she was just a substitute for his wife. But that didn't matter. He treated her with kindness, and, yes...could you believe it...love. Of all things to find in this God forsaken place, love!

And he loved Joe too. He actually liked babies, he told her. He was a rough working man, but he had a tender nature. He liked making Joe gurgle with pleasure as he swung him up in the air and down again. And Ernie looked after Joe when she went out.

At first she had slept downstairs in the front room, with little Joe in a basket that Ernie had found for the purpose.

Each evening, after dark, she went out to seek a customer of two in the public houses. She had to have money to buy food. She offered money to Ernie.

But instead of just taking it, as she had expected, he had a long talk with her. He told her he wanted her to give up the game, and to move into his bed. He earned enough money for them both to live on, and he very much wanted her to himself, for as long as she wanted to stay, and no longer. She could leave whenever she wanted.

What did he want in return?

Just your company, your warmth, he told her. I love to have love with you, you know that already. I've really taken to you and little Joe. I lay in bed last night, and I thought how empty this house and my life would be without you.

"I couldn't stand the thought of it. So I'm asking you to stay and be my wife if you will, but to stay anyway, if you won't marry me."

CHAPTER 32

1805

Marriage was something Isabella Mayer had not seriously thought about since she was a girl. And that seemed a long time ago. Seemed? It *was* a long time!

Let me see now...how long? Well I was only fifteen when the Marshall got me, and I was locked up in Newgate.

I'd always been cocky about never being caught. Dan had always told me that he'd be on hand to take the goods off me and get them to the receiver so fast that if the City Marshall himself came to arrest me within two minutes, there wouldn't be nothing to find on me – no evidence! And no evidence meant no charge – that's what Dan told me, time and time again he told me.

Only this time he wasn't there to take the goods away. And the Marshall and his men did come, and found I had the gentleman's pocket watch.

It wouldn't have been so bad if it had been a buttock and twang job. The man was a regular toff, and he probably wouldn't have dared to have me charged if he'd have had to face standing up in court and admitting that he'd been caught with his breeches down with a common prostitute, and that's how I'd been able to steal his watch.

But I had foolishly taken the opportunity to nick it when he stopped me and asked directions. He told me he was in a terrible rush, so I should have known that as soon as he stepped away from me he'd want to check the time.

He turned and caught hold of me before I could make myself scarce, and the Marshall heard his shouts for help because by a stroke of bad luck he was just round the corner, and he was there within moments.

He told the Marshall what had happened, and because it was early and I hadn't had no customers yet, it was very easy for the Marshall to personally check that what the man said was true – he'd only asked me directions and nothing more.

He checked me personally and very thoroughly, while his men held me...and them asking if they could have a check too, after him, the cheeky sods!

Anyway, that was in 1780...June, I'm pretty certain. I'll never forget that night. The clerk at the prison read the out the charge to me.

I was terrified, I'll admit it. And the stink inside the prison was horrible – even worse than it always is in the streets round Newgate. I felt I couldn't breathe properly. I cried. I pleaded with them to let me go, I was only fifteen, and I'd never do anything wrong again. I said I'd let them do anything they wanted with me, free, if they'd let me go.

But they threw me into Newgate, and they told me I'd hang, for sure.

I'd seen a lot of hangings at Tyburn...I'd been there lots of times. It's all like a carnival at first. Men facing hanging are usually drunk, so they're all bravado...laughing and pretending they're not frightened...taking more drink and promising to pay their turn on the way back! You had to laugh.

And even when the noose went round their necks, they still fooled...bowing to the hangman...waving to the crowd of people.

But when they were hanging by the neck...when they were kicking and going purple and messing themselves and struggling, for a long time sometimes...so long that their wives and or husbands or other people pulled on their legs to try to kill them and end their agony...it wasn't funny no more.

Thinking about me being there at Tyburn and that happening to me terrified me, I admit it. And they kept saying I shouldn't worry, I wouldn't be in jail for long...I'd be tried and hanging as fast as they could arrange it. They kept laughing about it...it was so funny, they thought!

I probably would have been hanged, too, but that very night there was that riot and the jail was burned down. I got away, like lots of others.

But when I got home to Dan he told me to get away from him – he wasn't going to be charged with hiding a prisoner who'd escaped in the riots. Hundreds of people had been killed...something to do with a Lord Gordon and protests against Catholics, I remember him saying. They were hunting for the rioters and the escaped prisoners, and anybody that harboured them. And home was the first place they'd come, wasn't it.

He yelled at me that he wasn't going to hang for what I'd done. He kicked me out and shouted after me not to come back...ever.

I know that was 1780. It's 1805 now. My God, that's twenty-five years! I must be...let me see...God! I'm more than forty now, I suppose.

After Ernie talked to me about living with him I remember thinking perhaps I should get wed now. I don't suppose I'll ever get the chance again, I thought.

And Ernie was a good man. It was Ernie who insisted that I must take Joe to the parish church to be christened. It was his proper right to be brought up as a Christian, he told me. It is important, he said. It would be wrong to exclude him from heaven at some time in the future just because I had neglected to take him to be baptised.

It surprised Isabella to hear Ernie talking like that. She was not used to men who cared for such niceties. He had hidden depths of thoughtfulness.

I've seen prettier men, and he is rough, that's true, I remember thinking. But he works hard and earns his wages. And in his way I think he loves me. Imagine that! It doesn't mean very much, perhaps. Except that he treats me well.

I thought: he's kind. And he treats Joseph well too. When will I find his like again?

*

So Ernie and Isabella Mayer were married. At the church they did not even have a witness, until the verger stepped in. It was not unusual for him...marriages came in all sorts.

They had left Joseph in the care of Ernie's next door neighbour, an elderly widow.

Isabella gave her address as the house next door, as she had for the reading of the banns. There were no problems. They put her down in the parish register as "sojourner,"

And she found that there were few problems after the ceremony. Living with Ernie was easy. Finding herself an ordinary wife of an ordinary working man in a dull midland town took some mental adjustment, certainly. And Ernie's wages were barely adequate to keep the household in food and other necessaries.

She was aware of the undercurrents of questioning in the minds of other women who lived in the street. Who and what was this woman, who spoke so strangely, and who suddenly appeared with a baby, lived with Ernie Betton, then married him. He'd told neighbours that she was a widow who came as a lodger in his spare room until they got married.

"Oh yes! I've heard that one before. She doesn't come from these parts, nor anywhere near here, anyone can tell that from the way she speaks.

"She's not what she seems, mark my words."

"Wouldn't surprise me if she was nothing better than a prostitute."

"Well she's married Ernie Betton...I feel sorry for anybody that does that. He's a real ugly man. If nothing else is wrong with her, I'll tell you what...her eyesight can't be any good!"

But Isabella was not worried by the cackling women. Suddenly she was legitimate, even if Joseph wasn't. God only knew which of her customers had given her Joe. She didn't know why she had decided to keep him and feed him and love him...she only knew that from the moment she'd known she was pregnant, she was sure she wanted him. Her first baby had died. There was nothing unusual about that. It happened all the time.

The woman who had helped her had said that it couldn't breathe, properly. She'd died because she couldn't breathe, you see. She'd been told that it was best she didn't see it dead. The woman had taken good care of it.

Isabella remembered she had cried at first, but she soon got over it. She was only fourteen. Things seem different when you are young. That baby had taken so long to be born, and it had hurt so much.

Like a lot of other girls, she had gone to the workhouse to have the baby. It was the only real help you could get. Workhouses were different then, though. People were quite kind. And sometimes the parish would send a girl's unwanted baby to be nursed in the country – there were women who would feed babies for a fee.

*

She took a job cleaning at a pub in the mornings. She enjoyed making Ernie happy. And less than three years later she had his child, a girl. They called her Martha. It sealed the marriage and Ernie was a happy man.

Despite her initial fears and worries about how she would cope with living a humdrum life in an ordinary and none-too-attractive town in what she now found was called the Black Country, Isabella was content too.

She wouldn't have believed it herself, but she loved being a mother, looking after the little, helpless things, watching them grow and respond to her; and to watch as they started to crawl, and then learn to walk and begin to talk. Above all, she loved talking to Joe, and then Martha as she grew, watching them become little people in their own right, with their own ways and thoughts.

More than three years after the birth of Martha, Isabella found she was pregnant again. Then, two months before the baby was due, a man came and told her that Ernie had been killed in an accident at the brickyard where he worked.

It was sudden, brutal, and Isabella's new world crashed down around her in an instant, like the bricks that had killed Ernie.

*

1805

Her job at the pub would not pay the rent on the two-bedroom terraced house which had been their home.

There was no money put by. She was going to have to get out within a week.

There was only one place to go: the workhouse.

She did not expect there to be a problem – most people didn't want to go in until they became too old to work and support themselves, or they had fallen on hard times due to the loss of a husband to support a woman with small children. For Isabella it was all there was.

But she found that as a person with no residential status in her own right, not having been born in the parish, and having no settlement certificate, questions were asked, and entry to the workhouse was by no means certain.

A settlement certificate was the one important document for anybody moving to live outside the parish in which they had been born. It was in effect a guarantee that your birth parish would take you back if you were unable to support yourself - another parish obviously would not want to take on the expense.

No settlement certificate? Right we'll escort you out of the parish...you're no concern of ours. On your way!

Living in the workhouse was an expense on the parish, and its ratepayers, and Isabella obviously came from somewhere else. Where was her settlement certificate?

I have the right of settlement here because I was married to a local man.

No. Ernest Betton was not born here. You must instantly leave the parish. You have no right to be here. Go back to where you were born, or find out where your husband was born...that parish might take you.

Isabella pleaded that she was heavily pregnant and could not make any journey. She had no money, and her two children would be in danger with no chance of getting food and shelter on the way.

"I am a pauper. I have nothing. Do not turn me away!"

In despair, when she found she was getting nowhere with the parish overseers, she went to see the parson who had married her and Ernie, to plead her case.

He simply repeated what she had already been told – she had admitted when she married Ernest Betton that she was from the parish of St. Sepulchre in London, which must now take on the cost of caring for her and her children – that was the law.

But I have no-one there...I haven't lived in London since I was young and I have no family or friends there. I have worked here in Castle as a cleaner for nine years. That gives me a right of settlement. I was married to a man who lived in this parish for years and years. My son and daughter were born here – you christened them yourself! So they have a right to stay. And my unborn baby's father was settled here – surely my new babe when it is born, will have a right to stay.

"Your new baby can stay here if it is born here and if it lives. We can put it out to nurse. The older girl can stay too...here in the workhouse. And your bastard son. They were all born here. But you must leave this parish."

But these infants cannot stay without me!

"You must leave this parish. I know the churchwardens will insist on it. You might have had some grounds for settlement, but there is talk of your being a woman of easy virtue. They say you were a prostitute. If this is the case you can not stay in this parish. I am sorry. That is the law!"

It would be murder to turn us away from this parish with nowhere to go!

She felt defiance rising within her. "Not only that, it would surely be unchristian, settlement certificate or not!"

But the desperate position for herself, her children, and her unborn child, was becoming terribly clear. Isabella sank to her knees in front of the clergyman. Please, your reverence! You must let us stay together in the workhouse! We will die if you do not...it will be murder to turn us away. You must see that I am telling the truth!

Her plea was met with silence. The vicar stood like a stone. It was like pleading to God. Like God's, his word, or lack of it, carried the power of life or death.

He placed his hand upon her head and gently stoked her hair, as in sympathy, for he was a caring man: but to Isabella his gesture seemed like a final, funereal blessing on her misfortune.

Suddenly Isabella felt angry. He was not a statue. He was not God. He was a man. All her years of experience had taught her about men. She knew that a woman, in an attitude of supplication and weakness can be an appealing thing to a man.

As she knelt his manhood was at her eye level. She reached round his legs and pulled herself to him. Now he would repel her, command her to cease such profanity. She expected to be repelled. But he made no move, uttered no sound.

Isabella had been a whore for a long time. She had many skills. It took her little time to make the reverend minister change his mind.

*

He stroked her hair. But it was different now. I'll see what I can do about letting you stay in Newcastle. Your husband lived and worked here for a good many years. I think we can say he had established himself as a permanent resident...his widow should be able to stay, especially as she has young children who were born here.

He talked as if he had thought it all out for himself.

I could be your housekeeper, she had said.

No! It might be seen as scandalous, and I could never allow that.

But I am sure I can find a place for you at the workhouse. I will make sure you are well treated there. It is a very good workhouse.

But you will need to be seen to be taking religious instruction. Once a week, I think would be right.

Each week, mind, you must come to me at the rectory for...for...instruction. Each week. And I will see what I can do for you.

So they went to live in the workhouse. And Isabella, who had tried so hard to be an ordinary housewife, an ordinary mother, was a whore again.

CHAPTER 33

1807

Lying there in the cold darkness of the workhouse night, Isabella knew that safety there would not be for ever. Ann was only four, true, but how long would her "arrangement" with the vicar last?

When Ann was nine or ten she would be taken away to be an apprentice – God knows where. Martha is nearly eight now. Two years more at the most for her to be with me.

But if they are lucky they might learn a trade, my girls. They might grow to be skilled, so they can earn their keep. They might stay pretty, and marry a good man. They might.

Well I may be a whore, but I've given them a chance, at least. I can do no more. I wonder how Joseph is faring? How I miss my Joe. I wish I could see him now – but I don't expect I ever shall.

He was cheeky, and sharp as a knife. I loved him so much. I'm sure he'll come back and find me if ever he gets a chance...and if I'm still here.

Newcastle is an ugly place. But no uglier than London. I was so glad to get away from there, and I don't want ever to go back.

Of course some places in London were beautiful, but not where we lived! And anyway if they ever find me, an escaped prisoner, I'm sure to hang...and all for a pocket watch.

I bet that man I stole it from could afford another watch, too. You could tell from the way he was dressed.

In London there were lots of rich people...still are, I shouldn't wonder. But for the likes of me, no matter how hard you work, even if it's proper, legal work like tradesmen or skilled people like weavers...we never get any better off.

I don't know how all the rich people ever get rich in the first place. But if you are well-off, I suppose London is the place to be. Big houses, carriages, theatres and coffee houses and clubs and shops where they buy expensive things...the ladies wear such beautiful dresses! And such hats! And jewellery!

All people like me can do is to look at it all and wonder how we can nick some of it off them.

Well that's all in the past as far as I'm concerned. I got away from that. Only by being on the game, though. You can be on the game *and* live in some nice places. Now...what was that first place where I ended up...Portsmouth! That's it. It was the first time I'd ever seen the sea! Now that *was* a place for a girl like me.

Trade was good there, I should say so! Matelots home from the sea, with money in their pockets – and all they wanted was drink and women. Boat after boat coming into port, sailors galore, and their wages in their pockets. It was non-stop alright.

Pity that customer of mine got into a fight. He was taken off to the court, and I was lucky not to be dragged off with him.

And he had the cheek to blame me for the fight...just because I showed my ankle to another sailor who was giving me the look. It was just fun. Me and my friend Molly used to have a lot of fun. We were always laughing in those days.

Anyway it was wise to get out of town before my matelot got out of the lockup. His mates told me he was likely to be vicious and they said he would come after me with his knife.

That's when Moll and me went to Bristol. Another good town. More sailors! And they sure were starved of what women can give them – even more than the matelots coming into Portsmouth, I reckon. I should be rich, all the hard work I had there!

Molly said the Bristol men were so ardent that she even enjoyed it with one or two of them. She was a card, though. There's lots of seamen in Bristol, she kept saying. I didn't get the joke at first, and that made Moll giggle all the more. I'd never heard it called that!

It was Molly that had to get out of Bristol, though, in the end. She nicked one sailor's cash when he was asleep, and crept away with it.

It was one of his mates that warned me that he was on the lookout for her, and she wouldn't live long if he caught her. Some people have a nasty streak, and the sailor she'd robbed was one.

So we decided to leave. Molly had been told about this place up north where there were iron-men. And money. It sounded the place to set up in our business, alright...and Moll liked the sound of iron men!

How to get there, that was the question. We didn't fancy walking. Then we heard that you could get there by boat – there were plenty of them sailing up the River Severn.

It was true, and we didn't have any difficulty getting the men to give us a ride...as long as we gave them one too! That's how we paid for our journey.

My, we had some fun with those boat-men, rough as they were. And the travelling was so smooth.

But it was funny...something happened to me on that journey. I don't know whether it was the countryside that we sailed through, or what. It certainly was beautiful. We stopped in some places I'd never heard of. Gloucester was the biggest. Quite a town it was – that's where we left that boat and got on another.

But it was the hills, and the fields and the forests and little cottages lost in the greenery that I couldn't take my eyes off. The weather happened to be good, and I could sit on the top of the boat in the sunshine and watch it all slowly passing by.

I think that was the first time in my life I'd ever envied folks that lived in those little cottages, so far away from crowded places and terrible, angry people.

I bet they never had to worry about the law catching up with them. Or vicious cut-throats out to get them. Or anything except looking after themselves and caring for their children as they watched them grow healthy and strong. That's what I thought.

It was daft. Here's me, brought up to the kind of life that I've had, carefree despite the dangers...until the law caught up with me, that is. A

259

business girl you might say. Definitely not a housewife and mother. Never that. Then, suddenly, that's what I find myself hankering for.

Not only that...I'm a city girl...always have been...and I'm thinking that what I'd like is a cottage in the country, miles from anywhere.

Why? Search me! But that's how I felt. All of a sudden: me! Thinking about living in the country doing nothing but look after children. Blessed if I could say why I suddenly got these thoughts. All I know is that I did.

One of the barge men, Sam, was real nice to me – he talked to me and told me things. He told me what places we were passing, and he told me about the goods the boats were carrying.

He was such a nice man. He wasn't always wanting me to lie down with him, like some did; perhaps he was too old to want it, although I've known lots of men who were a lot older, and it didn't seem to be a hindrance to them! In fact it's the older men who are keener than most...I suppose their wives aren't interested any more.

He smoked a pipe. Smelt nice. And he seemed to like talking to me. I suppose he was like a father would be. Mind you, I don't know much about fathers coz I never had one. Maybe he never had a daughter, and really wanted one.

He told me the boat was taking iron ore from the Forest of Dean to that place with that long name...Coalbrookdale.

I'd never heard of it, but he said there was great employment there, with good wages for the tough men who worked in the forges and blast furnaces. And that is where we'd find the iron men.

Suddenly Sam put his hand on my arm. I won't forget what he said: "You're not a skittish young 'un any more, you know Isabella – you might do worse than find a young feller there who'd marry you and look after you and give you a home to rear some youngsters in.

"You can't keep on in your line of work for ever. I know it's not my place to say so, but you should think about it, you know."

In Coalbrookdale it seemed that some wealthy man called Darby had invented a new way of making iron. They'd even made a new bridge, the first to be made only of iron, across a great gorge where the River Severn flowed through.

The new ways were cheaper, and it was driving foreign iron out of the market. It meant more work for Englishmen.

He said there was noise and smoke everywhere, and the sky was sometimes turned red by the glow from the furnaces and forges...a lot of people were going there just to see the picturesque prospect.

They were making all sorts of things from iron. He said it was a sight to see.

And when we eventually got there, it was as Sam had said. First, the bridge over the gorge was not like any bridge I'd ever seen before.

I'd expected it to be ugly, being made or iron. But it was a beautiful thing to see. It wasn't solid. It didn't look strong enough to stand any great weight. It looked too fragile. But somehow you could tell – I don't know how - that it had a hidden strength.

There was smoke pouring from dozens of tall chimneys, and strange buildings with red heat and steam where the iron was made. Inside it was so hot that men drank beer all day and never got drunk – it was all sweated out. So Sam said.

And when they finished work in the forges and furnaces they moved into the pubs and drank some more. Big, muscular men. For Molly and me this was what we'd come for. Business was good. The iron men weren't as eager as the matelots, but they were still keen enough once they'd taken the hint.

CHAPTER 34

1807

Life was good there for two years and more. We were enjoying ourselves no end.

When I realised I was pregnant of course I told Molly. "There'll be someone who can help you to get rid of it," I remember her saying.

And I remember her shocked look when I took a deep breath and told her I intended to keep the baby.

"Yes, there's always some women who can't have children of their own who'll adopt a healthy baby," she said.

"No. I don't just mean I am going to keep the baby till it's born. I mean I am keeping the baby always, Moll. I want to have a child and I want to love it and feed it from my own breast, and nurse it and care for it and watch it grow and love me.

"That's what I want. That's what I'm going to do. I've thought about it over and over. I don't know how I'll manage, but I'm going to do it somehow."

It was strange. Molly stopped being surprised and became delighted at what I'd said. I hadn't expected her to be so, but she was. She threw her arms round me and hugged me and said she was pleased.

And she got excited as she thought about it. I'll always remember how excited she got. We'd been friends for so long. She told me she would stay by me and help me, and we'd live together, two women and their own child, with her working to bring in the money we'd need and me at home nursing the baby.

I'd never thought of such an idea, but I was so happy and relieved. I told Molly I loved her. We were like young lovers, to be honest – heads in the clouds, so full of new thoughts and things to talk about.

As the days and weeks went by it filled our thoughts. We talked and talked about it, and made plans about where we'd live and how we'd manage. I was all new to us. It was a wonderful, exciting time. I became big as a balloon, Molly said, but somehow I didn't mind. I was just looking forward to having my own baby, very soon now.

Then Molly disappeared.

I wasn't worried at first – being out all night was quite an ordinary thing. Even two nights, if the customer was keen and had a bit of money.

But I did start to worry about her when three nights had gone by and she still hadn't appeared. I started to ask people if they'd seen her, but nobody had.

I kept thinking she might have struck lucky and gone off with some wealthy man who had a big house a few miles off, and couldn't bear to let her go...sometimes we girls have that effect on men who have such a good time with us that they think they're in love, and they want us to stay with them.

It was a week before someone told me a woman had been found drowned in the river three miles away. I knew straight away that it was Molly.

I had to go and see if it *was* her. I got a ride on a boat going that way. And of course it was poor Molly. It was terrible. My best friend in all the world, lying there, cold as ice, and so pale and dead.

I walked back to our lodgings, and I cried all the way. Nobody knew how she'd come to be drowned. Might have been an accident, falling in the river - we'll never know. That's what the man said where she was lying in a boathouse on the river bank.

But as I walked back home I kept thinking about those men, out to get her. Had they caught up with her? Would they be looking for me next?

I knew I couldn't stay there. I had to get away fast. There was my baby to protect. I could feel her moving inside me. Nobody was going to kill me.

So I packed my few belongings into a bag and left before daylight next day, saying nothing to anybody. Yes, I was scared all right: scared and lonely and sad, all together.

But I had an idea where I wanted to go. I had seen some beautiful crockery made in a place called Etruria by a man called Josiah Wedgewood. I was told he was getting quite a reputation for his pottery.

I had seen them in a shop in Coalbrookdale and they were the loveliest things I'd ever seen...so delicate and pretty. I had never seen their like.

I had made up my mind to save some money for a change so I could buy one of those plates. I really wanted it.

I wanted more than that really. I wanted to have a home where I could put it – a home I could call my own, and I could ask my friends to come to tea and to admire my baby. It was a strange longing for me to have, I'll admit. I don't know where such a feeling came from.

Anyway it had made me start to put some money aside. I'd never done so before. Earn it – spend it...that had been my way.

But now I had a feeling that I needed to save for things I needed. There was the pottery, of course. But there were the other things I had begun to think about...a home I could call my own...a baby...it would all need money.

At that time I'd been earning enough to live on and I began putting some in a secret place in the bag I had used for my clothes when we had moved from Bristol. Now I knew I might need that little hoard of mine.

I had asked about Etruria - such a strange, kind of foreign name. It sounded wonderful. I was told it was not far from a town called Stoke, north of Stafford. So now I made up my mind to find Etruria...I just wanted to see for myself the place where Josiah Wedgewood was making his beautiful tea-sets.

And now I had to make myself scarce. I knew it was a long way. But the way I was feeling about Molly being drowned, I wanted to be a long way away from Coalbrookdale.

I set out on foot early in the morning. I didn't want anybody to know which direction I took. I walked all day. I went through a place called Shifnal and then got on a road that was called Watling Street – so an old woman told me.

That night I slept in a wood, on a dry area under some bushes. I didn't like it, and it was uncomfortable and cold. But it was the fear of being hunted by whoever had drowned Molly that made me determined. I was sure she had been murdered. I wasn't going to be next - me and my baby - not if I could help it!

But the next day my feet hurt so much that I could hardly walk. I was hobbling painfully when a man in a cart asked me if I wanted a ride. At first I was afraid that he might be from Coalbrookdale and he might be looking for me.

But he kept calling me "missus" so I knew that he didn't know anything about me. He told me he was taking some goods to Stafford. He took me all the way there.

He was a nice, kind man. But I didn't tell him where I was going. Just in case he met somebody who was trying to find me. I told him my husband was a sailor who'd gone off down the river Severn, but I knew his ship would be going to places on the east coast, so I was determined to find him there.

"Well the east coast is a big place missus," he said. "I wish you luck."

The next day I walked to a place called Stone. I was weary. I found a lodging house where I could eat and sleep in comfort. And I felt safe. Nobody knew where I had come from, nor where I was going.

But I was lucky. There was a carter staying at the lodging house who was going to a place he called Castle which he said was near Stoke. I told him I was walking that way. He said I shouldn't be walking that far in my condition, and I could ride on his cart. He said he'd be glad of the company.

That's how I came to be in Newcastle. Newcastle under Lyme – that's its real name. But round here people call it Castle. The big trade is hat making.

I was wondering where to go next when I felt the baby start to come. The pains started to come quickly. A woman came out of a tavern and saw me. She was the wife of the landlord, and she took me inside and helped me when the baby came on the floor of her back parlour.

God, it hurt! But I had beautiful baby boy! All along I thought it would be a girl. Until the last few days. Then I knew it would be a boy – don't ask me why. And he was so lovely! He was perfect, with all the right numbers of little pink fingers and toes, and quite a lot of black hair. The woman was so good to me...it was funny, she was almost as proud as I was.

What are you going to call him? "Joe. It was his father's name."

It was a moment's decision. I just liked the name. My husband is dead. I was making my way north to find my husband's family in Manchester. That's what I told her.

She let me stay for ten days. She wouldn't take no money. She gave me a blanket to wrap the baby in. And I walked out into the wide world, with nowhere to go.

I still had some money, so I found a cheap place to stay in the town, and for a month I just looked after my little baby. Joe. Joseph. Joseph Mayer. He'd have a fine name when he grew up. He didn't cry much. My milk came easily. He was everything I wanted.

But I knew that I had to get more money. I had to get back to work. I went back on to the streets, leaving Joe in my lodgings, usually. There were men with money in their pockets and there were beer houses.

Put them together and they'd emerge with women on their minds...it is a well-known fact. And there I was, ready to help!

I needed the money. So I went into business in Castle. That's how I met Ernie. Dear, sweet, Ernie. It's true he was no oil painting. In fact he was ugly to look at. But he was kind, and caring, and loving – that was something special. To me, he was beautiful.

He's a good memory. So is Joe. I had him for nine years. He was a lovely boy. Everybody said so. Especially me! He has gone now. But I know he'll have a good life. I know he will. But now it's my girls I have to think about.

When sleep came Isabella was still thinking about them.

*

1807

"Goodbye, Joe," that's what we called after him, me and my two little girls. He looked so brave, as he left us, riding on the cart, to be an apprentice in a cotton mill up north, in Cheshire.

Well, it isn't all that far away. Perhaps we will see him again, some day. He's eleven now.

I can't bear to think how sad it made me to see him go. I had one baby before him. I was only 14 then. I'll never forget it. I was frightened. The pain was terrible...a lot worse than my mother had told me. The baby wouldn't come out, not for hours and hours. It hurt so bad. I cried and I screamed, but this woman told me it wouldn't help. I thought I was going to die. I really did.

Isabella lay on her bed in the workhouse and remembered. A whole day and a night it took, before she was born. A girl. She. They took her away so I could sleep.

When I woke up they told me the baby was dead. I was glad, and that's the honest truth. I was younger...not much more than a girl myself with that first one. I never really thought of it as a person. I never wanted squawking babies. I'd seen lots of them...they were hard work...all that looking after them that it took.

I didn't want that: not me!

But Joe was different. Through her pregnancy she had felt a strange need. What was growing within her was not just a baby – but something she had never felt before: an urgent need to love him.

Joe wasn't the name of his father. I wonder who *was* his father? It could have been anybody. No. Joe was just a name I like. I've always liked it. It's short and it sounds like a man's name *should* sound – solid and dependable, that's what I think.

*

All I can do is to stay here in the workhouse, my place here protected by the dear old vicar, until my girls are taken from me to go God knows where to be apprentices.

Then will they throw me out?

The vicar will be even older then, and he might not need to give me weekly instruction like he's been doing these past five years. How long can I keep him interested? He's mentioned religion a couple of times, recently. I hope that doesn't mean his conscience is getting the better of him.

No. He's a man like all other men. He needs a woman. His wife died years ago, that's what he told me. So I look after his needs, no questions asked.

I go to him for his special instruction and he likes having me. He certainly does. But will it last another five years or so till Ann is old enough to leave? Joe will be eighteen in seven years. He'll come back then. It could just work out fine.

Let's hope so. I don't want to be pushed out and have to go on the streets again. I'm not as young as I was.

But I'm certain Joe will come and find me when he's free of his apprenticeship. He'll be a man earning a man's wage after that, and he'll be able to look after me in my old age.

We'll be able to live together, and I'll cook for him and wash and mend his clothes. Me and Joe. That's what I've got to hope for. Me and my son.

He'll probably get married to some nice girl. And they'll have children...I'll be their grandma! They'll probably name their first girl after me. Maybe my girls will come back too after they've finished their apprenticeships. We'll all live together as one happy family. What more could any woman want?

*

1809

When death took Isabella, aged 45, a victim of pneumonia, they laid her in a pauper's grave. No stone marked her eternal resting-place; no message of love or biblical quotation perpetuated her memory.

But the few people who were present at the funeral service – Mrs. Hugget from the workhouse and Isabella's daughters Martha and Ann and half a dozen unknown citizens who were probably there just to get out of the cold - heard the Reverend Michael Smith speak on the theme of the forgiveness of sins.

He said that the deceased had been a woman who had strayed from the paths of righteousness, but had come, in the last few years of her life, back to the Lord our saviour, who forgave all who repented.

At her request he himself had given her special instruction to help her to find the way back to the arms of God, and there was no doubt in his mind that she would now be welcomed into heaven's eternal embrace.

Therein, he said, was a lesson for us all. In particular, Martha and Ann should always remember it as a guide for the future.

Nor should they fear, he added, that being poor was a bar to paradise. Jesus himself had told the disciples that it is easier for a camel to pass through the eye of a needle than for a rich man to enter the kingdom of heaven.

Certainly Isabella had been one of the poor. That is why she had been forced, after the death of her husband, to live with her children in the parish workhouse.

But there was no shame in this. For it was God, in his infinite wisdom, who had made some people to be poor, and others to be rich.

All had their part to play in the Almighty's mysterious works. Everyone must bear whatever burden He placed upon them in this life, knowing only that it suited His divine purpose.

Just as the rich had to bear their heavy responsibilities for the governance of their estates and their manufactories, so must the poor accept their lot, and bear the rigours of their lives with the knowledge that as they were made by God, under His eternal decree, it was not for any man to doubt that the Heavenly Father wished them to be poor and ignorant of the tribulations of their betters.

Some there may be who were ever hungry and pinched with cold. But by submitting to His will...by accepting with humility their lowly role in the Lord's eternal plan...and by going at the end to the grave in the knowledge that they had bent to their Maker's command...thus were they assured of an eternity in heaven.

"So that's all right, then," the girls alone heard Mrs Hugget mutter, sotto voce.

Then the children were taken back to the workhouse. Martha was told that now she was nearly ten she was being sent, the following week, to Nottingham to be an apprentice in the lace-making.

She was assured that Ann would follow her in three years' time when she, too, achieved the age of ten. Martha's tears were assuaged with the promise of a reunion with her sister in the fullness of time.

But Ann followed her mother to heaven when she was eight, taken by the measles. So Martha never did see her sister again.

CHAPTER 35

1984

The drive to Stafford took less than two hours. In the Staffordshire County Records Office Geoff found a Joseph Mair entry. But his mother was named as Isabella Betton. There were two other children, Martha and Ann Betton in the record of baptisms. He queried Isabella's surname with the helpful lady on the desk in the search room. She guessed that Joseph's father might have died, and his mother remarried. So Joseph would have kept his father's name. The girls might be the daughters of the second husband.

To progress his family history, Geoff needed to find Isabella's first marriage – to a man with the Mayer or Mair surname. He didn't really know where he was going to find this.

But initially it seemed to be a good idea to check out the second marriage, to someone called Betton. He got out the microfilm of Newcastle marriages, using the older girl's age as a guide. he had learned that in the old days there was usually little more than a year after a marriage before a christening was being recorded in the parish records...and sometimes it was considerably less than a year.

He had little trouble finding the marriage – to Ernest Betton, widower of this parish, labourer, on 22nd of November 1796. But what shook him was the description of the bride: Isabella Mayer, spinster, age 32, of the parish of St. Sepulchre-without-Newgate, London.

Spinster! Born in London!

So despite already having a son, she had never been married before.

Presumably it was this Ernest Betton who obliged...and he had to marry her, Geoff mused. No. I don't think that can be right, because surely Joseph would have been given the surname Betton, wouldn't he?

271

Maybe. Or maybe not. Joseph's baptism in the Newcastle parish baptism records said 1st December 1796, Joseph, bastard son of Isabella Mair, sojourner. The name was spelt differently, but everything else fitted. It had to be Joseph Mayer!

To make sure, he checked through five years of the baptism records, and there was no other Isabella Mair. No: his great-great-great grandfather Joseph was a bastard. "As the record so delicately puts it," Geoff said quietly to himself.

He checked through the death records. Ernest Betton was buried, he noted, on 19th December 1803.

He thought about it during the drive home. Perhaps she had had a passionate affair with some man who then dumped her, or who turned out to be married when she told him she was pregnant. So she married Ernest on the rebound.

"One thing's for certain: we'll never know!" he told his car. Then another thought came.

Oh my God! Hanna isn't going to be exactly jumping for joy when she hears about this! If she hears about it. Well she isn't going to hear this one from me! Not likely!   But how does a girl from London come to marry a labourer in Newcastle-under-Lyme? I thought people didn't travel very far from their birthplace in the old days. Well this woman did. I wonder why. Makes no real sense. Obviously there are always things you don't know, going back into the past.

The thought now occurred to Geoff: this Isabella was his direct ancestor. She was his great-great-great-great grandmother. And how the hell am I going to trace her in London? I somehow expected all my forebears to come from the northern half of the country, I don't know why. But sure as hell I haven't got the time to go hunting through records for hour after hour in London.

It's all very intriguing, but I think this is the end of the line as far as my family history is concerned. True I know the parish of her birth, but there's no way I can get down there time and time again just to pursue it.

272

It was during the next few days that Geoff, finding that he was regretting reaching the end of the road insofar as his family history was concerned, and intrigued by the mysterious London connection, hit on the answer.

On a whim he had bought a family history magazine that he saw on the newsagent's shelf. It was of only general interest to him, however, for none of the circumstances highlighted in the various articles touched on matters that might help him in tracing his family tree. Then, reaching the last few pages, he saw some small ads for professional genealogists to carry out research for a fee.

Most seemed to concentrate on specific areas of the country. But some were offering research in no particular region. So he chose one based in London, phoned the number, and, in the space of a few minutes' conversation, had arranged to write to the genealogist, giving all the details he had, to see if anything could be done to trace Isabella Mayer.

The fee was, Geoff thought, a bit steep – and it left things a bit too open-ended for Geoff's liking. But considering that the alternative would be to travel to London, arrange overnight accommodation, and feed himself while he was there, he reasoned that it was cheaper to pay the professional...and it had a lot greater chance of success.

He also decided to say nothing of it to Hanna. He knew that if he did tell her where he was up to, it would lead to further disparaging remarks about his ancestry, and somehow he knew that if he argued with her he would lose.

But when he was alone, Geoff did spend quite a lot of his leisure time thinking about these strangers that he had traced back as far as Isabella, whose genes were part of the fabric of his own being.

His research hadn't gone the way he had expected. He couldn't help smiling to himself as he thought how he had believed naively that he would quickly establish beyond any doubt that he had noble ancestors.

Even now, he accepted, the thought had crossed his mind that Isabella might have come from a wealthy or even an aristocratic family who had cruelly cast her out when she admitted to being with child as a result of some forbidden love, or from some terrible fate in which the lord so-and-so had forced himself upon her, aided by his evil retinue. That was the way it happened in 18th century novels.

Well, he would just have to wait and see what the researcher came up with. But somehow a mighty doubt had come into his mind.

No. It isn't logical. Go back far enough and maybe they were well-to-do. After all, I'm working backwards in time. All the people I've found have been descendants of Isabella. If she was poor – and she must have been poor to have ended up in the workhouse – then her children, and then their children, would probably be poor too, because of the bad start they'd have had.

"These days they call it the poverty trap," said Geoff to himself. Somehow he had always thought of people caught in the poverty trap as being at fault. But maybe it isn't as simple as that.

And, anyway, my family pulled itself up and out of poverty...even though it took...let me see...four generations to get from Isabella to my grandfather. Four generations and over a hundred years. A hell of a long time.

Hanna is scathing all the time about the working class. It's as if she has a built-in hatred of people who work with their hands. OK, maybe it's true that it means a lot of manual workers haven't had the same level of education as people in white-collar positions, but so what? It's how useful you are that matters.

He thought of his talk at the airport with Eric Perkins. He was an old man, and a former farm labourer. For that, Hanna would presumably despise him, because he was working class by any definition, obviously educated only to a basic level of reading and writing, with a bit of arithmetic thrown in – that's how it was in the old days when Eric was young.

Hanna doesn't like people like that. She admits it...or, actually, boasts of it.

But Geoff had enjoyed his talk with Eric. They spoke the same language...an interest in the old days and a love of aeroplanes.

274

And although their backgrounds and experience were completely different, they had got on well, two strangers just chatting about things they were interested in.

*

"What makes me uneasy about Thatcherism is that there's a growing attitude of 'them and us' these days...I was just reading about it in a newspaper I picked up, and it's a feeling I've had from talking to people recently.

"A lot of people are feeling left out, despite the economic recovery."

"Good God, Geoffrey! I really do think you're turning socialist!"

"Don't be silly, Hanna. You know I'm absolutely anti-socialist."

"Well what does it matter if some people *are* left out? The whole point made by the government time and time again is that our country's well-being depends on people like us - the go-getters...the entrepreneurs...the people who manage and run businesses large and small...the wealth creators. It doesn't matter what they do at the opposite end of the scale. If they are missing out, tough. The fact is they haven't exactly deserved much ever since the war. Or before, come to that!"

"I'm not arguing with you there, love. But if there's going to be nothing but Conservative governments from now on, what is going to be the effect on all these people who feel excluded? If it goes on for years, it's bound to lead to alienation.

"And it's all right the government saying we're going to be a service economy in the future, but if factories keep closing down the way they have been recently, who is going to employ all the people who would normally work in them?

"You know, factory jobs may be looked down on as repetitive and boring, but for a lot of people that kind of work gives a decent income.

"If most of these jobs disappear, what employment are they going to find?

"They'll be left with no work. And that could lead to trouble if enough people become frustrated enough, and angry enough. Not now, of course, but in a few years' time."

Hanna snorted a little laugh. "You think there'll be civil war or something!"

"No. Don't be silly. But I do mean trouble...riots in the streets. Buildings set on fire. Shops looted.

"Three years ago there were those riots in cities all over England. South London, Toxteth, Moss Side. OK, some of it was racial trouble, but it showed what could happen if things ever get out of hand.

"And there were the race riots in America. That last big one in Miami, three or four years ago was it, twelve people died, I seem to remember, and hundreds were injured. There was serious trouble."

Hanna's amused tone showed her reaction. "Well I can't believe all the stuff the so-called experts say. And anyway, if it happened, rioters would be put down, just like the miners were.

"Look at it this way: it's 1984 now...but it's nothing at all like that '1984' book that George Orwell wrote. All these doom and gloom predictions bore me...they're always absolute rubbish!

"If you *are* determined to worry about it, at least put it off for ten or twenty years. But it seems like a waste of time to me! You know, you're turning into a regular little worrier!"

"OK. OK. Perhaps you're right. But I wouldn't like Margaret Thatcher to be remembered for creating a few very rich people and a vast underclass who didn't count for anything.

"Incidentally...change of subject: I don't think I told you, darling, about an interesting old chap I bumped into at the airport a couple of weeks back."

Geoff and Hanna were sitting down to Sunday lunch at home, a bit of a rarity, with his shift system of working, which tended to be busier at weekends as holiday traffic built up towards the summer.

"No. Who was he?"

"Chap called Eric Perkins. I was having a coffee break in the buffet lounge and he came and sat at the same table. Turned out he used to be a porter at the airport until he retired twenty-five years ago or more."

"An airport porter! What on earth made you talk to him?"

"Well he was telling me how the airport used to be in the 1950s. It was a regular air show then, with a lot of military aircraft mixing with the passenger flights.

"Right up my street, it must have been. I was quite envious, I can tell you. I'd love to have seen Manchester Airport then."

"Yes, but what could he tell you...a porter! I wouldn't have thought you'd have learned much from him! What would *he* know about aircraft?"

"Well he knew exactly what was going on. He'd worked at the airport since it opened in the nineteen-thirties...1938 I think it was.

"Before that he was a farm labourer on the land that became the airfield, and the amazing thing was, he had actually heard his grandfather talk of the old family whose farm my great-great grandfather worked on."

"What...the farm labourer ancestor? I wouldn't have thought that would excite you very much. You talk as if it was a big deal, talking to this yokel!"

"Well it might not seem much to you, my dear, but to me it was a real link to my family's past that I've been working on for months.

"I mean, it's just names and places and dates that I've been finding – OK, my own ancestors, but somehow not quite real-life. Then I talk to someone with a tangible connection to my forebears, and it's as if it brings them as step nearer...out of the shadows, if you like.

"And Eric Perkins had an enthusiasm about him...about the airport, and about the history of the place, going back well before aeroplanes were thought of...he could talk about Ringway right back to the 1840s via his own parents."

Geoff hesitated as he looked at Hanna's sceptical face. "I liked him. He might have been in his nineties, but he was bright and intelligent and interesting to talk to."

He added quickly: "It just goes to show that *all* the working class are not thick, lacking in conversation, or sent from the devil, as you would seem to have it.

"In fact some people see working class people as the life and soul and energy of the nation. I heard that said on the TV just the other day."

"My God! You'll be marching about waving a red flag next!"

"Don't be silly, Hanna. Perhaps you ought to be waking up to the idea that people might be on different levels, but that doesn't mean you have to absolutely despise the working classes.

"In this day and age it is just ridiculous."

"Well I think it's you who are making yourself look ridiculous. You don't have to become a friend of the working class just because your ancestors seem to have crawled out of the gutter."

Geoff looked hard at Hanna: "You know, over many decades, it was the Whigs and the old Tories who represented the views of a tiny minority of the people of this country – the landed gentry and the wealthy middle classes – and the unpleasant truth is that they shamelessly exploited the poor and powerless. That's what concerns me because I am absolutely committed to supporting the Conservatives, and reading about the early 19th century frankly embarrasses me."

"Oh come on!" Hanna responded. "Maybe that's how it was 150 years ago, but it's got nothing to do with here and now. Don't try and tell me that the modern Tories are keeping the poor at starvation level...the long-dead past is totally irrelevant!"

"Well OK, but it's not just our party...it's Britain as a whole," said Geoff. "I'm thinking that in the 1820s it was the boast of the manufacturers that we could undersell any other country...our prices were lower because wages in the mills and factories were so low.

"Now nations with much lower levels of pay than ours – in the Far East, for example – are underselling us. And I'm thinking: why, with all our know-how, our education, and the great start we had in the industrial revolution, haven't we ever been able to solve the problem of how to pay workers a decent wage and still keep our market-share?

"It's an important question, and that's why I think the 1800s are relevant. And frankly there's more than a suspicion that the central principle remains – isn't that why Thatcher wants to take us back to Victorian virtues?

"I mean, isn't it about putting the working class in their place? That's what *you* keep saying, isn't it?"

"Utter rubbish! I think I'm quite typical of the people who like to recognise the truth when they see it. All I say is that it is completely obvious that the kind of people who run big businesses, or become surgeons or judges, do so because they have the ability to reach the top. And obviously they *should* have salaries to match," countered Hanna.

"Nobody is going to tell me that your average labourer on a building site or on a farm is on a par with such people...because it is quite obvious they are not."

A new thought struck her: "Of course it is possible for someone to be born into the working class but to work hard and rise through the ranks and escape from it...in fact you yourself are the result of just that, when your grandfather became a doctor.

"But once you've escaped from the working class what do you do? You start banging on about them as if it is something wonderful to have sprung from ancestors who were poor and ignorant.

"I'd say they were probably poor and ignorant because they were too idle to do anything to improve their lot.

"That's the way I still feel about them...more than ever now we've got a Prime Minister who believes that it is hard work that makes wealth...and it is the creation of wealth that relieves poverty.

"She is prepared to put the shirkers back in their proper place instead of kow-towing to them like everyone has been doing since the war.

"The truth is that there are far too many people who are too lazy to work for their living...they're better off getting state benefits. It's a fact that the welfare system rewards idleness.

"It's business enterprise that ought to be rewarded. If benefits were cut a lot of people would have to work in order to eat and pay for a roof over their heads. And that's the truth."

She paused, then went on: "As to the way it was in the past, you can't deny that ordinary people are a damn sight better-off now than they were hundreds of years ago, which is when you're talking about. Of course it wasn't fair at the time – life isn't fair...it never has been. But you can't deny that it was all for the good in the long run."

"Well, I suppose you're right. But as to the unemployed being better off on benefits, remember with three million unemployed now, they're not all shirkers...and there just aren't many jobs to be found.

"A lot of the unemployed have simply been the unlucky ones to have been made redundant as their companies have cut back. None of it is their fault."

But Hanna rose from her chair and walked into the kitchen, muttering: "Excuse me...I've got better things to do than sit here and listen to you talking rubbish."

*

I seem to have lost the argument again. Geoff shook his head. But it's more than that. Who is this woman? I've been married to her for twenty-two years, but I swear I don't really know her.

Either I've changed out of all recognition or she has. Hanna wasn't always like this, I swear. All right, we've both been Conservative voters since we came of age. We've never been party members or anything like that. Yet lately she has become absolutely militantly Tory.

I suppose it's down to having Margaret Thatcher as Prime Minister. Well I'm absolutely in favour of what she has done. She's saved this country from absolute anarchy, if you ask me.

It's true the trade unions had to be brought under control – they were holding the country to ransom. Some of their leaders are communists and you can bet they have their own agenda. So I'm all for

Thatcher. She's right when she says the unions are pricing their members out of their jobs with their excessive pay demands.

But why the hell can't a decent balance be found between profits and wages...it must be possible?

Anyway Hanna seems to have developed an absolute revulsion for anybody who is a manual worker. She reckons most are lazy and irresponsible...and communists at heart. It just isn't reasonable. Or sensible.

And it isn't only that that's eating Hanna. She's extended her intolerance to the labouring classes in the past...and through them to me, because most of my ancestors were working class.

She is moving into being the same sort of person as that military man who wrote to *The Times* a few years ago fatuously saying that the letters N.H.S. stand for "National Homage to Stalin."

That's not a political view...I'd say it's more of a blind, delusive snobbery that represents the worst of the British upper classes.

He felt annoyance turning to anger. What the hell does she mean...I'm making myself look ridiculous...my ancestors crawled out of the gutter...what on earth made me talk to an airport porter?

Hanna and I are just not on the same wave-length any more. In fact I'm beginning to wonder if we're on the same planet.

Geoff sat silent, unhappy, angry as he thought over their conversation. What silenced him more was a single thought that came to him: I just don't like this Hanna.

It was followed by another thought: and what is damn sure is that she doesn't like me. In fact, if I were to be asked directly, I'd have to say that the attitude I sense from Hanna is utter loathing. It's nothing less.

What was it she said the other day...not from the right sort of family...my low breeding shows. What wife says that to her husband?

CHAPTER 36

1984

Hanna was definitely becoming more waspish: she seemed perpetually irritated by Geoff. God knows why, he thought. It manifested itself one evening when she complained that he hardly ever seemed to bring friends home since Adam had gone to Australia.

"You'd have thought that being deputy flight manager, you'd have people queuing up to be friends – instead you seem to have fewer than before," she remarked.

"Ah! It's the isolation of the leader!" he responded with a grin.

"I don't see anything funny about it. If I were in your position it would worry me. Apart from the Davidsons, we haven't entertained friends to dinner for ages...nor have we been invited out.

"I can't help wondering if it's something about you and your attitudes that is losing our friends. You're too damn serious! You're not fun any more. You don't seem to have the right attitude."

"Perhaps it's *your* attitude darling – not mine – that's the problem. If there is one."

"What on earth do you mean by that?" Hanna bristled.

"Well, if you didn't push your political views down people's throats, for a start. I mean, people don't necessarily agree with you, you know. And it puts them in a very difficult position if they don't."

"We should all be politicians! That is the big advantage of TV and the instant news we get these days, surely...we know what's going on and we should care, and be involved enough to want to talk about things that affect everybody's lives," Hanna blazed back.

"It was ignoring the Nazis and letting them get away with so much in Germany in the thirties that allowed the situation that led to the war," she declared firmly.

282

"Here and now, politics matter more than ever. And if people don't accept the very obvious fact that Maggie Thatcher is the saviour of this country, we don't want them as friends anyway," she added.

"She's the best Prime Minister we've ever had, and thank God, because we needed her, the state the country was in when she took over."

"Look, my love, I know that's how you feel. But everyone doesn't feel the same – or, at least, doesn't feel as strongly about it.

"And in any case, political views don't make good dinner conversation. Frankly, most people regard it as taboo. For goodness sake, there are plenty of other things to talk about."

"But nothing as important! This isn't just any old politician. Maggie Thatcher will go down in history as the woman who saved this country from national bankruptcy that was caused by socialism!"

Geoff couldn't help smiling. "Honestly, darling, you're starting to sound like a politician yourself. Come off it! I agree with you. But I don't go round sounding off about it.

"Christ! The politicians do enough of that. Keep your views, of course – but I think you should pipe down about it unless you intend to stand for parliament or something."

"I'll say whatever I like. So don't tell me to pipe down. And don't try to divert the point away from what I'm saying: you don't seem to have any real friends any more. That is your failing, not mine.

"Nothing you say will change my mind on that, so don't even try!"

*

It was three months before Geoff received the genealogist's findings. He had made a couple of phone calls, asking for more information on Isabella. And he had written two letters saying that he was making some progress towards tracing her in London, but giving no details.

It hadn't worried Geoff that it was taking a long time – he was dealing with the period long before the 1830s and 1840s, when it became relatively easy to trace people through countrywide indexes for

283

births, marriages and deaths, and though the decennial national censuses.

He had furnished the professional researcher with all the information on Isabella that he had gleaned from the Stafford county records office...where she came from in London, and her age, which, of course, told him when she was born.

But it would take many hours of patient searching through the parish records, Geoff reasoned. It was bound to take time.

Moreover, he was resigned to hearing that it was all very boring info on christenings, marriages and burials, with names and family events, and very little else. For his own short experience with family history told him that the working classes didn't leave much else by way of enlightenment about their lives.

It would be nice to find a will – they give all sorts of interesting details...family relationships for a start, and what wealth or belongings a person had, way back in the past.

There was William Shakespeare's will, in which he left his second-best bed to his wife, Geoff recalled reading. You can't help wondering who got his best bed!

But I don't expect any of my forebears to have had enough money to make it worthwhile writing a will.

Geoff turned out to be right: no will. But the genealogist's report, when it came, had more information on Isabella than he could have expected...and it shocked him like nothing else had.

Yes, there was some routine but interesting stuff about Isabella being the illegitimate daughter of Eliza Mair, baptised in the parish of St. Sepulchre-without-Newgate on the 13th of October, 1764.

It was plainly the same Isabella that Geoff had found in the Newcastle-under-Lyme records. The name was spelt differently, but it sounded the same, and the London parish was the same, and the spelling was the same as the one given to Joseph's mother Isabella in the Newcastle records. And the year of baptism was right, using Isabella's age when she married.

The genealogist said the different spelling of the surname was quite common in the 18th century and earlier, when there was no formal spelling of words. And since most people couldn't read, they wouldn't know the difference if the parish clerk changed the spelling of their name, as long as it sounded the same. That was what Rose had said, too.

But he had discovered something infinitely more interesting - there was an Isabella Mayer, aged 15, of St. Sepulchre, among the list of prisoners who escaped from Newgate prison when it was burned down by a mob on June 6th, 1780.

"Oh no! She was a criminal when she was young," he said out loud to himself as the words sank in. "Please don't tell me she was on the run from the law for the rest of her life."

He read on. "The mass escape of over 100 prisoners from Newgate was connected with the Gordon riots which began on 4th June, and lasted for five days. Troops had to be called out, with the artillery defending important buildings, and more than 400 people were killed in the disturbances, which were the most serious insurrection experienced in the 18th century."

The report added: "I can find no record of Isabella Mayer being subsequently captured. She seems to have disappeared. She probably fled to another part of the country.

"I am convinced that this is the Isabella, daughter of Eliza Mair, christened at St. Sepulchre's church on 13 October 1764 – that would make her age 15 in June 1780.

"I have checked the Newgate records, and she had been arrested only that night, charged with the theft of a gold watch. She is described as a common prostitute of St. Sepulchre, and daughter of Eliza Mayer.

"Almost certainly, had she stood trial, she would have been hanged. The death penalty was the standard punishment for anybody found guilty of robbery, and very few people of her station in life would have been found not guilty at that time.

"I can find no record of her being executed. If she was on the run it would, of course, explain why she was never heard of again, as far as

285

the London criminal records are concerned. But her name and age fit exactly with the information you gave me about your Isabella Mayer, and according to the records she was arrested in the area where Eliza Mayer lived, and had her baby Isabella christened in 1764.

"I have checked the parish records, and I can find no other person of that name who is unaccounted for. Whilst there is no absolute certainty, I believe it is very likely that this Isabella Mayer was your ancestor.

"On that basis I can continue to trace your family history through Isabella's mother, Eliza Mair or Mayer, if that is your wish, using the pricing framework that we discussed when you commissioned me to carry out the research."

Yes, go ahead, Geoff told him by phone.

But he didn't mention any of it to Hanna.

*

1769

"Where are we going, mother?"

"You'll see. Wait and see, Izzy."

Isabella and her mother were walking through the spring sunshine away from home in Cock Lane. Eliza saw some dandelions gleaming golden at the edge of a ditch, and she stopped to pick them.

"Why are you getting those flowers?"

"I think they're so pretty, don't you? And I want them for a special reason...you'll see why. Just wait until we get to where we're going...just wait."

They turned in among the graves in St. Sepulchre's churchyard. It was the church they went to each Sunday. But they never walked among the graves. Isabella couldn't be patient. She was only four, and she was puzzled.

"Why have we come here?"

"Just follow me. I have to do something."

She followed, as bidden, to a small corner of the graveyard. There were one or two small, upright stones in the ground, amid the untidy grass.

It was on the north side of the burial-ground, where the hapless were put to rest, the suicides and the unfortunates who had been put to death by the execrable 18th century English legal system which believed in hanging for crimes great and paltry...whether or not there was any proof of guilt.

At a small hump in the grass, in a gap between two of the roughly inscribed stones, Eliza stooped, and tenderly placed on the grass the little bunch of yellow flowers that she had picked. She went down on to one knee, and picked up some dead flowers, and patted the ground, then left her hand on the damp grass, silently.

"Why are you crying?"

Eliza wiped the tears away with her sleeve before turning to Isabella. "I'll tell you why I'm sad. Once, before you were born, I had a little boy baby, but he was deadborn. And this is where he is buried under the ground, where the dogs and pigs could not find his little body..."

She choked over the words, as fresh tears welled though her eyes and spilt down her cheeks, with barely suppressed sobs.

She reached out and pulled Isabella to her, hugging the questioning little girl to her bosom. "Oh, Izzy, he never lived on this earth. He lay in my arms and looked like other sleeping babies...he looked just like your poppet.

"He was a lovely boy. So lovely. But there was no life. I looked and looked at him and kissed him and cuddled him...and hoped that would open his eyes and be alive...but he didn't."

"Why?"

"I think God must have decided that he could go straight to heaven."

Eliza buried her face against her daughter as more tears burst forth.

"Do you understand, Izzy? He was dead when he was born. He couldn't be christened, so we had to bury him here. My mother told me not to think about him any more, because he had never been alive. But I can never forget him. I think about him nearly every day.

"My mother told me you can't love a dead baby – but you can. You can.

"That's why we came here."

Eliza took her daughter's hand, and led her into the church. Isabella watched silently as her mother knelt on the hard stone floor facing the altar, and prayed.

After a short while Eliza rose to her feet, took Isabella by the hand again, and they began their short walk homewards. Both were silent at first, the mother unable to let go of her sad thoughts, the girl knowing that these were things she didn't understand.

But soon Isabella's curiosity got the better of her, and her questions about the things they saw began to change Eliza's mood.

As she watched her daughter darting here and there to look at things she espied on the way, Eliza began thinking of the time when *she* was four. It was the time when she had begun to understand some of the things that were happening around her.

CHAPTER 37

1740

Eliza had two mothers.

She loved the kindly one who brought her up and looked after her with all the fondness you'd expect from your Mam – the one she lived with.

The other lived across the street. She was called Miriam.

And although Eliza was always being told that the lady who lived opposite was her *real* mother, and so she must love her, the little girl found the task impossible. For the lady they said was her real mother wanted nothing to do with her.

It had always been so, as far back as she could remember. To the growing toddler it was just one of the facts that you knew but didn't remotely understand. But now she was five, and she began to ask why.

The answer seemed to be something to do with busy-ness; or was it business?

Eliza didn't understand. She was a very happy girl with the parents she called Mam and Dad. David and Dora Blundell were caring and hard-working. She knew they loved her, just as she loved them.

At home they played with her and talked to her about things she asked about; they took her for walks; they took her to church on Sundays.

They made sure she washed her hands and face. They gave her good, clean clothes to wear, and shoes for her feet. Some children – even some who lived in the same street – wore dirty clothes that were hardly better than rags. And some went about in the earth streets with bare feet.

Because her mam had been a servant in a big house in the city when she was young, she spoke in a nicer, gentler way than a lot of people.

That manner of speaking, of course, was the way Eliza learned as she began to talk. She grew to know that she was one of the lucky children.

So it didn't really matter that the other woman was her real mother, because Eliza hardly knew her. But it seemed important to Mam and Dad that she was aware of it.

*

David and Dora had rescued Eliza when she was only a day old. They knew she would have died otherwise. They had noticed that each of Miriam's previous three babies had simply disappeared. Each time, after a few weeks, Miriam had carried on being a prostitute as if nothing had happened.

David and Dora knew that this time she had had a long and painful birthing, and they offered to look after the baby while she recovered from the ordeal.

Miriam had told them then that she did not want anything to do with the baby.

So they took her home with them. Their next-door neighbour had recently lost her three-week-old baby – nobody knew why the child had died, and they were grieving bitterly. The woman's copious breast milk was a problem, she had told Dora. So Dora knew she would feed Miriam's baby. But the neighbour refused to take the child in as her own permanently.

"It's 'er baby" she stated, indicating Miriam's home with a jerk of her thumb. "She should look after it.

"I'll feed 'er for now. But that's all. That tart!"

She was a rough-spoken woman, and to tell the truth, Dora was not over-fond of her neighbour. But her heart was in the right place, she had the milk, she needed to get rid of it, and Dora certainly did not accept the widespread belief that a child would absorb the personality of the woman who suckled her.

As the days went by Miriam was still adamant that she did not want the baby. So as soon as the little girl could be weaned on to cow's milk they knew they could keep her as their adopted child. Miriam said they could have her for all she cared.

They had been married for eleven years. But Dora had never become pregnant. She had an aching need for a baby, and the couple had despaired when they saw other people desperate to have no more children...just another mouth to feed in times that were hard enough already.

Everyone knew that if you couldn't stop having babies, you could get rid of them. Try everything to abort them, or if they insisted upon being born, there was always the expedient of taking a new-born baby to a distant area and leaving it there to die...on the street...in a ditch...on a rubbish-heap. Or there was always the Thames.

That is what David and Dora suspected had happened to Miriam's previous babies. She was an unmarried woman, and she had to earn her own money in order to survive. That her chosen means was prostitution was not a matter that they condemned her for...you had to live somehow.

They understood how difficult it must be to be a prostitute with a small child. But the thought of killing those little babies tore at Dora's heart.

This one they would save, and bring up as their own little girl...that's all they wanted.

So when they heard that Miriam was in labour, that night in 1735, and Dora went to help two neighbours who were assisting in the delivery, her mind was firmly set: this one would not just disappear. If Miriam didn't want the baby – she did!

Miriam was happy with the arrangement. The couple were more than happy, for David had a good income from his work as a chair carver, and they could afford the extra expense involved.

The important thing was that they were now a family. Dora, who had longed for a child, but had become used to the idea that she could not have one out of her own body, was content in her new role as mother.

291

Her life was focused on her baby. But the couple would always make it clear to their little girl that Miriam was her real mother. They didn't want to be accused of stealing the child...they were quite clear on that.

Another thing they made her aware of was her name. Shortly taking the baby into their home, David and Dora took her to the parish church of St. Sepulchre to be christened.

They had explained the circumstances to the minister, and because he knew them well as regular members of his congregation, he happily performed the baptism at the ancient stone font.

They named this child Eliza. And after the service, when they went into the vestry, the parish clerk wrote the name into his record book. Starting with the date, he wrote: "Eliza, dau of...."

He paused. "What is her mother's name?"

"Miriam," said Dora. "Miriam Ayre."

"How does she spell her second name?" the clerk asked.

The couple admitted that they didn't know – neither of them could read or write.

"Don't worry. I think I know that last name," he said.

And he completed the entry into the baptism register "...Miriam Mair."

*

1748

David and Dora Blundell were God-fearing people, who had, as children, been brought up to know right from wrong. They taught Eliza their ways.

They were intelligent too. They had formed their own views on the social scene that was the daily backdrop to their lives.

They could see the fine houses and beautifully-dressed people who lived in the more fashionable parts of the burgeoning city.

They could marvel at the wide, paved streets that were being built, sweeping away the narrow, muddy lanes and tumbledown houses...which were so old and badly-built that they often did tumble down.

Splendid new edifices were being erected – buildings that astounded foreign visitors by their magnificence, turning London into the most fashionable city in Europe.

David and Dora marvelled at the changes. But they saw that close by, the magnificence turned to squalor. Vile, stinking mud-streets still abounded, with their central kennels into which the nastiest effluences of mankind were tipped.

They saw the rich in their carriages, and the poor, begging and starving, working for pittances, clinging to life as long as they could...but often losing.

They saw the dead babies, left in the streets or on rubbish-heaps.

And their sense of right and wrong strained their sense of humble acceptance that God had made all things good.

But they taught Eliza to accept her station in life with a belief that all was part of the good Lord's plan.

Westminster and London, which had once been separate towns, had been completely joined for more than 30 years now. Their streets and houses had, in effect, become one metropolis. And it was expanding so much that some people thought that rural areas such as Hackney, Bermondsey and Bethnal Green would one day be absorbed into the city too – just as the villages of Chelsea, Kensington, Hampstead, and Islington already had.

This great centre of life and trade brought riches to the rich, and an income that gave a degree of comfort to the skilled artisan and tradesman.

But farther down the scale, life in London was hard. And to make it more so, the wealthy folk derided the desperate poor as laughable objects who wore rags and whose faces were filthy and whose hair was matted and louse-ridden, purely to appeal to the pity of their betters, so that their begging might be more effective.

293

They were forthright in their view that the poor were poor simply because they were too lazy to work. Some undoubtedly were. But many were certainly not.

David and Dora saw it all around them, and wondered whether it was right. It made them no less determined to protect their pretty, adopted girl, and to give her a good start in life.

David's trade kept him busy, and brought in an income that helped. Dora was a hard-working wife who made sure their room was clean...it was next to godliness. For Eliza, it all meant security and a childhood that was happy.

She could see some of the wrongs that surrounded them...she could occasionally see the strange woman who was her real mother. For Miriam was usually drunk now. She had taken to the highly-popular gin-drinking craze of the time with enthusiasm and stamina.

But Eliza knew that there was nothing that she could do about it. It did not touch her life with her dependable and loving mam and dad.

So when her dad died, one April morning, only days after first feeling sick, the shock and the grief were all the greater.

Dora had called in a physician...she had money to pay him. But he could do nothing, other than to inform her that her husband was dying. Probably typhus. Sorry. Nothing anybody can do. Good day.

When David breathed his last, twelve hours later, Dora was distraught. Eliza, through the bitter, aching tears that matched her mam's, found it impossible to believe. Yet she knew it must be true.

What she did not know – and did not for one moment think about – were the effects on their lives...hers and Dora's.

The funeral came and went with its sombre ceremonial, leaving a terrible vacuum in their room.

Eliza didn't know what to do or what to say. But suddenly she was aware that her mam had become decisive, practicalities having shut out the empty pointlessness of grief.

In front of the flickering of the fire, two nights after the burial, she put a protective, loving arm round Eliza's shoulders, and the two leaned against each other in mutual comfort as they stared, unspeaking, into the warm, red glow.

"We shall have to leave this house," Dora said, after several minutes of silence.

"What!"

"I want you to be brave, Eliza, as I must be brave. I will find a nice family where you can go into service."

As the 13 year-old stared, aghast, she added, in the same considered, gentle tones: "I shall have to go into the workhouse. I have no income, you see. How would I pay the rent? But we will be able to see each other quite often. And maybe, one day, you'll get married to a nice young man, and I'll be able to come and look after you again.

"I've thought about it. It's the best thing that we can do."

Eliza could not stop tears running from her eyes. "No. It can't be true, can it?"

"Don't cry, my little one. I love you so much. I'll always be nearby...I'll always love you. But we must do as I say because, really, there is no choice. You will have to find work to support yourself, and I will have to find shelter in the workhouse.

"I'm lucky because the workhouse in this parish is well-run and caring for women like me. I'm sure I'll be well-treated, and I can do whatever work they ask of me. And I'll always have somebody to talk to...I couldn't bear living alone in this room."

She paused. "There's one thing you must do before you leave. Once I've found a place for you, you must let Miriam...you must let your real mother...know where you'll be, in case she ever needs you."

For Eliza, it was all too much to take in. It was all so sudden, so unexpected, so unwanted, so unbelievable. She wept bitterly, in inconsolable shock.

*

Eliza settled quickly into her new life as a servant of all work in the amazingly large house of Mr. Edward Lavington esquire and his wife

Celia, way over to the west in Westminster. They had a son, Samuel, aged fourteen.

Not only was the house large: it was filled with such beautiful furniture and ornaments. In a display cabinet there were real silver flasks and dishes and large spoons that gleamed like moonlight on the river. Eliza had never seen anything like it. It was wonderful. Even the servants' parts of the house were better than Eliza had ever dreamed of.

Her mam had found this family by going to see her own former mistress, where Dora had been a servant 30 years earlier. Old now, still mistress of her house in her widowhood, she knew of a lady who was looking for a well brought-up girl servant...a Mrs Lavington.

She knew that Mrs. Lavington was a good and kind woman, who would take good care of her servants' well-being, she assured Dora. She immediately penned a note to the lady, who lived only a short distance away, and within the hour received a favourable reply, suggesting that Dora took Eliza to be seen two days later.

The interview in the fine terraced house in New Burlington Street, in St. James Westminster, had gone well. Mrs. Lavington was such a nice lady, Dora saw at once. More importantly the lady took to Eliza, seeing that she was clean and having heard that she was a churchgoing girl, daughter of an artisan. And she had had the note from Dora's former employer, an elderly woman of some repute, recommending Eliza as the daughter of a faithful former servant.

Eliza had always helped her mam with the housework. She knew how to light a fire, and how to clean and dust, taking care of Dora's few precious ornaments. She knew about the importance of washing the pottery, and of washing under-garments.

And, as importantly, she was eager to please, and willing to work hard. That was as well, for the other six servants made sure that she had the biggest burden of work. She thought she would never stop washing floors! She did feel homesick, and she missed her mam and dad.

In truth it was exhausting for the first six months. But Eliza developed a friendship with another young servant, Maria, and she did not feel so alone.

After that, she was much happier. On her days out she always went to the workhouse to see her mam, who was surprisingly cheerful, despite – as she told Eliza – having to live alongside some terrible people...beggars and thieves, some of them. But they were, she knew, all God's children, and one had to see them in that light. All were poor, but that was often no fault of theirs.

"Always bear that in your mind, Eliza, when you behold some poor wretch, begging for a crust, or even being dragged off to Tyburn for stealing in order to eat – that might be your lot, but for the grace of God."

*

Maria had been caught stealing one of Mrs. Lavington's lace handkerchiefs, and was dismissed, despite her tearful pleas that she meant to return it - she had secretly borrowed it in order to impress a young man with whom she had been keeping company on her free days.

What would she do, without a place? Where could she go? She would never do such a thing again, she pleaded. She loved her work here. She had never done such a thing before.

But it was all in vain. She was dismissed and that was that. One could not abide dishonest servants.

To Eliza, it underlined the point made by Dora: the line was very thin between some degree of comfort and the disgrace of being reduced to poverty and homelessness in a city that would become instantly hostile and friendless.

Maria's dismissal was a blow to Eliza, who thus lost her friend. But there was one advantage: Eliza was no longer the most junior menial in the house – she had advanced one step up the ladder of the servants' hierarchy. Another girl was employed to do the dirty work.

CHAPTER 38

1752

Eliza's life in the Lavington household was a happy one in the main. Four years had gone by so quickly since she became a servant there that she could hardly believe it.

Mr. Lavington was a stockbroker who left the ordering of the household affairs to his wife. He was out at the Exchange for most of the day, but in the evenings, dressed for dinner and often entertaining important guests, who sometimes included noble lords and ladies and members of parliament, he was the grand head of the household.

At holiday times when Samuel, their son, was down from Oxford University, he was treated with enormous respect by the servants. He was only a year older than Eliza. He was unfailingly polite, in a rather uppish manner, Eliza thought...he had become a little over-grand...more so than his parents.

When guests were being entertained Eliza and her two fellow housemaids waited at table, serving the rich variety of food served up by cook – an expert and tyrannical mistress of the kitchen, a formidable woman who would brook no interference except from Mrs. Lavington herself.

Eliza was now a housemaid, and wore a striped cotton dress, a long apron, and a mob cap. She knew she looked smart...but not too smart: it wouldn't do to compete with her mistress.

Although there was still some hard physical work, most of the menial tasks were done by two younger girls who had been employed as other, older servants, had left – one being Maria and the other an eighteen year-old girl named Alice, who had fallen into the deep disgrace of becoming pregnant.

Mrs. Lavington had been full of sympathy and advice, and had urged Alice to name the father of her unborn child so that she could marry him, or at least get financial support when the baby was born.

However, Alice would not say who the father was, and in any case she had to leave the Lavingtons' employment. She had wept, but seemed to accept her fate with a resignation that seemed foolish to Eliza.

She refused to talk about it, even to her fellow-servants.

They were a friendly team, eating and living in the servants' quarters, three men and two older women, Eliza, and the two girls who had joined the household after her, and all felt the sadness at Alice's fate.

*

Home from Oxford for the summer, Master Samuel came and went, visiting mysteriously wonderful friends in distant shires, and sometimes entertaining male friends from university. They ranged through the house in uproarious fun, creating havoc for the servants who had to clean and tidy up after their pranks and drunken breakages.

But when he was alone in the house, Master Samuel was kindness itself. He would chat to the servants in a way that his father would never do. He seemed to enjoy their company, especially the females.

So Eliza was not overly surprised when, one day when Mr. Lavington was out at business, and Mrs. Lavington had taken the family's town coach to visit an aristocratic friend some distance away in Chelsea, Master Samuel knocked on the door of her room in the servants' area of the house.

Not knowing at first who was knocking, and calling "Come in!" Eliza, who was busy on some repairs to her apron at the time, found the young master stepping inside and closing the door behind him, a finger on his lips to request quiet.

"Sorry to barge in. I'm at a loose end. I wondered if we could have a chat to relieve the boredom...do you mind? I so much enjoy your company, and we don't have to have any of that master and servant stuff up here, in private, do we?"

Eliza felt embarrassed. It was a situation that she had not encountered before. Hastily putting away her needlework, she asked Master Samuel to sit on the chair she had vacated – the only chair in the tiny attic room. She stood, respectfully, until he said: "Do sit down, Eliza. Tell you what...we'll both sit on the bed...friendlier that way."

In your own room or not, an order is an order from the family son and heir.

They sat side by side on the tiny bed, and he asked her politely how she was today, and upon being assured that she was quite well, he told her she was lucky to be such a beautiful girl, and he assumed she had many admirers.

"Oh no. I have no admirers at all," she said, with a kind of finality of tone that she thought would bring this line of talk to an end.

Instead, it seemed to spur him on. "I cannot believe this! You know, you are such a lovely girl. I believe I am in love with you myself!"

His hand suddenly rested on her knee. It moved downward as he spoke, and she replied: "Oh, no!"

Suddenly the hand was now at her ankle, and then moving up, under her skirt, caressing the inside of her leg, quickly, up to her knee.

"Oh, no!" she repeated. But this time the tone was one of indignation. And in truth there was a fear in her voice, too. She tried to rise from the bed, but suddenly he was trying to push her backwards on to it.

Showing a physical strength that surprised him, Eliza twisted herself round, grabbed the metal bars of the bed-head, and heaved herself to her feet.

Before he could speak again she told him severely: "Master Samuel! You should not be doing this! What would your parents say!"

"But they're not going to know, are they, dear Eliza. Because it would certainly cost you your position here. You know that. And where would you go, as a servant dismissed without references. Or, even

300

worse, with information from your previous employers that you had tried to seduce their son!"

"Your parents would give no such information, because it would not be true."

"It would be true if I told them it was."

"I would most certainly deny it and tell them exactly what happened."

"And who would they believe, d'ye think? Me, or you...nothing but a servant girl."

He grabbed her skirt, and tried to pull her towards him, still seated on the bed. But she took hold of her skirt and wrenched it from his grasp.

"Master Samuel, please stop this! I have done nothing to deserve such treatment from you!"

"Yes you have. You have inflamed my passion."

"I am sure I have done nothing to encourage you in any way. As the son of the master of this house you are a gentleman. But this is not gentlemanly behaviour."

"I'm not sure you're right there, Eliza, from what I hear all around me!"

He tried to take hold of her skirt again.

"Stop it! Please, Master Samuel! At least consider my feelings."

"Feelings! You are a servant – what feelings could you have?"

Anger took hold of Eliza, at last. "I have the same feelings as you, or any person of any rank in society," she said determinedly.

"How dare you try to force yourself on me, and then complain that I am incapable of feelings! Let me tell you, I have feelings all right...of absolute disgust at what you are doing.

"And I promise you now, that if it should cost me my place or no, I shall scream aloud unless you leave this room this instant...I have suffered you enough!"

He rose to his feet and stepped towards the door. "You will regret this, I promise you!"

But at last he was gone.

*

The encounter with Samuel was followed by an uneasy lack of response. But several times he smiled as he caught Eliza's eye going about her duties. It was not a natural smile, she saw instantly. What was it? It was as if they shared a secret that nobody else knew about.

Well perhaps they did. But what was worrying her, and causing her to lose sleep at nights, was the question of what the son of the master was going to do about it.

All she could do for the moment was to avoid being alone with Samuel.

Then, one day when she was on her way back to the Lavingtons' after visiting her mother in the workhouse, she met Alice.

They greeted each other like lost sisters. But Alice was desperate, Eliza could see that at once. She had not been able to get employment. Without references it was hopeless.

Then she took Eliza's hand, and said: "I have had to lie with men for money."

Eliza was dumbstruck.

"It is the only way of getting money if you cannot get employment. I hate doing it. But I have no choice."

"But why don't you name the father of the child you're going to have? Surely that would be a much better thing to do."

"It wouldn't alter my position."

"Why not?"

"Because the father is Samuel! I thought it would be obvious to everyone at the Lavingtons'. But there was no point in saying anything, because when I told him I was pregnant he said he would tell his parents that I had seduced him in order to get money from them, and they would dismiss me for doing such a thing to their son.

"He was going to say it was all my fault. But honest to God, Eliza, he came up to my room on the quiet one day and forced himself on me. I tried to stop him, but I couldn't, and he had his way with me.

"After that it became a regular thing when he was home and he had an opportunity. He told me if I didn't agree to it, he'd tell his father that I was seducing him and he was too weak to avoid it. Imagine!

"Then I found I was pregnant, and I knew it was the end! There was no way to turn. So you see, telling Mrs. Lavington that Samuel was the father of my child would have done no good at all."

Eliza's mind was in a turmoil. She felt, first, great sympathy for Alice in the terrible fate that had befallen her. She told Eliza where she was lodging, and they promised to meet again.

Eliza could not get it out of her mind. It could have been her! And what was she going to do about this new knowledge? It was suddenly clear to her that something had to be done about Samuel. But how was she to take action without suffering the same fate as Alice?

*

For two days Eliza pondered. When she came up with an answer to the dilemma, she knew that it might work...or it could be disastrous. She decided to take the risk, great though it was.

Waiting for an opportune moment, when Samuel had gone back to Oxford, and Mr. Lavington was out at business, she approached her mistress and, secretly shaking with trepidation, asked if she might ask a favour.

Mrs. Lavington had grown to be fond of Eliza, now an experienced and thoroughly competent servant. She knew that Dora had health problems, and, believing that Eliza was going to ask for an extra day off in order to visit the workhouse, she immediately said that yes, of course she might ask a favour.

Eliza had turned into one her most reliable house servants, neat, clean, properly polite, and able to serve at table with the right balance of deference and a pleasant smile in responding to comments of dinner guests.

303

In fact Mrs. Lavington had recently been discussing Eliza with her husband, who had commented on her nice manner. She had told her husband that Eliza was one servant she would not want to lose.

"I don't think she has any followers – she is too busy looking after her mother's cares to be seeking the company of young men," she had said. "But she is a pretty girl, and I suppose it is inevitable that one day a young man will enter her life. Whoever it is, she will be a good catch. But, of course, she is only seventeen."

So Mrs. Lavington was deeply shocked when Eliza told her that she regretted that she was forced to leave her household, and would be very grateful if Madam would furnish her with a recommendation for a future employer.

"Eliza! What are you saying? Why must you leave? I hope you are not in any kind of trouble."

They both knew what she meant. "I am not in trouble, madam, but I very much regret that I cannot tell you why I must leave. It is something that I can not disclose."

"But Eliza, something has happened...can you not tell me about it...I would not like to lose you...and I promised your mother that I would take care of you while you are under my roof.

"Is there anything I can do to make you change your mind? Oh dear! I am utterly amazed! Will you not tell me what has brought this about?

"I would be most distressed if there is something wrong in my house. Is it something to do with the other servants?"

"No, Madam, it is not...although..."

"What is it, Eliza? Has there been trouble between you and someone else? If so, you really must tell me, for I cannot bear to have discord within my house. It is not fair to refuse me, you know."

Eliza realised that she must say something to avoid accusations being levelled at other servants. She paused. She thought. Is the time right? Do I dare?

It was too good an opportunity to miss.

"I saw Alice just the other day, Madam. All is not well with her. But she told me something that made me understand why she could not disclose who is the father of the child she is carrying."

"Oh?"

"Yes, Madam. I am not with child, nor am I anything but a virgin. But I am distressed to tell you that my case has some similarities with that of Alice, although I did not know this until my chance meeting with her."

She stopped. She sighed audibly. "Madam, I really can not say more.

"I do not wish to cause you any distress – I would do anything to avoid that, truly I would."

Mrs. Lavington was silent for a length of time...a full minute.

"Eliza, will you let me consider what you have said? I would at least like a little time to think about your request."

"Of course, Madam."

The interview was over. Eliza returned to the servants' quarters.

In the sitting-room, Mrs. Lavington remained seated, her brow furrowed.

She was no fool. Distress me? What can that mean? Why would something connected to Alice, who is with child, distress me? And why is Eliza's problem connected...and why should she say she is still a virgin?

Her fingers drummed the small table by her chair.

Her face assumed a grim look; her mouth hardened.

She rang the bell for Eliza, who soon arrived.

"Eliza. This is something to do with Samuel. Isn't it?"

"Madam, I can not tell. I must certainly not!"

"Eliza. You do not need to say more. I think I understand. And truly I am dismayed and shocked if my son's behaviour is behind all this...with both you and Alice.

"I will get to the bottom of this. If what I suspect is truly the case – and Mr. Lavington and I will make a judgement once we have talked to Samuel – I want you to reconsider your request to leave our service.

"And if my worst fears prove to be justified, I shall make proper recompense to Alice...for I fear she may have been dreadfully wronged."

"Madam, please understand I do not want to cause trouble for Samuel. I will willingly leave, rather than be the cause of dividing your family. He is but a young man. Everyone knows that young men have difficulty restraining themselves sometimes.

"Please do not be too hard on him, I beg you."

Back in her room, Eliza could not help feeling well pleased with what had been said...and what looked likely to be the outcome. She truly did not wish Samuel to be at enmity with his parents – and she had not actually accused him of anything.

But at the same time she was determined not to be trapped as Alice had been.

And it might be that her employers could help Alice. That was the best of all...they had enough money to provide for her, and to save her from the life she had been forced into would be something so worthwhile that the risk to her own livelihood would have been fully justified.

My father would have been proud that I have played such a role, if it is accepted by my master and mistress, she thought. With that I can only be satisfied.

CHAPTER 39

1752

Samuel was banished from the house, and then sent to Virginia to take up a post supervising transported criminals slaving on the tobacco plantations.

It was to be an experience that would make him or break him, his parents had told him. It would keep him under the surveillance of a man much trusted by Mr. Lavington, whilst subjecting him to hard work in difficult conditions.

He was to learn decency, or to stay away for ever.

For although Samuel's father, once told of Mrs. Lavington's suspicions, had at first attempted to pass it off as a minor misdemeanour such as young men do get up to, the lady of the house was accepting no such excuse.

"The matter is quite simple, Edward," she told her husband. "I will not have a rapist living under my roof.

"These servants are all under *your* protection when they come to be employed here. And I give my word personally that I will care for the young women in the absence of their parents.

"If Samuel cannot give us a satisfactory denial - and I know in my heart that he will be unable to do so – then in the first case I am determined that we must provide financial support for poor Alice for the rest of her life.

"I cannot bear to think of her fate without it.

"As to Eliza, I believe he made an attempt on her which seems to have been unsuccessful. But if I am right it is a despicable thing.

"Put together, it means that Samuel might well descend into a way of life that presents propriety when he is in society, yet reveals a complete lack of morals when he is not.

"If that is to be the pattern of his life, then I despair of him. I would always suspect him and be ashamed to be his mother.

"I repeat, I will not accept such a son. He must somehow learn that manhood involves more than the satisfaction of carnal instincts.

"And lastly, I wonder if you have considered that eventually such behaviour might ruin not only his reputation, but yours and mine also. Your fortune relies on trust and goodwill at the Exchange. Consider what would be the consequences if you were to lose that good will through the outrageous behaviour of your son."

When Samuel was summoned from Oxford to be confronted by his parents' cold and implacable questions, he had been unable to hide his guilt.

He then made the mistake of trying to pass it off as a bit of harmless fun with women who, being servants, didn't really matter.

He had never faced his mother's anger before. Now he found that it was something to be feared. No son expects to face the utter contempt of his mother...and Samuel could not bear it.

But his late conversion to contrition was brushed aside.

He was dismissed to his room. After an hour he was summoned before his parents again. His father informed him that the law degree for which he was studying would have provided him with an honourable profession. But as the law plainly meant nothing to him – a confessed rapist – he would not return to Oxford, nor any other university.

He would be informed of his fate in due course. In the meantime he was not to be allowed into his parents' home or presence. They would find a suitable place for him to stay under supervision until arrangements were made to send him to the Colony.

He had brought shame upon his parents, and now he could accept the punishment that they would provide, or find himself cut off without a penny. It was his choice.

He chose the punishment. He was sent to Virginia. And he was never seen in England again.

At first he wrote to his parents every month, as he had been instructed to do. The letters were full of misery and complaint about the heat, the food, the terrible people he had to work with...in fact about almost everything.

Then he began to write less often. Eventually the letters stopped. When they enquired about him, they were told that he had left, and nobody knew where he had gone.

*

1757

Five years had passed since Samuel's banishment. That time had left its mark on Mr. Lavington. Although he still entertained lavishly, the ebullience had gone from him.

Plainly, thought his wife, the loss of his son in this way had had its effect on her husband – it was to be expected.

Eliza found that far from blaming her for their son's disgrace, Mrs. Lavington seemed to take to her even more than before. She took an interest in her welfare. She enquired often about Mrs. Blundell, whom Eliza visited each week in the workhouse.

Her mam's condition had certainly deteriorated. She had become forgetful at first, then vague about most things that Eliza asked her about. It was just the effects of growing older, Eliza thought...after all her mam was now in her late fifties.

But what really distressed Eliza was that her mam had become untidy personally, in her dress and in her habits. She smelt of urine. Sometimes she did not seem to be fully aware of where she was.

And then, worst of all, she obviously did not really know Eliza. Her state of mind grew wild. Visits became difficult and upsetting. Eliza was talking to a brick wall, it seemed. It grew worse. One morning a letter told Eliza that her adopted mother had died.

The workhouse authorities arranged her funeral and burial. And Eliza's distress, she found, was tempered by the thought that for a long time her mam had not been the woman she had known and loved.

But her passing left a terrible gap in Eliza's life. It was Mrs. Lavington who comforted her, with consideration and kind words.

A few weeks after the funeral, it was a fine spring morning, the day when Eliza opened the door to find who was knocking so loudly. A rough-looking man asked her if this was the home of Mrs. Celia Lavington.

When told that it was, he demanded to see her. Eliza, alarmed by the man's manner, asked him to state his name and business, so she could tell her mistress.

"I'm from the bailiffs. I'm come to tell 'er, 'er 'usband's dead and we're taking possession of this 'ouse and its contents.

*

With a terrible suddenness it was Eliza who tried to comfort her employer. Yet what words could she find?

It was all too true. Mr. Lavington was dead. He had shot himself through the temple.

Over the next hours it became clear that he had been speculating in high-gain, high-risk shares with his clients' money...and they had crashed, yet another ridiculous venture that was becoming all too common.

In an attempt to make good the losses, he had tried again...and lost again. He desperately needed big returns.

But he seemed to have lost his ability to invest wisely. In the end, facing calamitous losses, he had mortgaged his house...and had lost yet again.

Faced with utter ruin, no friends who would not condemn him and demand reparation for the loss of their money, and the prospect of wasting his life rotting in a debtors' prison, he had taken the quickest way out...oblivion.

But if his death solved his problems, it cast his wife into a pit of despair. Before the crash she had had a wide social circle among the best of people. In a day, she was reduced from wealthy socialite to penniless outcast.

She quickly discovered that nobody wants to be associated with a homeless pauper...among other things most of the people she called her friends had lost money heavily from her husband's misadventures. So not only was she homeless...she was friendless too.

Everyone was forced out of the house in the face of writs which handed its legal ownership to the bank from which Mr. Lavington had taken a mortgage.

The servants, tears streaming down their faces, went away – except for Eliza. She could see that her mistress would never survive on the streets without a lot of help. "I will stay with you, madam," Eliza told her.

"But I am not your mistress now. I have no money. I have no home. I can not ask you to serve me now, Eliza."

"We will face life together, madam. I will see that we will not starve. I have talked to the other servants about how it is possible to live off the streets.

"But first we must find somewhere to shelter for the night."

For two days they wandered, with nowhere to go. Mrs. Lavington discovered that there were many other homeless people...flotsam in the whirlpool that was life for the poor and hopeless in London. All were looking for somewhere to pass the night sheltered from the weather. For although it was April, the nights were cold. The competition was fierce for the best places.

They slept the first night in a doorway. Eliza went off to the kitchen door of a tavern, and begged some half-chewed leftovers from someone's dinner. She found some more scraps in the tavern dustbin.

She brought back the prize to the doorway where Mrs. Lavington cowered, hopeless and terrified. She didn't explain where the morsels of meat came from. But they staved off the worst of their hunger.

311

The next day Eliza, by now footsore and weary in her search for shelter, struck gold: a bare, filthy room in a derelict house which looked so close to collapse that nobody else had dared to enter.

But some areas of the room were dry! She persuaded Mrs. Lavington to move in. "Oh it is hopeless, Eliza. How are we to find food?"

"You must leave that to me, madam. I said that I would look after you, and I will, never worry."

So Eliza joined London's thousands of poor beggars. She was not successful. It takes skill, cunning, or some special advantage – like having only one arm or leg or eye – to make a success of it. Children were often better beggars...many had been deliberately mutilated as babies by their parents in order to give them a better appeal to the kind-hearted with money.

Yes! That was the main thing, Eliza reasoned: you have to go where you'll find people who have money, and are prepared to spend it.

No good going into areas of the wealthy houses such as the one they had recently left...for the moneyed classes tended to step from their door directly into their chariots and away.

The taverns were already full of beggars, she found in her first forays. She did have some small success. However there were conditions attached, all too often.

"So, my pretty one...you'd like me to give you some money, would you?" Here a big wink to the man's drinking companions. "And what do I get for my shilling?

"Here it is...come and sit on my knee...I always like to handle the goods before I pay for them.

"You won't! Well, no sale then. Be off with you! There are plenty more harlots around!"

And Eliza found herself retreating from the gales of coarse laughter and ribald shouts.

She tried the coffee houses. They tended to be more refined, if you went to the right ones. But the result was often the same. You want money. I want sex for it.

After two weeks, it became clear to Eliza that her mistress was starving, and would not last long without solid food. Solid food costs money. Agreeing to men's demands would bring money.

So she became a prostitute.

Her first time was, for her, the torn fabric of nightmares...here she was with a strange man doing something that, yes, she had dreamed about in her romantic thoughts of her first and only lover.

But she was lucky: he was kind, and first bought her a drink. Then he took her to his room nearby, he talked to her, and was actually gentle with her. But he wanted his money's worth, and he got it. Eliza could not stop tears coursing down her face.

He gave her three shillings, for she was well-dressed, if a little grimy, and her hair was not infested with the lice that you expected on a prostitute.

She didn't know that a man would pay ten guineas for a virgin. Many whores made a profession for years out of being a virgin, it was so lucrative!

Distressed, yet successful, she bought some bread, milk, and a small amount of cold meat, and took them to her mistress.

It did not take more than a few minutes for Mrs. Lavington to work out how Eliza had got the food. She was horrified. Even worse, she refused to touch the food thus obtained. But Eliza insisted. "Madam, you must eat! We cannot lie here and die when I have the means to feed us."

Both women wept. But they ate the food. In the end the choice was simple.

Over the next few weeks Eliza earned enough to save them from starvation. But Mrs. Lavington, already plunged into deep despair at their situation, sank ever deeper into depression with which there was no reasoning.

The weather became warmer, and at least that gave some relief to Eliza's concerns. But her mistress's state of mind could not respond. She seemed unable to eat much of the food that Eliza brought, no matter how tasty.

One warm day in early August Eliza knew that she was pregnant. She would have to tell Mrs. Lavington sooner or later. She persuaded her mistress to take a walk with her in the sunshine. The sad older woman needed support each step of the way. They sat down on a bench in a small green park. And there Mrs. Lavington died.

For Eliza there was one last duty she had to perform for her mistress. She had discovered that, as a prostitute with a good turn of phrase as well as a face and figure that attracted men, she could demand higher fees.

She was determined that there would be no pauper's burial for her beloved mistress. So she set to work. And she was able to provide Mrs. Lavington with a funeral and a nice headstone for her grave.

CHAPTER 40

1757

She had been the only mourner at the funeral. Now Eliza was left alone, standing at the side of the grave as the men began filling it with earth.

But her mind was busy. She was pregnant. She was homeless. She had to do something. She was going to need decent shelter. She was going to need help.

Her real mother! Was she still in the same house in Cock Lane, opposite where Eliza had lived as a child? Even if she were not there, she might be found: with luck, somebody would know where she had gone.

After a longish walk Eliza found that Miriam was still living in the same house. It was nearly ten years since she had seen her mother, and Miriam had become an old woman.

And when Eliza explained who she was, and why she was there, it did not entirely surprise her that Miriam was not welcoming.

"You've got a sauce! You live with someone else full of airs and graces, you get pregnant, and left alone, then you come back here after all these years and expect me to provide you with a home. You can bugger off! I want nothing to do with you. I have enough of a hard time providing for myself!"

But Eliza was not a little girl, to be turned away. "Look. Whether you like it nor not you are my mother. You have never looked after me...ever.

"It's true I lived with someone else, simply because you gave me away as soon as I was born. It's no thanks to you that I'm still here. But here I am...and it is time you carried out some of your responsibilities."

"Of all the nerve! Go away! Go! Or I'll kick you down the street."

"No, mother. I am not leaving. You say you're having a hard time providing for yourself, and I'm not surprised. You may have been a beauty when you were young...and so you'd get a fair living from being a bunter. But just think, you are now how old? Turned forty, I'm sure.

"Like any woman of that age, you're past your best. You can't keep on the game for ever. And the gin hasn't helped! You'll need me in your old age.

"I'll be honest...I need you now. But once I've had this baby, I will be the one to bring in the money. You won't need to be laced mutton until you die of starvation."

"Oh! 'Ark at 'er! Laced mutton indeed! Where did you learn that kind of talk? Not at Dora Blundell's - 'er with her 'igh and mighty ways!"

She paused suddenly.

"'Ere...I see it all now! You're on the game too! That's it, ain't it! Fancy...Eliza Ayre a buttered bun!

"Eliza Mair, not Ayre, don't you know your own name, mother!"

"Ayre, Mare...what do I care. I've always said Ayre."

"Well, can I come in and live with you? You can be the madam and I'll go out on the town after I've had the baby. What do you say?"

So Eliza moved in to Miriam's room. And her first task was to start cleaning it up. "I've been living rough, but I'm not putting up with this mess," she said bluntly.

And in those few words she told her ageing, drunkard mother that she was now in charge.

*

1758

The birth of her baby was a torment of agony for Eliza. It went on...and on. All one day. All the night. Eliza was exhausted, bathed in sweat, full of fear as well as pain. Miriam's offers of gin were turned down at first. But as the excruciating waves returned and returned she was

316

prepared to take anything that might bring some relief...it was rough firewater that coursed through her.

But it didn't help. Eliza lost concentration, and she lost co-ordination. Eventually it was a younger woman from a room upstairs in the same house who came to her assistance after listening for hours to the inevitable din.

Miriam was elbowed out of the way. The neighbour, Bella, was only twenty, but she had already had a baby of her own, so she knew what was what.

At last, though, as the top of the baby's head could be seen, and she knew the final stage had been reached, she had to go back upstairs to feed her small baby whose furious crying could be heard.

Miriam helped to lift the baby clear. She knew what to do now. Before it could cry, she held her hand on to its face, holding it down, feeling the baby go limp under her.

And as Eliza began to try to see what was happening, and asked "Is it a boy?" Miriam told her that yes, it was, but it was dead...born dead.

Eliza's tears mingled with her exhaustion and a feeling of anger that it had all been for nothing. "I want to hold him," she pleaded.

"Oh! He is perfect. He can't be dead! Can we rub him alive...he must be alive....he is so lovely...he can't be dead!"

But he was. And when the young neighbour from upstairs returned, she confirmed it. She put her arm round Eliza's shoulders and kissed her and stroked her hair to try to comfort her in her terrible distress.

"There's nothing we can do. Give him to me...I'll get rid of him," said Miriam.

"No! No you won't! I love him and I want to hold him!"

"You can't love a baby that's born dead," her mother told her. "You mustn't think so. You need it out of the way, so you won't see it no more."

But Eliza was determined. She put the poor dead mite into a little cradle that she had borrowed, and rocked it. "He's asleep now," she said.

"Eliza, you have to face it...it's dead. You can't keep on pretending!"

"I'm pretending for now...I'm keeping him by me until I can make arrangements for him to be buried properly in the churchyard.

"I won't let him be thrown on to a rubbish heap to be eaten by dogs and pigs, like I've seen happen to dead babies.

"So don't try and take him away. He's my baby, even if he is dead. And I will look after him. He's in my care...till I can give him back to God."

She was as good as her word. Five days after the birth, she watched as her dead baby was put into his little grave in the north side of the churchyard of St. Sepulchre's, a place forever sacred to Eliza.

*

1764

It was nearly two years before Eliza had another baby. "It's what happens when you're on the game," her mother said philosophically.

"It's like I told you – babies are no good to a bunter. This time send it straight off to a country nurse, if it lives. It wrings your heart a bit at first, but it's the best way, and that's the honest truth."

It still hurt Eliza to think of that poor little dead baby of hers, seemingly perfect, yet dead. But she had become hardened to the ways of the world since then...a tough world, where, she had begun to admit, babies had no place if you were working the streets.

They needed money to live. A baby couldn't be kept, because it would stop her working.

And she had to keep on working. For Miriam didn't ply the streets now, except rarely...and she didn't have much success. Old, half-crazed by gin, missing a front tooth, she didn't attract too much trade...and the odd man who was desperate enough wasn't going to pay very much for his few minutes with Miriam.

So it did make sense. If this baby lived, it was best it should be farmed out to be nursed in the country...that seemed to give babies the best chance in life. The parish would arrange it, and pay for the service, too. They reckoned that it cost less than looking after the children of poor parents in the workhouse.

So when the new baby was born - a girl this time – Eliza wept a little, but was ready to bid the baby goodbye when Miriam took it away to hand over to the parish. The birthing had not been so bad this time, and much shorter. Eliza was back at work in three weeks.

Sixteen months later, it all happened again.

It was nearly two years later, when she was expecting her fourth child, that Eliza was confronted by the truth about babies sent out to countrywomen to nurse.

It was in a tavern one day, before the men were in the mood, when Eliza and two other street-women she had got to know, were drinking a bowl of coffee against the early-Spring chill, when the subject cropped up.

Eliza was clearly pregnant, and the three women were discussing babies...and what to do with them. They were definitely unwanted. "My last two have been sent to the parish to be nursed in the country...you never know what's happened to them, but at least I feel they've been given a chance," said Eliza.

"But not much of chance, from what I hear," said one of her friends.

"What do you mean?" asked Eliza.

"I've heard that hardly any of them live. The country women take their half-crown a week pay from the parish, then let them starve to death when they're ready to take another baby.

"The parish couldn't care less...it's cheaper for the babies to die than to be raised and then given back to the workhouse to feed and clothe before being sent out as apprentices...which is another expense for the parish."

"You mean these country nurse-women let them die on purpose, just to get a few shillings from the parishes?" said the third woman. "That is bloody murder, if you ask me...just bloody murder!"

319

"Yes, but it's no different from throwing new-born babies in the Thames, is it?"

"No. I suppose not. And, let's face it, we don't want the babies ourselves, do we?

"And at least the river is a quicker end then leaving babies to starve and get eaten by hogs on the rubbish heaps."

"I had my first baby buried decently in the churchyard, even though he was born dead," said Eliza. "Since then, my mother has taken the other two to the parish for nursing. I thought it gave them a chance."

"How do you know where your mother took them?" said one of her friends. "For all you know she may have just dumped them...on the rubbish or in the river. You don't really know, do you?"

Eliza thought about that. "No, I suppose I don't know for sure...only what my mother told me."

She thought about it a lot.

*

Thinking about her babies, especially the first one, the lovely little deadborn boy, played havoc with Eliza's emotions. *Had her mother told her the truth?* The question would not go away. It troubled Eliza's dreams at night; and by day it became a constant, nagging, doubt.

She knew that confronting Miriam over it would do no good. It would simply be denied that she had harmed the baby. Of course it would. And yet...

And what of her other babies? What would have become of those children if they had lived, and lived with her? How she would have loved to have seen them respond as babies, then learn to crawl and walk and talk, loving their mother. What would they have said to her?

Eliza had taken to visiting her upstairs neighbour Bella – it was short for Isabella, she was told. Bella lived with her husband John and their three little children, aged six, two and six months.

They were such nice people, and the children were a delight, Eliza found. Bella was obviously a good mother, for her children plainly

320

loved her as much as she loved them...clinging to her skirts...holding out their arms to be picked up...saying such funny things. Bella was happy with them.

Eliza pictured herself with little ones. It was, she found, a pleasing thought. And it kept coming back to her. It became a need, a pressing, urgent need within her, one that she could not suppress.

She wanted a child of her own.

Eliza was eight months pregnant before she told her mother that she had decided to keep this baby.

Miriam, by now, had become a drink-raddled old woman of 51. She pooh-poohed the very idea. Who would look after the child while Eliza was out working? Don't expect me to become a nursemaid at my age, for I shan't. Anyway it might be too weak to live...a lot of 'em are.

Eliza soothed her with assurances that she had some money put aside, and that would tide them over until she could get back to work again.

After that, she'd arranged for Bella to look after the baby. She was already at home with her own three little ones, and she'd be glad of the small amount Eliza would give her to look after her new baby too.

"Don't try to alter my mind, mother. I am quite decided."

By the time the baby was due, Eliza had arranged for Bella to help with the birth. She was as good as her word. She stayed until she was sure the new baby girl was safe in Eliza's arms, alive and squawking and obviously healthy.

But Miriam, her brain wandering goodness knew where, kept harping on about getting rid of the child before she became attached to it.

She was wasting her time. Eliza was ecstatic with her new baby. Two weeks after the birth she carried the little girl child to church to be christened Isabella, named after the neighbour-turned-friend who had helped with the birth...and, Eliza couldn't prevent herself from thinking, who had helped with keeping the baby out of Miriam's clutches while she herself was recovering from the birthing ordeal.

It was two days after the christening when Eliza, who had stepped outside to hang up some washing, returned to find the baby missing...and Miriam too.

In an instant sweat of panic she ran from the house. Which way? Miriam could have carried the baby anywhere. This way led towards the parish workhouse. No! The river! She had only been outside the house for a few minutes...she couldn't have got very far. Could she?

Fear – like a cold rat-bite somewhere deep inside – threatened to overwhelm Eliza. But she was not going to lose her baby without a fight. Her brain reasoned instinctively that if Isabella had been taken to the workhouse she could check that later. If she was thrown on to a rubbish-heap she could be found.

But the instant threat was that Miriam was taking her to throw into the Thames...and the river was more than a quarter of a mile away.

She could run faster than her old mother! It was a few moments to run into Pie Corner, then Giltspur Street. Picking up her skirts Eliza legged it past St. Sepulchre's, and down Old Bailey to Ludgate Hill, fear dominating everything else in her being.

Hardly noticing other people, her heart threatening to beat its way out of her chest, her breathing forced against its gasping desire to stop, she made her legs hurry down the narrow alley that faced her, then though a winding court that led into Broad Way, then Water Lane. There! At the end of Water Lane ahead, she saw a figure turn right and disappear: she was sure it was Miriam.

Scarcely able to breathe at all she staggered out of Water Lane to the path alongside the Fleet...and caught a glimpse of a figure heading down the stairs leading to the Thames waterside...Miriam!

No! Oh no! Please God! Leaping down the stone steps, Eliza launched herself at the figure of her mother. Miriam tottered, struggling to retain her balance, then fell on to one knee, still holding the baby. From behind, Eliza grasped her round the neck...tightening her arm under her mother's throat...twisting until she forced the older woman to the ground. Miriam was scratching and kicking to fight Eliza away.

Quickly Eliza jumped with her knees crashing on to her mother's side. Ignoring Miriam's groan of pain she grabbed her baby and hugged the child to her chest. But Miriam had got hold of Eliza's skirt, and was trying with demoniac persistence to pull herself up. Eliza was just as determined that she was not going to reach the baby. The two women wrestled...Miriam trying to scratch and punch in an insane fury.

Eliza pushing Miriam away, pushing, kicking out at the older woman as she fell to her knees again. This was not a struggle that could just stop at stalemate. It was a fight for life - Isabella's life. Eliza knew she had to stop her mother. With all her strength she kicked at her as she tried to get to her feet...kicked and pushed with her foot until Miriam fell sideways...and rolled into the rushing, unforgiving water...floating at first, a mess of dark clothes and a waving arm...a gurgle of a cry...and silence.

Isabella! My baby! Eliza's tears brushed her baby's face as she hugged her close: "There, there...you're all right now...you're all right my darling...my lovely...my little one."

But Isabella just gurgled contentedly, apparently happy at all that had gone on. She wasn't even crying.

For Eliza, breathless and battered, it was different. What have I done? I've killed her! Oh God! I have murdered my own mother! She looked round in her anguish and guilt. There's nobody who saw it. The struggle had been punctuated by gasps and yelps of pain from both women, but there had been no great noise to bring their fight to the attention of any passers-by. Is there a boat...can I save her? No. It's too late now. She's gone. I've killed her...my own mother! Oh God, forgive me. I didn't mean to kill her.

But even as that thought went through her mind, Eliza knew that she had felt glad when she kicked Miriam and watched her roll into the water. At that moment she had been glad!

And I'd do it again if she were to reappear and try to drown my baby again! For Eliza knew that was the only reason her mother could have had to carry Isabella all this way and to descend to the waterside, here, where nobody would see her. Surely that is true. Isn't it?

Maybe the baby had been crying and Miriam had taken her in her arms for a walk outside to comfort and quieten her! No. Quieten her for good! Of course Miriam would not have headed so quickly so far to the river if she was comforting the baby. I was right to do what I did. Of course I was...I have saved my baby's life, and that is what matters

It made Isabella all the more precious to her. But Eliza never had a day when the dreadful vision of her mother floating to her death failed to come into her mind. Nor a night when she did not dream of a fearsome, endless fight with Miriam.

CHAPTER 41

1770

Isabella was used to being left alone while her mother was out, working. She was six now, a bright little girl, and she had become quite able to look after herself, Eliza knew.

One floor above, there was always Bella who could be called on if Isabella needed help.

But it was not enough. Eliza was thirty-five. She had always been single. She needed a man to share her life. She had never set out to remain single.

She had often thought about it. If she could find the right man, a man she could love, and one who earned enough, she might be able to give up working, and look after her growing daughter all the time.

It was a pleasing thought. In that frame of mind Eliza found a man to fall in love with. But he wasn't what she needed.

Dan Moore was a bad choice. He moved in with Eliza and Isabella, sharing the one room. He was strong and quick-witted and funny, and kind to both. He seemed to have money. But he was keen to keep Eliza at work, just a little, to help with his business ventures, which were going through a thin time.

As time went on it became clear that what he wanted was to live off Eliza, while he dabbled in something he described as buying and selling.

It took trusting, open Eliza a while to realise that Dan was a receiver of stolen property, making a profit by moving it on. He wasn't a big-time crook. He dabbled. When he felt like it.

So he became Eliza's bully, taking care of her, he said, when she was on the streets, loitering within hailing distance...ready to rush to her aid if needed. Except that on the one or two occasions when she did have a problem with a client, he didn't happen to be around, just at that moment.

But at home Dan was good company, Eliza had to admit. And Isabella adored him. In bed he kept Eliza happy, too. She could enjoy sex with him.

So he became part of the household, useless or not. And Eliza kept on working as a prostitute, to support herself, Isabella, and Dan.

*

1777

At 42 Eliza might have expected a few more years. But syphilis and its horrors were mercifully virulent enough to make short work of her.

More than ten years earlier she had first noticed a strange ulcer. It had cleared up in a week. But a month later she had developed a rash of sores on her body and legs.

That had been more troublesome, because it was accompanied by aches and pains. It was one of her prostitute friends who warned her that it might be the great pox.

Eliza's anxiety on that score abated when the sores and the pains disappeared after a few weeks.

They came back from time to time. But they didn't seem to be anything to worry about.

In the last two years, though, Eliza's health had deteriorated. She had great pain in her limbs. And sometimes Isabella noticed that she had difficulty remembering things, and her speech became slurred as if she had been drinking.

Dan and Isabella had always been friends, despite the difference in their ages. Eliza's problems, which made every conversation with her a discussion of her ills, brought them even closer. They shared a joke; they told each other about funny things they had seen, or heard about: it was light relief from Eliza, her sickness, and her complaints.

Dan, who had always been a small-time crook, fascinated Isabella with his revelations about the way the underworld worked.

He told her, one day, about the Twang, in which a street walker - he called her a buttock – who was trained in picking pockets, would pull in a cull, and persuade him that a quiet corner against a wall in the darkness would be the place to get his pleasure. During initial fumbling she would take anything of value from his pocket, and once his trousers were down, round his ankles, her accomplice would come along, knock the man to the ground, making it look like an accident, and in the melee the woman would scarper with the items she had stolen.

It was one of many things he told Isabella. To a girl of thirteen it was eye-opening, fascinating...a glimpse of the adult world that she knew little about till now. To Isabella, Dan seemed to be the father she had always wanted.

Meanwhile life at home became more difficult. Eliza became very short of breath. Walking was a trouble to her. Sometimes she could not raise the energy to go to work. It caused rows with Dan, who didn't like to think that his income was threatened.

It was after such an argument, one day, that Eliza collapsed without warning. A physician was called, but she was dead. She had had a heart attack, he told a stunned Dan and Isabella after examining her. And by ways of comfort he added that it did not seem that she could have suffered...it looked as if she had been dead before her body struck the floor.

The attack, he added, had undoubtedly been brought on by her condition of lues. Never having heard the word, they did not know that it was the physician's term for syphilis.

The speed of her demise may have meant that Eliza did not suffer, but Isabella and Dan did. It was the most terrible shock. For Isabella the loss of her mother left her numb with grief...a thirteen year-old left alone in the world.

Dan's prime concern was for his livelihood. How were they to live?

*

That night, Dan was the instant comforter to Isabella. As she wept, he came and lay down with her on her mattress, stroking her hair, whispering gently that all would be well...kissing her and caressing her, stroking her shoulders, her back, her buttocks. She felt a strange new warmth. She felt a need that she had not experienced before. She turned to him and he was kissing her...not like a father.

They became entwined. She felt an ecstasy of surging sensations that made her forget her grief.

So they became lovers. But Eliza wasn't quite forgotten: Dan kept thinking about her loss, and how they would earn enough to support themselves.

And he came up with an answer quite quickly – in fact he had been considering it for weeks now. He reminded Isabella about it.

"We've got to pay the rent. I can teach you how we can get money by going on the buttock and twang. We'll be a team," he told Isabella.

"But first you'll have to learn how to pick a man's pockets...I can send you to a good teacher. Then you pretend to be a street woman.

"Remember what I told you: we choose our place, and you suggest to the cull that you stand against the wall, and he starts to fumble you. You fumble back. That's when you'll find it easier to pick his pocket. When he gets his breeches down round his ankles, I come blundering up, pretending to be drunk, crash into him and knock him to the ground, and while we're trying to get to our feet you make off with the valuables.

Works a treat, I'm told.

"You'd have the easy part. If the cull realises that we are a team he's liable to attack me.

"And in any case I'll be left with the problem of getting rid of the goods – I'll be classed as a receiver of stolen property if I'm caught...and that's a hanging offence."

Isabella didn't like the sound of it. "I'd be a common thief," she said. "And if you don't arrive at exactly the right time, I'll be a prostitute too.

"That's one thing I don't want to be...I only want to make love to you...ever. And look what happened to my mother!"

But Dan was persuasive. He kept on telling her about it. He kept on asking her how they were to live, bearing in mind that his business was going through such a difficult time again.

Yes, he loved her. Yes, they could always make love. Of course it was wonderful and he too felt the magic of it. But they had to pay the rent, and his business interests are going through a very thin time. They had to buy food. They had to find a way of getting money. Why won't you try what I'm suggesting? Or would you prefer to go out begging? At least, learn how to be a pickpocket – it might be a handy thing to know anyway.

So Isabella went to learn the tricky art of a clouter. In a cellar under a warehouse near the river there was this man – Jem he was called – who passed on his know-how for a fee.

But talking was not enough. You had to practise. And to do this he had devised a dummy figure, wearing a coat and trousers, with items in the pockets. But from each pocket hung a small bell: make a mess of taking the things from a pocket and you'd make at least one bell tinkle.

With three other pupils, all younger than Isabella, she listened to Jem's advice, and tried to lift the things from the dummy's pockets. At first they all failed. The bells rang every time. But they all got better, with the help of constant advice from their teacher.

After a month, during which Eliza's savings – which Dan had found hidden in an old pot - had all but been used up, Isabella began to find she could get into the dummy's pockets without ringing the bells.

Another two weeks of concentrated practise, and she was ready to set out with Dan on her first foray into the world of buttock and twang robbery. She had been coached by Dan on the art of being a buttock, but God! was she frightened!

In the event it was amazingly easy – and successful. The elderly man who fancied this obviously young prostitute was easy meat for the twang. He had plainly been drinking, and Isabella got a coin from his coat pocket and made off with it when Dan barged into her cull. The man thought it was an accident and when last seen making his way unsteadily into the darkness, brushing himself down, he had apparently not noticed his loss.

It became a way of life for Dan and Isabella. But sometimes her cull got his way with his pleasure and Dan failed to show up...he always had an excuse: the watch was too near; too many people were about; a business acquaintance had stopped to talk to him. So Isabella became the third in line in her family to become a woman of the streets, after Eliza and Miriam.

Dan, the man she thought of as her father, was now her business partner as well as her lover. Thinking about it all, Isabella had mixed feelings. It wasn't what she had ever intended. But it was paying the rent, and feeding them too.

She was sure her mother would not have approved. But her mother had gone now, and Isabella had to live.

My mother – I'll never forget her. She told me about her own life, and things didn't always go according to plan for her either. But she was a sweet lady. I'll never forget her – or the stories she told me about her life.

I don't think she ever thought about it, but what she told me showed that she was decent, and loyal. Unlike what she told me about her own mother...Miriam, she called her. Not only did Miriam give her away as a baby, but she seems to have been a bitter, cantankerous old biddy.

I wonder what made her so?

*

1984

Geoff had never seriously questioned the permanence of his marriage. Now there was an indefinable feeling of emptiness. In all the years, and despite the kind of tiffs that happen to everyone - and Hanna's growing acerbity that had become more and more noticeable recently - it had never occurred to him that their marriage was heading for the rocks.

But suddenly he couldn't help wondering what had happened to their relationship. There wasn't anything there any more.

With startling clarity he could see that he had learned to live with Hanna's contempt.

What on earth had made this change? I know there's the politics that she feels strongly about, but what I can't stomach is this terrible attitude against the working class...and its ridiculous transference to me because of the lowly status of my ancestors.

And it isn't just a touch of cynicism as she gets older. Sometimes I have the feeling that Hanna actually despises me. Why?

Now I think about it, it's been going on for a while now. And that's why, if I'm absolutely honest, I no longer feel there's any love between us...after all these years. I just can't believe it.

It was simply a fact that she was getting more and more critical.

Of course she's always been something of a nag. But then, a lot of women are. It's about keeping their men-folk in line.

That's what my friends tell me, anyway. But this seems more than just nagging. It's as if she can't refrain from destructively criticizing my every action, word, and suggestion.

Suddenly he remembered his "Fart Theory Extended."

Geoff had read somewhere about some sage – he couldn't remember who, but he thought he was a writer – who had stated that people like the smell of their own farts.

Of course, if true, then it followed naturally that people don't like other people's farts.

But it had occurred to Geoff at the same time that you could extend that statement to say that people don't like other people's farts *unless you like that person.*

A good friend's fart can be something to laugh about. Otherwise it is disgusting.

With an inward smile, he called it his Fart Theory.

For some reason that thought had returned to him later, and the idea had occurred that you could generalize the idea to most events in daily life.

Then he and Hanna went to the recently opened Royal Exchange Theatre in Manchester to see Shakespeare's "Hamlet," and Geoff found himself dwelling on the line "there is nothing either good or bad but thinking makes it so."

It looked as if the bard had had pretty well the same thought as the one that kicked off his Fart Theory!

Something done or said by a person you dislike becomes intolerable and you hate it: the same action or statement by someone you really like may be controversial, but it is just a matter for debate, maybe even of laughter.

He called it his Fart Theory Extended. It was mildly amusing to him. It wasn't something he'd ever mentioned to anyone else.

But he had, from time to time, used his theory in his role as deputy flight manager. Again, it was for nothing more than his secret amusement. Now, suddenly and with great clarity, it occurred to him that he fell into the category of people that Hanna disliked.

One day, he recalled, he had told her a joke that he had heard. He thought it was extremely funny. But when he told Hanna the joke she stayed po-faced, and said that she didn't think it funny at all.

A month or so later, having evidently forgotten his attempt at humour, Hanna told him that a friend had told her an absolutely hilarious joke. She related it to Geoff, and it was exactly the same joke. She laughed uproariously when she came to the punch-line.

It was the same joke that Geoff had told her...the one she had found so unfunny.

When he had pointed this out to her, Hanna said she couldn't remember his telling her any such story, and she certainly would have done if, in fact, he had told her. It must be his memory going – she had noticed of late that he was getting forgetful and vague.

Did he think he ought to go to the doctor's and have himself checked – perhaps he was getting Alzheimers.

Apart from the barbed nonsense about his memory, he could see that here was a case of the Fart Theory Extended.

It was true her constant harping was getting very irritating. That was something Geoff couldn't deny to himself.

He could think of loads of occasions when, in recent times, she had annoyed him by her barbed comments, unnecessary criticism, and attitudes that you had to say were actually nasty.

Has it always been like this? No, of course not. Yet for as long as he could remember it had been there to a lesser degree.

It was just more marked now. Since when? Was there any event that had happened that might have made her so critical? None that he could think of.

Take the time of that Malta flight, over a year ago now. One didn't like to blow one's own trumpet, but everybody said he had done a good job there. Yet Hanna had never once said "Well done" or even "Good job."

If anything, her tone had been vaguely critical, or, at least, she welcomed him with the air of one who wasn't impressed at all.

It's just the way she is. OK. But I don't have to like it.

CHAPTER 42

1725

Miriam Ayre remembered her mother quite well, even though she was only six when she was hanged.

Her mother had been so lovely and kind, and everything was nice, until the day some rough men came and took her away to prison because she was a thief.

Miriam was taken to live in the parish workhouse, and no matter how much she cried they told her she could not have her ma because she had been hanged. So she'd have to make the best of it.

So she got used to living in the workhouse. The other children said that most people were thieves, but didn't get caught...if you did you were put to death by being hung up by your neck at a place called Tyburn.

Lots of people went to see hangings. It was encouraged by the government because the ruling class thought it would be a deterrent to the lower orders.

But the mob made a party out of the hanging days, so it didn't actually cut crime. Only the loved ones of the hanged seemed horrified by the terrible sight of the agonizing, prolonged choking, as death usually took about ten minutes.

Sometimes the family of the condemned got permission from the hangman to hold on to their legs and pull down, so as to shorten the agony and speed up the death.

Miriam heard all this and was glad they hadn't allowed her to see her mother's hanging.

The workhouse women were quite kind, but very strict, she recalled. One of the women in charge told Miriam that she must never be a thief – if she was ever tempted to steal she must remember what had happened to her mother.

So she never was a thief. She decided, when she was twelve, to earn her living as a prostitute. And that is what she did.

The other girls had told her about it. It was easy. You let men do what they wanted, and they gave you money for it.

She was advised to try it out first with some of the workhouse boys, and after she got used to it she found that she really liked it.

So then she went out with two other girls, and instead of begging in the streets – which was what they were encouraged and expected to do - they went into a tavern, and they became prostitutes because it was so easy. And they all got money for it, and they were all very pleased.

Soon after that Miriam was sent away from the workhouse to be an apprentice with a woman who was a fishmonger. But the woman kept hitting her and shouting at her, and she got no money for being an apprentice – just food and lodgings, she was told when she first arrived.

The only food she was given were scraps that otherwise would have been thrown away. And what was meant by lodgings was sleeping on the hard floor of the shop when her mistress went upstairs to her room after locking up at night.

So Miriam ran away and worked full time as a prostitute, haunting the taverns and earning enough to rent a room in Cock Lane, Newgate – just a little way from the house she remembered as a little girl. She earned enough to live quite well. It was much better than being an apprentice.

*

Miriam never quite understood how her mother got money to live by.

But she assumed that she was given money by her father, who was wealthy as well as famous. Her ma, whose name was Lucy Ayre, was proud of telling her many times that her father was Jonathan Wild, the famous Deputy Under-Marshall of the City, and the best thief-taker in London. Probably the best in the world!

Sounded grand. And renowned he might have been, but he never married my mother, did he, she reasoned. I was born out of wedlock, that's for certain, for I'm Miriam Ayre, not Wild.

But ma doted on him...she had a strange sort of look in her eyes when she mentioned his name, I remember that. Thinking about it now when I'm older and can understand these things, she was very much in love with him.

So why would she have to steal? Perhaps he didn't give her so much after all. I'll never know.

But Jonathan Wild is dead now too, hanged for all sorts of devilry, so I was told. Just a month or two back. Everybody was talking about it. He was a very famous man, right enough.

Miriam was mulling over these thoughts as she made her way to a tavern where she picked up many of her customers. But it was too early to expect much business yet.

Inside the Boar's Head she saw an old man sitting by himself, and sipping at an ale tankard. She quickly sat beside him and said: "You look like a kind man, sir...would you buy two penn'orth of crank for a thirsty young girl that has no home and no parents."

It was her standard approach.

"How did you lose your parents?"

"Both hanged. My mother when I was only six years old, and my father just a month or two back...Jonathan Wild, he was called."

Now the old man sat back in his chair and looked carefully at Miriam. "Jonathan Wild was your father? Are you sure?"

"I only know that is what my mother told me. She seemed sure enough, because she told me so many times. She seemed to be very proud of him, although I'm sure they never were married."

"What was your mother's name?"

"Lucy Ayre."

"Well I knew Jonathan Wild, and I never heard tell of Lucy Ayre, although to tell the truth he did have many women in his life. He must have been married half a dozen times, sometimes to more than one at the same time!"

"What was he like?"

"Wait a minute – I'll get you that gin you wanted...and another ale for me, I think."

*

"What do you know about him already?"

"I only know that my mother seemed to be in love with him. And that he was hanged a month or two back. I was told he was up to all sorts of terrible things."

"Let me tell you, he was the absolute master of crime. But for years he fooled a lot of people into thinking that all he did was to catch criminals!

"He called himself by a grand title – Thief Taker General of Great Britain and Ireland. And it's true that he had agents all over the land.

"Even the government took his advice on catching thieves.

"It made him a rich man. In the end he went about in a coach and six, when it suited him. And he owned a ship to take stolen booty to Flanders and Holland to be sold there...and to bring valuables and brandy back to London to be sold here!

"He was the biggest organiser of crime in this city. But at the same time, mark you, he made his reputation as the man who fought crime...the best thief-taker that has ever been. He even petitioned to be given the freedom of the city of London.

"Fact is, he was an absolute genius, and no mistake."

"I don't understand how he could have been on both sides of the law at the same time," said Miriam.

"Well he was! He fooled the judges and he fooled the aldermen and he even fooled the government and the king. And I'll tell you how, if you've got an hour or two to spare!

"When he was a young man he came to London from up north somewhere, and he soon got into debt...ended up in debtors' prison...the Wood Street Compter I'm pretty sure it was.

337

"I believe the conditions in there were terrible. And he was inside for two years or more. I'm not sure what goes on in those places, for I've never been in one. But all I do know is that when he got out he had learned enough to become a master criminal.

"He went and lived with a prostitute that he'd met in the compter, and she completed his education, that's what I heard."

"When was this? Because my mother told me she'd been put inside Wood Street for debt...it was all a mistake, but they put her inside all the same."

"Aye, they all say that...there's never a man or woman in prison but that there're innocent! But when was it? I don't know for sure, but I reckon it would have been 1712 or 13 when Wild got out."

"Well I was born in 1713. I bet that's where they met...in the compter. I wonder if that's where they got together so that I came along nine months later!"

"From what I hear, it's quite likely. He had a charm about him, and a tongue that could persuade you to believe that black was white.

"The thing was, once he was freed he worked at getting to know all the criminals and the way they worked. Through the woman he lived with he got to know a lot of them, because she knew everybody. Crime was big business in London at that time. Thieving, highway robbery, cut-pursing...anything.

"He managed to become assistant to the Under Marshall – a man called Hitchens who was a famous thief-catcher. You got a big reward for catching thieves, once they were convicted...still do for that matter.

"Jon realised he could use his knowledge of who was in whose gang and put it to good use.

"Also he could see that he was smarter than his boss. So he set up on his own, catching thieves and getting them hanged, and mostly getting £40 for each one, and as much as £140, so I've heard."

Miriam was puzzled: "But isn't that doing good? Why did they say he was such a bad man if he caught lots of thieves?"

"I know it doesn't sound likely, but you see, all the time, he had a lot of thieves working for him. He only caught the thieves that were not

338

working for him. And remember, most of these crimes resulted in hanging. If they didn't hang he didn't get his reward money.

"And here's where it got nasty: if one of his own gang was taken before the court for stealing, Jon Wild always seemed to be able to find witnesses to swear that the theft was committed by someone else that he'd name – it might be a man from another gang, or even some poor innocent who had never committed a crime.

"You have to remember he pretended to a sort of official job of catching the criminals, so the courts believed his word, more often than not.

"And every now and again he had to let one of his people get caught and hanged or transported – the ones that he reckoned weren't much good to him, I suppose.

"I'll tell you straight: Jon Wild sent more innocent people to Tyburn than you could ever believe possible.

"And it didn't bother him none – not him! He seemed to have the power of life or death over people – and criminals were frightened of him. It scared his own thieves into working harder to bring in the valuables that gave him his rich style of life...he really lived the gentleman!

"He was into every sort of crime you can name...blackmail, forgery, smuggling...while he strutted around as the best in the land at catching the criminals...and perhaps he was, too!

"Anyway, that's how he managed to be the chief law-keeper and the chief law-breaker, both at the same time!

"Now that takes genius, if you ask me."

"But why did people steal for him? Why didn't they just steal for themselves?"

"Well at first, when he was making his name, crime was a lot easier because getting rid of stolen goods was easier. Theft was a hanging crime, but fencing stolen things was not.

"So all you had to do was to sell the things to a pawnbroker or a dealer and you were in the clear. I did a bit of it myself, then, when I was younger – that's how I got to know Jon Wild.

"Then, the law was changed, and they made it a hanging offence to receive stolen goods. That made life really difficult for the thieving trade...the threat of the noose round the neck was over all of us. I got out of it.

"But what does Jon Wild do? He calls a meeting of all the big criminals that he can persuade to come, and tells them he's got a scheme to restore their income.

"The idea was, that if they let him know what they had stolen, he would advertise in the newspapers to restore the goods to their owners!

"In the advertisements he claimed that in his capacity as a thief-taker he had chanced across information about the stolen items.

"So when he got a reply, he would tell the owner that through his contacts he had a good idea where he might locate their belongings, and he'd be in touch in a day or two.

"He would say that some honest pawnbroker had told him that he was suspicious when a stranger who looked too poor to own much had tried to sell him valuables.

"He always stressed that his sole interest was in restoring stolen property to its rightful owner, so if he could, he'd return the goods, no questions asked.

"But when he did return them, he naturally expected any reward to be paid to the 'honest pawnbroker' – who, of course, didn't exist. He'd stress that he didn't want anything for himself. To the owner, it was worth it - otherwise would never see his belongings again.

"It meant that Jon wasn't in danger of being prosecuted for receiving...for it was true that he hardly ever saw the things that had been stolen. But he got the reward money, and of course he didn't pass all of it on to the thieves who'd stolen the goods.

"He chose his thieves very carefully. If anybody tried to dispose of their booty themselves, he'd tell them that he knew all about their crimes. They could come under his protection, or if they chose not to, he would prosecute them, and they would undoubtedly hang.

"As a thief-taker he was greatly feared, so his words carried a real threat.

"Oh, he had crime at his fingertips! As a thief catcher he was second to none. His reputation was such that a few years ago the government consulted him about how to do something about the huge number of highway robberies that were happening.

"His advice was simple – he told them to increase the reward payable for catching the highwaymen. They did increase the reward...and it brought him more money for catching the robbers!

"For a time it seemed that whatever happened, he was bound to make money out of it.

"It made him famous, and it made him rich.

"Yes, that's the man who seems to have been your father."

"So why did they hang him?"

"Well for years he relied on fooling the magistrates into believing that he was their best upholder of the law. But at his game, he made some powerful enemies – friends of innocent people that he'd sent to be hanged.

"In the end he was taken to court for theft from a shop. Some say he was set up for revenge by the widow of a man he'd had hanged.

"And he faced a judge who was not to be fooled by his protestations...a judge who seemed to know a lot about him and his career...about his lying and cheating and sending innocent people to be hanged for crimes his own people had committed.

"Jon even tried writing to the king to appeal for mercy. He could read, and he could write a beautiful letter.

"He claimed that he shouldn't hang because he'd done so much public good by catching criminals. And it is true he had destroyed some rival gangs.

"But it didn't get him anywhere. He was tried, found guilty and hanged, and that was that.

"He did do some good in fighting crime. But he sent innocent people as well as guilty to the gallows without any qualms.

"So if you ask me, I'd say he deserved to end up at Tyburn, where so many of his victims went."

"Well I think it's a terrible end for anybody," said Miriam. "My mother was hanged there, and I've often wondered what must have been her terrors as she was taken to be hanged.

"I don't know what she stole or why she stole it. But I only wish Jon Wild had been able to save her. I do.

CHAPTER 43

1728

The old man's story about Jonathan Wild only reinforced Miriam's determination to stay out of crime. She refused to steal. And she refused to beg.

She saw her role as a prostitute as good, honest work.

On more than one occasion her clients, doubtless thinking kindly and trying to be helpful, asked her how she had been forced into being a whore.

She told them the truth: "I wasn't forced into it...I choose to do it. I like it. It's much better than working your fingers to the bone at some so-called honest employment, yet still starving because you don't get paid enough to live by.

"Since I was a girl of twelve I've earned my own living fair and square, and paid my way, and never been in debt to anyone.

"Kind gentlemen like you, sir, take pleasure from me, and give me enough for my pains to ensure that I can dress and eat proper, and enjoy the occasional six-penn'orth of crank to keep the cold out, and I don't have to beg.

"Why would I have to be forced into such a life?"

Despite her protestations, though, Miriam knew that being a bunter brought its problems.

Not all her clients were good and kind; not all paid her properly.

There were diseases to worry about.

And there were babies.

*

What to do with unwanted babies: it was one of the mighty problems.

There were no means of stopping yourself having babies, so they kept on coming, wanted or not.

Miriam ran the risk many times a day. She had always been a bright girl, and when she became a bunter she could see instantly that babies would become a problem soon or later.

She considered the options: you could keep them; you could make a payment to the parish to take them and farm them out to be suckled by country women; you could let them die; you could throw them away on to a rubbish heap or into the river; you could kill them as soon as they were born; or you could leave them in the streets where they might be found and cared for...or not.

Keeping a child was the last thing Miriam wanted.

All the alternatives meant, in effect, killing them...because everyone knew that parish babies rarely survived.

Why pay the parish to do what you can do yourself at no cost, she thought.

I'll get rid of any babies the quickest and easiest way, as it seems at the time, she decided. It'll be quite easy. It's having the babies that's the hard part. But there's nothing a woman can do about that.

Her first baby, which she had when she was barely fifteen, was certainly the hardest of all. The slow-down in her work as she became big and unattractive to the customers was bad enough; the pain and fear in giving birth was terrible. She had a neighbour in the same house to help her. When it was done, Miriam thanked her before she left, then put a cloth over the baby's face, and suffocated him.

She waited a while, then told the woman who had helped her that the baby had died. Then she wrapped the body and took it to a nearby trash heap.

There! That's that! As soon as I'm ready I can get back to work.

It was just part of the daily scene in London...the city that was becoming so much admired by foreign visitors for its splendid buildings, its wide new streets, its well-dressed people, its trade, and its impressive Royal Exchange.

Miriam had become friendly with the old man who had told her about Jonathan Wild. She quite often saw him in the Boar's Head. His name was William White. She liked to talk to him because he knew much that interested her.

Crime, he admitted was a huge problem. "But why is there so much robbing and thieving? I can't help thinking that it is because the ordinary people are so poor that they have to try desperate means to get money. Some out of envy of the rich, perhaps, but others simply because otherwise they'd starve. They lack the means to buy food, their wages being so low…if they have any wages.

"Of course, there's always begging…there are thousands of beggars on the streets.

"The rich see it as a lazy way of getting a living...another example of the idle poor doing anything rather than work for their living. I know a lot of better-off people think that way because I've seen and heard their contempt for those that beg.

"They might be right about some beggars. But the vast majority do it out of desperation. The spur that makes them do it is hunger.

"Thousands of them live out in the streets because they can't afford a penny for a flea-pit of a lodging. In winter I don't believe they do that out of choice.

"Of course that's of no interest to the Law, which is too busy taking a strong line on crime."

He added: "There are now hundreds of crimes that bring a death penalty. But it seems that the Law doesn't hang all criminals…crime is not so bad if them that commit it are rich or educated."

"Surely that can't be true,"

"It is, Miriam. That's why the courts used to have the Benefit of Clergy. If you could read the first verse of Psalm 51 – the neck verse, they called it – you were automatically spared hanging, no matter what the offence. Of course the idea was that anybody with education – who were usually the wealthy people or clergy – should be spared the worst rigours of the law."

"I don't see why that should make any difference," said Miriam.

"Well it did! What *should* make a difference, if you ask me, is *why* people steal. But the majesty of the law does not care that someone steals to buy bread because his children are crying out for food.

"In fact it regards that as a much worse crime than a theft committed in order to increase the riches of people who are already rich!

"You don't believe me? Well what about the case of the Earl of Macclesfield? He embezzled £100,000 of public money. He was taken to court only a few months ago, and fined £30,000. A massive sum indeed – but a lot less than he'd stolen.

"Yet nobody, as far as I know, asked for the earl to be hanged for his crime."

"I can't believe that can be true – can it be?"

"Yes it is! And what about that famous South Sea Company set up by the government fifteen or sixteen years back?"

"I heard about that. They called it the South Sea Bubble…and it ruined many rich people, I heard," said Miriam.

"Absolutely right. But from what I hear, not only rich people lost their money. Even people not so well-off lost their life-savings by investing in it."

"What was it, this company?"

"It was some mad-cap scheme thought up by the Chancellor of the Exchequer of the time. It was going to ship slaves to the Spanish colonies in South America, and the government's idea was that it would pay off the national debt.

"Government ministers let it be known that they were investing their own money in it, so everybody thought it must be a good thing. Hundreds of people who had money rushed to put their savings into it. It was crazy.

"When the bubble burst they lost it all. Some people committed suicide because they were ruined by it. There was big trouble. They had

346

to read the Riot Act. But they never did find out exactly why the company had gone bust because somebody had torn crucial pages out of the company's books.

"But I'm prepared to wager that a few people made vast fortunes out of it all...the investors' money must have gone somewhere.

"And what I'm saying is...it was a huge theft of people's money. Yet nobody was hanged for that either."

*

1740

Miriam had always taken a simple view of life. She liked it that way, and she took it that way. As a prostitute she was simply providing a service for which there was a demand. She gave the service. Men paid for it. So she could pay her rent and buy food for herself. Simple.

Thieving, gambling, religion, love? She didn't want them. Babies? She got rid of them. Men? She didn't want anybody else in her life: why should she give up any part of her life, freedom and cash by taking up with a man?

She liked the loneliness of her room. If she needed cheering up, there was always the crank. Gin was the cheapest thing to drink, and it was available everywhere you looked in London.

And in the terrible cold of this winter she needed it more than ever. The frost was so hard that the Thames froze, and shops and booths were opened on the ice in a big Frost Fair.

All such fun, it seemed...like a carnival! But for many people the cold brought misery, and in some cases, death. For coal supplies became short because ships bringing it from the northern coalfields could not get up the river to London.

Much outdoor work had to stop, not least for the fishermen. Their boats were icebound. Many people had no money for food and fuel. They had to beg. For nearly two months it went on. For some beggars living outdoors it brought desperate suffering.

For Miriam and for many others struggling to keep warm, gin was the only comfort. It brought an inner warmth that made the cold a little more bearable. Drink enough of it and it brought numbness, and sleep.

It was fortunate that gin was so cheap, and so readily available. It seemed that everybody was drinking gin now. You could buy it for very little at shops, street barrows, even ordinary houses. You didn't have to walk far to replenish supplies if you ran out of gin.

When the great frost was over, of course you didn't have to slow down on the drink. It made life more cheerful...until the morning. Then you needed more gin to cheer you up again, Miriam found.

For it was a little depressing to see what was happening around you: drunken men and women, people begging, people spending far too much on gambling...and nobody seemed to get any better-off.

A working girl needed to give herself a bit of comfort.

Then there was the day she saw her reflection in a tavern window, and hardly recognised herself. The reflection was that of a middle-aged woman! She tried moving her hand up to her face in case it was some sort of trick or illusion: but no, it was her all right.

Of course I am not a girl any more. I'm twenty-seven. Oh my God! Soon I'll be thirty! That was a little depressing, too. I need a gin...mustn't be gloomy about growing old.

Some people say you shouldn't drink so much. Well I say why the hell not? It's good for you. It certainly makes me feel better, every time! Of course, some people who have skilled work, like carpenters, for instance, it's important that they are not too drunk to do good work. But for me, it makes me more cheerful and funny, and my customers like it.

Mind you, there don't seem so many of them these days. Well, so what! A girl has to slow down a little as she gets older, that's what I say!

*

1764

The older you get, the harder it is. Life, I mean. And one thing's certain – you can't live like you did when you were young.

As a bunter, it's hard to grow old. I'm fifty-one now, and you see men take a look and decide not…they want something younger.

I can stand the looks. But when they start making remarks about my age to get a laugh from other tavern customers – and other bunters too, I've noticed – it gets nasty.

Mind you, if I get depressed, I can always go home and have a gin or two to cheer myself up. Then I go out again and head for Drury Lane. It's a bit of a walk but sometimes I try my luck on the streets like the low-class smut in their ragged, dirty clothes.

But I have a better chance than them, because I have my nice dress and I look so much better. I always keep my dress up-to-date…when one gets old-looking I go up to Rag Fair and I've never failed to get a newer one there.

I don't like the street trade. I've always used the taverns. Yet I don't do so well there any more.

So though I always said I want nothing to do with children, I can't say I was unhappy when Eliza turned up. She was the only one of all my babies that didn't die…all because those people across the street took her in and raised her. I didn't want anything to do with her. I made that clear.

But I was young then.

When she arrived at my door and asked if she could stay with me, I'll admit I told her to go away. But it only took a few minutes to realise that this might be the best thing for me…her out working the taverns and me spending more time taking my ease at home.

349

I was good for her too. The trouble with Eliza is that she's sentimental. She couldn't have got rid of her babies…not by herself. It was lucky for her that I was here. Now she's having another, and this time she's telling me she's determined to keep this one. So stupid!

Well, we'll see when the time comes. And afterwards, when it's gone, she'll thank me, I swear.

CHAPTER 44

1984

What was it like to live in the eighteenth century? Geoff had never thought about it. But since he had got to know something about his ancestors that far back, he had been doing some reading.

History had never been one of his favourite subjects at school. Now it became a lot more interesting as he tried to get an understanding of life more than 200 years ago.

He was determined not to mention it to Hanna, but he began to form some unpalatable conclusions.

OK. So a lot of people were poor because they were too lazy or thick to work hard and better themselves. I'm sure that must have been true, he mused.

But as I read it, whatever the cause of being poor, the fact is that at every period of history they have been shamelessly used and exploited by the better-off.

Maybe that's natural economics – although exploiting them to the point of starvation, and beyond, sometimes, is not exactly something to be proud of.

But having reduced the labouring poor to desperate poverty, I can not for the life of me see why they had to humiliate them even more by treating them almost as a sub-human species.

The wealthy seemed to have nothing but contempt for the people they had certainly helped to make poor. And not content with contempt, I read that many of the rich were openly derisive...they found it a matter of hilarity that poor people were dressed in rags and were begging for want of food.

That sort of thing caused the revolution in France, and it damn nearly caused one here. Why it didn't is a mystery.

Later, while he was reading a copy of William Cobbett's *Rural Rides*, he wondered about another mystery: why churches in isolated areas miles from any town or decent-sized village, were built so big...some of them capable of holding hundreds of people.

He voiced his puzzlement to Hanna. "Perhaps the local lord of the manor wanted to impress the next manor with his wealth," she suggested.

"More like he was trying to get a passport to heaven!"

"Well we'll never know," said Hanna. "Until we get there ourselves, of course. We must remember to ask!"

Geoff seemed to change the course of the conversation: "I was thinking about my ancestors – have you ever wondered what happens to all the good things that people do in their lives?

"I mean the little acts of kindness and thoughtfulness that are part of daily life, and don't really get noticed."

"Well what should happen to them? Nothing, I should say. What do you mean? What do you think happens to them, for goodness sake?"

"Well, we were talking about going to heaven. Quite honestly it's something said every day in churches, but it's a very strange idea, that you should die and then go to start a new kind of eternal life in paradise.

"I've been thinking that maybe all the little kindnesses that you do, might live on, in a way. People who barely notice it at the time might be influenced in some small way, so that they become more thoughtful, more kind themselves over a period of time because of the way you acted towards them...your children, for instance.

"Perhaps they become part of those double helixes that form the genes...I don't know. Maybe it is the inner you...your soul, if you like – living on in other people. Perhaps that *is* your eternal life."

"My God! You get some strange ideas, Geoffrey! I'm seriously concerned that you're going doolally."

"Perhaps you're right – I don't know what made me think of it. But it's the same thing essentially as the churches say...only it's a damn sight more likely than going and living in eternal bliss with angels for company."

*

1712

London! I never thought to see such a place! I never thought I would go so far from home...from my mother, and from my father.

Lucy Ayre's thoughts were interrupted by her trying to stop herself breaking into sobs as she remembered how her parents had turned her away in her hour of need.

She had been twelve when she went into service in the mansion house not far from her home near Canterbury. It was hard work, being a junior servant. Scrubbing, cleaning, lighting fires, endless polishing, until her arms ached and all she wanted was some sleep.

She seemed to be treated harshly by all, especially the more senior servants. And everyone was senior to her!

But she had applied herself to her work, just as her mother and father had told her to do. And over five years, she moved up the servant ranks, though not very far.

The big difference she noticed was that she did get treated better by some of her fellow-servants...especially the young men.

One or two risked a little squeeze of her waist, or patted her here and there in quiet corners in the servant areas of the big house. One or two tried giving her a kiss. And more than one made her blush by whispering compliments about her beauty!

It was nice to be appreciated. She told her parents about it when she made her occasional visits home. They warned her against becoming the sort of girl who would allow young men to touch her.

They were very strongly influenced by the Bible. There was, they averred, damnation for young women who fell into the Pit.

Lucy came to understand that contact with the opposite sex was the reserve only of the safely married...and then only rarely.

So that terrible day when Sir William raped her was all the more traumatic for Lucy. Once he had gone she gathered her few belongings, and, under cover of darkness, fled back home to tell her parents of the awful thing that had happened to her.

She didn't know what she had thought their reaction might be. But she certainly did not expect the anger, the condemnation, the rejection that she faced.

And all this was aimed at her! It was all her fault! She was a wicked, evil girl! Go from this house and never return! What will people say? What will his reverence the rector say? And him a friend of Sir William!

What if you should be with child as a result? You are no longer our daughter! Go!

Sodom and Gomorrah were thrown into the welter of biblical righteousness and condemnation, as was the wrath of Our Gracious Lord. Confused, frightened, hurt, unbelieving, Lucy couldn't make out whether they meant God or Sir William.

Only from her mother did she receive any abatement in their anger...secretly she pressed into her hand a gold guinea when she gave her a small box containing her belongings. The guinea was Mrs. Ayre's special savings for the time when Lucy should be married.

"Go. Go to London and find a mistress you can trust," her mother whispered.

*

The cart that had carried Lucy and two other people, a married couple, from Canterbury, stopped outside an inn. "Here we are – here's journey's end," sang out the carter, a cheerful man called Tom. "The Bell, Ludgate Hill. You'll find good refreshment inside."

Tom had chatted to his passengers for much of the two-day journey, and by this time knew quite a lot about each of them. He helped them down and handed them their bags.

There were people waiting in the cobbled yard to meet them. Strange, thought Lucy, there are more people waiting than there are people on the cart.

She got down, took her box, and hesitated, not knowing what to do or where she was going. Immediately a gaudily-dressed older woman, with rouged cheeks and startlingly red lips stepped up to her and said: "Are you seeking a place to stay and easy, well-paid employment, my dear?"

Lucy, startled by being addressed by such a fine lady, hesitated for a moment, looked at the woman briefly, and admitted, that yes, she was seeking work.

But carter Tom was suddenly by her side. "Sorry, dear madam, this young lady is being met," he said brusquely.

Several other women and a young man tried to talk to her, but Tom held her arm and guided her away. Bewildered, Lucy felt embarrassed at his treatment of the people who were obviously welcoming to a stranger.

"Tom, I'm not being met," she said. "And I do want employment."

"I know, Lucy, but you want nothing to do with them people. I'll see if I can find someone that'll help you."

"Tom! They were only being polite and helpful!

"Yes, but they were offering you a life of slavery as a prostitute...that's their game. Just a moment."

He looked around. After a few moments he led her over to a woman standing at the back of the little crowd. She was wearing a long, bodiced dress of dark green, plain, material, with a white neckerchief that fastened at the front; and over her head was a sort of lace veil, which, however, did not hide her face.

She had a sharp, probing gaze. As they approached she was plainly assessing Lucy up and down. "Are you looking for domestic servants, madam?" Tom asked her.

"Yes I am."

"I'm sorry to ask this, but young women have to be careful, arriving in the big city: where do you live?"

"That is none of your business, my man. Why do you ask such an impertinent question?"

"I'm sorry, but I am determined that this young woman will not find herself in the wrong hands...she is a country girl who has never been in London before.

"She needs to find employment with the right kind of person."

"I am housekeeper for Mrs. Pemburey, of Golden Square, in St. James's."

"You are a good distance from home, then...that's out Westminster way isn't it?"

"It is. I come here because I have always found that girls from Kent are good workers, and honest."

Lucy now found herself directly addressed: "Can you work hard? Have you any experience of domestic service?"

"Yes ma'am. I was in service for five years back home in Kent. I know about the work, and I have always worked hard."

She hesitated. "But I have no references."

"Why have you no references?"

"I had good reason to leave my previous service without notice. But I was not dismissed."

"This does not sound good."

"Ma'am, I know it seems bad. But..."

Lucy paused. She felt her face reddening. But she knew she had to say it. "The master...used me...in secret. He had his way with me, against my will, I swear. I had to get away."

The lady seemed to be considering what Lucy had said. "You poor thing! I am prepared to take a chance with you. I will take you on trial. If you don't fit in, or fail to work well, I shall not hesitate to dismiss you.

"Do you understand? Your wage will be twenty-five shillings per annum for the first year. Do you accept those terms?"

"Yes, ma'am. And thank you."

She turned to Tom: "And thank you too."

"I'm content that you have found a proper place. Goodbye Lucy. Goodbye ma'am."

*

For the first time in her life Lucy was told to climb aboard a small, open sort of trap pulled by a single pony. On the way across London, through what seemed to Lucy to be a journey through a never-ending succession of streets, she was informed that the lady who had taken her on was Mrs. Williams. Her employer was Mrs. Pemburey, a widowed gentlewoman whose house was near St. James's Square in Westminster.

It was a fine, tall house, one of a terrace, with a portico over the steps leading to the front door. But Lucy was led to steps at the side, leading down to a small door below street level.

Mrs. Williams had a key, and she opened the door and led Lucy in. She found herself in a dimly-lit passageway which led to the servants' parlour, where a fire burned brightly and everything was neat and clean.

But without pausing, Mrs. Williams led her upstairs into the fine parts of the house, and into the sitting room. There she was shown to Mrs. Pemburey, who eyed her up and down, then asked her name.

"You have some experience, I should think, at your age?"

Upon being assured that this was the case, she looked at Mrs. Williams, and said: "Show her round the house and tell her what her duties are. And for goodness sake find her something proper to wear."

Interview over, she was employed.

*

For four months life was so happy in the household that Lucy could hardly believe it. Work, compared with the manor house in Kent, was easy. Mrs. Pemburey did not entertain so much; and then only in the

357

afternoon, usually for widowed women like herself to take tea; occasionally for elderly married couples. All were quite genteel.

There were six women servants, including cook and Mrs. Williams. There was one male servant, Will Webster, who served as general repair-man, errand-boy, and groom-in-charge of Mrs. Pemburey's pony and trap.

She had no pretence to grandeur, being left very well-off and with nothing to prove.

From the start Lucy got on well with her fellow-servants. Will took a shine to her straight away, for Lucy had a pretty face and a comely figure.

It was only after the first few months, when Will began to show his feelings towards her, that Lucy began to experience some animosity from one of the other girls.

Until Lucy's arrival Will had tended to flirt with this other servant, Molly Masters. Seeing his attentions diverted to Lucy, Molly took it ill, naturally.

There was no open warfare, but Molly did all she could to make Lucy feel bad...the odd word here...the odd accusation that some item of Lucy's work was not well done...something was missing – had Lucy misplaced it? The unspoken question: had Lucy simply taken it?

*

The women servants were allowed a day off each month. They were to go out two at a time, for their own protection, immediately after breakfast, on days when no guests were coming to take tea with Mrs. Pemburey.

It was a fine early-Autumn day, sunny and warm, when Lucy found herself with Molly – for they were given no choice as to companion - setting out for a day free of household chores.

Lucy was conscious that her wardrobe was not up to the same standard as those of her fellow-servants, who had all been with Mrs.

Pemburey for several years, and were, consequently, better-paid than Lucy.

She suggested that they might go as far as Rag Fair, on Rosemary Lane, near the Tower of London, to see if she could invest part of her guinea in a better dress. She was expecting some opposition from Molly, for it was a long walk, but was pleasantly surprised when Molly said she wouldn't mind...she might buy something for herself too.

Rag Fair was well-known for the second-hand bargains that were to be had. Sometimes, wealthy women's cast-offs - by no means worn-out or even out of fashion – found their way on to the stalls...not always by legal means.

The walk took quite a part of the morning to Rosemary Lane, for they stopped to look at every interesting sight. At last they saw the Tower of London, and, just beyond, the start of Rosemary Lane. Tired as they were, both Lucy and Molly quickened their pace with anticipation.

There were shops, but most of the people thronging the lane were looking at the stalls in the street itself. There was an exciting air of curiosity...of bargains to be snapped up by the buyers with the sharpest eye for value for money. It seemed to bring out the competitive urge. It wasn't just clothes that were for sale. There was hardware, boots and shoes, children's toys, even furniture.

But Lucy's mission was a gown that would make her feel on a par with the other servants at Mrs. Pemburey's. They quickly found that much of what was on offer was unpleasant, dirty and smelly...as were many of the customers.

Molly was for leaving quickly. But we've come all this way! At least let us see what we can find...we've heard you can get good clothes here. We may be lucky!

When Lucy saw the dress she knew she had been right. It must have belonged to a gentlewoman. In fact the woman on the stall said it had belonged to a Lady Somethingorother. She knew that for a fact!

It was of a pale blue material, decorated with red edging to sleeves and neck. It was the dress of her dreams, and Lucy could see that it was her size. The woman eyed Lucy's respectable if country-plain dress and in an instant decided on her price range. She wanted three shillings for it! Oh! Far too much for me!

Well look, my dear, I have one that's not so much, should fit you too...where is it...yes, here it is...twelve pence, that should suit you...you'll never get a better dress for that price, I'll be bound!

Lucy realised that she would have to settle for something cheaper, like this. She held the dress up against herself, and asked for Moll's approval. Yes, I'm sure that would look nice on you...offer her six pence!

The woman had a small place where Lucy could put the dress on. It fitted. It was better than the dress she had been wearing. "Keep it on dear, if you like. I'll take that in exchange and settle for ten pence."

Immediately she showed Lucy's old dress to a woman who snapped it up after a few seconds bargaining, for six pence, and disappeared into the crowd.

The deal done, Lucy reached for her purse.

It had gone! The ribbon that held it secure, hidden in the pocket of her coat, had been cleanly cut! Oh, Moll, what am I to do...it's all I had in the world! Tears streamed down her face in her anguish.

But Moll said: "You sure you had it, Lucy? I never saw it. Maybe you forgot to bring it."

Quickly the stall woman, big and rough, was on her. "'Ere...I've had that trick before, young woman! You trying to cheat me?"

"No! I swear I had a guinea in my purse...look...it is gone!"

"So you say! 'Ere. Constable! This lass is trying to get away without paying for her dress...just like that one I had a couple of weeks ago...just the same!

"She says she had a guinea in her purse...likely! Even her friend says she didn't have it! She'll tell you. 'Ere...where's she gone?"

But Moll didn't want to be seen as accomplice to a thief. She was out of sight in the crowd which was gathering rapidly at the sound of some trouble.

"There you are...I'm right! They're a pair, those two are! Well this one isn't going to get away! Ten shillings, that dress!"

People were crowding round, eager, it seemed, to get involved in stopping a thief. Arrest her! She's been here before. Taking the bread out of poor people's mouths! Sling her inside! Put her in the stocks!

Lucy's protests of injured innocence seemed pale by comparison with the accusations. The constable was not loath to make an arrest and receive the general approval of the surrounding crowd.

Molly! Where are you? Tell them I am no thief! Moll! Moll!

She's well away by now young woman...otherwise she would be arrested with you.

*

Lucy's initial dismay at having been robbed of her money, then indignation at being accused of trying to steal the dress, now changed to fear.

For outrageous though it was, the idea was now being taken entirely seriously. But the magistrate was kind. He refused to take it as theft...it was a matter of debt. Lucy could do no more than protest that it was all nonsense and untrue. But she was committed to the Wood Street Compter for debt.

Back at Mrs. Pemburey's, Moll's story had also slightly shifted the way it had happened. She told her mistress that Lucy had got into trouble over a dress that she had taken but could not pay for.

She did explain that Lucy had claimed someone had stolen her purse containing a guinea, but Moll said she had never mentioned a guinea to her, and she had seen no such money, and that was the truth of it.

"Who would have thought that Lucy would be a thief," said Mrs. Pemburey. "Well, the law will doubtless discover the truth of it, and if she is guilty she will suffer the consequences, I'm afraid."

361

CHAPTER 45

1713

Lucy's growing fear turned into terror when she was led into the Wood Street Compter, and experienced for the first time the stench, not unlike a pigsty gone rotten.

Inside, two unkempt men behind a desk demanded something called garnish. "I do not understand – what is it?" she asked fearfully.

"Money, miss, money!" one of the men said stridently. "Give us garnish or you'll end up in the hole. You won't like that, so don't mess us about. What money have you got?"

When told that she had none, the other man gave a twisted grin to his mate and cackled: "It's criminal, the way some people come in 'ere these days!"

He added: "We'll take that dress then…we must have payment."

But I have nothing under it…what will I wear?"

"You can have these," said the man, rummaging in a cupboard and handing her a pile of filthy brown rags that stank of some horror or other.

"I can't wear those."

"Very well…wear nothing! Somebody'll have the clothes off you soon enough anyhow!"

The two men cackled in a kind of laughter. In the cold terror that was creeping through her being, Lucy took off her dress and pulled on the rags that she had been offered, to the accompaniment of appreciative cries and feeling by their rough hands on her nakednesses.

It was then that another man entered. "What have we here?" he said, in a strange kind of accent. "What, no money for garnish, my beauty?

"Gentlemen, allow me to assist this young lady."

The man was unkempt, like the two jailers. But he handed over some coins, and Lucy was given back her dress. She noticed one of the two men giving the other an obvious wink.

Taking her arm in his, and carrying the dress, her saviour led her out of the vestibule and into an open yard. Numerous filthy and wretchedly clothed men and women were standing about, or sitting on the ground.

There were some raucous shouts,

And one man yelled: "Got another wife already, 'ave you, Jon?"

"Don't worry about them, my dear," said her new friend. "They're ill-mannered people, and uncouth, most of them. Just come with me to my quarters and you'll be able to put your own dress on and get out of these rags. Just keep walking."

He led her into a room that was dingy and unclean. But it had in it a mattress on the floor, and a small table and two chairs.

"My humble abode," said the man, bowing slightly. He held out his hand and took hers. "Jonathan Wild at your service. And whom do I have the pleasure of addressing?"

"What?"

"What's your name?"

"Lucy. Lucy Ayre, sir."

"Don't address me as sir! I'm a prisoner just like you. Call me Jon. The only difference between me and that rabble outside is that I have no intention of being dragged down to their level.

"Now. What brings a nice young woman like yourself into a terrible place like this? What are you in for? Debt, or thieving?"

Lucy told Jon what had happened at Rag Fair. "I am innocent, I swear it."

"Ah, 'tis all too often the case, Lucy. You are the victim of a miscarriage of justice, right enough. But I'm afraid that once you are in the compter the only way out is to pay off your debts...or what are claimed to be your debts.

"For the time being allow me to offer you a share of my quarters..."

Lucy interrupted him: "Oh no, I couldn't possibly!"

"Listen Lucy, you've never been in prison before, I can tell that. You don't know what happens. Let me advise you to take my offer...I can see you're a sweet girl, and innocent.

"With no money you'll be put in the Hole. It's a filthy dungeon, with no light, no air, and certainly no privacy. Not to waste words, you'll become the common property of all who wish to use you.

"A lass like you will not last long in there. Let me help you...you'll be well advised. I've been in the compter for more than two years, and I started out in the Hole, so I know what I'm talking about.

"Now I've worked my way into getting the liberty of the gate, and I've got this room, one of the best in Wood Street Compter.

"I had a friend sharing it with me. But that friend has now got freedom and gone. You can come in with me...and I think you'll need a bit of looking after unless I'm much mistaken."

"But I can't share a room with...with a man, Mr Wild. What would people say?"

Jonathan laughed. He had nice, even teeth, Lucy noticed, and a nice smile. He was not so handsome, though, and he was not tall – hardly any taller than she was.

"They'll say you're no fool...and lucky!

"I'll tell you what, though: let me show you where you'll be put if you turn me down. Come...I'll show you the Hole."

He led her across the yard and into a door-way, then down some stone steps. "Oh the smell!" gasped Lucy. "It is too horrible. I can hardly breathe. What is it?"

"Your abode...unless you come in with me," said Jonathan grimly. "That's what the smell is. And here is what it looks like."

He walked to a door, and inside, through the bars across a square hole, Lucy could just make out, in the darkness, uncovered beds, one

364

above the other, stretching into the darkness. And there was the occasional movement of something...people.

The rank, offensive odour overwhelmed Lucy. "Let me get out of here!" she gasped, gagging with the awful stench of excrement, sweat, filth, and God knows what else.

"You are surely not telling me that you don't want to move into the Hole to live," smiled Jonathan as they retreated back to the daylight.

"Is there no other place for me to go?" asked Lucy.

"You see, you have to buy your accommodation in the compter," he told her. "But for folks who have no money, that's where they have to live...in the Hole."

"I can't go in there! She gasped.

"No? That's why I offered you a share of my room. Because I took to you as soon as I first saw you, Lucy. Well, the offer's still open.

"We could be very good friends together, you and me. What do you say?"

"It would be allowed?"

"Certainly! I've paid your garnish for you. I'm allowed quite a bit of freedom now. And there's something really good to tell you – I'm going to get out of here soon. There's been a pardon offered for some that have been here for a long time, and I've applied. I'm only waiting for the December Sessions to be told I can go.

"If we became really good friends, then once I'm free and able to make some money, I'll be able to pay off your debt and get you out too.

"It would all be part of the service!"

The quiet dread that had held Lucy in its grip from the moment she had entered the compter suddenly seemed lighter. There was some hope!

But Lucy was not so naïve as to be unaware what the bargain involved. There was only one mattress on the floor of Jonathan's room. Another kind of fear...

"I have never been with a man before...except..."

"Except what?"

Back in his room, Lucy told Jonathan something of her story – of how she had been raped by Sir William, and how she came to be in London.

He took her gently in his arms, and stroked her hair. "You have had a terrible time. But you are safe with me, I promise you. Stay with me and I'll have you safely out of Wood Street Compter. Trust me."

*

Jonathan was so gentle, so kind, so loving, that Lucy could easily imagine that she was married to him. For three months they were as man and wife, and Lucy, aware of the terrible fate he had saved her from, grew to love him more each passing day.

He was her support and saviour as well as her lover. When the time came for them to part, in mid-December, after her Jon had been freed under an Act of Parliament for the relief of debtors, she felt empty – and more alone than she had ever been in her life.

And her hopeless, terrible emptiness grew all the more a month later when she realised she was with child.

But she dreamed that he would come soon and rescue her, and they could be properly married, and live together in loving bliss with their growing family.

He brought her money for food. He had not deserted her! She knew he never would. He declared his love for her. They retired to the room that he had bequeathed her, and they made love, just like before.

But he needed time to get all the money he needed for his business before he could pay off her debts.

It was an agonising eight months before he came and saw his baby daughter for the first time, and paid off Lucy's debt and her leaving garnish.

"The jailers have to live...they've paid to get their positions, and they must profit by it," he explained when she asked why garnish money had to be paid. He seemed content to live with the ways of the compter. And he seemed to have money to spare.

He appeared to be overjoyed with the baby, and more than happy that Lucy had called her Miriam, after her grandmother.

For Lucy the baby was her joy and her wonder. It mattered little that she was in prison...her world was the space between herself and Miriam, a bright-eyed alert little thing that seemed to take in everything around her with a grave interest.

Lucy loved having this tiny being, totally dependent on her, needing to be loved and cared for. When, at six weeks old, Miriam had actually smiled when Lucy pulled a cloth away from her face and said "boo!" it had been instant happiness in that dingy room.

But her joy turned to alarm when Jon told her: "I've found you a nice room in Lewkenor's Lane...it's where I've been living myself until a week or so back."

"But Jon – are we not to live together? It is all I have thought about ever since your deliverance from the comptor...you and me and our baby."

"Lucy, you must understand, I have other commitments now. I have to follow my business interests. How else can I pay the rent? I must earn money...and that involves living...at my place of work, you know."

He comforted her tears. He took her to Lewkenor's Lane in Covent Garden , and saw her and Miriam safely installed in one of the old, ill-built houses, and with enough money for food.

Then he had to leave, for he had pressing business to attend to. "I'll come again soon," he said as he walked away.

*

1714

Lucy soon discovered that Lewkenor's Lane, Covent Garden, was not the most desirable address in town. A dark, muddy street, at night it was drunkenly peopled for the most part with prostitutes' customers, making their unsteady way from the adjoining Drury Lane to the numerous brothels.

But what shocked her more, was finding, from a woman neighbour who had a room in the same building, that her Jon had used the house as a brothel when he lived there with a prostitute called Mary Milliner in the months after his release from the compter.

He was not faithful to her! She could not accept the thought. She declared her absolute disbelief that this could be her Jon…the loving father of her baby.

"Well it's true…it 'im right enough," she was told.

"If I was you I'd steer clear of 'im. He's a bad 'un."

The next time Jon called on her, Lucy asked him if it was all true. Instead of denying it, or at least being evasive, as she had been expecting, Jon confirmed the facts and cursed nosey neighbours.

"She's the friend who shared my room in the compter before you arrived – I told you about her," he said calmly.

"You said a friend shared with you – but you didn't say it was a woman," she said in despair. "Oh Jon, I thought we'd be married and live together and have more children when I got out of the compter," she added.

"Lucy, I have never spoken to you of marriage. I can not marry you because I am already married."

"Oh no!"

"I haven't seen my wife these many years, and that is the truth. But in the eyes of the law I am still married to her."

"But now it seems you have gone back to another woman. What am I to do if you abandon us…me and our baby? What worse thing could happen to a mother?"

"I'd say a lot of things could be worse!" he exclaimed.

"What can you mean?"

"Well I have to be with this woman – this prostitute – because she is my means of earning a living. She also knows a great many people who may be of use to me in the future…by way of business, you understand.

"So I need to be with her. But I come here to see you and the baby – and I bring you money for living, and I pay the rent for you

"That's better than being in the compter, or even in the parish workhouse, isn't it? It's not perfect…but I say it could be worse."

"How can you expect a woman to live in this situation , Jon?"

"I expect it because that is what I have arranged for you. If you can't live in it you'd better go and beg admittance to the workhouse where you have a settlement. That would be in Kent, where you were born, I think.

"That's the alternative, Lucy."

CHAPTER 46

1719

It was a bitter blow to Lucy that she was not to live with the man she loved. But she was forced to admit to herself that she preferred his intermittent visits, and his financial support, to none at all.

She had had an early upbringing that was sheltered from the harsh realities of life in the big city.

Now she had been confronted with some of the terrible things that can happen. But at twenty she still retained some of her naivety intact; and her ability to trust to the goodness of everyone until proved otherwise, was largely unsullied.

So she swallowed her pride, and continued to love and to trust Jonathan Wild, who, after months of her complaints about Lewkenor's Lane, now moved her to live in Cock Lane, near Newgate Prison. But even nearer was the church of St. Sepulchre, and it was there where Lucy took little Miriam to be christened.

She was happier because Wild was living only a short walk away, just off Red Cross Street. Lucy knew little of Jonathan's day-to-day activities. But she knew he kept moving.

Lucy did not know when he took up as assistant to the Deputy City Marshall, Charles Hitchen, whose business was to fight crime. They worked together as thief-takers – capturing thieves for money.

That brought him more income. But once he realised that he could out-think Hitchen, Jonathan set up his own thief-taking business – so successfully that he had to move to bigger premises to cope with it all. He bought himself a silver-headed cane to emphasise his authority. He had a fine criminal mind and great expertise, and during the next few years he brought at least sixty men and women to the gallows, and many others to transportation.

They were not necessarily guilty of the crimes for which he charged them. But the courts were content that there had been a crime and somebody had been hanged for it, or transported to Maryland.

Lucy did not know when he took a sword and cut off one of his prostitute lover's ears in the course of a furious argument. That might have sounded a warning.

But she would never have believed that her beloved Jon was only looking after her and his baby until he needed an easy dupe.

He occasionally needed innocents to sacrifice to the courts in place of one of his trusted criminals, if they ever faced serious accusations – and he had seen from the first that naïve Lucy would be ideal for the purpose.

For sometimes his own people were caught thieving, and were arrested. If he saw them as valuable to his criminal enterprises, he would set out to save them from the gallows. So he would arrest quite innocent people – usually minor criminals who had come to his notice – and charge them with the offences that his own people had committed.

He would get others that he could influence – straw men, he called them - to go to court to testify that they had seen the entirely innocent people commit the offences.

The court almost always accepted what he said, and condemned his prisoner to death or transportation.

Lucy knew none of this. But she did become aware how famous her lover was becoming.

For he was now the central figure in the capital's crime scene. For him crime paid. And his new brilliant and audacious scheme to advertise for the owners of stolen goods to contact him, brought him a further good income when they paid him reward money.

Of course he almost always was able to find the stolen property and return the items to their legitimate owners because it was his own team of thieves who had taken them in the first place.

He shared part of the reward with them…and so kept everyone happy..

He became so well-known that he set up and advertised a "lost property office" where people could apply for help in tracing their stolen goods. It was a big success. The money rolled in. He was a figure of some renown.

His growing wealth enabled him to provide her with more money for food and the odd luxury for herself and Miriam. Miriam was growing, and taking more and more interest in all around her She became better-dressed and better-fed.

She was, as her mother was pleased to tell anybody who would listen, a lovely little girl, and so happy.

Many times Lucy told her daughter about her kind and famous father, and how she must always be proud of him.

And Lucy's devotion to Jonathan grew. She never questioned that her love for him was returned, despite the unusual circumstances of his living apart from her and Miriam.

*

When the men came to arrest her for stealing valuables from a shop, of course she protested her total innocence, for in the whole of her life she had never stolen anything.

"My little girl! I can not leave her alone! She is only six – what is to happen to her if you take me away? It is all a terrible mistake! I have done nothing wrong! Where are you taking me?"

They told her they were taking her to Newgate Prison to await her trial. It was even worse than the horrors of the Hole at the Wood Street Compter.

Miriam, they assured her, would be well cared for in the parish workhouse.

Lucy's horror at the terrible Newgate stench, the degradation, the vile and disgusting prisoners around her, did not last long. Her trial came quickly – the day after her arrest.

She was taken to the Old Bailey court, and kept at first in a press of people so smelly that she was relieved it was in the open air.

When she was brought before the bewigged judge to face trial someone remembered the allegations that she had stolen a dress from a stall at Rag Fair in 1712. It was recalled that then the court had commuted the offence to a term of imprisonment for debt – that of being unable to pay for the dress she had taken.

She did not know that it was one of Wild's men who had "remembered" it, and told the judge. Knowing looks in court. It did not help her plea of innocence now,

She tried telling the judge that she knew nothing of the theft for which she was charged…that she could not understand why she had been arrested.

A witness was called. He identified Lucy as the thief.. Yes, he was absolutely certain.. There was no doubt. He saw her clear as day, and there she is now, standing in the dock.

Guilty as charged! Sentence: death.

"No! It cannot be! I have done nothing at all!"

A thought came to her: the judge would know of Jonathan Wild, the father of my child – the famous Jonathan Wild. He will tell you I am innocent!

She did not know it was another of Jonathan Wild's men who had testified that she had committed the offence.

Please! Send someone to tell him what has happened. He will know it is a mistake. He will come and save me…ask him to help me…please, I beg you.

Terrified, unable to comprehend what was the cause of her awful predicament, she was taken back to Newgate. And a week later they put her in a cart along with six other condemned prisoners and took her to Tyburn to be hanged, pleading to the last for her Jon.

But Wild didn't come. He was getting on with his unlawful business, happy in the knowledge that he had saved one of his better women thieves at the expense of the useless Lucy Ayre.

*

Geoff had been passed over for the job of Manchester Flight Manager. Sunjet had brought in a younger man from Gatwick.

Of course Geoff had applied for the job on the retirement of old Dave Tomkins, who had been with the airline since it had been founded in 1973.

He thought he had made a pretty good case for himself to step up from deputy.

But it cut no ice with the directors, although they were very kind in their comments about his ability, and how much they appreciated his excellent work.

"Of course, the problem is that I'm up here in Manchester – they're down there in Gatwick. We don't see each other every day. This new guy is obviously somebody they've decided to groom for stardom. So that's that," he told Ron Davidson.

Ron was full of genuine sympathy. The two men had been friends for quite a while.

But at home, Hanna was a different proposition. "Bloody Hell!" she ranted. "Well, I'm not entirely surprised.'

"I'll tell you one good reason you haven't got the job: your bloody northern accent!

"How many times have I told you to stop saying words like bath and path with a short "a"? They rhyme with 'car' not 'cat'. Everybody knows that it is just not the Queen's English to talk like somebody from the backwoods, for God's sake."

"Hanna, that is laughable! I'm damned if I'm going to suddenly start saying baarth and paarth. The long aa is simply the remnant of the drawly accents of the peasants in the south of England in the old days.

"The fact that people in different regions speak with different accents should be seen as a good and proper diversity: not as an insult; not as illogical; and certainly not as a reason for awarding or not awarding a job."

And even as Hanna drew breath to reply, he said: "There is nothing in English grammar that says that the letter 'a' should be pronounced long rather than short. Frankly I find the triphonic aaa illogical, and it is no more valid than the short, northern bath and path pronunciation."

"Absolute piffle!"

And before he could frame an adequate reply she moved on to her second topic of denunciation: "It goes to prove that I'm right about your lack of savoir faire to get to the top.

"God! I'll be the laughing stock for all the Sunjet people – their wives, anyway!

"Just don't ever come whining to me again about not getting promotion. Frankly you're nothing but a bloody failure!"

And with that she swept out of the room, grabbing her coat and her car keys, and drove off.

"Thank you so much," said Geoff to the departing rear number plate. "Just the sort of reaction I'd hoped for…I don't think! The very least I could have deserved was sympathy and support."

CHAPTER 47

1985

It was late when Hanna came back. She went to sleep in the spare room. It didn't make Geoff feel any better.

The next morning, she slept late. When she did wake up, and Geoff could hear the radio in her room, she still didn't get up. He took her a cup of tea. She spoke to him in a kind of expressionless voice.

He knew it was intended to demonstrate that she couldn't care less about what he had said the previous day.

Suddenly she appeared downstairs, put on her coat, and, without saying a word, went out. A few moments later her BMW swept out of the drive, leaving Geoff alone with his puzzlements. What the hell is she up to? His thoughts were interrupted by the arrival of the postman.

There was a letter from the London genealogist. Despite everything, it was a bright spot in the gloomy day, the first of two days off duty for Geoff.

Using as a guide the baptism of Isabella, daughter of Eliza Mair, on 13 October, 1764, in the parish of St. Sepulchre-without-Newgate – that he had found in his first report - he had made further progress.

In the same parish, he had found the christening of Eliza, daughter of Miriam Mair, on 19 May 1735.

Working further back, he had failed to find any marriage of anybody called Miriam to any man with the surname Mair, or any christening of any child named Miriam Mair.

But what he had found, on 21 September 1714, was the baptism of Miriam, daughter of Lucy Ayre, at the parish church of St. Sepulchre.

"There may, at first glance, appear to be no connection between this Miriam Ayre and our Miriam Mair," the genealogist's letter said.

"But the way it is entered into the baptism register is: 'Eliza, daughter of...' then the name of the mother.

"The mother in this case might have said her name was 'Miriam Ayre' – but because of the letter 'm' at the end of Miriam, it might have been heard as 'Miriam Mair.'

"Because the mother was probably illiterate, she wouldn't know the difference when her name was written down.

"It is not an uncommon occurrence in family history."

The genealogist added that there was no way of finding Lucy Ayre's origins. He had checked the St. Sepulchre parish records, and those of surrounding parishes, without find her baptism. She might not have been born in London. It would be unrealistic to continue searching in the hope of taking Geoff's family history further back.

"My God, not only have a got a load of bastards, prostitutes and criminals as ancestors – even my name looks as if it should be Ayre and not Mayer," he said to himself, looking around the room guiltily, as if to see if Hanna had heard him. But of course she was out.

Geoff turned back to his letter. There was much worse news to come.

"Assuming that Miriam and her mother Lucy Ayre are your direct ancestors – as I think is a reasonable conjecture– I have some interesting information for you," the letter added.

"In the records of Newgate prison I found that Lucy Ayre was imprisoned after a jury at the Old Bailey found her guilty of theft.

"She was hanged at Tyburn on 19 June 1719."

*

Rose was enthusiastic about the report. Geoff had phoned her: he wanted to talk about it. They met in a café in Bramhall, near her home. He passed the genealogists letter to her to read.

"This is brilliant! It tells you where she lived – St. Sepulchre's parish. That makes it much easier to follow it up yourself if and when you have the chance. Without that it would be like looking for a needle in a haystack in London. And, of course, it gives you all this information about the people themselves – among the poorer classes that kind of thing is very difficult to find...in fact it's usually impossible for the amateur family tree searcher."

"But I've got a common prostitute, a woman wanted for breaking out of jail, and worst of all, a woman hanged for more thieving!" exclaimed Geoff.

"I'll tell you what, Hanna won't like this one bit! She's been trying to make me give up family history because it shows my ancestors were working class!

"This'll really put the lid on it."

Rose looked Geoff in the eye. She said: "I often think how you have to admire the people at the bottom of the heap who did well to survive through terrible conditions in times past.

"Their lives must have been so very hard. These days you hear about women turning to prostitution to get money to buy drugs. In the eighteenth century it would have been for survival at all costs.

"How old was this girl, Isabella? Fifteen! My God! What kind of pressures was she under, at that age? And then in Newgate – it was notorious – she would almost certainly have faced a death sentence. She must have been terrified.

"I suppose if you had a choice between hanging and escape, most of us would make a run for it. And she'd have lived in fear of being caught for the rest of her life.

"No wonder she ended up in a place like Newcastle-under-Lyme. She'd probably see safety in anonymity in a small town so far from London and her friends and family. It's a heartbreaking story, I'd say."

"But Hanna will hate it. She can't stand the thought of being lower class – much less prostitution and robbery! Honestly, I think it would threaten our marriage. It's everything she hates."

"But you can't escape the past. Like it or not, it's where you came from, genealogically speaking."

"Yes, but it's the fact that I've got the genes of somebody like Isabella that gives Hanna the heebie-jeebies. It offends her sense of who we are. She can't stand it, to be honest...she feels she's above that, and probably quite rightly."

Rose paused before she responded. "Well it sounds as if she hates a heck of a lot of people, because most of us sprang from working-class roots.

"To me, it's part of the fascination of tracing my family tree. It's all part of me. I can't change it anyway.

"And finding out about them – where they lived, who they married, how many children they had and how many survived, what they did for a living...it all opens a window into the past, because the lower ranks don't get much of a mention in school history books.

"If I were you, I'd be really pleased to get this information. Your family history could have ended in the 1790s, but now there's a whole new area to find out about, and maybe take you much further back. It's brilliant!"

And she gave Geoff's arm a squeeze of encouragement. She's very tactile. Not like Hanna. I can't remember when she last squeezed my arm. When did she last give me a day-time kiss – just because she was pleased about something?

With a slight shock he realized it must have been a long time ago.

He looked at Rose – slightly wind-blown Rose, he suddenly thought wryly – and said: "Well, thanks for your encouragement. It's nice to hear that for a change. You're right of course: I'll just have to live with my ancestors whether I or anybody else likes it or not!"

*

Two days later he told Hanna about it.

"Bloody hell!" she shouted, "That is the last straw!

"I've put up with every type of low-life in your family. But to have an ancestor strung up for thieving...that's just too much!

"Just tear up all your family history nonsense and throw it on the fire before anybody hears about it! I'm not joking! I will not stand for this any more.

379

"If you won't burn it, I will!"

Hanna simply could not understand why Geoff, far from wanting to burn his family history, found the latest piece of information really interesting.

She was deadly serious about destroying the family tree that he was compiling, and pretending that it had never existed. Certainly nobody else should ever know anything about Geoff's ancestors, she kept demanding.

"Look, even if you don't like it, our son might want to know these things," he pointed out.

"David has no interest whatsoever in your family history," said Hanna firmly. "I can tell you that!

"And even if becomes interested, I'm sure he wouldn't want to be told that he might have descended from a common criminal who was hanged...and a string of whores who should have been.

"Wonderful pedigree that would be to lumber him with! I can see him boasting about it to his friends: 'Oh yes, I'm from a long line of criminals and harlots, you know. But they really came good in more recent times...weavers and farm bloody labourers. Really good stock!'

"So get rid of it all now, or I'm leaving. Leaving for good this time. I've had enough!

"It's either me or your family bloody history!"

Geoff made the mistake of smiling: it struck him suddenly that she really was so ridiculous that it was funny.

"Spinners, actually, not weavers."

"Right! Now you're laughing at me. Well you'll see if it is amusing. You seem to have made your choice. So you live here with your thieves and your whores and other riff-raff ancestors and I'll have my own life with a bit of class and decency."

*

The sight of Hanna storming off out of the house had become part of life for Geoff. It didn't worry him – he knew she'd be back...perhaps a

380

little frosty at first, but their relationship was strong enough to withstand the occasional storm.

"Into every life a little rain must fall," he found himself saying, with a smile to himself.

He had been going to suggest that they take a drive out into the Peak District, to find a nice place for lunch. Now that idea had gone up in the smoke of Hanna's departure, he was at a loose end.

I'm damned if I'm just sitting at home and waiting for Hanna to return...in any case it's often after my bed-time when she comes home. God knows which friend she'll be sheltering with this time.

He decided on the spur of the moment to head for the Central Library in Manchester. The idea of starting to look into his mother's family history had been hovering at the back of his mind for some time now. He might as well make this the day he'd start on it.

In the library's family history room he quickly realized that it wasn't going to be easy. He didn't really know enough to make a start with her death. But he did know approximately when his parents had married. So that was his first search.

He remembered that his birth certificate had given his mother's maiden name as Pendleton. But he didn't know where she had been born. Nor did he know her year of birth, or the place where she had died. Of course the censuses wouldn't help, for you couldn't see them until they were at least 100 years old.

Suddenly Rose walked in, and came over when he waved to her. He explained what he was doing, but admitted that he'd suddenly lost interest. "Do you fancy a cup of tea?" he asked.

Somehow it seemed better to have someone to talk to, rather than find ancestors' births, marriages and deaths. Over the tea in the café they chatted, and he found himself telling Rose about the tiff he'd had with Hanna.

"She is demanding that I burn all my family history research. She says either it goes or she goes."

"Why on earth would she say that?"

381

"Hanna equates my failure to rise through the management ranks to the lowly position of most of my ancestors."

"You're not being serious!"

"No. It's quite logical, Rose. She says that if we inherit so much through our genes, then my make-up must include the genes of people who, in all fairness, were low-life losers.

"I don't just mean that they were of the labouring class. There were the prostitutes and thieves...and the one who escaped from Newgate. And the other who was actually hanged at Tyburn for stealing.

"Hanna's point is that having their genes explains why I'm not top management material. I can see her point. But actually I wouldn't want to get any promotion that took me away from flying...I like being a pilot: it's what I want to do."

"Well, there you are then – you're a pilot, not a thief or a vagabond. But I'm sure she's just joking...nobody actually thinks that DNA makes you a carbon-copy of your ancestors! In any case, you have dozens of ancestors...which ones would you be a copy of, and which not?"

*

The note, written on Hanna's pad that she had filched from some hotel, was short and to the point. He could see that before he walked across the kitchen to read it.

It'll say something like "I'm out at Jenny's" or "I'm in the spare room – don't wake me up" - that's the kind of thing they always say, Hanna's notes.

But these words said something else. They said: "I'm leaving you. I've had enough. You've made my life a misery. I want a divorce."

Geoff still held the flowers that he had bought as a "let's be friends" gesture.

In his numb shock, he found her favourite Moorcroft vase, part-filled it with cold water, and carefully put the flowers in, arranging them till they looked nice. He carried them into the lounge and put them on the small table.

The room suddenly looked strange: cold and pointless. It wasn't a place to sit in and be comfortable. It was alien territory. She'd chosen every piece of furniture, every ornament, every table-lamp. He'd let her because he thought it would please her.

The house was full of Hanna. Only an hour ago Rose had said she'd be back when I got home. She won't ever be back. Hanna always means what she says. She wouldn't leave a note like that if she intended to come back.

A new thought. He went upstairs. In their bedroom her wardrobe looked half-empty. Another thought. Her knicker drawer was empty. Well, that's it. She's gone for good, and taken her knickers with her. Through his grief he couldn't help a small, grim smile. It's a bit like a modern poem. Doesn't scan, but it's got all the right sentiments.

He took his jacket off, and nearly threw it on the bed. He stopped, just in time. Hanna doesn't like that. He hung it on a hanger in his wardrobe. They had his and hers. His and hers.

I need a drink. I'm not flying tomorrow. Just as well. But I don't want to get drunk. I want to think this out. What the hell do you do in a situation like this? At least she's not dead. I don't have to inform the authorities or get a certificate.

Certificates! Bloody family history. That's what has caused all this.

Who should I inform? David! He'll have to be told. He's just approaching his finals, too. God knows what effect it'll have on him. No rush, though. Unless he rings. I'd have to tell him then.

Who else? At least we don't have a milkman anymore. "Half a pint a day from now on please."

The milkman would know what it meant. They must meet it all the time. Do they still have half-pints? Don't be silly...of course not. OK, the note would have to say "One pint every other day."

Anyway, it doesn't matter – we get our milk from the supermarket in Macclesfield these days. We. I mean *I* will be getting milk from the supermarket. No. Sod it. I'll get my milk from wherever I choose! I can please myself now.

Oh God, why am I worrying about milk? My Hanna has walked out on me. She wants a divorce. The only woman I've ever loved.

*

He decided not to tell anybody, at least for the time being. So two days later he flew his rostered early departure Manchester-Ibiza route, with an immediate return flight.

Uneventful. Ordinary. He was a professional. He forced his mind to concentrate on the job.

Back at Ringway he drove home to Prestbury. In the post was an envelope posted in Manchester and bearing Hanna's handwriting. His heart sank. He knew he'd been secretly hoping she'd have come back. If she'd written, it kyboshed any such thought.

He poured himself an Irish whiskey, added as much water, and sat down to read it. It told him nothing, except that he would shortly be hearing from a solicitor whom she had consulted. Any communication should be through the lawyer. He took a swig at his whiskey. Too much to swallow. It made his eyes water. He felt the gloom press on him, a weight that he had never known before.

I can't believe it. I have done nothing whatsoever to deserve this. Why the hell are my eyes so wet? I'm bloody well not crying, if that's what you're thinking. He had to talk this over with someone. He rang Ron Davidson. No reply. Of course: he and Mary were on holiday. Why? I know we had some arguments, but don't all married couples? Surely a woman isn't going to walk out on her marriage because her husband is doing family history, is she? It'll make a good story for the newspapers. Prestbury woman sues for divorce citing her husband's ancestors as co-respondents!

CHAPTER 48

1985

The trouble with someone doing something ridiculous to you is that you can't rationalise it.

So you keep turning it over and over in your mind, trying to make sense of it...in the car, taking a walk, lying in bed, trying to sleep.

Geoff Mayer could not explain it to himself. What had gone wrong? We've been happily married for twenty-three years. It would have been our silver wedding in a couple of years! I've been secretly planning a round-the-world holiday to celebrate it. Another thing lost.

Everything that I counted as precious is gone. I wish I could just shrug my shoulders and say it doesn't matter. But it means so much that now nothing else matters. Call me a wimp, but I really can't stand it. You can't just forget a quarter of a century of your life, as if it didn't matter. It matters like hell!

Yes, we had some rough little arguments, but we had years of real happiness. Don't they count for anything to Hanna? How can she just walk out on all that, just over a silly row over my ancestors' being poor?

For God's sake, it isn't logical.

*

Geoff's decision not to tell anyone that Hanna had left him changed when he bumped into Sharon. He was on an "M" shaped route-pattern of flying duty: Manchester, Mahon, Gatwick, Palma, Manchester. He had a break at Gatwick in the middle of his flight programme. And there was Sharon, who had just completed her working day!

They greeted each other warmly, as old friends. They had time for a coffee and a quick chat. And when Sharon asked how was Hanna, he decided he couldn't lie to her.

"I haven't told anybody else, but she has gone and it looks like we'll end up divorced, after twenty-three years of marriage," he said quietly.

"So you found out about her," said Sharon.

"What do you mean?"

"You found out that she was playing away."

Sharon saw Geoff's face. "Didn't you?"

"Playing away?"

"Yes."

"What exactly do you mean, Sharon?"

"I saw her with another man. Some time ago."

"You knew!"

Geoff's voice was suddenly harsh...accusatory.

Oh hell! This was suddenly embarrassing. "Well, perhaps I'm speaking out of turn, and I couldn't prove it, but I saw her one evening in a restaurant in Didsbury with a man, and they were holding hands and billing and cooing like love-birds...I wondered if they were going to get on with it there and then on the table-top!"

"You...when was this?"

"Oh about a year ago...it was just after I'd come to Gatwick and you came to a company dinner where I was serving champagne...you remember? Just a week or so after that, when I was in Manchester for my mother's birthday."

"Are you sure it was Hanna?"

"Absolutely...I'd only just met her, remember, and I'd had a good look at her during that evening at Gatwick.

"She didn't notice us, but I was sitting in the restaurant where I could see her very clearly. I'm one hundred percent certain it was Hanna."

To her surprise, she saw Geoff growing overtly angry. "You saw all this a year ago? You didn't think of telling me!"

"How could I? I didn't know...I still don't know for sure that anything improper was going on between Hanna and this man. I'd certainly have bet on it, but I couldn't swear to it.

"I couldn't just come running to you and telling you what my suspicions were on the basis of what I saw of them in public. And I haven't actually seen you since that company event at Gatwick.

"What I saw wouldn't have stood up in a court of law, you know."

"Yes you could have told me! At least I could have asked Hanna about it. I wouldn't have had to tell her how I knew.

"I thought we were friends. But you simply decided to keep me in the dark, like a damned fool...and a cuckold if you're right."

"Geoff, what could I have told you?"

"In future Captain Mayer to you! I'm bloody furious! You could most certainly have told me, and you didn't. So don't come talking to me again – any friendship I thought we had is over."

Knocking the table and spilling coffee as he rose and stormed off didn't make his departure any more dignified. It didn't look good to passengers and airline staff in the buffet area, whose eyes were drawn to what was plainly a public tiff between two uniformed airline crew.

Sharon busied herself cleaning up the mess with a couple of paper napkins. But her embarrassment was clear. Her face was red. And there was more than a suspicion of tears welling up in her eyes.

She finished wiping up the mess, stood up, picked up her bag, and left with as much dignity as she could muster with a dozen pairs of eyes watching, fascinated...one smart jet-set lady obviously upset.

For one brief half-moment Sharon thought of stopping and announcing: "No need to stare! There's nothing going on between us, you know!"

But she thought better of it, relying on dignity to sweep her out of the buffet.

She walked away into the anonymity of the airport terminal, satisfying herself with the thought that she didn't have to explain anything to all those staring people.

"They're probably the kind of people who go running up to watch dog-fights!" she said to herself.

And although she had long ago given up all thoughts of herself and Geoff as lovers, she knew that this marked the end of a beautiful friendship, and it upset her very much.

God! What made me say that? she asked herself. I thought he was telling me that it had all come out into the open, and that he'd found out that Hanna was unfaithful.

For God's sake, *he didn't know*! He hadn't got a clue!

So I blew it, just when he was about to come on to the market! Bloody hell! Bloody, bloody hell!

*

Hanna's car was in the drive when Geoff arrived home from his day's flying duty.

What awaited him? He suddenly felt a second of nervousness...an apprehension of what was going to happen. He did not like confrontations.

But only for a second. He had just finished a day of being in command during the flights, and as if his airline uniform, with its four captain's stripes, was bound to put him in control, he walked firmly from his car, turned his key in the Yale, and went in.

Hanna, plainly, was upstairs. And her voice floated down: "Is that you, Geoffrey?"

"No. It's a burglar."

Silence. Then a bit of noise, of drawers being closed, and wardrobe doors. I'm damned if I'm going to run upstairs after her.

If she can't come down to talk to me, I am not going to become her lap-dog.

He sat down and turned to the back page of the Daily Telegraph. The first couple of clues in the big crossword came instantly to him. He forced himself to concentrate on working out an anagram.

"Geoffrey?" The voice from above.

"Yes?"

"Can you give me a hand to get these heavy suitcases down stairs?"

So that's how it is. She isn't here to stay. And damn me if she doesn't expect me to do the heavy work of her removals! The absolute bloody nerve!

"Certainly. I'll be up in a minute."

He walked into the kitchen, filled the kettle, and switched it on. He got a mug from the cupboard, and put a tea-bag in. He waited till the kettle boiled. He poured the water into the mug. He got some milk from the fridge. He poured some into the mug. He stirred until the tea was the right colour.

Then he walked slowly upstairs.

*

"So you really are determined to clear off for good?"

"You made your choice – me or your family history. You didn't choose me. You didn't expect me to come crawling back after a few days, surely. I'd have thought you knew me better than that."

"That really is ridiculous! And why the hell should I be ashamed of my ancestors? Let's face it: all this is your choice, not mine. And precious little to do with family history, I'd say.

"Obviously I can't do anything to stop you leaving, if that's your intention.

"But as you're here, I think it might be a good opportunity to talk about some of the practicalities. I think we're civilized enough for that, after nearly 25 years of marriage."

"Fine by me. Nothing you can say will make me change my mind."

Geoff lugged the heavy suitcase downstairs, while Hanna made herself a cup of tea. They sat down in the lounge.

"What about your mail? Can you give me a forwarding address?"

"No. I'd rather not."

"Why not?"

"Frankly, I don't want you to be able to contact me direct. I'd like everything to be done via my solicitor after today."

"Is that because you have moved in with somebody else...another man?"

"What gives you that idea?"

"Somebody told me that you were seen a while back with a man in a restaurant...holding hands and billing and cooing."

"What rubbish!"

"No it isn't. It is quite true, and you know it."

Hanna paused. "Well, if you must know. Yes, there is somebody else. I don't think anybody could blame me after the shabby way I've been treated recently."

"Leaving the 'shabby treatment' aside for a moment, it wasn't recently. It was about a year ago. So it's been going on for quite a while, hasn't it?"

"Look, I'm not being given the third degree. That's not why I'm here."

"Well I think I've a right to know. After all, I'm the one being cuckolded, remember."

"Oh God, how quaint! That's one of your troubles: you're so old-fashioned."

"Well, I believe in keeping my wedding vows, if that's what you mean by 'old fashioned'. It seems you don't."

"Oh, come off it. Nobody believes in that 'till death do us part' nonsense these days. And as to wedding vows, nobody can promise that they'll love somebody for ever – situations change and people change. It's nonsense!

"The fact is, nobody stays faithful to one partner these days.

"Of course men don't like it. But men have always had a bit on the side at every opportunity while the little woman stayed at home looking after the children, cooking, ironing and cleaning.

"Don't tell me you've never strayed. Anyway, now – it's our turn. The pill has made it possible for women to have sex when we want it, with whoever we want, without the fear of pregnancy. It's simply made us free at last."

"I can't believe I'm hearing this! From a woman who admires Maggie Thatcher, among other things, for saying that the permissive society is wrecking family life!"

"The trouble is that you men don't like women being assertive – even the fact that we have a woman prime minister hasn't made you see that we women are no longer going to sit at home being the good housewife."

"What is marriage for, then?"

"I agree! There's no point in it any more. Most women don't want it, and I predict that in another twenty years or so hardly anybody will bother."

"So you're saying you don't love me any more?"

"I don't love you. I have never loved you. And I never will love you."

"So why did you marry me?"

"Well at the time I thought you might be going places. I suppose I thought it would be an advantage."

"So you're sitting there and telling me that all this time our marriage has been a sham."

"No more than other people's."

"Throughout our marriage I have loved you and been completely faithful to you."

"Well more fool you."

"What about David?"

"I don't think it will worry him either way. Once he's got his degree he'll be flying the nest anyway...he has already told me so."

"You've already spoken to him about...getting a divorce?"

"Yes. I thought he should know. He just said it was up to us. He didn't think it was his business."

"My God! He is a cool one. If it had been me, I'd have been really cut up about my parents splitting up."

"Anyway, I'm going now. Get the house on the market soon. I need the cash."

CHAPTER 49

1985

Of course she'd gone. After that he was glad. There was absolutely nothing more to be said. He'd told her that if she wanted out, he would not contest a divorce. Why fight a lost battle? He'd even carried her suitcases to the car and put them in the boot.

The helping hand wasn't demeaning. It was symbolic: you're leaving me for good...let me help you!

He went upstairs to survey the damage. Typical! She hadn't even closed the drawers and cupboards that she'd taken things from.

He began tidying up.

She'd stuffed a lot of papers in the waste basket. It was full to overflowing. He carried it downstairs to dump it in the bin. He noticed a corner of an airmail letter poking up. Idly he drew it out to look at it.

He instantly recognized the hand-writing. It was his friend Adam's, who had written to them several times from Australia.

This was just the last page of a letter, in hand-writing that he recognised. But it wasn't any letter Geoff had read before. It said:

> "Weary with toil I haste me to my bed
> The dear repose for limbs with travel tired;
> But then begins a journey in my head
> To work my mind when body's work's
> expired
> For then my thoughts, from far where I abide,
> Intend a zealous pilgrimage to thee
> And keep my drooping eyelids open wide,
> Looking on darkness which the blind do see;
> Save that my soul's imaginary sight

Presents thy shadow to my sightless view,
Which like a jewel hung in the ghastly night
Makes black darkness beauteous and her old
face new.
Lo, thus by day my limbs, by night my mind,
For thee, and for myself, no quiet find.

Shakespeare
Sonnet 27."

Of all the absolute low-down creeps! It took one moment for the penny to drop. This could only be part of a love letter sent from his best friend Adam to Hanna!

It could only mean that they had been lovers before Adam and his family emigrated.

The thoughts clicked into place. It had been Hanna's suggestion that he should make a pal of Adam. And like a damn fool he'd fallen for it.

The conniving...she'd planned it...no, *they'd* planned it - so I wouldn't be suspicious if Adam rang! If I answered the phone, he would be ringing to talk to me. If I wasn't there...well, the coast was clear!

"What an absolute bloody Judas! No. That's a calumny against Mr. Iscariot," he said aloud, to the empty room.

But it can't be Adam she's just moved in with...it was a couple of years ago when he moved to Australia. So that's at least two men that I know of, and at least two years that she's been putting herself around. I wonder how many more. Looks like she's been prepared to open her legs to anybody who was polite enough to ask! My God, all this time – maybe for years – she's been the bloody village bicycle!

*

Geoff put the phone down, stunned beyond belief. Not angry. Just empty. And this time they were tears that blurred his vision.

394

He had phoned David, determined to talk man-to-man, to reassure him that whatever happened he could always rely on his father...for accommodation, advice if needed, money...he'd always be his father.

It was David's quite cool reply - almost matter-of-fact, it seemed – that silenced Geoff. "Well thanks for the assurance. But mother told me that you're not actually my father, biologically speaking. He was some feller she met twenty-odd years ago."

"*What!*"

"She assured me it was true, Dad. I'm sorry...I don't know what to say...didn't you know?"

"No! No. I didn't."

He paused. "You're not my son? Oh God! I never expected...I can't think what..."

Geoff's voice tailed off into nothing.

"Dad, are you OK? Look, don't worry. It makes no difference to us. You'll always be Dad to me."

In the shattering silence after putting the phone down the overwhelming thought in Geoff's mind was that he was left with absolutely nothing.

Two weeks ago I had a family life...a wife to come home to, a son, a reasonably happy family. Now...nothing left of it at all.

The enormity of it left Geoff unable to think. And for the best part of an hour, unable to move, incapable of action. The sudden bleak emptiness of his life was overwhelming...soul-crushing.

He was our future...he was my future. It's what you live for. It's the greatest hope in anybody's life. It's the thing that drives life forward – even the animals and birds know it's the one thing that matters: passing life on. And now it's gone. What's left? Nothing.

And yet, what about David? Can I just turn my back on him...cut him out of my life because he's not my son? Well of course I must. Must I? He's grown up with me as his father...not A.N.Other. The betrayal is Hanna's – not his. What happens to all the love and trust and happy times we've had? Aren't they still there? Am I expected to obliterate them?

Geoff had an overwhelming sense of helplessness in the face of events, because the answer, he knew, was not in his hands. It depended on David, and what he felt. He saw a glimmer of hope: if what we have made between us is strong enough, it will survive, won't it?

At last he spoke to the room.

"What the hell am I going to do?"

There was despair in the question. There was an agony in the question. And there was no answer.

My whole bloody life has been for nothing. It's been a fiction. And not written by me.

It is all down to that bloody woman. I've spent twenty-odd years in love with a woman who cared not one jot. I've been faithful to a woman who was unfaithful the whole time.

I've been a total bloody fool. And I've brought up a son...I've loved a son...who isn't my son at all.

How can I have been so stupid? So bloody stupid!

But even more of a question is how could Hanna do it?"

The thought that was paramount was: she has lied her way through twenty-three years of marriage. How can anyone do that?

I just can't believe it. In my wildest dreams I don't think I could have got into a nightmare like this!

*

Night was worse than day. He'd wake up, remember the situation, and night thoughts would take over, thinking him into despair.

He would find himself on a wild ride through revenge, suicide, killing Hanna.

His will would need changing. That was a night thought. I'll obviously cut Hanna out, and David too...he's not my son!

But who do I leave all my worldly goods to? There isn't anybody else.

And David: all right, there's Hanna's betrayal involved, but that wasn't David's fault, was it. All his life I have been his father.

396

OK, he's turned twenty-one, and he hasn't been at home much for the last three years – and obviously he'll be off soon, making his own life, and very likely not in north Cheshire or the Manchester area. So I'm going to see even less of him. Does that relationship matter so much. Does he still want to regard me as his dad? He said so.

He'll get married. Eventually he'll have children. Will they be my grandchildren? Certainly not biologically. But I think I'd like to have little children calling me grandpa. Well David's children will be the only possibility there.

Oh my God! My family tree! I hadn't thought of that. It ends with me! I was doing all that family history for David as well as for myself. Now it simply doesn't include him.

Well not really, although David is registered as my son. I mean, what rights does that give him? I could cut him out of my will...that was my first thought, wasn't it. But do I want to do that?

*

In the morning Geoff couldn't remember exactly at what point sleep had overtaken him. But he could remember most of his night thoughts.

It didn't alter much. It didn't stop his agony. But, being daytime, he could push it into the back of his mind as he got on with his work, either in his office at the airport, or seated in the cockpit, flying airliners. He was a professional. That came first.

Until he got home at the end of his working day. It seemed empty and cold. He didn't want to live there any more. He had already called in an estate agent, and put the house up for sale.

Seeing the sign outside made his spirits sink as he reached home. Home? It wasn't home any more: not really. It was just where he happened to live for the time being.

Where the hell was he going to live? He couldn't make himself think about that seriously. He should be looking for a new place. But he had no enthusiasm. What the hell am I going to do?

A lot of men might have turned to drink. Geoff didn't do that: he was a professional pilot, and he did not drink the day before flying – it had been a mantra throughout his career.

He picked up the telephone, and dialled Rose's number.

*

She'd invited him to her home in Bramhall.

Something about his tone – "Rose, I need to see you" – told her that the café where they'd met before might not be a good idea.

It was a modest detached house, similar to the other houses in the road. There was nothing special about it...a bit like Rose, he thought wryly.

So why was he here to talk to her? Because he had a feeling that she would know what to do...she'd understand. Maybe all the ordinary houses were little palaces inside. Then Rose opened the door.

She invited him to sit in the lounge while she made a cup of tea. It was a cosy sort of room, much smaller than his own. Two armchairs and a matching settee were fat and comfy, covered in a flowered material. There were real flowers in a cut-glass vase on a small table, and a small lamp on another. The lamp base seemed to be of a ceramic material, mainly white with flowers on it in a pattern.

There was a bookcase, not too tidy, and a fire burning in the grate, and it felt warm and comfortable, despite the restrictions in space.

There was a folded newspaper on the arm of one of the chairs, and Geoff got up from the settee and took the newspaper. Unfolded, it turned out to be the *Daily Telegraph.*

He was looking at its front page when Rose came in with two small china mugs of tea. "Sounded as if this was going to be a job for a mug of tea rather than a cup," she offered by way of explanation.

"I don't know why, but I thought you might be a *Guardian* reader."

"I might be, but I can't do the *Guardian* crossword," she said. "I can usually get through this one."

Her voice changed: "Have you got a problem, Geoff?"

398

He poured out his story to her. Hanna...divorce...David not being his son.

"The fact is that while I've been stitching together my family history at one end, my own family has been unravelling at the other."

He admitted: "I can't deny I'm absolutely devastated, Rose. Here I was, a family man, quite contented with life. Suddenly I've lost it all. And I just don't know why. I don't understand.

"I have to admit...I looked around me at home after I'd put it up for sale and I thought what the hell do I do now. I don't know. I honestly could have wept.

"I truly feel that I've got nothing to live for now...oh Christ! I'm sorry. I shouldn't be loading my problems on to you like this."

Rose paused before saying anything. Then: "I don't know Hanna, so I suppose I shouldn't judge her. But I can say one thing after what you've told me: she is a cruel woman."

Geoff started to speak, then stopped. Rose went on: "All right, she wants a divorce: there's probably nothing you can do about that. But she didn't have to say anything about David.

"That is a woman with the definite intention of hurting and humiliating. It may be a lie anyway...she's already had to tell a lot of lies, that's obvious.

"But even if it is true that he was biologically fathered by somebody else, your relationship with him is father and son. I think she's trying to break that, just as she's breaking your marriage.

"Well I wouldn't let her. It may be hard to accept, but David is the boy you raised and loved. In the end nothing has changed there. It is just the same for people who have adopted a child. You just don't have to think too much about the biology...surely it's the relationship that matters above all.

"If Hanna had not said anything, you wouldn't know now, and nor would David. Then your relationship would have been just as it has always been.

"How many people are walking about at this moment unaware that their biological father isn't the man they thought he was? And how many in the past...millions, I should guess.

"How does the old saw go: it's a wise child who knows its own father.

"Do you want to cut him out of your life because Hanna says so? Because it really looks like one last nasty kick at you as she leaves."

"No. I suppose you're right, Rose. It's just very hard to accept.

"But since you mention the past, I have to say that it was my family history that caused all this conflict with Hanna. She couldn't stand my being from a poor background, way back."

Again Rose paused. "Geoff, I may be wrong, but I find it very hard to believe that Hanna has left you for that reason alone.

"I'd say she was looking for an excuse...for a reason to go. I thought it when you told me before about how she hated your ancestors. It doesn't make sense. I'm prepared to bet there's a more basic reason...like another man."

"Well, as a matter of fact she's already admitted that. And I've good reason to think she has had at least two other affairs in recent years...one with the man I thought was my best friend who emigrated to Australia.

"It's one of the things that floors me...I never suspected it...she's made an absolute fool of me. And here I was, never thinking of being unfaithful to her! God, she must have been laughing!

"The irony is that we first met Adam and his wife at church. You get married in church. You make solemn vows. If that means anything in your life, you'd think it means faithfulness and family values. You stand there and you reject adultery, don't you.

"It's one of the ten commandments – it's basic."

"Maybe God intended it this way," said Rose quietly. Her eyes were fixed on his. "They say God has it all planned, don't they? There's a divine purpose in everything if only we could see it?

"Once when we were talking you told me you believed in God because there's evidence everywhere of an intelligence in the design of the universe and how it works."

"I still believe that. I mean, just look at the way a bird's wing is made, perfect for enabling it to fly...that couldn't have just happened."

Again Rose spoke quietly, carefully: "Yes. I see. Just like God decreed and designed cereals so that they can be made into bread. And bread was designed so that it could be sliced and made into toast, to go with the butter and the marmalade that he had made possible by designing oranges and sugar."

"You are enormously cynical!" said Geoff, shocked by her response.

"No. Just practical. I stopped believing in fairies a long time ago. I refuse to worry about who designed the flowers' petals and the butterflies' wings. I just enjoy seeing them.

"We find life as it is and we must deal with it as best we can. I think we all have to find our way despite everything that life can throw at us...it is allowing yourself to believe that fate will win that destroys you."

She added: "You say Hanna made a fool of you. You could argue that not knowing what she was up to simply shows your trust in her. It is a reflection of your faithfulness...that's why it would never cross your mind.

"Women can be extremely good at deceit, you know. Much better than men."

*

"Anyway, Rose, I obviously don't need my family history now. I'm the end of the line! It was always in my mind that it's for my son...for posterity, if you like. Now it doesn't matter, biologically. It means nothing now.

"It's not as if my ancestors were anything special. Mostly they were just very ordinary people, and some were worse than that. Their lives

401

all seem pointless. And to be honest I can't help feeling that so does mine."

Rose looked hard at Geoff. She paused only briefly. "OK. Ordinary people. But what did they think? How did they cope with life's difficulties? We'll never know. But I don't think you should make the mistake of imagining, because they were ordinary and poor, that they were stupid and incapable of thinking and loving and hoping and wanting better. Or of thinking that their existence was empty and meaningless.

"Of course we know so little about them...they are just shadows. But I've always been fascinated by shadows – I think it goes back to my childhood when my mother read to me about Peter Pan losing his shadow!

"I've often looked at sundials, with their shadow silently telling the passing hours and leaving no trace when the sunshine stops...just as our shadowy ancestors give us a fleeting bit of information, then are gone."

Geoff started to speak, but she went on determinedly: "Another thing that interests me is that since our physical and maybe intellectual characteristics are passed on by our genes, am I – are you – close to being a copy of some of our ancestors, at least mentally?

"Is that where the idea of the phoenix comes from? Have we, in effect, lived before? And will again? In different times and conditions, of course, but essentially all that we are – our personality - may have been here before.

"Was there a person, way back before our times, who thought and felt just like me? It's a fascinating idea. Or is it just imagination run riot?"

Geoff spoke immediately: "No. I don't think it is. In fact I've had exactly the same thought. I mentioned it to Hanna. She pooh-poohed it, of course. But I agree, it is not impossible.

"If DNA transfers personality from one generation to the next, it follows that we must think like some of our ancestors, to some extent, bearing in mind that their times were very different...and so was their situation, certainly."

Said Rose: "Have you ever had the momentary feeling that something has happened before – yet you know it can't have? Or that somewhere you just arrived for the first time is familiar and you suddenly feel you've been there before?

"Could it go back to our DNA? Is it an echo of the past that we suddenly sense?"

She paused, then added: "You've concentrated on the male line in your family history, especially in the nineteenth and twentieth centuries, as is natural at first because you want to follow your name back. But what about the women in their lives – what about your mother, and the other women who brought up the children and played the biggest part in forming their characters? They form an equal part of your family tree.

"There's so much to find out...and so much we can only guess at. It's tantalizing but it's there, just out of reach of what we can learn from the records. What drove them? What inspired or terrified them?

"You're experiencing anguish now...and you can bet that your ancestors faced anguish too, many times. Even fear for their lives, perhaps. Almost certainly hunger and deep unhappiness at times. How did they survive it all?

"Like them, you can only pick up the pieces and carry on. At least you have the chance of enjoying your life. How many of your ancestors had that chance? You've still got your health. You have a profession that you love. You've got a lot going for you. You've got friends, and that counts for a lot. Don't let yourself forget how lucky you are.

"So let's have a fresh cup of tea. And one of those cream cakes I bought yesterday. It's almost as if I knew beforehand that you'd be coming to help me eat them."

*

1987

The divorce took the best part of a year, mostly due to wrangling over money. Whether it was Hanna or just her lawyers, Geoff didn't know, but this woman who had never loved him, had betrayed him, and had walked out on him for no good reason as far as he was concerned, now wanted him to pay her very large sums for his enormous sins.

He had to admit, in the end he did his best to make it awkward for her: he felt aggrieved and he felt embattled. And when there was a settlement on their disputes he felt that the law favoured Hanna simply because she was a woman and the assumption was that it was always the man who must have been the cause of the marital breakdown. It was a huge relief when it was over..

It was a year after that when he and Rose were married.

Geoff had slowly realised how much he relied on Rose...on her judgement, her views, her feelings...and on an unspoken friendship, a feeling of togetherness that was about being comfortable with each other...a feeling that at last he recognized as love.

Suddenly life was different...and better.

How could I have been depressed because Hanna was out of my life, he asked himself: it's the best thing that's happened to me for years. David occasionally calls from Los Angeles, where he's got a job with a high-tech computer company. But more important: he still calls me "dad." I'm not sure if he realizes how important that is to me.

And there were important discoveries when he took up his family history again, encouraged by Rose.

He had the idea that it would have pleased his father if he researched his mother's family. He sent for his mother's death certificate, and was astounded to find that she had died only in 1977, in the psychiatric unit of North Manchester General Hospital. There could be only one conclusion: his father had lied when he told him his mother had died giving birth to him. It was a huge betrayal.

All those years she had been alone in the asylum, forgotten by everyone after his father died. Geoff never knew her. He could have visited her...got to know her...comforted her. How often did she wait and hope endlessly for a visit from her son?

But above it all, Geoff found himself always looking forward to getting home to be with Rose, rediscovering the joy of life.

Marrying her had been a journey of discovery, with many shared interests, and a shared friendship. There was always something to talk about. There was a complete lack of the sort of tension that had so marked his life with Hanna. Life was so much better.

And there was a future to look forward to, as well as a past.

End

Printed in Great Britain
by Amazon

32472476R00229